FEATURING THE SAINT

FOREWORD BY JACK KERLEY

THE ADVENTURES OF THE SAINT

Enter the Saint (1930), *The Saint Closes the Case* (1930), *The Avenging Saint* (1930), *Featuring the Saint* (1931), *Alias the Saint* (1931), *The Saint Meets His Match* (1931), *The Saint Versus Scotland Yard* (1932), *The Saint's Getaway* (1932), *The Saint and Mr Teal* (1933), *The Brighter Buccaneer* (1933), *The Saint in London* (1934), *The Saint Intervenes* (1934), *The Saint Goes On* (1934), *The Saint in New York* (1935), *Saint Overboard* (1936), *The Saint in Action* (1937), *The Saint Bids Diamonds* (1937), *The Saint Plays with Fire* (1938), *Follow the Saint* (1938), *The Happy Highwayman* (1939), *The Saint in Miami* (1940), *The Saint Goes West* (1942), *The Saint Steps In* (1943), *The Saint on Guard* (1944), *The Saint Sees It Through* (1946), *Call for the Saint* (1948), *Saint Errant* (1948), *The Saint in Europe* (1953), *The Saint on the Spanish Main* (1955), *The Saint Around the World* (1956), *Thanks to the Saint* (1957), *Señor Saint* (1958), *Saint to the Rescue* (1959), *Trust the Saint* (1962), *The Saint in the Sun* (1963), *Vendetta for the Saint* (1964), *The Saint on TV* (1968), *The Saint Returns* (1968), *The Saint and the Fiction Makers* (1968), *The Saint Abroad* (1969), *The Saint in Pursuit* (1970), *The Saint and the People Importers* (1971), *Catch the Saint* (1975), *The Saint and the Hapsburg Necklace* (1976), *Send for the Saint* (1977), *The Saint in Trouble* (1978), *The Saint and the Templar Treasure* (1978), *Count On the Saint* (1980), *Salvage for the Saint* (1983)

FEATURING THE SAINT

LESLIE CHARTERIS

SERIES EDITOR: IAN DICKERSON

The characters and events portrayed in this book are fictitious. Any similarity to real persons, living or dead, is coincidental and not intended by the author.

Introduction to "The Wonderful War" originally published in *The First Saint Omnibus* (Doubleday Crime Club, 1939)
Introduction to "The Man Who Could Not Die" originally published in *Paging the Saint* (1945)

Published by Thomas & Mercer, Seattle

www.apub.com

ISBN-13: 9781477842645
ISBN-10: 1477842640

Cover design by David Drummond, www.salamanderhill.com

Printed in the United States of America.

To Barbara
London, November 1930

PUBLISHER'S NOTE

The text of this book has been preserved from the original edition and includes vocabulary, grammar, style, and punctuation that might differ from modern publishing practices. Every care has been taken to preserve the author's tone and meaning, allowing only minimal changes to punctuation and wording to ensure a fluent experience for modern readers.

FOREWORD TO THE NEW EDITION

I intended to write this introduction wearing my scholar's cloak, with an academically freighted deconstruction utilizing references to Sir Arthur Conan Doyle, Sir Walter Scott, the chivalric code, and inevitably, Freud. The erudition of my arguments and analyses would not only elucidate the psycho-ontological motivations behind Simon Templar, but make me look pretty damn smart as well.

Then I picked up one of my ancient copies of Saint stories, selected "The Wonderful War," and read about a banana republic invaded by one man with a delicious vision for justice. I smiled a lot and laughed aloud almost as often. I reread passages to be tickled yet again. I set the book aside when finished, but had it back in my hands within an hour.

In short, I read with the giddy joy of a thirteen-year-old. Which makes perfect sense, since I was thirteen when I met the Saint. A reader leaning heavily toward the mystery/suspense genre, I had early immersion in the Bobbsey Twins, Seckatary Hawkins, and the Hardy Boys. I had read them to tatters when my father appeared in my bedroom one evening. "I think you'll like these stories," he said, bearing *The First Saint Omnibus*. "They concern a man named Simon

Templar, the Saint. They're more sophisticated than you're used to, and certainly racier, but I suspect you'll enjoy that aspect."

With those cryptic words he set the book in my palms and retreated, singing an odd song about the bells of hell. Hoping my old man had not gone fully 'round the bend, I opened the book and, in my own way, have never closed it.

I have read all the Saint sagas, including the three gems in *Featuring the Saint*, at least a dozen times each. If there is anything I as a writer have taken from my father's prescient gift—and I've taken as much from Leslie Charteris as from John D. MacDonald, Robert Parker, and James Lee Burke—it is that a good hero always has a moral code (though it not might be yours or mine), the innocent must be protected, and when the bad get a comeuppance, it should fit the crime.

Oh . . . and beautiful women never detract from a story.

"The Wonderful War" is an all-time favorite, boasting nearly all of the hallmarks of a Saint mini-epic: a comely lady, a masterful plan, a Saintly versification, racy quotes regarding the actress and the bishop, and The Song. Per a good Saint yarn, the malefactors are suitably venal and unattractive and—perhaps most irritating to Simon Templar—rude. All that's missing is an appearance by Inspector Teal, though I suspect he might not be much at home in a South American bananocracy.

And what grand invention is the country of Pasala . . . Charteris's setting is a rip-roaringly comic and deviously accurate caricature of the era and locale. The world stops for siesta. The army is five-hundred strong, with a general or colonel for every nine men. The navy consists of . . . well, you get the idea.

The Saint stories are not for analysis, I realize, at least not by me. Not for deconstruction or preconstruction or anything akin to psychobabble. They're simply masterworks of delight, asking only that you pick up the pages of a champion storyteller, hold your breath, and step within.

You don't analyse joy. You revel in it.

—Jack Kerley

FEATURING THE SAINT

PREFACE

Eighteen years went by between the first Sherlock Holmes book, *A Study in Scarlet* (1887), and the last, *The Return of Sherlock Holmes* (1905), and Sir Arthur Conan Doyle went on to live twenty-five years after that, during which he saw great changes in the world. Throughout that time, so far as I know, the popularity of his detective was undimmed, and the books were always in print in some edition or other, as they are to this very day. But Sir Arthur never seems to have thought of revising them to keep them in touch with the changing times, and apparently found nothing incongruous in leaving Baker Street to the gaslight and hansom cabs which had long since been replaced by electricity and motor cars, to say nothing of radio in the home and airplanes roaring overhead.

The stories in this volume were written almost an equivalent quarter-century ago, during which the changes in the world have been more drastic even than in Doyle's. The radio has been supplanted by television, a science-fiction fantasy now made commonplace with commercials; aircraft still ply overhead, but they are jets at least, threatening to become supersonic, if they are not already rocket-launched satellites; and the automobiles, paradoxically, are mechanically capable of travelling about as fast on a good road as the planes that Doyle saw, but crawl through London traffic today at a pace which would have made one of those old horse carriages seem airborne. And I must admit that I don't have Doyle's self-restraint and that I have often been tempted to bring the oldest Saint stories up to date, and in a few cases have done something about this when they were reprinted.

But that is a labour which could be endless, as my slothful instincts finally realized in the nick of time, and ultimately pointless anyhow, if my Immortal Works outlive me by a few centuries, as I expect them to.

Therefore, let this book go out as another period piece in the making. I only ask readers not to be beguiled by any accidental modernitics into forgetting how venerable the stories actually are, and how embryonic was the technology of the world in which they were laid.

And also, if you would be critically tolerant, how young was the author, and how correspondingly youthful was his hero.

—Leslie Charteris (1969)

THE LOGICAL ADVENTURE

1

If there must be more stories of the Saint, I prefer to choose them from among his later exploits, from the days when he was working practically alone—although Patricia Holm was never far away, and Roger Conway was always within call at times of need. I often think that it best suited the Saint's peculiar temper to be alone: he was so superbly capable himself, and so arrogantly confident of his own capability, that it irked him to have to deputise the least item of any of his schemes to hands that might bungle it, and exasperated him beyond measure to have to explain and discuss and wrangle his inspirations with minds that leapt to comprehension and decision less swiftly and certainly than his own. These trials he suffered with characteristic good humour, yet there is no doubt that he suffered sometimes, as may be read in other tales that have already been told of him. It is true that the Saint once became something perilously like a gang; there came about him a band of reckless young men who followed him cheerfully into all his crimes, and these young men he led into gay and lawless audacities that made the name of the Saint famous—or infamous—over the whole world; but even those adventures were no more than episodes in the Saint's life. They were part of his development, but they were not the end. His ultimate destiny still lay ahead; he knew that it still lay ahead, but he did not then know what it was. "The Last Hero" he was called once, but the story of his last heroism is not to be told yet, and the manner of it he never foresaw even in his dreams.

This story, then, is the first of a handful that I have unearthed from my records of those days of transition, when the Saint was waiting upon Fate. They were days when he seemed to be filling up time, and, as might have been expected of the man, he beguiled the time in his own incomparable fashion, with his own matchless zest. But it is inevitable that his own moods should be reflected in these tales which are exclusively his—that the twist of the tales should write what he himself felt about them at the time, that they were not really important, and yet that they were none the less fantastically delightful interludes. For Simon Templar was incapable of taking anything of life half-heartedly—even an interlude. And it may be that because of all these things, because he had that vivid sense of the pleasant unimportance of all these adventures, the spirit of laughing devil-may-care quixotry that some have called his greatest charm dances through these tales as it does through few others.

I am thinking particularly of the story that stands first upon my list—a slight story, but a story. Yet it began practically from nothing—as, indeed, did most of the Saint's best stories. It has been said that Simon Templar had more than any ten men's fair share of luck in the way of falling into ready-made adventures, but nothing could be farther from the truth. It was the Saint's own unerring, uncanny genius, his natural instinct for adventure, that made him question things that no ordinary man would have thought to question, and sent him off upon broad, clear roads where no ordinary man would have seen the vestige of a trail, and some volcanic quality within himself that started violent action out of situations that the ordinary man would have found stillborn. And if there is any story about the Saint that illustrates this fact to perfection it is this story which opens—ordinarily enough—upon the American Bar of the Piccadilly Hotel, two Manhattans, and a copy of *The Evening Record.*

"Eight to one," murmured the Saint complacently, "and waltzed home with two lengths to spare. That's another forty quid for the old oak chest. Where shall we celebrate, old dear?"

Patricia Holm smiled.

"Won't you ever take an interest in something outside the racing reports?" she asked. "I don't believe you even know whether we've got a Conservative or a Labour Government at the moment."

"I haven't the faintest idea," said the Saint cheerfully. "Apart from the fact that a horse we've never seen has earned us the best dinner that London can provide, I refuse to believe that anything of the least importance has happened in England today. For instance"—he turned the pages of the newspaper—"we are not at all interested to learn that 'Evidence of a sensational character is expected to be given at the inquest upon Henry Stobbs, a mechanic, who was found dead in a garage in Balham yesterday. I don't believe the man had a sensational character at all. No man with a really sensational character would be found dead in a garage in Balham . . . Nor are we thrilled to hear that 'Missing from her home at South Norwood since January last, the body of Martha Danby, a domestic servant, was discovered in a disused quarry near Tavistock early this morning by a tramp in an advanced state of decomposition.' Not that we don't feel sorry for the tramp—it must be rotten for the poor fellow to have to cruise about the world in an advanced state of decomposition—but my point is . . ."

"That'll do," said Patricia.

"O.K.," said the Saint affably. "So long as you understand why I'm so . . . Hullo . . . what's this?"

He had been folding the paper into a convenient size for the nearest waste-basket when his eye was caught by a name that he knew, and he read the paragraphs surrounding it with a sudden interest. These paragraphs figured in that admirable feature "Here and There" conducted by that indefatigable and ubiquitous gossip "The Eavesdropper."

"Well, well, well!" drawled the Saint, with a distinct saintliness of intonation, and Patricia looked at him expectantly.

"What is it?"

"Just a little social chatter," said Simon. "Our friend is warbling about the progress of civil aviation, and how few serious accidents there have been since light aeroplane clubs started springing up all over the country, and how everyone is taking to the air as if they'd been born with wings. Then he says, 'There are, of course, a few exceptions. Mr. Francis Lemuel, for instance, the well-known cabaret impresario, who was one of the founders of the Thames Valley Flying Club, and who was himself making rapid progress towards his "A" licence, was so badly shaken by his recent crash that he has been compelled, on medical advice, to give up all idea of qualifying as a pilot.' The rest is just the usual kind of blurb about Lemuel's brilliant impresarioning. But that is interesting, now, isn't it, to know that dear Francis was sighing for the wings of a Moth!"

"Why?"

The Saint smiled beatifically, and completed the operation of preparing *The Evening Record* for its last resting-place.

"There are many interests in my young life," he murmured, "of which you are still in ignorance, dear lass. And little Fran is one of them, and has been for some time. But I never knew that he was a bold bad bird-man, outside of business hours . . . And now, old Pat, shall we dine here or push on to the Berkeley Arms?"

And that was all that was said about Francis Lemuel that night, and for ten days afterwards, for at that time, bowing before Patricia's pleading, Simon Templar was trying to lead a respectable life. And yet, knowing her man, she was a little surprised that he dropped the subject so quickly, and, knowing her man again, she heaved a little sigh of rueful resignation when he met her for lunch ten days later and showed quite plainly in his face that he was on the trail of more trouble. At those times there was a renewed effervescence about the Saint's always electric personality, and a refreshed recklessness about the laughter that was never far from the surface of his blue eyes, that were unmistakable danger-signs. The smooth sweep of his patent-leather hair seemed to become sleeker and slicker than ever, and the keen brown face seemed to take on an even swifter and more rakish chiselledness of line than it ordinarily wore. She knew these signs of old, and challenged him before he had finished selecting the hors d'oeuvre.

"What's on the programme, Saint?"

Simon sipped his sherry elegantly. "I've got a job."

"What's that?"

"You know—work. Dramatis persona: Simon Templar, a horny-handed son of toil."

"Idiot! I meant, what's the job?"

"Private Aviator Extraordinary to Mr. Francis Lemuel," answered the Saint, with dancing eyes. "And you can't laugh that off!"

"Is that what you've been so mysterious about lately?"

"It is. I tell you, it wasn't dead easy. Mr. Lemuel has an eccentric taste in aviators. I got a lot of fun out of convincing him that I was really a shabby character. Try to imagine the late lamented Solomon applying, incog., for the job of 'Ask Auntie Abishag' on the staff of *The Lebanon Daily Leader* . . ." The Saint grinned reminiscently. "But as an ex-RAF officer, cashiered for pinching three ailerons, four longerons, and a brace of gliding angles, I had what you might call a flying start."

"And what are you supposed to do?"

"Propel him about the bright blue sky."

"Where?"

The Saint bisected a sardine with precision and dexterity.

"That," he answered, "is the point. According to rumours, Francis is proposing to extend his cabaristic activities into the other capitals of Europe. But why by air? 'The latest and most rapid means of transport,' says you, intelligent-like. Oh, every time. But the whole of civilised Europe is served by very comfortable public airways—very comfortable—and my researches into Mr. Lemuel's character never made me think he was the sort of cove who'd sacrifice his arm-chair in a pukka flying Pullman and go batting through the blue in an open two-seater air-louse just to save an hour here and there. Mystery Number One. That's why I was so interested to read that Brother Francis had been trying to aviate solo . . . you remember?"

Patricia nodded. "I wondered . . ."

"Never give tongue before you've got the blue-bottle by the blunt end," said the Saint. "That's my motto. But I always believe in taking two looks at anything that seems to have slipped the least bit off the main line, and that was a case in point. Particularly with a man like Francis Lemuel. I've always thought he was far too respectable to be above suspicion. Now we may start to learn things."

She tried to find out how he had contrived to discover that Mr. Lemuel had been searching for a disreputable aviator; she was equally curious to know how the Saint had contrived to present himself for the job, but Simon Templar still had his own little secrets. About some of the preliminary details of his adventures he was often absurdly reticent.

"I heard about it," he said, "and a bloke I met in a pub out at Aldgate landed me on the front door, so to speak . . . Mystery Number Two, of course, is why the aviator should have been disreputable . . . "

He talked energetically about this problem, and left her first questions otherwise unanswered. And with that she had to be content—until, abruptly, he switched off the subject altogether, and for the rest of that day refused to talk any more about what he was pleased to call "affairs of state."

Other things happened afterwards—very shortly afterwards. A few other people entered the story, a few other threads came into it, a few diverting decorations blossomed upon it, but the foundations of the story were already laid, and it is doubtful whether any of the subsequent events herein described would have evented at all if Simon Templar had not chanced to catch sight of that innocent paragraph in *The Evening Record*. For of such material were the Saint's adventures made.

And nothing can be more certain than that if the Saint had not been a man of such peculiar genius and eccentric interests he would not to this day carry an eight-inch scar on his right forearm as a memento of the adventure, and Mr. Francis Lemuel would not have experienced such a sudden and cataclysmic elevation, and one Jacob Einsmann might still have been with us, and M. Boileau, the French Minister of Finance, would not have been put to considerable inconvenience—and (which is perhaps even more important) a girl whose name used to be Stella Dornford would not now be married to a bank clerk with very ordinary prospects, and living in a very ordinary apartment in Battersea, and perfectly happy in spite of that.

2

The Calumet Club is situated (as the estate agents so beautifully put it) in a spacious basement in Deacon Street, Soho. This statement should be taken at its face value. There are, in fact, no premises whatsoever in any way ostensibly appertaining to the said club on the street level, or on any of the floors above. Entrance to the club is by means of a narrow flight of stone steps leading down into a microscopic area, and through a door opening upon this area one may (if one is known to the management) obtain access to the club itself, via a room which only an estate agent would have the nerve to describe as a vestibule, and past a porter who has been other things in his time.

The Calumet Club has an extensive if curiously exclusive membership. Things are discussed there—fascinating things. Money, and other objects of vertu, changes hands there. And, sometimes, strange things are said to have happened there—very strange things. The Saint was distinctly interested in the Calumet Club. It was one of the irregular interests of his young life.

Nevertheless, the visit he paid to it on a certain evening began as a mere matter of routine, and was embarked upon without immediate malice premeditated.

For thus is the way paved for adventure, as far as human ingenuity can contrive it, with good sound non-skid tarmac. Upon learning, almost beyond dispute, that Mr. Phineas Poppingcove is a saccharine smuggler, you do not, whatever your principles and prowess, immediately invade his abode, beat him vimfully about the head with some blunt instrument, and so depart with the work of discouragement satisfactorily accomplished. If you discover, after patient investigation, that the rooms in which Miss Désirée Sausage professes to teach the latest ballroom dances (h. & c.) are in reality the dens where foolish men are fleeced of their fathers' money at wangled games of halma, you do not, even if you are the Saint, instantly force your way into those rooms, shoot the croupier, denounce Miss Sausage, and take the stake-money home with you as a souvenir. Or, if you do, your promising career is liable to terminate abruptly and in a manner definitely glutinous. The Saint, it should be remembered, had been in that sort of game for some time and he knew, better than anyone, the value of painstaking preparation. When everything that could possibly be known about the lie of the land and the personal habits of its denizens was known, and the line of subsequent retreat had been thoroughly surveyed, mapped, dressed, ventilated, and upholstered—then, oh, yes, then the blunt instrument, wielded with decisive celerity and no uncertain hand. But not before.

This visit to the Calumet Club was definitely "before" and the Saint was therefore prepared and even expecting to behave himself with all the decorum that the occasion demanded.

He passed to a corner table, ordered a drink, lighted a cigarette, and settled himself comfortably.

It was then barely eleven, and the club would not begin to do real business for about another half-hour. The nucleus of an orchestra was rhythmically, if a trifle unenthusiastically, insisting that it didn't care how much some lady unspecified made it blue. To the accompaniment of this declaration of an unselfish devotion of which the casual eye, judging the orchestra solely by appearances, would never have believed them capable, four self-appointed ladies, in two pairs, and two other self-appointed ladies paired with an equal number of temporary gentlemen, were travelling in small circles round a minute section of inferior parquet. At other tables round the floor a scattering of other clients, apparently male and female, were absorbing divers brands of alcohol in the lugubrious fashion in which alcohol is ordinarily absorbed in England during the hours in which the absorption is legal. In fact, the Calumet Club was just yawning and stretching itself preparatory to waking up for the night's festivities.

The Saint sighed, inhaled cigarette-smoke luxuriously, tasted the modest glass of beer which the waiter brought him, paid twice the usual retail price for it, added a fifty per cent bonus, and continued to inspect his fellow-members with a somewhat jaundiced eye.

One by one he dismissed them. Two men whom he had met there several times before saluted him, and he smiled back as if he loved them like brothers. An unattached damsel at an adjacent table smiled sweetly at him, and the Saint smiled back just as sweetly, for he had a reputation to keep up. And then, in another corner, his gaze came to rest upon a man he had seen before, and a girl he had never seen before, sitting together at a table beside the orchestra.

Simon's gaze rested upon them thoughtfully, as it had rested upon other people in that room, and it only rested upon them longer than it had rested upon anyone else that night, because at that moment, when his glance fell upon them, something stirred at the back of his brain and opened its inward intangible eye upon the bare facts of the case as conveyed by the optic nerves. The Saint could not have said what it was. At that moment there was nothing about that corner of the scenery to attract such an attention. They were talking quite ordinarily, to judge by their faces and, if the face of the girl was remarkably pleasant to look upon, even that was not unprecedented in the Calumet Club and the entourage of Baldy Mossiter. And yet, in spite of these facts rather than because of them, Simon Templar's queer instinct for the raw material of his trade flicked up a ghostly eyelid in some dim recess of his mind, and forced him to look longer, without quite knowing why he looked. And it was only because of this that the Saint saw what he saw, when the almost imperceptible thing happened in the course of one of Mr. Mossiter's frequent and expressive gestures.

"Have you got a cigarette?" murmured the unattached damsel at the adjacent table, hopefully, but the sweetness of the smile which illuminated the Saint's features as she spoke was not for her, and it is doubtful whether he even heard.

He lounged out of his chair and wandered across the room with the long, lazy stride that covered ground with such an inconspicuous speed, and the man and the girl looked up together as he loomed over their table.

"Hullo," drawled the Saint.

He sat down in a vacant chair between them, without waiting to be invited, and beamed from one to the other in a most Saintly way.

"Beautiful weather we're having, aren't we, Baldy?"

"What the devil do you want, Templar?" snarled Mr. Mossiter, with no cordiality. "I'm busy."

"I know, sweetheart," said the Saint gently. "I saw you getting busy. That's why I came over."

He contemplated Mr. Mossiter with innocent blue eyes, and yet there was something in the very innocence of that stare, besides its prolonged steadiness, that unaccountably prickled the short hairs on the back of Mossiter's bull neck. It did not happen at once. The stare had focused on its object for some time before that cold draught of perplexedly dawning comprehension began to lap Mossiter's spinal column. But the Saint read all that he wanted to read in the sudden darkening of the livid scar that ran down the side of Mossiter's face from his left temple to his chin, and the Saintly smile became dazzlingly seraphic.

"Exactly," said the Saint.

His gaze shifted over to the girl. Her hand was still round her glass—she had been raising it when the Saint reached the table, and had put it down again untasted.

Still smiling, Simon took the girl's glass in one hand and Mossiter's in the other, and changed them over. Then he looked again at Mossiter.

"Drink up," he said, and suddenly there was cold steel in his voice.

"What d'you mean?"

"Drink," said the Saint. "Open your mouth, and induce the liquid to trickle down the gullet. You must have done it before. But whether you'll enjoy it so much on this occasion remains to be seen."

"What the hell are you suggesting?"

"Nothing. That's just your guilty conscience. Drink it up, beautiful." Mossiter seemed to crouch in his chair.

"Will you leave this table?" he grated.

"No," said the Saint.

"Then you will have to leave the club altogether . . . Waiter!"

The Saint took out his cigarette-case and tapped a cigarette meditatively upon it. Then he looked up. He addressed the girl.

"If you had finished that drink," he said, "the consequences would have been very unpleasant indeed. I think I can assure you of that, though I'm not absolutely certain what our friend put in it. It is quite sufficient that I saw him drop something into your glass while he was talking just now."

He leaned back in his chair, with his back half-turned to Mr. Mossiter, and watched the waiter returning across the floor with the porter who had been other things in his time, and added, in the same quiet tone, "On account of the failure of this bright scheme, there will shortly be a slight disturbance of which I shall be the centre. If you think I'm raving mad, you can go to hell. If you've got the sense to see that I'm telling the truth, you'll stand by to make your bolt when I give the word, and meet me outside in a couple of minutes."

Thus the Saint completed his remarks, quite unhurriedly, quite calmly and conversationally, and then the waiter and the porter were behind his chair.

"Throw this man out," said Mossiter curtly. "He's making a nuisance of himself."

It was the porter who had been other things in his time who laid the first rough hand upon the Saint and Simon grinned gently. The next moment Simon was on his feet, and the porter was not.

That remark needs little explanation. It would not be profitable to elaborate a description of the pile-driving properties of the left hook that connected with the porter's jaw as Simon rose from his chair, and, in fact, the porter himself knew little about it at the time. He left the ground momentarily, and then he made contact with a lot more ground a little farther on, and then he slept.

The elderly waiter, also, knew little about that particular incident. The best and brightest years of his life were past and over, and it is probable that he was growing a little slow on the uptake in his late middle age. It is, at least, certain that he had not fully digested the significance of the spectacle to which he had just been treated, nor come to any decision about his own attitude to the situation, when he felt himself seized firmly by the collar and the seat of his pants. He seemed to rise astonishingly into the air, and, suspended horizontally in space at the full upward stretch of the Saint's arms, was for an instant in a position to contemplate the beauties of the low ceiling at close range. And the Saint chuckled.

"How Time flies," murmured the Saint, and heaved the man bodily into the middle of the orchestra—where, it may be recorded, he damaged beyond repair, in his descent, a tenor saxophone, a guitar, and a device for imitating the moans of a stricken hyena.

Simon straightened his tie, and looked about him. Action had been so rapid, during those few seconds that the rest of the club's population and personnel had not yet completely awoken to understanding and reprisal. And the most important thing of all was that the sudden sleep of the porter who had been other things in his time had not only demoralised the two other officials who were standing in the middle distance, but had also left the way to the exit temporarily clear.

Simon touched the girl's shoulder.

"I should push along now, old dear," he remarked, as if there was all the time in the world and nothing on earth to get excited about. "Stop a taxi outside, if you see one. I'll be right along."

She looked at him with a queer expression and then she left her chair and crossed the floor quickly. To this day she is not quite sure why she obeyed, but it is enough that she did, and the Saint felt a certain relief as he watched her go.

Then he turned, and saw the gun in Mossiter's hand. He laughed—it was so absurd, so utterly fantastic, even in that place. In London, that sort of thing only happens in sensational fiction. But there it was and the Saint knew that Baldy Mossiter must have been badly upset to make such a crude break. And he laughed, and his left hand fell on Mossiter's hand in a grip of steel, but with a movement so easy and natural that Mossiter missed the meaning of it until it was too late. The gun was pointed harmlessly down into the table, and all Mossiter's strength could not move it.

“You had better know me,” said Simon quietly. “I’m called the Saint.” Baldy Mossiter heard him, staring, and went white.

“And you must not try to drug little girls,” said the Saint.

A lot of things of no permanent importance have been mentioned in this chapter, but the permanently important point of it is that Baldy Mossiter’s beautiful front teeth are now designed to his measure by a gentleman in a white coat with a collection of antediluvian magazines in his waiting-room.

3

A few moments later, the Saint strolled up into the street. A taxi was drawn up by the kerb, and the Saint briefly spoke an address to the driver and stepped in.

The girl was sitting in the far corner. Simon gave her a smile, and cheerfully inspected a set of grazed knuckles. It stands to the credit of his happy disposition that he really felt at peace with the world, although the evening's amusement represented a distinct set-back to certain schemes that had been maturing in his fertile brain. As a rough-house it had had its virtues, but the truth was that the Saint had marked down the Calumet Club for something more drastic and profitable than a mere rough-house, and that idea, if it was ever to be materialised now, would have to be tackled all over again, from the very beginning and a totally different angle. A couple of months of shrewd and patient reconnaissance work had gone west that night along with Baldy Mossiter's dental apparatus, but Simon Templar was incapable of weeping over potential poultry annihilated in the egg.

"Have a cigarette," he suggested, producing his case, "and tell me your name."

"Stella Dornford." She accepted a light, and he affected not to notice the unsteadiness of her hand. "Did you—have much trouble?"

The Saint grinned over his match.

"Well, hardly! I seemed to get a bit popular all at once . . . that was all. Nobody seemed to want me to go. There was a short argument—nothing to speak of."

He blew out the match and slewed round, looking through the window at the back.

There was another taxi close behind, which is not extraordinary in a London street and, hanging out of the window of the taxi behind, was a man—or the head and shoulders of one—which, to the Saint's suspicious mind, was quite extraordinary enough. But he was not particularly bothered about it at the moment, for he had directed his own driver to the Criterion, and nothing would happen there.

"Where are we going?" asked the girl.

"Towards coffee," said the Saint. "Or, if you prefer it, something with more kick. Praise be to the blessed laws of England, we can drink for another half-hour yet, if we hire a sandwich to put on the table. And you can tell me the story of your life."

In the better light of the restaurant, and at leisure which he had not had before, he was confirmed in the impression which he had formed at the Calumet. She was undeniably pretty, in a rather childish way, with a neat fair head and china-blue eyes. A certain grace of carriage saved her from mere fluffiness.

"You haven't told me your name," she remarked, when he had ordered refreshment.

"I thought you heard Mossiter address me. Templar-Simon Templar."

"You seem to be rather a remarkable man."

The Saint smiled. He had been told that before, but he had no objection to hearing it again. He really had very simple tastes, in some ways.

"It's rather lucky for you that I am," he answered. "And now, tell me, what were you doing at the Calumet with Baldy?"

He had some difficulty in extracting her story—in fact, it required all his ingenuity to avoid making the extraction look too much like a cross-examination, for it was evident that she had not yet made up her mind about him.

He learned, after a time, that she was twenty-one years old, that she was the only daughter of a retired bank manager, that she had run away from the dull suburban circle of her family to try to find fortune on the wrong side of the footlights. He might have guessed that much, but he liked to know. It took some much more astute questioning to elicit a fact in which he was really much more interested.

" . . . He's a junior clerk in the branch that used to be Daddy's. He came to the house once or twice, and we saw each other occasionally afterwards. It was all rather sweet and silly. We used to go to the pictures together, and once we met at a dance."

"Of course, you couldn't possibly have married him," said the Saint cunningly, and waited thoughtfully on her reply.

"It would have meant that I'd never have got away from all the mildewed things that I most wanted to run away from. I wanted to see Life . . . But he really was a nice boy."

She had got a job in a revue chorus, and another girl in the same show had taken her to the Calumet one night. There she had met Mossiter, and others. She was without friends in London, and sheer loneliness made her crave for any society rather than none. There had been difficulties, she admitted. One man, a guest of Mossiter's—a German—had been particularly unpleasant. Yes, he was reputed to be very rich . . .

"Don't you see," said the Saint, "that Mossiter could only have wanted to drug you for one of two reasons?"

"One of two?"

"When does this German go back to Germany?"

"I think he said he was going back tomorrow . . . that's Friday, isn't it?"

Simon shrugged.

"Such is life," he murmured, and she frowned.

"I'm not a child, Mr. Templar."

"No girl ever is, in her own estimation," said the Saint rudely. "That's why my friends and I have been put to so much trouble and expense in the past, and are likely to go on being bothered in the same way."

He had expected her to be troublesome—it was a premonition he had had about her from the first—and, as was his way, he had deliberately preferred to precipitate the explosion rather than fumble along through smouldering and smoke. But he was not quite prepared for the reaction that he actually provoked, which was that she simply rose and left the table.

"I'm perfectly capable of taking care of myself, thank you," was her parting speech.

He beckoned a waiter, and watched her go with a little smile of rueful resignation. It was not the first time that something of that sort had happened to him—cases of that type were always liable to be trying, and fulfilled their liability more often than not.

"And so she swep' out," murmured Simon wryly, as he pocketed his change, and then he remembered the men who had followed them from the Calumet. "Men"—it was unlikely to be a "man." The Calumet bunch were not of that class.

There were, as a matter of fact, two of them, and their instructions had been definite. They were merely to obtain addresses. It was therefore doubly unfortunate for the one who was concerned to follow Stella Dornford that, when he grasped part of the situation, he should have elected to attempt a coup on his own.

Stella Dornford tenanted a minute apartment in a block close to the upper end of Wardour Street. The block was in the form of a hollow square, with a courtyard in the centre, communicating with the street by a short passage, and the entrances to all the main staircases opened on to this courtyard. Standing in this courtyard, facing the doorway by which the girl had entered, the sleuth glanced up curiously at the windows. A moment later he saw one of the windows light up.

It was then that he decided upon his folly. The window which had lighted up was a French window, and it gave on to a narrow balcony—and, most tempting of all, it stood ajar, for the night was warm. And the building had been designed in the style that imitates large blocks of stone, with substantial interstices between the blocks. To reach that balcony would be as easy as climbing up a ladder.

He glanced about him. The courtyard was deserted and the light was poor. Once off the ground, he was unlikely to be noticed even if some other tenant passed beneath him. In the full blaze of his unconscious foolishness the man buttoned his coat and began to climb.

Standing in the shadows of the passage communicating with the street, Simon Templar watched him go. And, as he watched, with a newborn smile of sheer poetic devilment hovering on his lips, the Saint loaded up his newest toy—a small but powerful air-pistol.

He had acquired it quite recently, out of pure mischief. It wasn't by any means a lethal weapon, and was never intended for the purpose, but its pellets were capable of making a very painful impression upon the recipient. It had occurred to Simon that, adroitly employed from his window, it might serve as a powerful discouragement to the miscellaneous collection of professional and amateur sleuths whom from time to time he found unduly interested in his movements. But this occasion he had not anticipated, and his pleasure was therefore all the keener.

As the man on the wall reached the level of the second floor and paused for breath, Simon took careful aim.

The bullet smacked into the man's hand with a force that momentarily numbed his fingers. With a sharp gasp of pain and fear, he became aware that his hold was broken, and he had not enough strength in his uninjured hand to support himself with that alone. He gasped again, scrabbling wildly at the stone—and then his foot slipped . . .

The Saint pocketed his toy, and stepped quickly back into the street—so quickly that the man who was waiting just outside the passage had no time to appreciate his danger before it was upon him. He felt his coat lapels gripped by a sinewy hand, and looked into the Saint's face.

"Don't follow me about," said the Saint, in a tone of mild and reasonable remonstrance, and then his fist shot up and impacted crisply upon the man's jaw.

Simon turned and went back down the passage, and crossed the courtyard swiftly and the first window was flung up as he slipped into the shadow of the doorway opposite.

He went quickly up the dark stone stairs, found a bell, and pressed it. The door was opened almost immediately, but the girl was equally quick to shut it when she saw who her visitor was.

The Saint, however, was even quicker—with the toe of his shoe in the opening.

"There's something outside you ought to see," he said, and pushed quickly through the door while she hesitated.

Then she recovered herself.

"What do you mean by bursting in like this?" she demanded furiously.

"I told you . . . there's a special entertainment been put on for your benefit. Come and cheer."

He opened the nearest door, and went through the tiny sitting-room as if he owned the place. She followed him.

"If you don't get out at once I shall shout for help. There are people all round, and a porter in the basement, and the walls aren't very thick, so you needn't think no one will hear."

"I hadn't bothered to think," said the Saint calmly. "Besides, they're all busy with the other attraction. Step this way, madam."

He passed through the open window and emerged on to the balcony. In a moment he found her beside him. "Mr. Templar . . ."

Simon simply pointed downwards. She looked, and saw the little knot of people gathering about the sprawled figure that lay moaning at the foot of the wall. "So perish all the ungodly," murmured the Saint.

The girl turned a white face.

"How did it happen?"

"He, and a pal of his, followed us from the Calumet. I meant to tell you, but you packed up in such a hurry and such a naughty temper. I followed. He was on his way up to this verandah when I hypnotised him into the belief that he was a performing seal and I was a piece of ripe herring, whereupon he dived after me."

He turned back into the sitting-room, and closed the window after her.

"I don't think you need join the congregation below," he remarked. "The specimen will be taken for a promising cat burglar who's come down in the world, and he will probably get six months and free medical attention. But you might remember this incident. . . it will help you to take care of yourself."

She looked him in the eyes for several seconds. Then, "I apologise," she said quietly.

"So do I," answered the Saint. "That remark was unnecessarily sarcastic, and my only defence is that you thoroughly deserved it."

He smiled and then he reached for his cigarette-case.

"Gasper? . . . Splendid . . . By the way, I suppose you don't happen to have such a thing as a kipper about the place, do you? I was going to suggest that we indulge at the Cri, but you didn't give me time. And this is the hour when I usually kip . . ."

4

A few days later, Mr Francis Lemuel made his first long flight with his new pilot. They went first to Paris, and then to Berlin, in a week of perfect weather, and of the Saint's share in their wanderings abroad, on that occasion, there is nothing of interest to record. He drank French and German beers with a solid yearning for good English bitter, and was almost moved to assassinate a chatty and otherwise amiable Bavarian who ventured to say that in his opinion English beer was zu stark. Mr Lemuel went about his own business, and the Saint only saw him at sporadic meal-times in their hotels.

Lemuel was a man of middle age, with a Lombard Street complexion and an affectation of bluff geniality of which he was equally proud.

Except when they were actually in transit, he made few calls upon his new employee's time.

"Get about and enjoy yourself, Old Man,"— everyone was "Old Man" to Mr Lemuel. "You can see things here that you'll never see in England."

The Saint got about, and, in answer to Lemuel's casual inquiries, magnified his minor escapades into stories of which he was heartily ashamed. He made detailed notes of the true parts of some of his stories, to be reserved for future attention, but the Saint was a strong believer in concentrating on one thing at a time, and he was not proposing to ball up the main idea by taking chances on side-issues—at the moment.

He only met one of Lemuel's business acquaintances, and this was a man named Jacob Einsmann, who dined with them one night. Einsmann, it appeared, had a controlling interest in two prosperous night-clubs, and he was anxious for Lemuel to arrange lavish cabaret attractions. He was a short, florid-looking man, with an underhung nose and a superfluity of diamond rings.

"I must have it der English or American girls, yes," he insisted. "Der continental—pah! I can any number for noddings get, aind't it, no? But yours . . ."

He kissed excessively manicured fingers.

"You're right, Old Man," boomed Lemuel sympathetically. "English or American girls are the greatest troupers in the world. I won't say they don't get temperamental sometimes, but they've got a sense of discipline as well, and they don't mind hard work. The trouble is to get them abroad. There are so many people in England who jump to the worst conclusions if you try to send an English girl abroad."

He ranted against a certain traffic at some length and the Saint heard out the tirade, and shrugged.

"I suppose you know more about it than I do, sir," he submitted humbly, "but I always feel the danger's exaggerated. There must be plenty of honest agents."

"There are, Old Man," rumbled Lemuel. "But we get saddled with the crimes of those who aren't."

Shortly afterwards, the conversation reverted to purely business topics and the Saint, receiving a hint too broad to be ignored, excused himself.

Lemuel and the Saint left for England the next morning, and at the hour when he took off from Waalhaven Aerodrome on the last stage of the journey (they had descended upon Rotterdam for a meal) Simon was very little nearer to solving the problem of Francis Lemuel than he had been when he left England.

The inspiration came to him as they sighted the cliffs of Kent.

A few minutes later he literally ran into the means to his end.

It had been afternoon when they left the Tempelhof, for Mr Lemuel was no early riser, and even then the weather had been breaking. As they travelled westwards it had grown steadily worse. More than once the Saint had had to take the machine very low to avoid clouds, and although they had not actually encountered rain, the atmosphere had been anything but serene ever since they crossed the Dutch frontier. There had been one very bumpy half-hour during which Mr Lemuel had been actively unhappy . . .

Now, as they came over English ground, they met the first of the storm.

"I don't like the look of it, Templar," Mr. Lemuel opined huskily, through the telephones. "Isn't there an aerodrome near here that we could land at, Old Man?"

"I don't know of one," lied the Saint. "And it's getting dark quickly—I daren't risk losing my bearings. We'll have to push on to Croydon."

"Croydon!"

Simon heard the word repeated faintly, and grinned. For in a flash he had grasped a flimsy clue, and had seen his way clear; and the repetition had confirmed him in a fantastic hope.

"Why Croydon?"

"It's the nearest aerodrome that's fitted up for night landings. I don't suppose we shall have much trouble with the Customs," added the Saint thoughtfully.

There was a silence, and the Saint flew on, as low as he dared, searching the darkening country beneath him. And, within himself, he was blessing the peculiar advantages of his favourite hobby.

Times without number, when he had nothing else to do, the Saint had taken his car and set out to explore the unfrequented byways of England, seeking out forgotten villages and unspoilt country inns, which he collected as less robust and simple-minded men collect postage-stamps. It was his boast that he knew every other inch of the British Isles blindfolded, and he may not have been very far wrong. There was one village, near the Kent-Surrey border, which had suggested itself to him immediately as the ideal place for his purpose.

"I say, Old Man," spoke Lemuel again, miserably.

"Hullo?"

"I'm feeling like death. I can't go on much longer. Can't you land in a field around here while there's still a bit of light?"

"I was wondering what excuse you'd make, dear heart," said the Saint, but he said it to himself. Aloud, he answered cheerfully, "It certainly is a bit bumpy, sir. I'll have a shot at it, if you like."

As a matter of fact, he had just sighted his objective, and he throttled off the engine with a gentle smile of satisfaction.

It wasn't the easiest landing in the world to make, especially in that weather, but the Saint put the machine on the deck without a mistake, turned, and taxied back to a sheltered corner of the field he had chosen. Then he climbed out of the cockpit and stretched himself.

"I can peg her out for the night," he remarked, as Lemuel joined him on the ground, "and there shouldn't be any harm done if it doesn't blow much harder than this."

"A little more of that flying would have killed me," said Lemuel, and he was really looking rather pale. "Where are we?"

Simon told him.

"It's right off the map, and I'm afraid you won't get a train back to town tonight, but I know a very decent little pub we can stay at," he said.

"I'll phone for my chauffeur to come down," said Lemuel. "I suppose there's a telephone in this place somewhere?"

"I doubt it," said Simon, but he knew that there was.

Again, however, luck was with him. It was quite dark by the time the aeroplane had been pegged out with ropes obtained from a neighbouring farm, and a steady rain was falling, so that no one was about to watch the Saint climbing nimbly up a telegraph-pole just beyond the end of the village street . . .

Lemuel, who had departed to knock up the post office, rejoined him later in the bar of the "Blue Dragon" with a tale of woe.

"A telegraph-pole must have been blown down," he said. "Anyway, it was impossible to get through."

Simon, who had merely cut the wires without doing any damage to the pole, nevertheless saw no reason to correct the official theory.

Inquiries about possible conveyance to the nearest main-line town proved equally fruitless, as the Saint had known they would be. He had selected his village with care. It possessed nothing suitable for Mr Lemuel, and no traffic was likely to pass through that night, for it was right off the beaten track.

"Looks as if we'll have to make the best of it, Old Man," said Lemuel, and Simon concurred.

After supper, Lemuel's spirits rose, and they spent a convivial evening in the bar.

It was a very convivial evening. Mr Lemuel, under the soothing influence of many brandies, forgot his day's misadventures, and embarked enthusiastically upon the process of making a night of it. For, he explained, his conversation with Jacob Einsmann was going to lead to a lot of easy money. But he could not be persuaded to divulge anything of interest, though the Saint led the conversation cunningly. Simon smiled, and continued to drink him level—even taking it upon himself to force the pace towards closing time. Simon had had some opportunity to measure up Francis Lemuel's minor weaknesses, and an adroit employment of some of this knowledge was part of the Saint's plan. And the Saint was ordinarily a most temperate man.

"You're a goo' feller, Ole Man," Mr Lemuel was proclaiming, towards eleven o'clock. "You stick to me, Ole Man, an' don' worrabout wha' people tell you. You stick to me. I gorra lotta money. Show you trick one day. You stick to me. Give you a berra job soon, ole man. Pallomine . . ."

When at length Mr Lemuel announced that he was going to bed, the Saint's affable "Sleep well, sir!" would have struck a captious critic as unnecessary, for nothing could have been more certain than that Mr Lemuel would that night sleep the sleep of the only just.

The Saint himself stayed on in the bar for another hour, for the landlord was in a talkative mood and was not unique in finding Simon Templar very pleasant company. So it came to pass that, a few minutes after the Saint had said good night, his sudden return with a face of dismay was easily accounted for.

"I've got the wrong bag," he explained. "The other two were put in Mr Lemuel's room, weren't they?"

"Is one of them yours?" asked the publican sympathetically.

Simon nodded.

"I've been landed with the samples," he said. "And I'll bet Mr. Lemuel's locked his door. He never forgets to do that, however drunk he is. And we'd have to knock the place down to wake him up now—and I'd lose my job if we did."

"I've got a master key, sir," said the landlord helpfully. "You could slip in with that, and change the bags, and he wouldn't know anything about it."

Simon stared.

"You're a blinkin' marvel, George," he murmured. "You are, really."

With the host's assistance he entered Mr Lemuel's room, and emerged with the key of the door in his pocket and one of Lemuel's bags in his hand. Mr Lemuel snored rhythmically through it all.

"Thanks, George," said the Saint, returning the master key. "Breakfast at ten, and in bed, I think . . ."

Then he took the bag into his own room, and opened it without much difficulty.

Its weight, when he had lifted it out of the aeroplane, had told him not to expect it to contain clothes, but the most superficially interesting thing about it was that Mr Lemuel had not possessed it when he left England, and it was simply as a result of intensive pondering over that fact that the Saint had arrived at the scheme that he was then carrying out. And, in view of his hypothesis, and Mr Lemuel's reaction to the magic word "Croydon," it cannot be said that the Saint was wildly surprised when he found what the bag actually held. But he was very, very interested, nevertheless.

There were rows and rows of neatly-packed square tins, plain and unlabelled. Fishing one out, the Saint gently detached the strip of adhesive tape which sealed it, and prised off the lid. He came to a white, crystalline powder . . . but that had been in his mind when he opened the tin. Almost perfunctorily, he took a tiny pinch of the powder between his finger and thumb, and laid it on his tongue, and the Saintly smile tightened a little.

Then he sat back on his heels, lighted a cigarette, and regarded his catch thoughtfully.

"You're a clever boy, Francis," he murmured.

He meditated for some time, humming under his breath, apparently quite unmoved. But actually his brain was seething.

It would have been quite easy to dispose of the contents of the bag. It would have been quite easy to dispose of Mr Lemuel. For a while the Saint toyed with the second idea. A strong solution of the contents of one of the tins, for instance, administered with the hypodermic syringe which Simon had in his valise . . . Then he shook his head.

"Try to remember, Old Man," he apostrophised himself, "that you are a business organisation. And you're not at all sure that Uncle Francis has left you anything in his will."

The scheme which he ultimately decided upon was simplicity itself—so far as it went. It depended solely upon the state of the village baker's stock.

Simon left the "Blue Dragon" stealthily, and returned an hour later considerably laden. He was busy for some hours after that, but he replaced Lemuel's grip looking as if it had not been touched, opening the door with Lemuel's own key.

It is quite easy to lock a door from the outside and leave the key in the lock on the inside—if you know the trick. You tie a string to the end of a pencil, slip the pencil through the hole in the key, and pass the string underneath the door. A pull on the string turns the key and the pencil drops out, and can be pulled away under the door.

And after that the Saint slithered into his pyjamas and rolled into bed as the first greyness of dawn lightened the sky outside his bedroom window, and slept like a child.

In the morning they flew on to Hanworth, where Lemuel's car waited to take them back to London.

The Saint was dropped at Piccadilly Circus and he walked without hesitation into the Piccadilly Hotel. Settling himself at a table within, he drew a sheet of the hotel's note-paper towards him, and devoted himself with loving care to the production of a Work of Art. This consisted of the picture of a little man, drawn with a round blank head and straight-lined body and limbs, as a child draws, but wearing above his cerebellum, at a somewhat rakish angle, a halo such as few children's drawings portray. Then he took an envelope, which he addressed to Francis Lemuel and omitted to embellish with a stamp. He posted his completed achievement within the hotel.

At half past one he burst in upon Patricia Holm, declaring himself ravenous for lunch. "With beer," he said. "Huge foaming mugs of it. Brewed at Burton, and as stark as they make it."

"And what's Francis Lemuel's secret?" she asked.

He shrugged.

"Don't spoil the homecoming," he said. "I hate to tell you, but I haven't come within miles of it in a whole blinkin' week."

He did not think it necessary to tell her that he had deliberately signed and sealed his own death-warrant, for of late she had become rather funny that way.

5

There are a number of features about this story which will always endear it—in a small way—to the Saint's memory. He likes its logical development, and the neat way in which the diverse factors dovetail into one another with an almost audible click. He likes the crisp precision of the earlier episodes, and purrs happily as he recalls the flawless detail of his own technique in those episodes, but particularly is he lost in speechless admiration when he considers the overpowering brilliance of the exercise in inductive psychology which dictated his manner of pepping up the concluding stages of the adventure.

Thus he reviewed the child of his genius:

"The snow retails at about sixty pounds an ounce, in the unauthorised trade, and I must have poured about seventy thousand pounds' worth down the sink. Oh, yes, it was a good idea—to fetch over several years' supply at one go, almost without risk. And then, of course, according to schedule, I should have been quietly fired, and no one but Uncle Francis would have been any the wiser. Instead of which, Uncle's distributing organisation, whatever that may be, will shortly be howling in full cry down Jermyn Street to ask Uncle what he means by ladling them out a lot of tins of ordinary white flour. Coming on top of the letter, which will be shot in by the late post tonight, this question will cause a distinct stir. And, in the still small hours, Uncle Francis will sit down to ponder the ancient problem: What should 'A' do?"

This was long afterwards, when the story of Francis Lemuel was ancient history. And the Saint would gesture with his cigarette, and beam thoughtfully upon the assembled congregation, and presently proceed with his exposition:

"Now, what should 'A' do, dear old strepsicocco? . . . Should he woofle forth into the wide world, and steam into Scotland Yard, bursting with information? . . . Definitely not. He has no information that he can conveniently lay. His egg, so to speak, had addled in the oviduct . . . Then should he curse me and cut his losses and leave it at that? . . . Just as definitely not. I have had no little publicity in my time and he knows my habits. He knows that I haven't finished with him yet. He knows that, unless he gets his counter-attack in quickly, he's booked to travel down the drain in no uncertain manner . . . Then should he call in a few tough guys and offer a large reward for my death-certificate? . . . I think not. Francis isn't that type . . . He has a wholesome respect for the present length of his neck, and he doesn't fancy the idea of having it artificially extended in a whitewashed shed by a gentleman in a dark suit one cold and frosty morning. He knows that that sort of thing is frequently happening— sometimes to quite clever murderers . . . So what does he do?"

And what Francis Lemuel did was, of course, exactly what the Saint had expected. He telephoned in the evening, three days later, and Simon went round to Jermyn Street after dinner—with a gun in his pocket in case of accidents. That was a simple precaution; he was not really expecting trouble, and he was right.

The instructions which he actually received, however, were slightly different from the ones he had anticipated. He found Lemuel writing telegrams, and the impresario came straight to the point.

"Einsmann—you remember the fellow who came to dinner—seems to have got himself into a mess. He's opening a new night club tomorrow, and his prize cabaret attraction has let him down at the last minute. He hasn't been able to arrange a good enough substitute on the spot, and he cabled me for help. I've been able to find a first-class girl, but the trouble is to get her to Berlin in time for a rehearsal with his orchestra."

"You want me to fly her over?" asked the Saint, and Lemuel nodded.

"That's the only way, Old Man. I can't let Einsmann down when he's just on the point of signing a big contract with me. You have a car, haven't you?"

"Yes, sir."

"I'll give you this girl's address." Lemuel took a slip of paper, and wrote. "She's expecting you to pick her up at nine o'clock tomorrow morning. You must go straight to Hanworth . . ."

Simon folded the paper and stowed it carefully away in his pocketbook, while Lemuel gave further instructions.

Lemuel was showing signs of the strain. There was a puffiness about his eyes, and his plump cheeks seemed to sag flabbily. But he played his part with a grim restraint.

Leaving Jermyn Street, the Saint found himself heading mechanically for the Piccadilly Hotel. There he composed, after some careful calculations with the aid of a calendar, a brief note:

> *Unless the sum of £20,000 (Twenty Thousand Pounds) is paid into the account of J. B. L. Smith at the City and Continental Bank, Lombard Street, by 12 noon on*

Saturday, I shall forward to the Public Prosecutor sufficient evidence to assure you of five years' penal servitude.

The note was signed with one of the Saint's most artistic self-portraits, and it was addressed to Francis Lemuel.

This was on Thursday night.

As he strolled leisurely home the Saint communed with himself again.

"Uncle Francis wanted a disreputable aviator so that if anything went wrong the aviator could be made the scapegoat. But when he deduced that I was the Saint, that idea went west. What should I have done if I'd been Uncle Francis? . . . I should have arranged for Mr Templar to fall out of an aeroplane at a height of about four thousand feet. A nasty accident—he stalled at the top of a loop, and his safety belt wasn't fastened . . . And Uncle knows enough about the game to be able to bring the kite down . . . And that's what I thought it was going to be, with a few drops of slumber mixture in my beer before we went up next time . . . But this is nearly as good. I do my last job of work for Uncle, and doubtless there is an entertainment arranged for my especial benefit in Berlin tomorrow night—or a man hired to file my elevator wires ready for the return journey on Saturday. Yes—perhaps this is even cleverer than my own idea. The commission to take this girl to Berlin is intended to disarm my suspicions. I am meant to think that I'm not suspected. I'm supposed to think that I'm absolutely on velvet, and therefore get careless . . . Oh, it should be a great little weekend!"

The only trouble he expected the next morning would not be directly of Lemuel's making—and in that, again, his deduction was faultless.

Stella Dornford was surprised to see him. "What do you want?" she asked.

"I want you to fly with me," said the Saint dramatically, and she was taken aback.

"Are you Lemuel's man?"

Simon nodded.

"Extraordinary how I get about, isn't it?" he murmured.

"Is this a joke?"

He shook his head. "Anything but, as far as I'm concerned, old dear. Now, can you imagine anyone getting up at this hour of the morning to be funny?" He grinned at her puzzled doubts. "Call it coincidence, sweetheart, and lead me to your luggage."

At the foot of the stairs he paused, and looked thoughtfully round the courtyard.

"They seem to have scraped Cuthbert off the concrete," he said, and then, abruptly, "How did you get this job?"

"Lemuel was in front the other night," she answered. "He sent his card round in the interval . . ."

"Told you he was struck by your dancing, bought you out, signed you up . . ."

"How did you know?"

"I didn't. But it fits in so beautifully. And to make me the accessory—oh, it's just too splendiferous for words! I didn't know Francis had such a sense of humour."

"What do you mean?"

"I'm right, am I? Listen. He said, 'It's one of the worst shows I've ever seen, old man' . . . no, I suppose he'd vary that . . . 'but your dancing, old woman, is the elephant's uvula.' Or words to that effect. What?"

"He certainly said he liked my dancing . . ."

"Joke," said the Saint sardonically.

She caught him up when he was loading her two suitcases into the back of his car. "Mr. Templar . . ."

"My name."

"I don't understand your sense of humour."

"Sorry about that."

"I'd be obliged if you'd leave my dancing alone."

"Darling," said the Saint kindly, "I'd like to maroon it on a desert island. After I'd met you for the first time I made a point of seeing your show, and I must say that I decided that you are beautiful and energetic and well-meaning, and your figure is a dream—but if your dancing is the elephant's uvula, then I think the R.S.P.C.A. ought to do something about it."

Pale with fury, she entered the car, and there was silence until they were speeding down the Great West Road.

Then Simon added, as if there had been no break in his speech, "If I were you, old dear, I'd be inclined to think very kindly of that nice boy in the bank."

"I don't think I want your advice, Mr. Templar," she said coldly. "Your job is to take me to Berlin—and I only wish I could get there in time without your help."

All the instinctive antagonism that had come up between them like barbed wire at their first meeting was back again. After the accident to the amateur mountaineer there had been a truce, but the Saint had foreseen renewed hostilities from the moment he had read the name and address on the paper which Lemuel had given him, and he had been at no pains to avert the outbreak. Patricia Holm used to say that the Saint had less than no idea of the art of handling women. That is a statement which other historians may be left to judge. The Saint himself would have been the smiling first to subscribe to the charge, but there were times when Simon Templar's vanity went to strange extremes. If he thought he had any particular accomplishment, he would either boast about it or disclaim it altogether, so you always knew where you were with him. So far as the handling of women was concerned, his methods were usually of the this-is-your-label-and-if-you-don't-like-it-you-can-get-to-hell-out-of-here school—when they were not exactly the reverse—and in this case, at least, he knew precisely what he was doing. Otherwise, he might have had a more entertaining journey to Berlin than he did, but he had developed a soft spot in his heart for the unknown nice boy who used to take Stella Dornford to the movies—and, bless him, probably used to hold her hand in the same. Now, Jacob Einsmann would never have thought of doing a thing like that . . .

There was another reason—a subsidiary reason—for the Saint's aloofness. He wanted to be free to figure out the exact difference that had been made to the situation by the discovery of the identity of his charge. A new factor had been introduced which was likely to alter a lot of things. And it was necessary to find out a little more about it—a very little more.

So they travelled between Hanworth and the Tempelhof in a frost-bitten silence which the Saint made no attempt to alleviate, and in the same spirit he took Stella Dornford by taxi to the address that Lemuel had given him.

This was a huge, gloomy house nearly two miles away from the centre of fashionable gaiety, and anything less like a night club Simon Templar had rarely seen.

He did not immediately open the door of the taxi. Instead, he surveyed the house interestedly through a window of the cab and then he turned to the girl.

"I'm sure Jacob Einsmann isn't a very nice man," he said. "In fact, he and I are definitely going to have words. But I'm ready to leave you at a hotel before I go in."

She tossed her head, and opened the door herself.

The Saint followed her up the steps of the house. She had rung the bell while he was paying off the taxi, and the door was unbarred as he reached her side.

"Herr Einsmann wishes to see you also, sir."

The Saint nodded, and passed in. The butler—he, like the porter at the Calumet Club, of hallowed memory, looked as if he had been other things in his time—led them down a bare sombre hall, and opened a door.

The girl passed through it first, and Simon heard her exclamation before he saw

Einsmann.

Then her hand gripped his arm. "I don't like this," she said.

Simon smiled. He had read the doubt in her eyes when she first saw the house, and had liked the dam'-fool obstinacy that had marched her into it against his advice and her better judgment. But, while he approved her spirit, he had deliberately taken advantage of it to make sure that she should have her lesson.

"So!" Jacob Einsmann rose from his chair, rubbing his hands gently together. His eyes were fixed upon the girl. "You vould not listen to it vot I say in London, no, you vere so prrroud, but now you yourself to me hof come, aind't it?"

6

"Aye, laad, we've coom," drawled the Saint. "So you hof got it vot you vanted, yes, no, aind't it?"

Einsmann turned his head.

"Ach! I remember you . . ."

"And I you," said the Saint comfortably. "In fact, I spent a considerable time on the trip over composing a little song about you, in the form of a nursery rhyme for the instruction of small children, which, with your permission, I will now proceed to sing. It goes like this:

"Dear Jacob is an unwashed mamser.
We like not his effluvium, sir;
If we can tread on Jacob's graft,
Das wird ja wirklich fabelhaft."

"For that effort in trilingual verse I have already awarded myself the Swaffer Biscuit."

Einsman leered. "For vonce, Herr Saint, you hof a misdake made."

"Saint?" The girl spoke, at Simon's shoulder, startled, half incredulous.

He smiled round at her. "That's right, old dear. I am that well-known institution. Is this the Boche you mentioned at the Cri—the bird who got fresh at the Calumet?"

She nodded. "I didn't know . . ."

"You weren't meant to," said Simon coolly. "That was just part of the deception. But I guessed it as soon as Lemuel gave me your name."

"You vos clever, Herr Saint," Einsmann said suavely.

"I vos," the Saint admitted modestly. "It only wanted a little putting two and two together. There was that dinner the other day, for instance. Very well staged for my benefit, wasn't it? All that trout-spawn and frog-bladder about your cabarets, and Lemuel warbling about the difficulty of getting English girls abroad . . . I made a good guess at the game then and I'd have laid anyone ten thousand bucks to a slush nickel, on the spot, that it wouldn't be long before I was asked to ferry over a few fair maidens in Lemuel's machine. I had your graft taped right out a few days ago, and I don't see that the present variation puts me far wrong. The only real difference is that Francis is reckoning to have to find another aviator to carry through the rest of the contract—aind't it?"

His hand went lazily to his hip pocket, and then something jabbed him sharply in the ribs, and he looked down at a heavy automatic in the hand of the imitation butler, who had not left the room.

"You vill bring your gun out verree slowly," said Einsmann, succulently. "Verree slowly . . ."

Simon smiled—a slow and Saintly smile. And, as slow as the smile, his hand came into view.

"Do you mind?" he murmured.

He opened the cigarette-case, and selected a smoke with care. The butler lowered his gun.

"Let us talk German," said the Saint suddenly, in that language. "I have a few things to say which this girl need not hear." Einsmann's mouth twisted.

"I shall be interested," he said ironically.

With an unlighted cigarette between his lips, and the cigarette-case still open in his hands, Simon looked across at the German. Stella Dornford was behind the Saint, the imitation butler stood a little to one side, his automatic in his hand.

"You are a man for whom there is no adequate punishment. You are a buyer and seller of souls, and your money is earned with more human misery than your insanitary mind can imagine. To attempt to visit some of this misery upon yourself would do little good. The only thing to do is to see that you cease to pollute the earth."

His cold blue eyes seemed to bore into Einsmann's brain, so that the German, in spite of his armed bodyguard, felt a momentary qualm of fear.

"I only came here to make quite sure about you, Jacob Einsmann," said the Saint. "And now I am quite sure. You had better know that I am going to kill you." He took a step forward, and did not hear the door open behind him.

Einsmann's florid face had gone white, save for the bright patches of colour that burned in either cheek. Then he spoke, in a sudden torrent of hoarse words. "So! You say you will kill me? But you are wrong. I am not the one who will die tonight, I know you, Herr Saint! Even if Lemuel had not told me, I should still have known enough. You remember Henri Chastel? He was my friend, and you killed him. Ach! You shall not have a quick death, my friend . . ."

With the Saintly smile still resting blandly on his lips, Simon had closed his cigarette-case with a snap while Einsmann talked, and was returning it to his hip pocket . . . He performed the action so quietly and naturally that, coming after the false alarm he had caused when he took it out of the same pocket, this movement of his hand passed almost unnoticed. Nor did it instantly seem strange to the audience when the Saint's hand did not at once return to view. He brought the hand up swiftly behind his back; he had exchanged the cigarette-case for a gun, and he nosed the muzzle of the gun through the gap between his left arm and his body.

"You may give my love to Henri," he remarked, and touched the trigger.

He saw Einsmann's face twist horribly, and the German clutched at his stomach before he crumpled where he stood, but Simon only saw these things out of the tail of his eye. He had whipped the gun from under his armpit a second after his first shot. There was no time to fetch it round behind his body into a more convenient firing position, and he loosed his second shot with his forearm lying along the small of his back and the gun aimed out to his left. But the butler's attention had been diverted at the moment when the Saint fired first, and the man's reaction was not quite quick enough. He took the Saint's bullet in the shoulder, and his own shot blew a hole in the carpet.

Then the door slammed shut and Simon turned right round.

The man who had seized Stella Dornford from behind a moment before the Saint's first shot was not armed, and he had not taken a second to perceive the better part of valour. Unhappily for his future, the instinct of self-preservation had been countered by another and equally powerful instinct, and he had tried to compromise with the two. Perhaps he thought that the armed butler could be relied upon.

The speculation is interesting but unprofitable, for the man's mental processes are now beyond the reach of practical investigation. All we know is that at that precise instant of time he was heading down the hall with an unconscious burden.

And the Saint had wrenched at the handle of the door and found it locked upon the outside. Simon jerked up his gun again, and the report mingled with a splintering crash.

He jerked the door open, and looked up and down the dark hall. At the far end, towards the back of the house, another door was closing—he saw the narrowing strip of brighter light in the gloom. The strip vanished as he raced towards it, and he heard a key turn as he groped for the handle. Again he raised his automatic, and then, instead of the detonation he was expecting, heard only the click of a dud cartridge. He snatched at the sliding jacket, and something jammed. He had no time to find out what it was; he dropped the gun into his pocket, made certain of the position of the keyhole, and stepped back a pace. Then he raised his foot and smashed his heel into the lock with all his strength and weight behind it.

The door sprang open eighteen inches—and crashed into a table that was being brought up to reinforce it. The Saint leapt at the gap, made it, wedged his back against the jamb, and set both hands to the door. With one titanic heave he flung the door wide and sent the table spinning back to the centre of the room.

The girl lay on the floor by the doorway. On the other side of the room, beyond the up-turned table, the man who had brought her had opened a drawer in a desk, and he turned with an automatic in his hand.

"Schweinhund!" he snarled, and the Saint laughed.

The Saint laughed, took two quick steps, and launched himself headlong into space in a terrific dive. It took him clear over the table, full length, and muddled his objective's aim. The man sighted frantically, and fired and the Saint felt something like a hot iron sear his right arm from wrist to elbow. Then Simon had gathered up the man's legs in that fantastic tackle, and they went to the floor together.

The Saint's left hand caught the gunman's right wrist and pinned it to the floor, then, his own right hand being numb, he brought up his knee . . .

He was on his feet again in a moment, gathering the automatic out of the man's limp hand as he rose.

The girl's eyes fluttered as he reached her, but the Saint reckoned that freight would be less trouble than first aid. He put his captured gun on a chair, and, as the girl started to try to rise, he yanked her to her feet and caught her over his left shoulder before she could fall again.

Quickly he tested his right hand again, and found that his fingers had recovered from the momentary shock. He picked up the gun in that hand.

A faint sound behind him made him turn swiftly, and he saw the gunman crawling towards him with a knife. He had not meant to fire, but the trigger must have been exceptionally sensitive, and the gunman rolled over slowly and lay quite still.

Then the Saint broke down the hall.

A gigantic negro loomed up out of the twilight. Careful of the trigger this time, the Saint snapped the muzzle of the gun into the man's chest, and the negro backed away with rolling eyes. Keeping him covered, Simon sidled to the door and set the girl gently on her feet. She was able to stand then and she it was who, under his directions, unbarred the door and opened it.

"See if there's a taxi," rapped the Saint, and heard her hurry down the steps. A moment later she called him.

He gave her time to get into the taxi herself, and then, like lightning, he sprang through the door and slammed it behind him.

The chauffeur, turning to receive his instructions through the little window communicating between the inside and outside of the cab, heard the shout from the house, and looked round with a question forming on his lips. Then something cold and metallic touched the back of his neck, and one of his fares spoke crisply.

"Gehen Sie schnell, mein Freund!"

The driver obeyed.

The fact that, having been given no destination to drive to, he was quietly steering his passengers in the direction of the nearest police station, is of no great historical interest. For, when he reached the station he was without passengers, and the officials who heard his story were inclined to cast grave doubts upon that worthy citizen's sobriety, until confirmation of some of his statements arrived through another channel.

Stella Dornford and the Saint had quietly left him in a convenient traffic block, for Simon had much more to do in the next twenty-four hours, and he was in no mood to be delayed by embarrassing inquiries.

7

"And if that doesn't learn you, my girl," said the Saint, a trifle grimly, "nothing ever will."

They were in a room in the hotel where the girl had parked her luggage before proceeding to the interview with Einsmann. The Saint, with a cigarette between his lips and a glass tankard of dark syrupy Kulmbach on the table beside him, was sitting on the bed, bandaging his arm with two white linen handkerchiefs torn into strips. Stella Dornford stood by shame-facedly.

"I'm sorry I was such a fool," she said.

Simon looked up at her. She was very pale, but this was not the pallor of anger with which she had begun the day.

"Can I help you with that?" she asked.

"It's nothing," he said cheerfully. "I'm never hurt. It's a gift . . ."

He secured his effort with a safety-pin, and rolled down his sleeve. Then he gave her one of his quick, impulsive smiles.

"Anyway," he said, "you've seen some Life. And that was what you wanted, wasn't it?"

"You can't make me feel worse than I do already."

He laughed, and stood up and she looked round as his hands fell on her shoulders.

"Why worry, old dear?" he said. "It's turned out all right—so what the hell? You don't even have to rack your brains to think of an unfutile way of saying, 'Thank you.' I've loved it. The pleasure of shooting Jacob in the tum-tum was worth a dozen of these scratches. So let's leave it at that." He ruffled her hair absently. "And now we'll beat it back to England, shall we?"

He turned away, and picked up his coat.

"Are you leaving now?" she asked in surprise.

Simon nodded. "I'm afraid we must. In the first place, this evening's mirth and horseplay is liable to start a certain hue and cry after me in this bouncing burg. I don't know that that alone would make me jump for the departure platform, but there's also a man I want to see in England—about a sort of dog. I'm sorry about the rush, but things always seem to happen to me in a hurry. Are you ready?"

They landed for a late meal at Amsterdam and they had not long left Schiphol behind when the darkness and the monotonous roar of the engine soothed Stella Dornford into a deep sleep of sheer nervous weariness. She awoke when the engine was suddenly silenced, and found that they were gliding down into the pale half-light before dawn.

"I think there's enough light to make a landing here," Simon answered her question through the telephones. "I don't want to have to go on to Croydon."

There was, at least, enough light for the Saint to make a perfect landing and he taxied up to the deserted hangers and left the machine there for the mechanics to find in the morning. Then he went in search of his car.

In the car, again she slept, and it is therefore not surprising that she never thought of Francis Lemuel until after he had unloaded her into one of the friendliest sitting-rooms she had ever seen, and after he had prepared eggs and bacon and coffee for them both, and after they had smoked two cigarettes together. And then it was Simon who reminded her.

"I want you to help me with a telephone conversation," he said, and proceeded to coach her carefully.

A few minutes later she had dialled a number and was waiting for the reply. Then, "Are you Piccadilly thrrree-eight thrrree-four?" she asked sweetly.

The answer came in a decorated affirmative. "You're wanted from Berlin."

She clicked the receiver hook, and then the Saint took over the instrument.

"Dot vos you, Lemuel, no? . . . You vould like to hear about it der business, aind't it? . . . Ja! I hof seddled it altogether der business. Der man vill not more trrouble gif, andt der samples I hof also received it, yes . . ."

A couple of lines of brisk dialogue, this time in German, between the Saint and an excellent impersonator of the Berlin exchange, cut short the conversation with the Saint hurriedly concluding, "Ja! I to you der particulars tomorrow vill wrrrite . . ."

"It's detail that does it," murmured Simon complacently, as he replaced the receiver.

Stella Dornford was regarding him with a certain awe.

"I'm beginning to understand some of the things I've read about you," she said, and the Saint grinned, for no false modesty had ever been numbered among his failings.

Shortly afterwards he excused himself, and when he returned to the sitting-room, which was in a surprisingly short space of time, he had changed out of the characteristically conspicuous suit in which he had travelled, and was wearing a plain and unnoticeable blue serge. The Saint's phenomenal speed of dressing would have made the fortune of a professional quick-change artist and he was as pleased with the girl's unspoken astonishment at his feat as he had been with her first compliment.

"Where are you going?" she demanded, when she had found her voice.

"To see you home, first," he answered briskly. "And then I have a little job of work to do."

"But why have you changed?"

The Saint adjusted a cheap black tie.

"The job might turn into a funeral," he said. "I don't seriously think it will, but I like to be prepared."

She was still mystified when he left her at the door of her apartment.

From there he drove down to Piccadilly, and left his car in St. James's Street, proceeding afterwards on foot. Here the reason for his change of costume began to appear. Anyone might have remarked the rare spectacle of a truly Saintly figure parading the West End of London at six o'clock in the morning arrayed in one of the most dazzling creations of Savile Row, but no one came forward to describe the soberly dressed and commonplace-looking young man who committed the simplest audacity of the season.

Nor could he ever afterwards have been identified by the sleepy-eyed porter who answered his ring at a certain bell in Jermyn Street, for, when the door was opened, Simon's face was masked from eyes to chin by a handkerchief folded three-cornerwise, and his hat-brim shaded his eyes. So much the porter saw before the Saint struck once, swiftly, mercifully, and regretfully, with a supple rubber truncheon . . .

The Saint closed the door behind him, and unbuttoned his double-breasted coat. There were a dozen turns of light rope wound round his waist belt-fashion, and with these he secured the janitor hand and foot, completing the work with a humane but efficient gag. Then he lifted the unconscious man and carried him to a little cubicle at the back of the hall, where he left him—after taking his keys.

He raced up the stairs to the door of Lemuel's apartment, which was on the second floor.

It was the work of a moment only to find the right key. Then, if the door were bolted . . . But apparently Lemuel relied on the security of his Yale and the watchfulness of the porter . . .

The Saint passed like a cat down the passage that opened before him, listening at door after door. Presently he heard the sound of rhythmic breathing and he entered Lemuel's bedroom without a sound, and stood over the bed like a ghost.

He was certain that Lemuel must have spent a restless night until the recent telephone call came through to calm his fears. There was a bottle, a siphon, a glass, and an ash-tray heaped with cigarette-ends, on a table by the bedside, to support this assumption, but now Lemuel must be sleeping the sleep of the dead.

Gently Simon drew the edge of the sheet over the sleeping man's face, and on to the sheet he dripped a colourless liquid from a flask which he took from his pocket. The atmosphere thickened with a sickly reek . . .

Five minutes later, in another room, the Saint was opening a burglar-proof safe with Lemuel's own key.

He found what he was expecting to find—what, in fact, he had arranged to find. It had required no great genius to deduce that Lemuel would have withdrawn all his mobile fortune from his bank the day before; if there had been no satisfactory report from Einsmann before morning, Lemuel would have been on his way out of England long before the expiration of the time limit which the Saint had given him.

Simon burned twenty-five thousand pounds' worth of negotiable securities in the open grate. There was already a heap of ashes in the fireplace when he began his own bonfire and he guessed that Lemuel had spent part of the previous evening disinfecting his private papers; it would be a waste of time to search the desk. With about forty thousand pounds in Bank of England notes cunningly distributed about his person, the Saint closed the safe, after some artistic work on the interior, and returned to Lemuel's bedroom, where he replaced the key as he had found it. Before he left, he turned the sheet back from Lemuel's face; the bedroom windows were already open, and by morning the smell of ether should have dispersed.

"By morning . . ." The Saint glanced at his watch as he went down the stairs, and realised that he had only just given himself enough time. But he stopped at the janitor's cubicle on his way out, and the helpless man glared at him defiantly.

"I'm sorry I had to hit you," said the Saint. "But perhaps this will help to console you for your troubles."

He took ten one-pound notes from his wallet, and hid them on the porter's desk, then he hurried down the hall, and slipped off his masking handkerchief as he opened the door.

Half an hour later he was in bed.

Francis Lemuel had arranged to be called early, in case of accidents, and the reassuring telephone message had come too late for him to countermand the order. He roused at half-past eight, to find his valet shaking him by the shoulder, and sat up muzzily. His head was splitting. He took a gulp at the hot tea which his man had brought, and felt sick.

"Must have drunk more whisky than I thought," he reflected hazily, and then he became aware that his valet was speaking.

"There's been a burglary here, sir. About six o'clock this morning the porter was knocked out . . ."

"Here—in this apartment?" Lemuel's voice was harsh and strained.

"No, sir. At least, I've looked round, sir, and nothing seems to have been touched." Lemuel drew a long breath. For an instant an icy dread had clutched at his heart. Then he remembered—the Saint was dead, there was nothing more to fear . . .

He sipped his tea again, and chuckled throatily.

"Then someone's been unlucky," he remarked callously, and was surprised when the valet shook his head.

"That's the extraordinary thing, sir. They've been making inquiries all round, and none of the other apartments seem to have been entered either."

Lemuel recalled this conversation later in the morning. He had declined breakfast blasphemously, and had only just managed to get up and dress in time to restore his treasures to the keeping of his bank.

He saw the emptiness of his safe, and the little drawing which the Saint had chalked inside it by way of receipt, and went a dirty grey-white.

The strength seemed to go from his knees, and he groped his way blindly to a chair, shaking with a superstitious terror. It was some time before he brought himself to realise that ghosts do not stun porters and clean out burglar-proof safes.

The valet, coming at a run to answer the frantic pealing of the bell, was horrified at the haggard limpness of his master.

"Fetch the police," croaked Lemuel, and the man went quickly.

Chief Inspector Teal himself had just arrived to give some instructions to the detective-sergeant who had taken over the investigations, and he it was who answered the summons.

"Sixty-five thousand pounds? That's a lot of money to keep in a little safe like this."

Teal cast sleepy eyes over the object, and then went down on his knees to examine it more closely. His heavy eyelids merely flickered when he saw the chalk-marks inside.

"Opened it with your own key, too." Lemuel nodded dumbly.

"I suppose he warned you?" said Teal drowsily—he was a chronically drowsy man.

"I had two ridiculous letters . . ."

"Can I see them?"

"I—I destroyed them. I don't take any notice of threats like that."

Teal raised his eyebrows one millimetre.

"The Saint's a pretty well-known character," he said. "I should hate to have to calculate how many square miles of newspaper he's had all to himself since he started in business. And the most celebrated thing about him is that he's never yet failed to carry out a threat. This is the first time I've heard of anyone taking no notice of his letters."

Lemuel swallowed. Suddenly, in a flash of pure agony, he understood his position. The Saint had ruined him—taken from him practically every penny he possessed—and yet had left him one fragile thing that was perhaps more precious than ten times the treasure he had lost—his liberty. And Lemuel's numbed brain could see no way of bringing the Saint to justice without imperilling that last lonely asset.

"What was the Saint's grouse against you?" asked Teal, like a sleep-walking Nemesis, and knew that he was wasting his time.

All the world knew that the Saint never threatened without good reason. To attempt to get evidence from his victims was a thankless task; there was so little that they could say without incriminating themselves.

And Lemuel saw the point also, and clapped quivering hands to his forehead.

"I—I apologise," he said huskily. "I see you've guessed the truth. I heard about the burglary, and thought I might get some cheap publicity out of it. There was nothing in the safe. I drew the picture inside—copied it from an old newspaper cutting . . ."

Teal heard, and nodded wearily.

But to Francis Lemuel had come one last desperate resolve.

8

There were many men in London who hated the Saint, and none of them hated him without cause. Some he had robbed; some he had sent to prison; some he had hurt in their bodies, and some he had hurt in their pride; and some, who had not yet met him, hated him because they feared what he might do if he learned about them all the things that there were to learn—which was, perhaps, the most subtle and deadly hatred of all.

Simon Templar had no illusions about his general popularity. He knew perfectly well that there were a large number of people domiciled between East India Dock and Hammersmith Broadway who would have been delighted to see him meet an end so sticky that he would descend to the place where they thought he would go like a well-ballasted black-beetle sinking through a pot of hot glue, and who, but for the distressing discouragements which the laws of England provide for such natural impulses, would have devoted all their sadistic ingenuity to the task of thus settling a long outstanding account. In the old days Simon had cared nothing for this; in those days he was known only as the Saint, and none knew his real name, or what he looked like, or whence he came; but those days had long gone by. Simon Templar's name and address and telephone number were now common property in certain circles; it was only in sheer blind cussedness, which he had somehow got away with, that he had scorned to use an alias in his dealings with Francis Lemuel and the Calumet Club. And there had already been a number of enterprising gentlemen who had endeavoured to turn this knowledge to account in the furthering of their life's ambition—without, it must be admitted, any signal success.

While there were not many men at large who in cold blood could have mustered up the courage to actually bump the Saint off (for British justice is notoriously swift to strike, and English criminals have a greater fear of the rope than those of any other nationality), there were many who would have delighted to do the Saint grievous bodily harm, and Simon Templar had no great wish to wake up in his bed one night and find someone pouring vitriol over his face, or performing any similar kindly office. Therefore he had made elaborate arrangements, in the converted mews where he had taken up his new headquarters, to ensure the peace and safety of his slumbers.

He woke up, a few nights after his raid upon Jermyn Street, to the whirring of the buzzer under his pillow. He was instantly alert, for the Saint slept and woke like a cat, but he lay still in bed for a few moments before he moved, watching the flickering of tiny coloured lights in the panel on the opposite wall.

Johnny Anworth knew all that there was to know about the ordinary kind of burglar alarm, and had adroitly circumvented the dummy ones which the Saint had taken care to fix to his doors and windows. But what Johnny did not understand was the kind that worked without wires. There were wireless alarms all over the Saint's home—alarms that relied upon an invisible ray projected across a doorway, a stairway, or a corridor, upon a photoelectric cell on the opposite side. All was well so long as the ray continued to fall thus, but when anything momentarily obscured it, the buzzer sounded under the Saint's pillow, and a tiny bulb blinked a coloured eye in the indicator panel on the Saint's bedroom wall to show the exact locality of the intruder.

Johnny Anworth had made absolutely no sound, and had heard none, and, when the Saint took him suddenly by the throat from behind, he would have screamed aloud if his larynx had not been paralysed by the steely grip of the fingers that compressed it. He felt himself being lifted into the air and heaved bodily through a doorway, and then the lights went on and he saw the Saint.

"Don't make a noise," drawled Simon. "I don't want you to wake the house."

He had slipped on a startling dressing-gown, and not a hair of his head was out of place. In defence of Simon, it must be mentioned that he did not sleep in a hair-net. He had actually stopped to brush his hair before he went in search of the visitor.

The capture was a miserable and unsavoury-looking specimen of humanity, his sallow face made even sallower by the shock he had received. The Saint, after a short inspection, was able to identify it.

"Your name is Anworth, isn't it, Beautiful? And I recently had the pleasure of socking you on the jaw—one night when you followed me from the Calumet."

"I never seed yer before, guv'nor—strite, I never. I'm dahn an' aht—starvin' . . ."

Simon reached out a long, silk-sheathed arm for the cigarette-box—he had heaved the specimen into the sitting-room.

"Tell me the old, old story," he sighed.

"I 'adn't 'ardly a bite to eat since Friday," Johnny whined on mechanically. "This is the fust time I ever went wrong. I 'ad ter do it, guv'nor . . ."

He stopped, as the Saint turned. Incredulous audiences Johnny Anworth had had, indignant audiences, often, and even sympathetic audiences, sometimes—but he had never met such a bleak light in any outraged householder's eyes as he met then. If he had been better informed, he would have known that there were few things to which the Saint objected more than being interrupted in his beauty sleep. This Simon explained.

"Also, you didn't come here on your own. You were sent." The cold blue eyes never left Johnny's face. "By a man named Lemuel," Simon added, in a sudden snap, and read the truth before the crook had opened his mouth to deny it.

"I never 'eard of 'im, guv'nor. I was near starvin' . . ."

"What were you told to do?"

"I never . . ."

On those words, Johnny's voice trailed away. For he had heard, quite distinctly, the stealthy footfall in the passage outside.

The Saint also had heard it. He had not expected a man like Johnny Anworth to be on a job like that alone.

"You're telling naughty stories, Precious . . ."

The Saint spoke gently and dreamily, stepping back towards the door with the silence of a hunting leopard, but there was neither gentleness nor dreaminess in the eyes that held the burglar half-hypnotised, and Johnny did not need to be told what would happen to him if he attempted to utter a warning.

"Naughty, naughty stories—you've brought me out of my beautiful bed to tell me those. I think I shall have to be very cross with you, Johnny . . ."

And then, like an incarnate whirlwind, the Saint whipped open the door and sprang out into the passage. Baldy Mossiter had a gun, but the Saint was too quick for him, and Baldy only just relaxed his trigger finger in time to avoid shooting himself in the stomach.

"Step right in and join the merry throng, Hairy Harold," murmured Simon, and Mossiter obeyed, the Saint speeding him on his way.

That Johnny Anworth, having started forward with the idea of taking the Saint in the rear, should have been directly in the trajectory of his chief, was unfortunate for both parties. Simon smiled beatifically upon them, and allowed them to regain their feet under their own power.

"You wait, Templar!" Mossiter snarled, and the Saint nodded encouragingly.

"Were you starving, too?" he asked.

There was some bad language—so bad that the Saint, who was perhaps unduly sensitive about these things, found it best to bind and gag both his prisoners.

"When you decide to talk, you can wag your ears," he said.

There was a gas fire in the sitting-room, and this the Saint lighted, although the night was already torrid enough. In front of the burners, with ponderous deliberation, he set an ornamental poker to heat.

The two men watched with bulging eyes.

Simon finished his cigarette and then he solemnly tested the temperature of the poker, holding it near his cheek as a laundryman tests an iron.

"Do you sing your song, Baldy?" he inquired—so mildly that Mossiter, who had an imagination, understood quite clearly that his own limits of bluff were likely to be reached long before the Saint's.

The story came with some profane trimmings which need not be recorded.

"It was Lemuel. We were to cosh you, and take your girl away. Lemuel said he knew for certain you'd got a lot of money hidden away, and we were going to make you pay it all over—while we held the girl to keep you quiet. We were going shares in whatever we got . . . What are you doing?"

"Phoning for the police," said the Saint calmly. "You must not commit burglary, particularly with guns."

The law arrived in ten minutes in the shape of a couple of men from Vine Street, but before they came the Saint had made some things painfully plain.

"I'd guessed what you told me, but I always like to be sure. And let me tell you, you pair of second-hand sewer-skunks, that that sort of game doesn't appeal to me. Personally, I expect the most strenuous efforts to be made to bump me off—I'd be disappointed if they weren't—but my girlfriends are in baulk. Get that. And if at any time the idea should come back to you that that would be a good way of getting at me—forget it. Because I promise you that anyone who starts that stuff on me is going for a long ride, and he'll die in a way that'll make him wish he'd never been born. Think that over while you're carving rocks on the Moor!"

Then the police came and took them away. They said nothing then, and went down for three years without speaking.

But the Saint was a thoughtful man at breakfast the next morning.

In the old days, Patricia Holm had shared his immunity. Now that his was gone, her own went also. The knowledge of her existence, and what she might be assumed to mean to the Saint, was free to anyone who took the trouble to watch him. The plan of campaign that the facts suggested was obvious; the only wonder was that it had not been tried before. For one thing, of course, the number of the Saint's enemies whose minds would take that groove was limited, and the number who would be capable of actually travelling along the groove was more limited still—but the idea must not be allowed to grow. And Lemuel had lost much—he would have a long memory.

"I don't think he's a useful citizen," concluded the Saint, out of the blue, and Patricia Holm looked up blankly from her newspaper.

"Who's that?"

"Uncle Francis."

Then she heard of the nocturnal visitors.

"He doesn't know that all the money I took off him has gone to Queen Charlotte's Hospital—a most suitable charity-less only our regular ten per cent fee for collection," said the Saint. "And if I told him, I don't think he'd believe me. As long as he's at large, he'll be thinking of his lost fortune—and you. And, as I said, I don't think he's a useful citizen."

"What can you do?" she asked.

Simon smiled at her. He really thought that she grew more beautiful every day. "Sweetheart," he said, "you're the only good thing this rolling stone's collected out of all the world. And there's only one logical thing to do."

But he left her to guess what that was; he had not worked out the details himself at that moment. He knew that Francis Lemuel owned a large country house standing in its own spacious grounds just outside Tenterden, and the next day he learned that Lemuel had established himself there—"to recover from a severe nervous collapse," the newspaper informed him—but it was not for another two days, when another item of news came his way, that the Saint had his inspiration for the manner in which Francis Lemuel should die.

9

I shall call on Wednesday at 3 p.m. You will be at home.

Francis Lemuel stared at the curt note, and the little sketch that served for signature, with blurring eyes. Minutes passed before he was able to reach shakily for the decanter—his breakfast was left untasted on the table.

An hour later, reckless of consequences, he was speaking on the telephone to Scotland Yard.

At the same time Simon Templar was speaking to Patricia Holm, what time he carefully marmaladed a thin slice of brown bread and a thick slice of butter.

"There are three indoor servants at Tenterden—a butler and a cook, man and wife, and the valet. The rest of the staff have been fired, and half the house is shut up—I guess Francis is finding it necessary to pull in his horns a bit. The butler and cook have a half-day off on Wednesday. The valet has his half-day on Thursday, but he has a girl at Rye. He has asked her to marry him, and she has promised to give her answer when she sees him next—which will, of course, be on Thursday. He has had a row with Lemuel, and is thinking of giving notice."

"How do you know all this?" asked Patricia. "Don't tell me you deduced it from the mud on the under-gardener's boots, because I shan't believe you."

"I won't," said the Saint generously. "If you want to know, I saw all that last part in writing. The valet is an energetic correspondent. Sometimes he goes to bed and leaves a letter half-finished, and he's a sound sleeper."

"You've been inside Lemuel's house?"

"These last three nights. The burglar alarms are absolutely childish."

"So that's why you've been sleeping all day, and looking so dissipated!"

Simon shook his head. "Not 'dissipated,'" he said. "'Intellectual' is the word you want."

She looked at him thoughtfully. "What's the game, lad?"

"Is your memory so short, old Pat? Why, what should the game be but wilful murder?"

Patricia came round the table and put her hands on his shoulders. "Don't do it, Saint! It's not worth it."

"It is." He took her hands and kissed them, smiling a little. "Darling, I have hunches, and my hunches are always right. I know that the world won't be safe for democracy as long as Francis continues to fester in it. Now listen, and don't argue. As soon as you're dressed, you will disguise yourself as an elderly charwoman about to visit a consumptive aunt at Rye. At Rye you will proceed to the post office and send a telegram which I've written out for you . . . here." He took the form from his pocket, and pressed it into her hand. "You will then move on to Tenterden."

He gave an exact description of a certain spot, and of an instrument which she would find there. "If you observe a crowd and a certain amount of wreckage in the offing, don't get excited. They won't be near where you've got to go. Collect the gadget and et ceteras, and push them into the bag you'll have with you . . . Then, returning to the blinkin' Bahnhof, you will leap into the first train in which you see a carriage that you can have all to yourself, and in that you will remove your flimsy disguise, disembark as your own sweet self at the next stop, catch the first train back to Town, and meet me for dinner at the Embassy at eight. Is that clear?"

She opened the telegraph form, and read it. "But what's the idea?"

"To clear the air, darling."

"But . . ."

"Uncle Francis? . . . I've worked that out rather brilliantly. The time has gone by, sweetheart, when I could bounce in and bump off objectionable characters as and when the spirit moved. Too much is known about me—and robbery may be a matter for the robbed, but murder is a matter for the Lore. But I think this execution ought to meet the case. Besides, it will annoy Teal—Teal's been a bit uppish lately."

There was no doubt that his mind was made up, yet it was not without misgivings that Patricia departed on her mission. But she went, for she knew the moods in which the Saint was inflexible.

It was exactly three o'clock when the Saint, a trim and superbly immaculate and rather rakish figure, climbed out of his car at the end of Lemuel's drive, and sauntered up to the house.

"Dear old Francis!" The Saint was at his most debonair as he entered the celebrated impresario's library. "And how's trade?"

"Sit down, Templar."

The voice was so different from Lemuel's old sonorous joviality that the Saint knew that the story of "a severe nervous collapse" was not a great exaggeration. Lemuel's hand was unsteady as he replaced his cigar between his teeth.

"And what do you want now?"

"Just a little chat, my cherub," said the Saint.

He lighted a cigarette, and his eyes roved casually round the room. He remarked a tiny scrap of pink paper screwed up in an ash-tray, and a tall Chinese screen in one corner, and a slow smile of satisfaction expanded within him—deep within him. Lemuel saw nothing.

"It's a long time since we last opened our hearts to each other, honeybunch," said the Saint, sinking back lazily into the cushions, "and you must have so much to tell me. Have you been a good boy? No more cocaine, or little girls, or anything like that?"

"I don't know what you mean. If you've come here to try to blackmail me . . ."

"Dear, dear! Blackmail? What's that, Francis? Or shall I call you Frank?"

"You can call me what you like."

Simon shook his head. "I don't want to be actually rude," he said. "Let it go at Frank. I once knew another man, a very successful scavenger, named Frank, who slipped in a sewer, and sank. This was after a spree; ever afterwards he was teetotal—but, oh, how unpleasant he smelt. Any relation of yours?"

Lemuel came closer. His face looked pale and bloated; there was a beastly fury in his eyes. "Now listen to me, Templar. You've already robbed me once . . ."

"When?"

"D'you have to bluff when there isn't an audience? D'you deny that you're the Saint?"

"On the contrary," murmured Simon calmly. "I'm proud of it. But when have I robbed you?"

For a moment Lemuel looked as if he would choke. Then, "What have you come for now?" he demanded.

Simon seemed to sink even deeper into his chair, and he watched the smoke curling up from his cigarette with abstracted eyes.

"Suppose," he said lazily, "just suppose we had all the congregation out in the limelight. Wouldn't that make it seem more matey?"

"What d'you mean?"

Lemuel's voice cracked on the question.

"Well," said Simon, closing his eyes, with a truly sanctimonious smile hovering on his lips, "I really do hate talking to people I can't see. And it must be frightfully uncomfortable for Claud Eustace, hiding behind that screen over there."

"I don't understand . . ."

"Do you understand, Claud?" drawled the Saint, and Chief-Inspector Claud Eustace Teal answered wearily that he understood.

He emerged mountainously, and stood looking down at the Saint with a certain admiration in his bovine countenance.

"And how did you know I was there?"

Simon waved a languid hand towards the table. Teal, following the gesture, saw the ash-tray, and the discarded pink overcoat of the gum which he was even then chewing, and groaned.

"Wrigley," sighed the Saint, succinctly.

Then Lemuel turned on the detective, snarling. "What the hell did you want to come out for?"

"Chiefly because there wasn't much point in staying where I was, Mr Lemuel," replied Teal tiredly.

Simon chuckled.

"It's as much your fault as his, Francis, old coyote," he said. "If you must try to pull that old gag on me, you want to go into strict training. A man in your condition can't hope to put it over . . . Oh, Francis! To think you thought I'd bite that bit of cheese—and land myself in good and proper, with Teal taking frantic notes behind the whatnot! You must take care not to go sitting in any damp grass, Francis—you might get brain fever."

"Anyway," said Teal, "it was a good idea."

"It was a rotten idea," said the Saint disparagingly. "And always has been. But I knew it was ten to one it would be tried—I knew it when I sent that note to Francis. I'm glad you came, Claud—I really did want you here."

"Why?" Lemuel cut in. His face was tense and drawn.

"Inspector, you know this man's character . . ."

"I do," said Teal somnolently. "That's the trouble."

"He came here to try to blackmail me, and he'd have done it if he hadn't discovered you. Now he's going to try to get out of it on one of his bluffs . . ."

"No," said the Saint, and he said it in such a way that there was a sudden silence.

And, in the stillness, with his eyes still closed, the Saint listened. His powers of hearing were abnormally acute: he heard the sound he was waiting for when neither of the other two could hear anything—and even to him it was like nothing more than the humming of a distant bee.

And then he opened his eyes. It was like the unmasking of two clear blue lights in the keen brown face, and the eyes were not jesting at all. He stood up.

"As you said—you know me, Teal," he remarked. "Now I'll tell you what you don't know about Francis Lemuel. The first thing is that he's at the head of the dope ring you've been trying to get at for years. I don't know how he used to bring the stuff into the country, but I do know that when I was his private pilot, a little while ago, he came back from Berlin one time with enough snow in his grip to build a ski-slope round the Equator . . ."

"It's a lie! By God, you'll answer for that, Templar . . ."

"Now I come to think of it," murmured Teal, "how do you know his real name?"

Simon laughed softly. The humming of the bee was not so distant now—the other two could have heard it easily, if they had listened.

"Don't haze the accused," he said gently. "He'll get all hot and bothered if you start to cross-examine him. Besides, the charge isn't finished. There's another matter, concerning a girl named Stella Dornford—and several others whose names I couldn't give you, for all I know . . ."

"Another lie!"

Teal turned heavy eyes on the man. "You're a great clairvoyant," he said, judicially.

"At this man's request," said the Saint quietly, "I flew Stella Dornford over to Berlin. She was supposed to be going to a cabaret engagement with a man called Jacob Einsmann. The place I took her to was not a cabaret—I needn't mention what it was. The Berlin police will corroborate that . . ."

Lemuel grated, "They want you for the murder of Einsmann . . ."

"I doubt it," said the Saint. "I certainly shot him, but it shouldn't be hard to prove self-defence." The bee was very much closer. And the Saint turned to Teal. "I have one other thing to say," he added, "for your ears alone."

"I have a right to hear it," barked Lemuel shakily. "Inspector . . ."

"Naturally you'll hear it, Mr. Lemuel," said Teal soothingly. "But if Mr. Templar insists on telling me alone, that's his affair. If you'll excuse us a moment . . ."

Lemuel watched them go, gripping the table for support. Presently, through the French windows, he saw them strolling across the lawn, side by side. The air was now full of the drone of the bee, but he did not notice it.

He stumbled mechanically towards the side-table where bottle and glasses were set out, but the bottle was nearly empty. Savagely he jabbed at the bell, and waited an impatient half-minute, but no one answered. Cursing, he staggered to the door and opened it. "Fitch!" he bawled.

Still there was no answer. The house was as silent as a tomb. Trembling with terror of he knew not what, Lemuel reeled down the hall and flung open the door of the servants' quarters. There was no one in sight.

On the table, he saw an orange envelope with a buff slip beside it. Impelled by an unaccountable premonition, he picked up the form and read.

Come at once. I want you. Eileen.

Fitch was already on his way to Rye. The Saint was thorough.

As Lemuel crumpled the telegram with furious hands, the bee seemed to be roaring directly over his head.

10

Simon Templar gazed thoughtfully at the sky.

"Cloudy," he remarked thoughtfully. "The weather forecasts said it would be cloudy today, and for once they're right."

Teal looked back over his shoulder.

"That aeroplane's flying pretty low," he said.

"Owing to cloud," said the Saint, and the detective glanced at him quickly.

"What's the big idea, Saint?" he demanded.

Simon smiled.

"I've been getting rather tired of answering that question lately," he said.

They had reached a clump of trees at the edge of the wide lawn, a couple of hundred yards away from the house, and here the Saint stopped. Both the men turned.

The aeroplane was certainly low—it was flying under five hundred feet, and the racket of its engine was deafening.

"I know your habits," said Teal sourly. "If you weren't here with me, Saint, I'd be inclined to think you were up there—getting ready to do some illegal bombing practice." He was watching the aeroplane with screwed-up eyes, while he took a fresh purchase on his gum, and then he added suddenly, "Do any of the other guys in your gang fly?"

"There ain't no gang," said the Saint, "and you ought to know it. They broke up long ago."

"I wouldn't put it above you to have recruited another," said Teal.

Simon leaned against a tree. His hand, groping in a hollow in the trunk, found a tiny switch. He took the lever lightly between his finger and thumb. He laughed, softly and lazily, and Teal faced round.

"What's the big idea?" he demanded again. "I don't know what it is, but you're playing some funny game. What did you fetch me out here to tell me?"

"Nothing much," answered the Saint slowly, "I just thought . . ."

But what he thought was not destined to be known. For all at once there came a titanic roar of sound that was nothing like the roar of the aeroplane's engine—a shattering detonation that rocked the ground under their feet and hurled them bodily backwards with the hurricane force of its breath.

"Good God!"

Teal's voice came faintly through the buzzing in the Saint's ears. Simon was scrambling rockily to his feet.

"Something seems to have bust, old water-melon . . ."

"F-ZXKA," Teal was muttering. "F-ZXKA; F-ZXKA . . ."

"Ease up, old dear!" Simon took the detective by the shoulder. "It's all over. Nothing to rave about."

"I'm not raving," snarled Teal. "But I've got the number of that machine . . ."

He was starting off across the lawn, and the Saint followed. But there was nothing that they or anyone else could do, for Francis Lemuel's house was nothing but a great mound of rubble under a mushroom canopy of smoke and settling dust, through which the first tongues of flame were starting to lick up towards the dark clouds. And the aeroplane was dwindling into the mists towards the north.

Teal surveyed the ruin and then he looked round at the crowd that was pattering up the road.

"You're arrested, Saint," he said curtly, and Simon shrugged.

They drove to Tenterden in the Saint's car, and from there Teal put a call through to headquarters.

"F-ZXKA," he said. "Warn all stations and aerodromes. Take the crew, whatever excuse they try to put up, and hold them till I come."

"That's the stuff," said the Saint approvingly, and Teal was so far moved as to bare his teeth.

"This is where you get what's coming to you," he said.

It was not Teal's fault that the prophecy was not fulfilled.

Simon drove him back to London with a police guard in the back of the car and Teal was met almost on the doorstep of Scotland Yard with the news that the aeroplane had landed at Croydon. The prisoners, said the message, had put up a most audacious bluff; they were being sent to headquarters in a police car.

"Good!" said Teal grimly, and went through to Cannon Row Police Station to charge the Saint with wilful murder.

"That's what you've got to prove," said the Saint, when the charge was read over to him. "No—I won't trouble my solicitor. I shall be out in an hour."

"In eight weeks you'll be dead," said the detective.

He had recovered some of his old pose of agonised boredom, and half an hour later he needed it all, for the police car arrived from Croydon as the newspaper vans started to pour out of E.C.4 with the printers' ink still damp on the first news of the outrage at Tenterden.

Two prisoners were hustled into Teal's office—a philosophical gentleman in flying overalls, and a very agitated gentleman with striped cashmere trousers and white spats showing under his leather coat.

"It is an atrrrrocity!" exploded the agitated gentleman. "I vill complain myself to ze Prime Ministair! Imbecile! Your poliss, zey say I am arrrrest—zey insult me—zey mock zemselves of vat I say—zey trreat me like I vas a criminal—me! But you shall pay . . ."

"And who are you pretending to be?" asked Teal, lethargically unwrapping a fresh wafer of his favourite sweetmeat.

"Me? You do not know me? You do not know Boileau . . ." Teal did not.

"Take that fungus off his face," he ordered, "and let's see what he really looks like."

Two constables had to pinion the arms of a raving maniac while a third gave the agitated gentleman's beard a sharp tug.

But the beard failed to part company with its foundations, and, on closer examination, it proved to be the genuine home-grown article.

Teal blinked as the agitated gentleman, released, danced in front of his desk, semaphoring with frantic arms.

"Nom d'un nom! You are not content viz insult me, you must attack me, you must pull me ze beard! Aaaaah!"

Words failed the man. He reeled against the desk, clawing at his temples.

Teal ran a finger round the inside of his collar, which seemed to have suddenly become tight.

Then the philosophical gentleman in overalls spoke.

"'E 'as say true, m'sieu. 'E is M. Boileau, ze French Finance Minister, 'oo come ovair for confer . . ."

Teal signed to one of the constables.

"Better ring up the Embassy and see if someone can come over and identify him," he said.

"Merde alors!" screamed the agitated gentleman. "I vill not vait! I demand to be release!"

"I'm afraid you'll have to be identified, sir," said Teal unhappily.

And identified M. Boileau was, in due course, by a semi-hysterical official from the Embassy and Teal spent the most uncomfortable half-hour of his life trying to explain the mistake.

He was a limp wreck when the indignation meeting finally broke up and the telephoned report of the explosives expert who had been sent down to Tenterden did not improve Teal's temper.

"It was a big aerial bomb—we've found some bits of the casing. We didn't find much of Lemuel . . ."

"Could it have been fired by a timing device?"

"There's no trace of anything like that, sir. Of course, if there had been, it might have been blown to bits."

"Could it have been fired electrically?"

"I haven't found any wires yet, sir. My men are still digging round the wreckage. On the other hand, sir, if it comes to that, it might have been fired by radio, and if it was radio we shan't find anything at all."

Teal had his inspiration some hours too late.

"You'd better search the grounds," he said, and gave exact instructions.

"Certainly, sir. But what about the aeroplane that went over?"

"That," said Teal heavily, "contained the French Minister of Finance, on his way to a reparations conference."

"Well, it couldn't have been him," said the expert sagely, and Teal felt like murder.

A few days later the Saint called on Stella Dornford. He had not seen her since the morning when he dropped her on his way to Jermyn Street, and she had not communicated with him in any way.

"You must think me a little rotter," she said. "It seems such a feeble excuse to say I've been too busy to think of any thing . . ."

"I think it's the best excuse in the world," said the Saint.

He pointed to the ring on her finger. "When?"

"Ten days ago. I—I took your advice, you see . . ."

Simon laughed. "'To those about to marry,'" he quoted softly. "Well, you must come round to a celebratory supper, and bring the Beloved. And Uncle Simon will tell you all about married life."

"Why, are you married?"

He shook his head. For a moment the dancing blue eyes were quiet and wistful. And then the old mocking mirth came back to them.

"That's why I'll be able to tell you so much about it," he said.

Presently the girl said, "I've told Dick how much we owe you. I'll never forget it. I don't know how to thank you . . ."

The Saint smiled, and put his hands on her shoulders.

"Don't you?" he said.

THE WONDERFUL WAR

INTRODUCTION

At various points in the chronicle of the Saint's exploits there are vague references to his adventures in the far corners of the earth. This particular story, however, is the only one of its kind which is completely on record, and his followers have mentioned it often enough to convince me that it is one of their favourite recollections of his early days. The Saint himself derives so much obvious fun from it that I am bound to believe that it must still be one of his most enjoyable memories. I suppose that one of the so-called "comic opera" South American republics has at one time or another been almost every man's imaginative playground, and it is only to be expected that Simon Templar would have used such a setting for one of his most riotous escapades.

—Leslie Charteris (1939)

1

The Republic of Pasala lies near the northward base of the Yucatan peninsula in Central America. It has an area of about 10,000 square miles, or roughly the size of England from the Tweed to a line drawn from Liverpool to Hull. Population, about 18,000. Imports, erratic. Exports, equally erratic, and consisting (when the population can be stirred to the necessary labour) of maize, rice, sugar-cane, mahogany, and—oil.

"You can hurry up and warble all you know about this oil, Archie," said Simon Templar briskly, half an hour after he landed at Santa Miranda. "And you can leave out your adventures among the Señoritas. I want to get this settled—I've got a date back in England for the end of May, and that doesn't give me a lot of time here."

Mr. Archibald Sheridan stirred slothfully in his long chair and took a pull at a whisky-and-soda in which ice clinked seductively.

"You've had it all in my letters and cables," he said. "But I'll just run through it again to connect it up. It goes like this. Three years ago almost to the day, a Scots mining engineer named McAndrew went prospecting round the hills about fifty miles inland. Everyone said he was crazy—till he came back six months later with samples from his feeler borings. He said he'd struck one of the richest deposits that ever gushed—and it was only a hundred feet below the surface. He got a concession—chiefly because the authorities still couldn't believe his story—staked his claim, cabled for his daughter to come over and join him, and settled down to feel rich and wait for the plant he'd ordered to be shipped over from New Orleans."

"Did the girl come?" asked Templar.

"She's right here," answered Sheridan. "But you told me to leave the women out of it. She doesn't really come into the story anyway. The man who does come in is a half-caste bum from God knows where, name of Shannet. Apparently Shannet had been sponging and beachcombing here for months before McAndrew arrived. Everyone was down on him, and so McAndrew, being one of these quixotic idiots, joined up with him. He even took him into partnership, just to defy public opinion, and, anyhow, he was wanting help, and Shannet had some sort of qualifications. The two of them went up into the interior to take a look at the claim. Shannet came back, but McAndrew didn't. Shannet said a snake got him."

Simon Templar reached for another cigarette.

"Personally, I say that snake's name was Shannet," remarked Archie Sheridan quietly. "Lilla—McAndrew's daughter—said the same thing. Particularly when Shannet produced a written agreement signed by McAndrew and himself, in which it was arranged that if either partner should die, all rights in the claim should pass to the other partner. Lilla swore that McAndrew, who'd always thought first of her, would never have signed such a document, and she got a look at it and said the signature was forged. Shannet replied that McAndrew was getting over a bout of malaria when he signed it, and his hand was rather shaky. The girl carried it right to the court of what passes for justice here, fighting like a hero, but Shannet had too big a pull with the judge, and she lost her case. I arrived just after her appeal was turned down."

"What about McAndrew's body?"

"Shannet said he buried it by the trail, but the jungle trails here are worse than any maze that was ever invented, and you can almost see the stuff grow. The grave could quite reasonably be lost in a week. Shannet said he couldn't find it again. I took a trip that way myself, but it wasn't any use. All I got out of it was a bullet through a perfectly good hat from some sniper in the background—Shannet for a fiver."

"After which," suggested Simon Templar thoughtfully, "Shannet found he couldn't run the show alone, and sold out to our dear friend in London, Master Hugo Campard, shark, swindler, general blackguard, and promoter of unlimited dud companies . . ."

"Who perpetrated the first sound company of his career, Pasala Oil Products, on the strength of it," Sheridan completed. "Shares not for public issue, and sixty per cent, of them held by himself."

Simon Templar took his cigarette from his mouth and blew a long, thin streamer of smoke into the sunlight.

"So that's what I've come over to deal with, Archibald?" he murmured. "Well, well, well I . . . Taken by and large, it looks like a diverting holiday. Carol a brief psalm about things political, son."

"Just about twice as crooked as anything south of the United States border," said Sheridan. "The man who matters isn't the President. He's under the thumb of what they call the Minister for the Interior, who finds it much more convenient and much safer to stay in the background—they never assassinate Ministers for the Interior, apparently, but Presidents are fair game. And this man—Manuel Concepcion de Villega is his poetic label—is right under the wing of Shannet, and is likely to stay there as long as Shannet's money lasts."

The Saint rose and lounged over to the verandah rail. At that hour (which was just after midday) the thermometer stood at a hundred and two in the shade, and the Saint had provided himself suitably with white ducks. The dazzling whiteness of them would have put snow to shame, and he wore them, as might have been expected of him, with the most cool and careless elegance in the world. He looked as if he would have found an inferno chilly. His dark hair was brushed smoothly back; his lean face was tanned to a healthy brown; altogether he must have been the most dashing and immaculate sight that Santa Miranda had set eyes on for many years.

Sheridan was in despair before that vision of unruffled perfection. His hair was tousled, his white ducks looked somewhat limp with the heat, and his pleasantly ugly face was moist.

"What about the rest of the white, or near-white, inhabitants?" inquired the Saint.

"A two-fisted, rip-roaring giant of a red-headed Irishman named Kelly," was the reply. "His wife—that's two. Lilla McAndrew, who's staying with them—I wouldn't let her put up at the filthy hotel in the town any longer—three. Four and five, a couple of traders, more or less permanently drunk and not worth considering. Six—Shannet. That's the lot."

The Saint turned away and gazed down the hillside. From where he stood, on the verandah of Sheridan's bungalow, he could look down on to the roofs of Santa Miranda—the cluster of white buildings in the Moorish style which formed the centre, and the fringe of adobe huts on the outskirts. Left and right of him, on the hill above the town, were other bungalows. Beyond the town was the sea.

The Saint studied the view for a time in silence, then he turned round again.

"We seem to be on to the goods," he remarked. "Shannet, the small fish, but an undoubted murderer—and, through him, our real man, Campard. I had a hunch I shouldn't be wasting your time when I sent you out here as soon as I heard Campard was backing Pasala Oil

Products. But I never guessed P.O.P. would be real till I got your first cable. Now we're on a truly classy piece of velvet. It all looks too easy."

"Easy?" queried Sheridan sceptically. "I'm glad you think it's easy. With Shannet's claim established, and the concession in writing at Campard's London office, and Lilla McAndrew's petition dismissed, and Shannet twiddling the Government, the Army, the police, and the rest of the bunch, down to the last office-boy, round and round his little finger with the money he gets from Campard—and the man calls it easy. Oh, take him away!"

The Saint's hands drove even deeper into his pockets. Tall and trim and athletic, he stood with his feet astride, swaying gently from his toes, with the Saintly smile flickering faintly round his mouth and a little dancing devil of mischief rousing in his blue eyes.

"I said easy," he drawled.

Sheridan buried his face in his hands.

"Go and put your head in the ice-bucket," he pleaded. "Of course, it's the sun. You're not used to it—I forgot that."

"How big is the Army?"

"There's a standing army of about five hundred, commanded by seventeen generals, twenty-five colonels, and about fifty minor officers. And if your head hurts, just lie down, close the eyes, and relax. It'll be quite all right in an hour or two."

"Artillery?"

"Three pieces, carried by mules. If you'd like some aspirin . . ."

"Navy?"

"One converted tug, with 5-9 quick-firer and crew of seven, commanded by two admirals. I don't think you ought to talk now. I'll put up the hammock for you, if you like, and you can sleep for an hour before lunch."

"Police force?"

"There are eleven constables in Santa Miranda, under three superintendents. And in future I shouldn't have any whisky before sundown."

The Saint smiled.

"I'm probably more used to the sun than you are," he said. "This is merely common sense. What's the key to the situation? The Government. Right. We don't propose to waste any of our good money bribing them—and if we did, they'd double-cross us. Therefore they must be removed by force. And at once, because I can't stay long. Long live the Revolution!"

"Quite," agreed Sheridan helplessly. "And the Revolutionary Army? This State is the only one in South America that's never had a revolution—because nobody's ever had enough energy to start one."

The Saint fished for his cigarette-case.

"We are the Revolutionary Army," he said. "I ask you to remember that we march on our stomachs. So we'll just have another drink, and then some lunch, and then we'll wander along and try to enlist the mad Irishman. If we three can't make rings round six hundred and fifteen comic-opera dagoes, I'm going to retire from the fighting game and take up knitting and fancy needlework!"

2

"My dear soul," the Saint was still arguing persuasively at the close of the meal, "it's so simple. The man who manages the Government of this two-by-four backyard is the man who holds the fate of Pasala Oil Products in his hands. At present Shannet is the bright boy who manages the Government, and the master of P.O.P. is accordingly walking around under the Shannet hat. We'll go one better. We won't merely manage the Government. We'll be the Government. And Pop is ours to play hell with as we like. Could anything be more straightforward? As the actress said when the bishop showed her his pass-book."

"Go on," encouraged Sheridan weakly. "Don't bother about my feelings."

"As the actress said to the bishop shortly afterwards," murmured the Saint. "Blessed old Archie, it's obvious that three months in this enervating climate and the society of Lilla McAndrew have brought your energy down to the level of that of the natives you spoke of so contemptuously just now. I grant you it's sudden, but it's the only way. Before I knew the whole story I thought it would be good enough if we held up the post office and sent Campard a spoof cable purporting to come from Shannet, telling him the Government had been kicked out, the concession revoked, and the only thing to do was to sell out his Pop holdings as quickly as possible. What time our old friend Roger, back in London, snaps up the shares, discreetly, as fast as they come on the market."

"Why won't that work now?"

"You're forgetting the girl," said Templar. "This oil is really her property, so it isn't good enough just to make Campard unload at a loss and sell back to him at a premium when the rumour of revolution is exploded. The concession has really got to be revoked. Therefore I propose to eliminate the present Government, and make Kelly, your mad Irishman, the new Minister of the Interior. That is, unless you'd take the job."

"No, thanks," said Sheridan generously. "It's not quite in my line. Pass me up."

The Saint lighted a cigarette.

"In that case Kelly is elected unanimously," he remarked with charming simplicity. "So the only thing left to decide is how we start the trouble. I've been in South American revolutions before, but they've always been well under way by the time I arrived. The technique of starting the blamed things was rather missed out of my education. What does one do? Does one simply wade into the Presidential Palace, chant 'Time, gentlemen, please!' in the ear of his Illustrious Excellency, and invite him to close the door as he goes out? Or what?"

"What, probably," said Sheridan. "That would be as safe as anything. I might get you reprieved on the grounds of insanity."

The Saint sighed. "You aren't helpful, Beautiful Archibald."

"If you'd settle down to talk seriously . . ."

"I am serious."

Sheridan stared. Then, "Is that straight, Saint?" he demanded.

"From the horse's mouth," the Saint assured him solemnly. "Even as the crowd flieth before the pubs open. Sweet cherub, did you really think I was wasting precious time with pure pickled onions?"

Sheridan looked at him. There was another flippant rejoinder on the tip of Archie Sheridan's tongue, but somehow it was never uttered.

The Saint was smiling. It was a mocking smile, but that was for Sheridan's incredulity. It was not the sort of smile that accompanies a test of the elasticity of a leg. And in the Saint's eyes was a light that wasn't entirely humorous.

Archie Sheridan, with a cigarette in his mouth, fumbling for matches, realised that he had mistaken the shadow for the substance. The Saint wasn't making fun of revolutions. It was just that his sense of humour was too big to let him plan even a revolution without seeing the funny side of the show.

Sheridan got a match to his cigarette.

"Well?" prompted the Saint.

"I think you're pots, bats, and bees," he said. "But if you're set on that kind of suicide—lead on. Archibald will be at your elbow with the bombs. You didn't forget the bombs?"

The Saint grinned. "I had to leave them behind," he replied lightly. "They wouldn't fit into my sponge-bag. Seriously, now, where and how do you think we should start the trouble?"

They were sitting opposite one another at Sheridan's bare mahogany dining-table, and at the Saint's back was the open door leading out on to the verandah and commanding an uninterrupted view of the approach to the bungalow.

"Start the thing here and now and anyhow you like," said Sheridan, and he was looking past the Saint's shoulder towards the verandah steps.

Simon Templar settled back a little more lazily into his chair, and a very Saintly meekness was spreading over his face.

"Name?" he inquired laconically.

"Shannet himself."

The Saint's eyes were half-closed.

"I will compose a little song about him immediately," he said.

Then a shadow fell across the table, but the Saint did not move at once. He appeared to be lost in a day-dream.

"*Buenos días*, Shannet," said Archie Sheridan. "Also, as soon as possible, *adios*. Hurry up and say what you've got to say before I kick you out."

"I'll do any kicking out that's necessary, thanks," said Shannet harshly. "Sheridan, I've come to warn you off for the last time. The *Andalusia* berthed this morning, and she sails again on the evening tide. You've been nosing around here too long as it is. Is that plain enough?"

"Plainer than your ugly face," drawled Sheridan. "And by what right do you kick me out? Been elected President, have you?"

"You know me," said Shannet. "You know that what I say here goes. You'll sail on the *Andalusia*—either voluntary or because you're put on board in irons. That's all . . . What's this?"

The Saint, perceiving himself to be the person thus referred to, awoke sufficiently to open his eyes and screw his head round so that he could view the visitor.

He saw a tall, broad-shouldered man of indeterminate age, clad in a soiled white suit of which the coat was unbuttoned to expose a grubby singlet. Shannet had certainly not shaved for two days, and he did not appear to have brushed his hair for a like period, for a damp, sandy lock drooped in a tangle over his right eye. In one corner of his mouth a limp and dilapidated cigarette dangled tiredly from his lower lip.

The Saint blinked.

"Gawd!" he said offensively. "Can it be human?"

Shannet's fists swept back his coat and rested on his hips. "What's your name, Cissy?" he demanded.

The Saint flicked some ash from his cigarette, and rose to his feet delicately.

"Benito Mussolini," he answered mildly. "And you must be one of the corporation scavengers. How's the trade in garbage?" His gentle eyes swept Shannet from crown to toe. "Archie, there must have been some mistake. The real scavenger has gone sick, and one of his riper pieces of refuse is deputising for him. I'm sorry."

"If you . . ."

"I said I was sorry," the Saint continued, in the same smooth voice, "because I'm usually very particular about the people I fight, and I hate soiling my hands on things like you."

Shannet glowered.

"I don't know who you are," he said, "and I don't care. But if you're looking for a fight you can have it."

"I am looking for a fight, dear one," drawled the Saint. "In fact, I'm looking for a lot of fights, and you're the first one that's offered. 'Cissy' is a name I particularly object to being called, O misbegotten of a pig!"

The last words were spoken in colloquial Spanish, and the Saint made more of them than it is possible to report in printable English. Shannet went white, then red.

"You . . ."

His answering stream of profanity merged into a left swing to the Saint's jaw, which, if it had landed, would have ended the fight there and then. But it did not land.

Simon Templar swayed back, and the swing missed by a couple of inches. As Shannet stumbled, momentarily off his balance, the Saint reached round and took the jug of ice water off the table behind him. Without any appearance of effort or haste, he side-stepped and poured most of the contents of the jug down the back of Shannet's neck.

Shannet swung again. The Saint ducked, and sent the man flying with a smashing jab to the nose.

"Look out, Saint!" Sheridan warned suddenly.

"Naughty!" murmured the Saint, without heat.

Shannet was getting to his feet, and his right hand was drawing something from his hip pocket.

The Saint took two steps and a flying leap over Shannet's head, turning in the air as he did so. Shannet had only got to his knees when the Saint landed behind him and caught his opponent's throat and right wrist in hands that had the strength of steel cables in their fingers. Shannet's wrist was twisted behind his back with an irresistible wrench . . .

The gun clattered to the floor simultaneously with Shannet's yelp of agony, and the Saint picked up the gun and stepped away.

"A trophy! Archie!" he cried, and tossed the weapon over to Sheridan. "Guns I have not quite been shot with—there must be a drawer full of them at home . . . Let's start, sweet Shannet!"

Shannet replied with a chair, but the Saint was ten feet away by the time it crashed into the opposite wall.

Then Shannet came in again with his fists. Any one of those whirling blows carried a kick that would have put a mule to sleep, but the Saint had forgotten more about ring-craft than many professionals ever learn. Shannet never came near touching him. Every rush Shannet made, somehow, expended itself on thin air, while he always seemed to be running his face slap into the Saint's stabbing left.

And at last the Saint, scorning even counter-attack, dropped his hands into his pockets, and simply eluded Shannet's homicidal onslaught by sheer brilliant footwork—ducking, swaying, swooping, as calm and unruffled as if he were merely demonstrating a few ballroom steps, and as light and graceful on his toes as a ballet dancer—until

Shannet reeled limply back against the wall with the sweat streaming into his eyes, utterly done in.

The Saint's mocking smile had never left his lips, and not one hair of his head had shifted.

"Want a rest?" he asked kindly.

"If you'd come in and fight like a man," gasped Shannet, his tortured chest heaving, "I'd kill you!"

"Oh, don't be silly!" said the Saint in a bored voice, as though he had no further interest in the affair. "Hurry up and get out—I'm going to be busy."

He turned away, but Shannet lurched after him.

"Get out yourself!" snarled the man thickly. "D'you hear? I'm going right down to fetch the police . . ."

The Saint sat down.

"Listen to me, Shannet," he said quietly. "The less you talk about police when I'm around, the better for you. I'm telling you now that I believe you murdered a man named McAndrew not so long ago, and jumped his claim on a forged partnership agreement. I'm only waiting till I've got the proof. And then—well, it's too much to hope that the authorities of this benighted republic will execute the man who pays half their salaries, and so in the name of Justice I shall take you myself and hang you from a high tree."

For a moment of silence the air seemed to tingle with the same electric tension as heralds the breaking of a thunderstorm, while the Saint's ice-blue eyes quelled Shannet's re-awakening fury; and then, with a short laugh, the Saint relaxed.

"You're a pawn in the game," he said, with a contrasting carelessness which only emphasised the bleak implacability of his last speech. "We won't waste good melodrama on you. We reserve that for clients with really important discredit accounts. Instead, you shall hear the epitaph I've just composed for you. It commemorates a pestilent tumour named Shannet, who disfigured the face of this planet. He started some fun, but before it was done he was wishing he'd never began it. That otherwise immortal verse is greatly marred by a grammatical error, but I'm not expecting you to know any better . . . Archibald—the door!"

Archie Sheridan had no reason to love Shannet, and the kick with which he launched the man into the garden was not gentle, but he seemed to derive no pleasure from it.

He came back with a grave face, and resumed his chair facing the Saint.

"Well," he said, "you've done what you wanted. Now shall we sit down and make our wills, or shall we spend our last hours of life in drinking and song?"

"Of course, we may be shot," admitted the Saint calmly. "That's up to us. How soon can we expect the Army?"

"Not before five. They'll all be asleep now, and an earthquake wouldn't make the Pasala policeman break off his siesta. Much less the Army, who are inclined to give themselves airs. We might catch the *Andalusia*," he added hopefully.

The Saint surveyed him seraphically.

"Sweetheart," he said, "that joke may now be considered over. We've started, and we've got to keep moving. As I don't see the fun of sitting here waiting for the other side to surround us, I guess we'll bounce right along and interview Kelly. And when you two have coached me thoroughly in the habits and topography of Santa Miranda, we'll just toddle along and capture the town."

"Just toddle along and which?" repeated Sheridan dazedly.

The Saint spun a cigarette high into the air, and trapped it neatly between his lips as it fell.

"That is to say, I will capture the town," he corrected himself, "while you and Kelly create a disturbance somewhere to distract their attention. Wake up, sonny! Get your hat, and let's go!"

3

The Saint's breezy way of saying that he would "just toddle along and capture the town" was a slight exaggeration. As a matter of fact, he spent nearly four days on the job.

There was some spade-work to be done, and certain preparations to be made, and the Saint devoted a considerable amount of care and sober thought to these details. Though his methods, to the uninformed observer, might always have seemed to savour of the reckless, tip-and-run, hit-first-and-ask-questions-afterwards school, the truth was that he rarely stepped out of any frying-pan without first taking the temperature of the fire beyond.

Even in such a foolhardy adventure as that in which he was then engaged, he knew exactly what he was doing, and legislated against failure as well as he might; for, even in the most outlandish parts of the world, the penalty of unsuccessful revolution is death, and the Saint had no overwhelming desire to turn his interesting biography into an obituary notice.

He explained his plan to Kelly, and found the Irishman an immediate convert to the Cause.

"Shure, I've been thinkin' for years that it was time somebody threw out their crooked Government," said that worthy, ruffling a hand like a ham through his tousled mop of flaming hair. "I'm just wonderin' now why I niver did ut meself."

"It's a desperate chance," Simon Templar admitted. "But I don't mind taking it if you're game."

"Six years I've been here," mused Kelly ecstatically, screwing up a huge fist, "and I haven't seen a real fight. Exceptin' one or two disagreements with the natives, who run away afther the first round."

The Saint smiled. He could not have hoped to find a more suitable ally.

"We might easily win out," he said. "It wouldn't work in England, but in a place like this . . ."

"The geography was made for us," said Kelly.

On a scrap of paper he sketched a rough map to illustrate his point.

Pasala is more or less in the shape of a wedge, with the base facing north-east on the sea-coast. Near the centre of the base of the wedge is Santa Miranda. In the body of the wedge are the only other three towns worth mentioning—Las Flores, Rugio, and, near the apex, Esperanza. They are connected up by a cart-track of a road which includes them in a kind of circular route which starts and finishes at Santa Miranda, for the State of Pasala does not yet boast a railway. This is hardly necessary, for the distance between Santa Miranda and Esperanza, the two towns farthest apart, is only 140 miles.

It should also be mentioned that the wedge-shaped territory of Pasala cuts roughly into the Republic of Maduro, a much larger and more civilised country.

"Of course, we're simply banking on the psychology of revolutions and the apathy of the natives," said the Saint, when they had finished discussing their plan of campaign. "The population aren't interested—if they're shown a man in a nice new uniform, and told that he's the man in power, they believe it, and go home and pray that they won't be any worse off than they were before. If we take off a couple of taxes or something like that, as soon as we get in, the mob will be with us to a man. I'm sure the Exchequer can stand it—I don't imagine Manuel Concepcion de Villega has been running this show without making a substantial profit on turnover."

"That'll fetch 'em," Kelly averred. "They're bled dhry with taxes at present."

"Secondly, there's the Army. They're like any other army. They obey their officers because it's never occurred to them to do anything else. If they were faced with a revolution they'd fight it. So instead of that we'll present the revolution as an accomplished fact. If they're like any other South American army, they'll simply carry on under the new Government—with a bonus of a few pesos per man to clinch the bargain."

They talked for a while longer, and then they went out and joined Archie Sheridan, who had not been present at the council, being otherwise occupied with Lilla McAndrew on the verandah.

The Saint had a little leisure to admire the girl. She was rather tall, fair-haired and blue-eyed, superbly graceful. Her sojourn in that sunny climate had coloured her skin a pale golden-brown that was infinitely more becoming than mere pink-and-white, but the peach-like bloom of her complexion had not had time to suffer.

It was plain that Archie Sheridan was fatally smitten with the inevitable affliction, and the Saint was mischievously delighted.

"You want to be careful of him, Miss McAndrew," he advised gravely. "I've known him since he was so high, and you wouldn't believe what a past he's collected in his brief career of sin. Let's see . . . There was Gladys, the golden-haired beauty from the front row of the Gaiety chorus, Susan, Beryl—no, two Beryls—Ethel, the artist's model, Angela, Sadie from California, Joan—two Joans—no, three Joans . . ."

"Don't believe him, Lilla," pleaded Archie. "He's been raving all day. Why, just before lunch he said he was Benito Mussolini!"

The girl laughed.

"It's all right," she told Simon. "I don't take him seriously."

"There's gratitude for you!" said Sheridan wildly. "After all I've done for her! I even taught her to speak English. When she arrived here she had a Scots accent that would have made a bawbee run for its life. She reeked of haggis . . ."

"Archie!"

"Haggis," persisted Sheridan. "She carried one around in her pibroch till it starved to death."

"What are pibroch?" asked the Saint curiously. "Are they something you wear under a kilt?"

When the girl had recovered her composure, "Is he really so impossible?" she exclaimed.

"I don't know you well enough to tell you the whole truth," said the Saint solemnly. "The only hope I can give you is that you're the first Lilla in his life. Wait a minute—sorry—wasn't Lilla the name of the barmaid . . ."

"Go away," said Sheridan morosely. "With sudden death staring you in the face, you ought to be spending your time in prayer and repentance. You'll be shot at dawn tomorrow, and I shall look over the prison walls and cheer on the firing squad."

He watched Kelly and the Saint retire to the other end of the verandah, and then turned to the girl, with his pleasant face unusually serious.

"Lilla," he said, "I don't want to scare you, but it isn't all quite as funny as we make out. The Saint would still be laughing in the face of the firing squad I mentioned, but that doesn't make the possibility of the firing squad any less real."

She looked at him with sober eyes.

"Then it's easily settled," she said. "I won't let you do it."

Sheridan laughed. "It isn't me you've got to deal with," he replied. "It's the Saint. Nothing you could say would stop him. He'd simply tell me to beat it with you on the Andalusia this evening if I was scared. And I'd rather face the said firing squad than have the Saint say that to me."

She would have protested further, but something in the man's tone silenced her. She knew that he was making no idle statement. She had no experience whatever of such things, and yet she realised intuitively what she was up against, recognised the heroic thing when she met it—the blind, unswerving loyalty of a man to his friend, the unshakable obedience of a man to a loved leader. And she knew that any attempt she made to seduce her man from that reality would only lower herself in his eyes.

Perhaps there are few women who could have shown such an understanding, but Lilla McAndrew was—Lilla McAndrew.

She smiled suddenly.

"I've always wanted to see a revolution," she said simply.

Moments passed before Sheridan could grasp the full wonder of her sympathy and acquiescence. And then his arms went round her, and her hands tousled his hair.

"Dear Archie!" she said, and found herself unaccountably breathless.

"I admit every girl the Saint mentioned," said Sheridan defiantly. "And a few more. But that doesn't alter the fact that I love you, and as soon as this comic revolution's over I'm going to marry you."

"I'll believe that when you do it," she teased him, but her heart was on her lips when he kissed her . . .

Some almost offensively discreet coughing from the Saint interrupted them ten minutes later.

"I tried to save you," said the Saint, declining to avert his shamelessly quizzical gaze from the girl's efforts to straighten her hair inconspicuously. "And I'm sorry to have to butt in on your downfall, but your boyfriend and I have work to do. If you look down towards the town you'll see a file of men advancing up the main street in our direction, led by two men on horseback in the uniform of commissionaires. The entire police force of Santa Miranda, as far as I can make out from this distance, is on its way up here to arrest me for assaulting and battering one of their most prominent citizens, and to arrest Archie as an accessory before, after, and during the fact. They have just woken up from their afternoon snooze, and have been put on the job by the aforesaid citizen with commendable rapidity. Will you excuse us if we escape?"

They went to the edge of the verandah and looked down. Below them, about a mile away, Santa Miranda, as yet hardly astir from its siesta, lay bathed in the afternoon sunshine.

The town, indeterminately vignetted at the edges, had a definite core of nearly modern white buildings ranged down its principal streets. These numbered two, and were in the form of a T. The top of the T ran parallel with the waterfront; the upright, half-way down which was the Presidential Palace, ran inland for nearly a mile, tailing off in the mass of adobe huts which clustered round the core of the town.

From where they stood they could look down the length of the street which formed the upright of the T, and the situation was even as the Saint had diagnosed it . . .

"One minute for the fond farewell, Archie," said the Saint briskly, and Sheridan nodded. Simon Templar drew Kelly inside the bungalow.

"By the way," he said, "do you happen to have such a thing as a good-looking pot of paint?"

"I've got some enamel," replied the mystified Kelly.

He produced a couple of tins, and the Saint selected one with every appearance of satisfaction.

"The very idea," he said. "It's just an idea of mine for dealing with this arrest business." Kelly was suspicious.

"I don't seem to have much to do," he complained aggrievedly. "It's hoggin' the best of the fightin' yez are. Now, if I had my way, I'd be sthartin' the throuble with these policemen right away, I would."

"And wreck the whole show," said the Saint. "No, it's too soon for that. And if you call being fifty percent of an invading army 'having nothing to do' I can't agree. You're one of the most important members of the cast. Besides, if your bus doesn't break down, you'll be back here just when the rough stuff is warming up. You get it both ways."

He adjusted his hat to an appropriately rakish and revolutionary angle on his head, and went out to collect Archie Sheridan.

They shook hands with the still grumbling Kelly, but the Saint had the last word with Lilla McAndrew.

"I'm sorry I've got to take Archie," he said. "You see, he's the one man I can trust here who can tap out Morse fluently, and I sent him out from England for that very reason, though I didn't know it was going to pan out as it's panning out now. But I'll promise to get him back to you safe and sound. You needn't worry. Only the good die young. I wonder how you've managed to live so long, Lilla?"

He smiled, and when the Saint smiled in that particularly gay and enchanting manner, it was impossible to believe that any adventure he undertook could fail.

"Archie is marked 'Fragile—With Care' for this journey," said the Saint, and went swinging down the verandah steps.

He walked back arm-in-arm with Sheridan to the latter's bungalow at a leisurely pace enough, for it was his last chance to give Sheridan his final instructions for the opening of the campaign.

Archie was inclined to voice much the same grievance as Kelly had vented, but Templar dealt shortly with that insubordination.

"I'm starting off by having the most boresome time of any of you," he said. "If I could do your job, I promise you I'd be making you do mine. That being so, I reckon I deserve a corresponding majority ration of excitement at the end. Anyway, with any luck we'll all be together again by Thursday, and we'll see the new era in in a bunch. And if you're going to say you've thought of another scheme that'd be just as effective, my answer is that you ought to have spoken up before. It's too late to change our plans now."

At the bungalow the Saint made certain preparations for the arrival of the police posse which to some extent depleted Archie Sheridan's travelling athletic outfit. That done, he sent Sheridan to his post, and himself settled down with a cigarette in an easy chair on the verandah to await the coming of the Law.

4

The *guindillas* came toiling up the last two hundred yards of slope in a disorderly straggle. The hill at that point became fairly steep, they were in poor condition, and, although the sun was getting low, the broiling heat of the afternoon had not yet abated, and these factors united to upset what might otherwise have been an impressive approach. The only members of the squad who did not seem the worse for wear were the two *comisarios*, who rode in the van on a pair of magnificent high-stepping horses, obvious descendants of the chargers of Cortes's invading Spaniards, the like of which may often be seen in that part of the Continent. The Saint had had an eye for those horses ever since he spied them a mile and a half away, which was why he was so placidly waiting for the deputation.

He watched them with a detached interest, smoking his cigarette. They were an unkempt and ferocious-looking lot (in Pasala, as in many other Latin countries, Saturday night is Gillette night for the general public), and every man of them was armed to somewhere near the teeth with a musket, a revolver, and a sabre. The Saint himself was comparatively weaponless, his entire armoury consisting of a beautifully-fashioned little knife, strapped to his left forearm under his sleeve, which he could throw with a deadly swiftness and an unerring aim. He did not approve of firearms, which he considered messy and noisy and barbarous inventions of the devil. Yet the opposition's display of force did not concern him.

His first impression, that the entire police force of Santa Miranda had been sent out to arrest him, proved to be a slight over-estimate. There were, as a matter of fact, only ten *guardias* behind the two mounted men in resplendent uniforms.

The hand came to a bedraggled and slovenly halt a few yards from the verandah, and the *comisarios* dismounted and ascended the short flight of steps with an imposing clanking of scabbards and spurs. They were moustached and important.

The Saint rose.

"*Buenos tardes, Señores,*" he murmured courteously.

"Señor," said the senior *comisario* sternly, unfolding a paper overloaded with official seals. "I regret that I have to trouble a visitor illustrious, hut I am ordered to request your honour to allow your honour to be taken to the *prevencion*, in order that in the morning your honour may be brought before the tribunal to answer a charge of grievously assaulting the *Señor* Shannet."

He replaced the document in his pocket, and bowed extravagantly. The Saint, with a smile, surpassed the extravagance of the bow.

"*Señor polizante,*" he said. "I regret that I cannot come."

Now the word "*polizante*" while it is understood to mean "policeman," is not the term with which it is advisable to address even an irascible *guardia*—much less a full-blown *comisario*. It brought to an abrupt conclusion the elaborate ceremony in which the *comisario* had been indulging.

He turned, and barked an order, and the escort mounted the steps and ranged themselves along the verandah.

"Arrest him!"

"I cannot stay," said the Saint sadly. "And I refuse to be arrested. *Adios, amigos*!"

He faded away—through the open door of the dining-room. The Saint had the knack of making these startlingly abrupt exits without any show of haste, so that he was gone before his audience had realised that he was on his way.

Then the *guardias*, led by the two outraged *comisarios*, followed in a body.

The bungalow was small, with a large verandah in front and a smaller verandah at the back. The three habitable rooms of which it boasted ran through the width of the house, with doors opening on to each verandah. The dining-room was the middle room, and it had no windows.

As the *guardias* surged in in pursuit, rifles at the ready, with the *comisarios* waving their revolvers, the Saint reappeared in the doorway that opened on to the back of the verandah. At the same moment the doors to the front verandah were slammed and barred behind them by Archie Sheridan, who had been lying in wait in an adjoining room for that purpose.

The Saint's hands were held high above his head, and in each hand was a gleaming round black object.

"*Señores,*" he said persuasively. "I am a peaceful revolutionary, and I cannot be pestered like this. In my hands you see two bombs. If you shoot me, they will fall and explode. If you do not immediately surrender I shall throw them—and, again, they will explode. Is it to be death or glory, boys?"

He spoke the last sentence in English, but he had already said enough in the vernacular to make the situation perfectly plain. The *guardias* paused, irresolute.

Their officers, retiring to a strategic position in the background from which they could direct operations, urged their men to advance and defy death in the performance of their duty, but the Saint shifted his right hand threateningly, and the *guardias* found the counter-argument more convincing. They threw down their arms and the *comisarios*, finding themselves alone, followed suit as gracefully as they might.

The Saint ordered the arsenal to be thrown out of the door, and he stepped inside the room and stood aside to allow this to be done. Outside, the guns were collected by Archie Sheridan, and their bolts removed and hurled far away into the bushes of the garden. The cartridges he poured into a large bag, together with the contents of the bandoliers which the Saint ordered his prisoners to discard, for these were required for a certain purpose. Then the Saint returned to the doorway.

"*Hasta la vista*!" he murmured mockingly. "Until we meet again!"

And he hurled the two gleaming round black objects he carried, and a wail of terror went up from the doomed men.

The Saint sprang back, slamming and barring the doors in the face of the panic-stricken stampede and the two tennis-balls, which he had coated with Kelly's providential enamel for the purpose, rebounded off the heads of the cowering *comisarios*, leaving great splashes of paint on the gorgeous uniforms and the gorgeous moustachios of Santa Miranda's Big Two, and went bouncing insolently round the room.

The Saint vaulted over the verandah rail and ran round to the front of the bungalow. Sheridan, his bag of cartridges slung over his shoulder, was already mounted on one of the police horses, and holding the other by the bridle. From inside the dining-room could be heard the muffled shouting and cursing of the imprisoned men, and on the panels of the barred doors thundered the battering of their efforts to escape. The Saint sprang into the saddle.

"*Vamos*!" he cried, and smacked his hand down on the horse's quarters.

The pounding of departing hoofs came to the ears of the men in the locked room, and redoubled the fury of their onslaught on the doors. But the mahogany of which the doors were made was thick and well-seasoned, and it was ten minutes before they broke out. And then, on foot, and unarmed, there was nothing for them to do but to return to Santa Miranda and confess defeat.

The which they did, collaborating on the way down to invent a thrilling tale of a desperate and perilous battle, in which they had braved a hundred deaths, their heroism availing them naught in the face of Simon Templar's evil cunning. But first, to restore their shattered nerves, they partook freely of three bottles of Sheridan's whisky which they found. And it may be recorded that on this account the next day found them very ill, for, before he left, Archie Sheridan had liberally adulterated the whisky with Epsom salts, in anticipation of this very vandalism. But, since *guardia* and *comisario* alike were unfamiliar with the flavour of whisky, they noticed nothing amiss, and went unsuspecting to their hideous fate.

But when they returned to Santa Miranda they said nothing whatever about bombs, wisely deeming that the inclusion of that episode in their story could not but cover them with derision.

Meantime, Simon Templar and Archie Sheridan had galloped neck and neck to Kelly's bungalow, and there Kelly was waiting for them. He had a kit-bag already packed with certain articles that the Saint had required, and Simon took the bag and lashed it quickly to the pommel of his saddle.

Sheridan dismounted. The Saint shook hands with him, and took the bridle of the spare horse.

"All will be well," said the Saint blithely. "I feel it in my bones. So long, souls! See you all again soon. Do your stuff—and good luck!"

He clapped his heels to his horse, and was gone with a cheery wave of his hand.

They watched him till the trees hid him from view, and then they went back to the bungalow.

"A piece of wood, pliers, screws, screwdriver, and wire, Kelly, my bhoyl," ordered Sheridan briskly. "I've got some work to do before I go to bed tonight. And while I'm doing it you can gather round and hear the biggest laugh yet in this revolution, or how the Battle of Santa Miranda was nearly won on the courts of Wimbledon."

"I thought you weren't coming back," said the girl accusingly.

"I didn't know whether I was or not," answered the shameless Archie. "It all depended on whether the Saint's plan of escape functioned or not. Anyway, a good-bye like you gave me was far too good to miss just because I might be coming back. And don't look so disappointed because I got away. I'll go down to the town and surrender, if that's what you want."

Towards sundown a squadron of cavalry galloped up to the bungalow, and the officer in command declared his intention of making a search. Kelly protested.

"You have no right," he said, restraining an almost irresistible desire to throw the man down the steps and thus precipitate the fighting that his fists were itching for.

"I have a warrant from the Minister of the Interior, *El Supremo é Ilustrisimo Señor* Manuel Concepcion de Villega," said the officer, producing the document with a flourish.

"El Disgustando y Horriblisimo *Señor*!" muttered Kelly.

The officer shrugged, and indicated the men who waited below.

"I do not wish to use force, *Señor* Kelly," he said significantly, and Kelly submitted to the inevitable.

"But," he said, "I do not know why you should suspect me to be hiding him."

"You are known to be a friend of the *Señor* Sheridan," was the brief reply, "and the *Señor* Sheridan is a friend of this man. We are looking for both of them." Kelly followed the officer into the house.

"What did you say was the name of this man you are looking for?" he inquired.

"To the *Señor* Shannet, whom he attacked," said the officer, "he gave his name as Benito Mussolini."

He was at a loss to understand Kelly's sudden earthquaking roar of laughter. At last he gave up the effort, and put it down to another manifestation of the well-known madness of all *ingleses*. But the fact remains that the joke largely compensated Kelly for the indignity of the search to which his house was subjected.

The officer and half a dozen of his men went through the bungalow with a small-toothed comb, and not a cubic inch of it, from floor to rafters, escaped their attention. But they did not find Archie Sheridan, who was sitting out on the roof, on the opposite side to that from which the soldiers had approached.

At last the search-party allowed themselves to be shepherded out, for barely an hour's daylight was left to them, and they had already fruitlessly wasted much valuable time.

"But remember, *Señor Kelly*," said the officer, as his horse was led up, "that both Sheridan and Mussolini have been declared outlaws for resisting arrest and assaulting and threatening the lives of the *guardias civiles* sent to apprehend them. In the morning they will be proclaimed, and the *Señor* Shannet, who has heard of the insolence offered to the Law, has himself offered to double the reward for their capture, dead or alive."

The troopers rode off on their quest, but in those latitudes the twilight is short. They scoured the countryside for an hour, until the fall of night put an end to the search, and five miles away they found the horses of the two *comisarios* grazing in a field, but of the man

Mussolini there was no trace. The Saint had had a good start, and what he did not know about the art of taking cover in the open country wasn't worth knowing.

He was stretched out on a branch of a tall tree a mile away from where the horses were found when the troop of cavalry reined in only twelve feet beneath him.

"We can do no more now," said the officer. "In the morning we shall find him. Without horses he cannot travel far. Let us go home."

The Saint laughed noiselessly in the darkness.

5

That night there came into Santa Miranda a *peón*.

He was dirty and disreputable to look upon. His clothes were dusty, patched in many places, and threadbare where they were not patched, and his hair was long, and matted into a permanent thatch, as is the slovenly custom of the labourers of that country.

Had he wished to do so, he might have passed unnoticed among many other similarly down-at-heel and poverty-stricken people, but this he did not seem to want. In fact, he went out of his way to draw attention to himself, and this he found easy enough, for his poverty-stricken appearance was belied by the depth of his pocket.

He made a fairly comprehensive round of the inferior cafés in the town, and in each he bought wine and *aguardiente* for all who cared to join him. Naturally, it was not long before he acquired a large following, and, since he seemed to account for two drinks to everybody else's one, there was no surprise when he became more and more drunk as the evening wore on.

It was not to be expected that such display of affluence on the part of one whose outward aspect argued against the probability that he would have more than a few *centavos* to his name could escape comment, and it was not long before the tongues that devoured the liquor which he bought were busy with rumour. It was whispered, as with authority, that he was a bandit from the Sierra Maduro, over the border beyond Esperanza, who had crossed into Pasala to spend his money and rest until the *rurales* of Maduro tired of seeking him and he could return to his old hunting-grounds with safety. Then it was remarked that on his little finger was a signet ring bearing a heraldic device, and with equal authority it was said that he was the heir to a noble Mexican family indulging his hobby of moving among the *peónes* as one of themselves and distributing charity where he found it merited. Against this, another school of thought affirmed that he was a *peón* who had murdered his master and stolen his ring and his money.

The *peón* heard these whisperings, and laughingly ignored them. His manner lent more support, however, to either of the two former theories than to the third. He was tall for a *peón*, and a man of great strength, as was seen when he bought a whole keg of wine and lifted it in his hands to fill his goblet as if it had weighed nothing at all. His eyes were blue, which argued that he was of noble descent, for the true *peón* stock is so mixed with the native that the eyes of that sea-blue colour are rare. And again, the bandit theory was made more plausible by the man's boisterous and reckless manner, as though he held life cheap and the intense enjoyment of the day the only thing of moment, and would as soon be fighting as drinking. He had, too, a repertoire of strange and barbarous songs which no one could understand.

"Drink up, *amigos*!" he roared from time to time, "for this is the beginning of great days for Pasala!"

But when they asked him what they might mean, he turned away their questions with a jest, and called for more wine.

Few of his following had seen such a night for many years.

From house to house he went, singing his strange songs, and bearing his keg of wine on his shoulder. One or two *guardias* would have barred his way, or, hearing the rumours which were gossiped about him, would have stopped and questioned him, but the *peón* poured them wine or flung them money, and they stood aside.

Towards midnight, still singing, the man led his procession up the Calle del Palacio. The crowd followed, not sure where they were going, and not caring, for they had drunk much.

Now, the Calle del Palacio forms the upright of the T which has been described, and half-way down it, as has been stated, is the palace from which it takes its name.

In the street opposite the palace gates the *peón* halted, set down his keg, and mounted unsteadily upon it. He stood there, swaying slightly, and his following gathered round him. "*Viva! Viva!*" they shouted thickly.

The *peón* raised his hands for silence.

"Citizens!" he cried, "I have told you that this is the beginning of great days for Pasala, and now I will tell you why. It is because at last we are going to suffer no more under this Manuel Concepcion de Villega. May worms devour him alive, for he is a thief and a tyrant and the son of a dog! His taxes bear you down, and you receive nothing in return. The President is his servant, that strutting nincompoop, and they are both in the pay of the traitor Shannet, who is planning to betray you to Maduro. Now I say that we will end this, tonight."

"*Viva!*" responded a few doubtful voices.

"Let us finish this slavery," cried the *peón* again. "Let us storm this palace, which was built with money wrung from the poor, where your puppet of a President and this pig of a de Villega sleep in luxury for which you have been tortured! Let us tear them from their beds and slay them, and cast them back into the gutter from which they came!"

This time there were no "*Vivas!*" The awfulness of the stranger's blasphemy had sobered the mob as nothing else could have done. It was unprecedented—incredible. No one had ever dared to speak in such terms of the President and his Minister—or, if they had, it was reported by spies to the *comisarios*, and *guardias* came swiftly and took the blasphemers away to a place where their treason should not offend the ears of the faithful. Of course, the *peón* had spoken nothing but the truth. But to tear down the palace and kill the President! It was unheard of. It could not be done without much discussion.

The stranger, after his first speech, had seen the sentries at the palace gates creep stealthily away, and now, over the heads of the awestruck crowd, he saw a little knot of *guardias* coming down the street at the double. Whistles shrilled, and the mob huddled together in sudden terror.

"*Amigos*," said the stranger urgently, in a lower voice, "the hour of liberation will not be long coming. Tonight you have heard me sing many strange songs, which are the songs of freedom. Now, when you hear those songs again, and you have thought upon the words I have said tonight, follow the man who sings such songs as I sang, for he will be sent to lead you to victory. But now go quickly, or you will be taken and punished."

The mob needed no encouragement for that. Even while the peón spoke many of them had sneaked away into the dark side-streets. As he spoke his last sentence, it was as if a cord had been snapped which held them, and they fled incontinently.

The *peón* straightened up and shook his fists at their backs.

"Fools!" he screamed. "Cowards! Curs! Is it thus that ye fight? Is it thus that ye overthrow tyrants?"

But his audience was gone, and from either side the *guardias* were closing in on him with drawn sabres.

"*Guarro!*" challenged one of them. "What is this raving?"

"I speak for liberty!" bawled the *peón*, reeling drunkenly on his pedestal. "I speak against the President, who does not know the name of his father, and against the Minister for the Interior, Manuel Concepcion de Villega, whom I call *Señor* Jugo Procedente del Estercolero, the spawn of a dunghill—*guarros, perruelos, hijos de la puts adiva* . . ."

He let loose a stream of the vilest profanity and abuse in the language, so that even the hardened *guardias* were horrified.

They dragged him down and hustled him ungently to the police station, where they locked him up in a verminous cell for the night, but even then he cursed and raved against the President and the Minister for the Interior, mingling his maledictions with snatches of unintelligible songs, until the jailer threatened to beat him unless he held his tongue. Then he was silent, and presently went to sleep.

In the morning they brought him before the magistrate. He was sober, but still rebellious. They asked him his name.

"Don Fulano de Tal," he replied, which is the Spanish equivalent of saying "Mr. So-and-So Such-and-Such."

"If you are impertinent," said the magistrate, "I shall order you to receive a hundred lashes."

"My name is Sancho Quijote," said the *peón* sullenly.

He was charged, and the sentries from the palace testified to the treason of his speeches. So also did the *guardias* who had broken up his meeting. They admitted, in extenuation of his offence, that he had been very drunk.

He was asked if he had anything to say.

"I have nothing to say," he answered, "except that, drunk or not, I shall spit upon the name of the President and the Minister for the Interior till the end of my days. As for you, *Señor jeuz*, you are no better than the *guindillas* who arrested me—you are all the miserable hirelings of the oppressors, paid to persecute those who dare speak for justice. But it will not be long before your pride is turned to humiliation."

"He is mad," whispered one *guardia* to another.

The *peón* was sentenced to seven years' imprisonment with hard labour, for there are no limits to the powers of summary jurisdiction in Pasala. He heard the verdict without emotion.

"It does not matter," he said. "I shall not stay in prison seven days. It will not be long before you know why."

When he reached the prison he asked to be allowed to send a message by telegraph to Ondia, the capital of Maduro.

"I am of Maduro," he confessed. "I should have returned to Ondia tomorrow, and I must tell my wife that I am detained."

He had money to pay for the telegram, but it was evening before permission was received for the message to be sent, for nothing is done hurriedly in Spanish America.

Twenty-four hours later there came from Ondia a telegram addressed to Manuel Concepcion de Villega, and it was signed with the name and titles of the President of Maduro. A free translation would have read:

> *I am informed that a citizen of Maduro, giving the name of Sancho Quijote, has been imprisoned in Santa Miranda. If he is not delivered to the frontier by Wednesday noon my armies will advance into Pasala.*

Shannet was closeted with de Villega when the message arrived, and for the moment he was no better able to account for it than was the Minister.

"Who is this man Quijote?" he asked. "It's a ridiculous name. There is a book called *Don Quijote*, Quixote in English, and there is a man in it called Sancho Panza."

"I know that," said Don Manuel, and sent for the judge.

He heard the story of the *peón*'s crime and sentence and was not enlightened. But he had enough presence of mind to accuse the magistrate of inefficiency for not having suspected that the name Sancho Quijote was a false one.

"It is impossible," said de Villega helplessly, when the magistrate had been dismissed, "By Wednesday noon—that hardly gives us enough time to get him to the frontier even if we release him immediately. And who is this man? A labourer, a stranger, of whom nobody knows anything, who suddenly appears in Santa Miranda with more money than he could have ever come by honestly, and preaches a revolution to a mob that he has first made drunk. He deserves his punishment, and yet the President of Maduro, without any inquiry, demands his release. It means war . . ."

"He knew this would happen," said Shannet. "The judge told us—he boasted that he would not stay in prison seven days . . ."

They both saw the light at the same instant. "An agent provocateur . . ."

"A trap!" snarled de Villega. "And we have fallen into it. It is only an excuse that Maduro was seeking. They sent him here, with money, for no other purpose than to get himself arrested. And then this preposterous ultimatum, which they give us no time even to consider . . ."

"But why make such an intrigue?" demanded Shannet. "This is a poor country. They are rich. They have nothing to gain."

Don Manuel tugged nervously at his moustachios.

"And we cannot even buy them off," he said. "Unless we appeal to the Estados Unidos . . ." Shannet sneered.

"And before their help can arrive the war is over," he said. "New Orleans is five days away. But they will charge a high price for burying the hatchet for us."

Don Manuel suddenly sat still. His shifty little dark eyes came to rest on Shannet.

"I see it!" he exclaimed savagely. "It is the oil! You, and your accursed oil! I see it all! It is because of the oil that this country is always embroiled in a dozen wars and fears of wars. So far Pasala has escaped, but now we are like the rest. My Ministry will be overthrown. Who knows what Great Power has paid Maduro to attack us? Then the Great Power steps in and takes our oil from us. I shall be exiled. Just now it is England, through you, who has control of the oil. Perhaps it is now America who tries to capture it, or another English company. I am ruined!"

"For God's sake stop whining!" snapped Shannet. "If you're ruined, so am I. We've got to see what can be done about it."

De Villega shook his head.

"There is nothing to do. They are ten to one. We shall be beaten. But I have some money, and there is a steamer in two days. If we can hold off their armies so long I can escape."

It was some time before the more brutally vigorous Shannet could bring the Minister to reason. Shannet had the courage of the wild beast that he was. At bay, faced with the wrecking of his tainted fortunes, he had no other idea but to fight back with the desperate ferocity of a cornered animal.

But even when Don Manuel's moaning had been temporarily quietened they were little better off. It was useless to appeal to the President, for he was no more than a tool in de Villega's hands. Likewise, the rest of the Council were nothing but figureheads, the mere instruments of de Villega's policy, and appointed by himself for no other reason than their willingness, for a consideration, to oppose nothing that he put forward.

"There is but one chance," said Villega. "A radio-gram must be sent to New Orleans. America will send a warship to keep the peace. Then we will try to make out to Maduro that the warship is here to fight for us, and their armies will retire. To the Estados Unidos, then, we will say that we had made peace before their warship arrived; we are sorry to have troubled them, but there is nothing to do."

It seemed a flimsy suggestion to Shannet, but it was typical of de Villega's crafty and tortuous statesmanship. Shannet doubted if America, having once been asked to intervene, would be so easily put off, but he had no more practical scheme to suggest himself, and he let it go.

He could not support it with enthusiasm, for an American occupation would mean the coming of American justice, and Shannet had no wish for that while there were still tongues wagging with charges against himself. But he could see no way out. He was in a cleft stick.

"Why not let this *peón* go?" he asked.

"And will that help us?" demanded Don Manuel scornfully. "If we sent him away now he would hardly have time to reach the border by noon tomorrow, and they would certainly say that they had not received him. Is it not plain that they are determined to fight? When they have taken such pains to trump up an excuse, will they be so quickly appeased?"

A purely selfish train of thought led to Shannet's next question.

"This man Sheridan and his friend—has nothing been heard of them yet? They have been at large two days."

"At a time like this, can I be bothered with such trifles?" replied de Villega shortly. "The squadron of Captain Tomare has been looking for them, but they are not found."

This was not surprising, for the searchers had worked outwards from Santa Miranda. Had they been inspired to work inwards they might have found Simon Templar, unwashed and unshaven, breaking stones in their own prison yard, chained by his ankles in a line of other unwashed and unshaven desperadoes, his identity lost in his official designation of Convicto Sancho Quijote, No. 475.

It was the Saint's first experience of imprisonment with hard labour, and he would have been enjoying the novel adventure if it had not been for various forms of microscopic animal life with which the prison abounded.

6

There came one morning to the London offices of Pasala Oil Products Ltd. (Managing Director, Hugo Campard) a cable in code. He decoded it himself, for it was not a code in general use, and his pink face went paler as the transliteration proceeded.

By the time the complete translation had been written in between the lines Hugo Campard was a very frightened man. He read the message again and again, incredulous of the catastrophe it foreboded.

> *Maduro declared war Pasala on impossible ultimatum. Believe deliberately instigated America or rival combine. Pasala army hopelessly outnumbered. No chance. Villega appealed America. Help on way but will mean overthrow of Government. Concession probably endangered. Sell out before news reaches London and breaks market.*
>
> *Shannet.*

Campard's fat hands trembled as he clipped the end of a cigar.

He was a big, florid man with a bald head and a sandy moustache. Once upon a time he had been a pinched and out-at-elbows clerk in a stockbroker's office, until his ingenuity had found incidental ways of augmenting his income. For a few years he had scraped and saved. Then, with five hundred pounds capital, and an intimate knowledge of the share market, he had gone after bigger game.

He had succeeded. He was clever, he knew the pitfalls to avoid, he was without pity or scruple, and luck had been with him. In fifteen years he had become a very rich man. Innumerable were the companies with which he had been associated, which had taken in much money and paid out none. He had been "exposed" half a dozen times, and every reputable broker knew his stock for what it was, but the scrip of the Campard companies was always most artistically engraved and their prospectuses couched in the most attractive terms, so that there was never a lack of small investors ready to pour their money into his bank account.

It is said that there is a mug born every minute, and Campard had found this a sound working principle. Many others like him, steering narrowly clear of the law, have found no lack of victims, and Campard had perhaps found more suckers than most.

But even the most triumphant career meets a check sometimes, and Campard had made a slip which had brought him into the full publicity of a High Court action. He had wriggled out, by the skin of his teeth and some expensive perjury, but the resultant outcry had told him that it would be wise to lie low for a while. And lying low did not suit Campard's book. He lived extravagantly, and for all the wealth that he possessed on paper there were many liabilities. And then, when his back was actually to the wall, had come the miracle—in the shape of the chance to buy the Pasala concession, offered him by a man named Shannet, whom he had employed many years ago.

Pasala oil was good. In the few months that it had been worked, the quality and quantity of the output had been startling. Campard enlisted the help of a handful of his boon companions, and poured in all his resources. More plant was needed and more labour, more expert management. That was now to be supplied. The directors of Pasala Oil Products sat down to watch themselves become millionaires.

And then, in a clear sky, the cloud.

Hugo Campard, skimming through his newspaper on his way to the financial pages, had read of the early manifestations of the Saint, and had been mildly amused. In the days that followed he had read of other exploits of the Saint, and his amusement had changed gradually to grave anxiety . . . And one day there had come to Hugo Campard, through the post, a card . . .

Each morning thereafter the familiar envelope had been beside his plate at breakfast; each morning, when he reached the offices of Pasala Oil Products, he had found another reminder of the Saint on his desk. There had been no message. Just the picture. But the newspapers were full of stories, and Hugo Campard was afraid . . .

Then, two days ago, the Saint had spoken.

Campard could not have told why he opened the envelopes in which the Saint sent his mementoes. Perhaps it was because, each time, Campard hoped he would be given some indication of what the Saint meant to do. After days of suspense, that had painted the black hollows of sleeplessness under his eyes and brought him to a state of nerves that was sheer physical agony, he was told.

On that day, underneath the crude outline, was pencilled a line of small writing:

In a week's time you will be ruined.

He had already had police protection—after the Lemuel incident there had been no difficulty in obtaining that, as soon as he showed the police the first cards. All night there had been a constable outside his house in St. John's Wood. All day a constable stood in the corridor outside his office. A plain-clothes detective rode in his car with him everywhere he went. Short of some unforeseeable masterpiece of strategy, or a recourse to the machine-gun fighting of the Chicago gangsters, it was impossible that the Saint could reach him as he had reached Lemuel.

Now, at one stroke, the Saint brought all these preparations to naught, and broke invisibly through the cordon. Against such an attack the police could not help him.

"In a week's time you will be ruined."

An easy boast to make. A tremendous task to carry out.

And yet, even while he had been racking his brains to find out how the Saint might carry out his threat, he had his answer.

For a long time he stared blindly at the cable-gram, until every letter of the message was burned into his brain as with a hot iron. When he roused himself it was to clutch at a straw.

He telephoned to the telegraph company, and verified that the message had actually been received from Santa Miranda via Barbados and Pernambuco. Even that left a loophole. He cabled to an agent in New York, directing him to obtain authentic information from Washington at any cost, and by the evening he received a reply confirming Shannet's statement. The *U.S.S. Michigan* was on its way to Santa Miranda in response to an appeal from the President.

There was no catch in it. Shannet's code message was not a bluff, not even from an agent of the Saint in Santa Miranda. It was a grimly sober utterance of fact.

But the gigantic thoroughness of it! The colossal impudence of the scheme! Campard felt as if all the strength and fight had ebbed out of him. He was aghast at the revelation of the resources of the Saint. Against a man who apparently thought nothing of engineering a war to gain his ends, he felt as puny and helpless as a babe.

His hand went out again to the telephone, but he checked the impulse. It was no use telling the police that. They could do nothing—and, far too soon as it was, the news would be published in the Press. And then, with the name of Campard behind them, P.O.P. shares would tumble down the market to barely the value of their weight in waste paper.

Before he left the office that night he sent a return cable in code to Santa Miranda:

> *Believe war organised by criminal known as Saint, who has threatened me. Obtain particulars of any strange Englishman in Pasala or Maduro. Give descriptions. Report developments.*

What the Saint had started, Campard argued, the Saint could stop. Campard might have a chance yet, if he could bargain . . .

But the declaration of war was announced in the evening paper which he bought on his way home, and Hugo Campard knew then that it was too late.

He had no sleep that night, and by nine o'clock next morning he was at the office, and speaking on the telephone to his broker.

"I want you to sell twenty thousand P.O.P.s for me," he said. "Take the best price you can get."

"I wish I could hope to get a price at all," came the sardonic answer. "The market's full of rumours and everyone's scared to touch the things. You're too late with your selling—the Bears were in before you."

"What do you mean?" asked Campard in a strained voice.

"There was a good deal of quiet selling yesterday and the day before," said the broker. "Somebody must have had information. They're covering today, and they must have made thousands."

During the morning other backers of the company came through on the telephone and were accusing or whining according to temperament, and Campard dealt with them all in the same formula.

"I can't help it," he said. "I'm hit twice as badly as any of you. It isn't my fault. The company was perfectly straight; you know that."

The broker rang up after lunch to say that he had managed to get rid of six thousand shares at an average price of two shillings.

"Two shillings for two-pound shares?" Campard almost sobbed. "You're mad!"

"See if you can do any better yourself, Mr. Campard," replied the broker coldly. "The market won't take any more at present, but I might be able to get rid of another couple of thousand before we close at about a bob each—to people who want to keep them as curios. A firm of wall-paper manufacturers might make an offer for the rest . . ."

Campard slammed down the receiver and buried his face in his hands.

He was in the same position three hours later when his secretary knocked on the door and entered with a buff envelope.

"Another cable, Mr. Campard."

He extracted the flimsy and reached out a nerveless hand for the code book. He decoded:

> *Maduro armies advancing into Pasala. Only chance now sell any price. Answer inquiry. Man arrived nearly four months ago . . .*

With a sudden impatience, Campard tore the cablegram into a hundred pieces and dropped them into the waste-paper basket. There was no time now to get in touch with the Saint. The damage was done.

A few minutes later came the anticipated message from the firm that he had induced to back him over Pasala Oil Products. Rich as he had become, he would never have been able to acquire his large holding in the company without assistance. How, with his reputation, he had got any firm to back him was a mystery. But he had been able to do it on the system known as "margins" —which, in this instance, meant roughly that he could be called upon immediately to produce fifty per cent of the amount by which the shares had depreciated, in order to "keep up his margin."

The demand, courteously but peremptorily worded, was delivered by special messenger, and his only surprise was that it had not come sooner. He scribbled a cheque, which there was no money in the bank to meet, and sent it back by the same boy.

He sent for his car, and left the office shortly afterwards. The paper which he bought outside told of the panic of P.O.P.s, and he read the article with a kind of morbid interest.

There was a letter, delivered by the afternoon post, waiting at his house when he got back.

> *I sold P.O.P.s and covered today. The profits are nearly twelve thousand pounds.*
>
> *The expenses of this campaign have been unusually heavy; but, even then, after deducting these and my ten per cent collecting fee, I hope to be able to forward nine thousand pounds to charity on your behalf.*
>
> *Received the above-named sum—with thanks.*

The Saint

Enclosed was a familiar card, and one Pasala Oil Products share certificate.

Hugo Campard dined well that night, and, alone, accounted for a bottle of champagne. After that he smoked a cigar with relish, and drank a liqueur brandy with enjoyment.

He had dressed. He felt the occasion deserved it. His mind was clear and untroubled, for in a flash he had seen the way out of the trap.

When his cigar was finished, he exchanged his coat for a dressing-gown, and passed into his study. He locked the door behind him, and for some time paced up and down the room in silence, but no one will ever know what he thought. At ten o'clock precisely the pacing stopped.

The constable on guard outside heard the shot, but Hugo Campard did not hear it.

7

The men serving sentences of hard labour in the prison of Santa Miranda are allowed an afternoon siesta of three hours. This is not due to the humanity and loving-kindness of the authorities, but to the fact that nothing will induce the warders to forgo the afternoon nap which is the custom of the country, and no one has yet discovered a way of making the prisoners work without a wide-awake warder to watch them and pounce on the shirkers.

The fetters are struck off the prisoners' ankles, and they are herded into their cells, a dozen in each, and there locked up to rest as well as they can in the stifling heat of a room ventilated only by one small barred window and thickly populated with flies. The warders retire to their quarters above the prison, and one jailer is left on guard, nodding in the passage outside the cells, with a rifle across his knees.

It was so on the third day of the Saint's incarceration, and this was the second hour of the siesta, but the Saint had not slept.

His cell-mates were sprawled on the bunks or on the floor, snoring heavily. They were hardened to the flies. Outside, the jailer dozed, his sombrero on the back of his head and his coat unbuttoned. Through the window of the cell a shaft of burning sunlight cut across the moist gloom and splashed a square of light on the opposite wall.

The Saint sat by the gates of the cell, watching that creeping square of light. Each afternoon he had watched it, learning its habits, so that now he could tell the time by it. When the edge of the square touched a certain scar in the stone it was four o'clock . . . That was the time he had decided upon . . .

He scrambled softly to his feet.

The jailer's head nodded lower and lower. Every afternoon, the Saint had noted, he set his chair at a certain point in the passage where a cool draught from a cross-corridor would fan him. Therefore, on that afternoon, the Saint had taken pains to get into the nearest cell to that point.

He tore a button off his clothes, and threw it. It hit the jailer on the cheek, and the man stirred and grunted. The Saint threw another button. The man shook his head, snorted, and roused, stretching his arms with a prodigious yawn.

"*Señor!*" hissed the Saint. The man turned his head.

"Loathsome disease," he growled, "why dost thou disturb my meditations? Lie down and be silent, lest I come and beat thee."

"I only wished to ask your honour if I might give your honour a present of fifty pesos," said the Saint humbly.

He squatted down again by the bars of the gate and played with a piece of straw. Minutes passed . . .

He heard the jailer get to his feet, but did not look up. The man's footsteps grated on the floor, and stopped by the cell door. In the cell the other convicts snored peacefully.

"Eater of filth and decomposing fish," said the jailer's voice gruffly, "did I hear thy coarse lips speak to me of fifty pesos? How hast thou come by that money?"

"Gifts break rocks," replied the *peón*, quoting the Spanish proverb. "I had rather my gifts broke them than I were compelled to break any more of them. I have fifty pesos, and I want to escape."

"It is impossible. I searched thee . . ."

"It was hidden. I will give it to your honour as a pledge. I know where to find much more money, if your honour would deign to release me and let me lead you to where it is hidden. Have you not heard how, when I was arrested, it was testified that in the town I spent, in one evening, enough to keep you for a year? That was nothing to me. I am rich."

The jailer stroked his stubbly chin.

"Verminous mongrel," he said, more amiably, "show me this fifty pesos and I will believe thee."

The Saint ran his fingers through his tangled hair, and there fell out a note. The jailer recognised it, and his avaricious eyes gleamed.

He reached a claw-like hand through the bars, but the Saint jerked the note out of his reach. The jailer's face darkened.

"Abominable insect," he said, "thou hast no right to that. Thou art a convict, and thy goods are forfeit to the State. As the servant of the State I will confiscate that paper, that thy low-born hands may defile it no longer."

He reached for his keys, but the Saint held up a warning hand.

"If you try to do that, *amigo*," he said, "I shall cry out so loudly that the other warders will come down to see what has happened. Then I shall tell them, and they will make you divide the fifty pesos with them. And I shall refuse to tell you where I have hidden the rest of my money. Why not release me, and have it all for yourself?"

"But how shall I know that thou dost not lie?"

The Saint's hands went again to his hair, and a rain of fifty-peso notes fell to the floor. He picked them up and counted them before the jailer. There were thirty of them altogether. "See, I have them here!" he said. "Fifteen hundred pesos is a lot of money. Now open this door and I will give them to you."

The jailer's eyes narrowed cunningly. Did this fool of a *peón* really believe that he would be given his liberty in exchange for such a paltry sum? Apparently.

Not that the sum was so paltry, being equal to about two hundred pounds in English money, but if any prisoner escaped, the jailer would be blamed for it, and probably imprisoned himself. Yet this simpleton seemed to imagine that he had only to hand over his bribe and the jailer would risk punishment to earn it.

Very well, let him have his childish belief. It would be easily settled. The door opened, the money paid over, a shot . . . And then there would be no one to bear witness against him. The prisoner was known to be violent. He attempted to escape, and was shot. It would be easy to invent a story to account for the opening of the cell door . . .

"*Señor peon,*" said the jailer, "I see now that your honour should not be herded in with these cattle. I will set your honour free, and your honour will give me the money, and I shall remember your honour in my prayers."

He tiptoed back to his chair and picked up his rifle. Then, with elaborate precautions against noise, he unlocked the cell door, and the *peón* came out into the passage.

The other prisoners still snored, and there was no sound but the droning of the flies to arouse them. The whole colloquy had been conducted in whispers, for it was imperative for the jailer as for the *peón* that there should be no premature alarm.

"Now give me the money," said the jailer huskily.

The Saint held out the handful of notes, and one broke loose and fluttered to the floor. As the jailer bent to pick it up, the Saint reached over him and slid the man's knife gently out of his belt. As the man straightened up the Saint's arm whipped round his neck, strangling his cry of fear before it could pass his throat. And the man felt the point of the knife prick his chest.

"Put thy rifle down against the wall," breathed the Saint in his ear. "If it makes a sound thou wilt not speak again."

No rifle could ever have been grounded more silently.

The Saint withdrew the knife and picked the man off his feet. In an instant, and without a sound, he had him on the floor, holding him with his legs in a ju-jitsu lock so that he could not move.

"Be very quiet," urged the Saint, and let him feel the knife again.

The man lay like one dead. The Saint, his hands now free, twisted the man's arms behind his back and tied them with the sling of his rifle. Then he rolled the man over.

"When you searched me," he said, "I had a knife. Where is it?"

"I am wearing it."

The Saint rolled up the man's sleeve and unstrapped the sheath from his forearm. With loving care he transferred it to his own arm, for he had had Anna for years, and she was the darling of his heart. That little throwing-knife, which he could wield so expertly, had accompanied him through countless adventures, and had saved his life many times. He loved it like a child, and the loss of it would have left him inconsolable.

With Anna back in her place, the Saint felt more like himself—though it is doubtful if anyone could have been found to agree with him, for he could never in his life have looked so dirty and disreputable as he was then. He, Simon Templar, the Saint, the man who was known for his invariable elegance and his almost supernatural power of remaining immaculate and faultlessly groomed even in the most hectic rough-house and the most uncivilised parts of the world, had neither washed nor shaved for nearly four days. There was no provision for these luxuries in the prison of Santa Miranda. And his clothes had been dreadful enough when Kelly had borrowed them off his under-gardener for the purpose; now, after having been lived in day and night on the stone pile and in the filthy cell which they had just left, their condition may be imagined . . .

His greatest wish at that moment was to get near some soap and water, and already the time of grace for such a diversion was getting short. The square of light on the cell wall told him that he had barely half an hour at his disposal before Santa Miranda would be rousing itself for the second instalment of its day's work, and the other warders would soon be lurching down, yawning and cursing, to drive the prisoners back to their toil. It was time for the Saint to be moving.

He unfastened the jailer's belt and used it to secure the man's legs, then he rolled him over and stuffed his handkerchief into his mouth for a gag. He straightened up, hands on hips, and the helpless man glared up at him with bulging eyes.

"But I had forgotten!" cried the Saint, under his breath, and stooped again to take his money from the jailer's pocket.

The man squirmed, and the Saint swept him a mocking bow.

"Remain with God, my little ape," he murmured. "There will now be nothing to disturb thy meditations."

Then he was gone.

He ran lightly down the corridor, and out at the end into the blazing sunlight of the prison courtyard. This he crossed swiftly, slowing up and moving a little more cautiously as he neared the gates. Within the courtyard, beside the gates, was a little sentry-box where the gatekeeper might take shelter from the sun.

The Saint stole up the last few yards on tiptoe, and sidled one eye round the doorway of the box.

The gatekeeper sat inside on a packing-case, his back propped against the wall. His rifle was leaning against the wall in one corner. He was awake, but his eyes were intent on a pattern which he was tracing in the dust with the toe of his boot.

The bare prison walls were too high to scale, and the only way out was by way of the gates.

The Saint's shadow suddenly blocked the light from the sentry-box, and the gatekeeper half-rose to his feet with a shout rising to his lips. It was rather like shooting a sitting rabbit, but the issues involved were too great to allow of making a more sporting fight of it. As the warder's head came up, the Saint hit him on the point of the jaw scientifically and with vim, and the shout died stillborn.

The Saint huddled the man back against the wall, and tipped his sombrero over his eyes as if he was asleep—which, in fact, he was. Then he scrambled over the gates, and dropped cat-footed into the dust of the cart-track of a road outside.

The prison of Santa Miranda lies to the east of the town, near the sea, among the slums which closely beset the bright main streets, and the Saint set himself to pass quickly through the town by way of these dirty, narrow streets where his disreputable condition would be most unnoticed, avoiding the Calle del Palacio and the chance of encountering a guardia who might remember him.

Santa Miranda had not yet awoken. In the grass-grown lanes between the rude huts of the labourers a child in rags played here and there, but paid no attention to his passing. In the doorway of one hut an old and wizened Indian slept in the sun, like a lizard. The Saint saw no one else.

He threaded the maze quietly but with speed, steering a course parallel to the Calle del Palacio. And then, over the low roofs of the adobe hovels around him, he saw, quite close, a tall white tower caught by the slanting rays of the sun, and he changed his plans.

That is to say, he resolved on the spur of the moment to dispense with making plans. His original vague idea had been to make for Kelly's bungalow, get a shave, a bath, some clean clothes, and a cigarette, and sit down to deliberate the best way of capturing the town. So far, in spite of his boast, the solution of that problem had eluded him, though he had no doubts that he would be given inspiration at the appointed time.

Now, looking at that tower, which he knew to be an ornament of the Presidential Palace, only a stone's throw away, the required inspiration came, and he acted upon it at once, branching off to his left in the direction of the tower.

It was one of those gay and reckless, dare-devil and foolhardy, utterly preposterous and wholly delightful impulses which the Saint could never resist. The breath-taking impudence of it was, to his way of thinking, the chief reason for taking it seriously; the suicidal odds against success were a conclusive argument for having a fling at bringing off the lone hundred-to-one chance; the monumental nerve that was plainly needed for turning the entertaining idea into a solemn fact was a challenge to his adventurousness that it was simply unthinkable to ignore. The Saint took up the gauntlet without the faintest hesitation.

For this was the full effrontery of his decision.

"Eventually," whispered the Saint, to his secret soul, "why not now?"

And the Saintly smile in all its glory twitched his lips back from his white teeth . . .

His luck had been stupendous, and it augured well for the future. Decidedly it was his day. A clean getaway from the prison, with no alarm. And he reached the high wall surrounding the palace grounds unobserved. And only a dozen feet away from the walls grew a tall tree.

The Saint went up the tree like a monkey, to a big straight branch that stuck out horizontally fifteen feet from the ground. Measuring the distance, he jumped.

The leap took him on to the top of the wall. He steadied himself for a moment, and then jumped again, twelve feet down into the palace gardens.

He landed on his toes, as lightly as a panther, and went zigzagging over the lawn between the flower-beds like a Red Indian. The gardens were empty. There was no sound but the murmuring of bees in the sun and the soft rustle of the Saint's feet over the grass.

He ran across the deserted gardens and up some steps to a flagged terrace in the very shadow of the palace walls. Eight feet above the terrace hung a low balcony. The Saint took two steps and a jump, hung by his finger-tips for a second, and pulled himself quickly up and over the balustrade.

An open door faced him, and the room beyond was empty. The Saint walked in, and passed through to the corridor on the other side.

Here he was at a loss, for the geography of the palace was strange to him. He crept along, rather hesitantly, without a sound. In the space of a dozen yards there was another open door. Through it, as he passed, the Saint caught a glimpse of the room beyond, and what he saw brought him to a sudden standstill.

He tiptoed back to the doorway, and stood there at gaze. It was a bathroom.

Only a year ago that bathroom had been fitted up at enormous cost for the delectation of the Saturday nights of His Excellency the President and the Minister of the Interior. A gang of workmen specially sent down by a New York firm of contractors had affixed those beautiful sky-blue tiles to the walls, and laid those lovely sea-green tiles on the floor, and installed that superlative pale green porcelain bath with its gleaming silver taps and showers and other gadgets. Paris had supplied the great crystal jar of bath salts which stood on the window-sill, and the new cakes of expensive soap in the dishes.

The Saint's glistening eyes swept the room.

It was not Saturday, but it seemed as if someone was making a departure from the usual habits of the palace household. On a rack above the wash-basin were laid out razor, shaving-soap, and brush.

On a chair beside the bath were snowy towels. On another chair, in a corner, were clothes—a spotless silk shirt, a sash, wide-bottomed Mexican trousers braided with gold, shoes . . .

For a full minute the Saint stared, struck dumb with wonder at his astounding good fortune. Then, in fear and trembling, he stole into the room and turned on a tap.

The water ran hot.

He hesitated no longer. War, revolution, battle, murder, and sudden death meant nothing to him then. He closed the door, and turned the key.

Blessings, like misfortunes, never come singly. There was even a packet of Havana cigarettes and a box of matches tucked away behind the bath salts . . .

Ten minutes later, already shaved, the Saint was stretched full length in a steaming bath into which he had emptied the best part of the Presidential jar of bath salts, innocently playing submarines with the sponge and a cake of soap.

A cigarette was canted jauntily up between his lips, and he was without a care in the world.

8

Archie Sheridan mopped his moist forehead and smacked viciously at a mosquito which was gorging itself on his bare forearm.

"Thank the Lord you're back," he said. "This blistered place gives me the creeps. Have you fixed anything?"

Kelly settled ponderously on the spread groundsheet.

"I have arranged the invadin' army," he said. "Anything come through while I've been away?"

"Nothing that matters. One or two private messages, which I duly acknowledged. I wonder what they're thinking at the Ondia end of the line."

"There'll be a breakdown gang along—some time," pronounced Kelly. "It's now the second day of the wire bein' cut. Within the week, maybe, they'll wake up and send to repair it. What's the time?"

Sheridan consulted his watch.

"A quarter-past eleven," he said.

They sat under a great tree, in a small clearing in the jungle near the borders of Maduro, some ten miles east of Esperanza. A mile away was the rough track which led from Esperanza across the frontier to Maduro, and which formed the only road-link between the two countries; and there Kelly's Ford, in which they had made most of the journey, waited hidden between the trees at a little distance from the road.

But for all the evidence there was to the contrary they might have been a thousand miles from civilisation. At the edge of the tiny clearing colossal trees laced together with vines and creepers hemmed them in as with a gigantic palisade; high over their heads the entangled branches of the trees shut out the sky, and allowed no light to pass but a ghostly, grey twilight, in which the glaring crimsons and oranges and purples of the tropical blooms which flowered here and there in the marshy soil stood out with a shrieking violence.

Now and again, in the stillness of the great forest, there would be a rustle of the passing of some unseen wild thing. Under some prowling beast's paw, perhaps, a rotten twig would snap with a report like a rifle-shot. Sometimes the delirious chattering of a troop of monkeys would babble out with a startling shrillness that would have sent a shudder up the spine of an impressionable man. And the intervals of silence were not true silence, but rather a dim and indefinable and monotonous murmur punctuated with the sogging sound of dripping water. The air was hot and steamy and heavy with sickly perfumes.

"You get used to it," said Kelly with a comprehensive wave of the stem of his pipe.

"Thanks," said Sheridan. "I'm not keen to. I've been here two days too long already. I have nightmares in which I'm sitting in an enormous bath, but as soon as I've finished washing a shower of mud falls on me and I have to start all over again."

Now this was on the morning of the day in the afternoon of which the Saint escaped from prison.

On Sheridan's head were a pair of radio headphones. On the ground-sheet beside him was a little instrument, a Morse transmitter, which he had ingeniously fashioned before they left Santa Miranda. Insulated wires trailed away from him into the woods.

The telegraph line, for most of its length, followed the roads, but at that point, for some inexplicable reason, it took a shortcut across country. They had decided to attack it at that point on grounds of prudence, for, although the road between Esperanza and the Maduro frontier was not much used, there was always the risk of someone passing and commenting on their presence when he reached his destination.

The afternoon before, they had cut the line and sent through to Esperanza, to be relayed to Santa Miranda, the ultimatum purporting to come from the President of Maduro. Since then, night and day, one of them had sat with the receivers upon his ears, waiting for a reply. The arrangement was complicated, for Kelly could not read Morse, while Sheridan's Spanish was very haphazard, but they managed somehow. Several times when Archie had been resting Kelly had roused him to take down a message, but the translation had had no bearing on the threat of war, except occasionally from a purely private and commercial aspect. There had been no official answer.

Sheridan looked at his watch again.

"Their time's up in half an hour," he said. "What do you say to sending a final demand? —the 'D' being loud and explosive, as in 'Income Tax.'"

"Shure—if there's no chance of 'em surrenders,'" agreed Kelly. "But we can't let anything stop the war."

The message they sent was worded with this in view:

> *Understand you refuse to release Quijote. Our armies will accordingly advance into Pasala at noon.*

While they waited for zero hour, Kelly completed the task of breaking camp, strapping their tent and equipment into a workmanlike bundle. He finished this job just before twelve, and returned to his prostrate position on the ground-sheet.

"I wonder what that blackguard Shannet is doin'?" he said. "I only hope he hasn't missed the news by takin' a thrip to the concession. It'd be unlucky for us if he had."

"I think he'll be there," said Sheridan. "He was in Santa Miranda when we left, and he's likely to stay there and supervise the hunt for the Saint."

"He's a good man, that," said Kelly. "It's a pity he's not an Irishman." Sheridan fanned himself with a handkerchief.

"He's one of the finest men that ever stepped," he said. "If the Saint said he was going to make war on Hell, I'd pack a fire extinguisher and go with him." Kelly sucked his pipe, and spat thoughtfully at an ant.

"That's not what I call your duty," he remarked. "In fact, I'm not sure that yez should have been in this at all, with a girl like Lilla watchin' for yez to come back, and worryin' her pretty head. And with a crawlin' sarpint like Shannet about . . ."

"He's tried to bother her once or twice. But if I thought . . ."

"I've been thinkin' a lot out here," said Kelly. "I'm not sayin' what I've thought. But it means that as soon as we've done what we're here to do we're goin' to hurry back to Santa Miranda as fast as Tin Lizzie'll take us. There's my missus an' Lilla without a man to look afther them, an' the Saint . . ."

Sheridan suddenly held up a hand for silence. He wrote rapidly on his little pad, and

Kelly leaned over to read. "What's it mean?"

"The war's on!" yelled Kelly ecstatically, "Don Manuel ain't the quitter I thought he was or maybe he didn't see how he could get out of it. But the war's on! Hooroosh! There's goin' to be fightin'! Archie, me bhoy, the war's on!"

He seized Sheridan in a bear-hug of an embrace, swung him off the ground, dropped him, and went prancing around the clearing uttering wild Celtic cries. It was some minutes before he could be sobered sufficiently to give a translation of the message.

It was short and to the point:

The Armies of Pasala will resist aggression to the death.

Manuel Concepcion de Villega, being a civilian official, had thought this a particularly valiant and noble sentiment. In fact, he was so pleased with it that he used it to conclude his address to the Army when, with the President, he reviewed it before it rode out of Santa Miranda to meet the invaders. Of course the speech should have been made by the President, but His Excellency had no views on the subject.

At lunch-time the news came through from Esperanza that the enemy were attacking the town.

Although there had been ample warning, few of the inhabitants had left. The bulk of the population preferred to stay, secure in the belief that wars were the exclusive concern of the professional soldiers and had nothing to do with the general public, except for the inconvenience they might cause.

There was a small garrison stationed in the town, and they had barricaded the streets and settled down to await the attack. It came at about one o'clock.

The "invading armies" which Kelly had prepared had been designed by Archie Sheridan, who was something of a mechanical genius.

In the woods on the east, three hundred yards from the front line of improvised fortifications, had been established a line of ten braziers of glowing charcoal, about twenty yards apart. Above each brazier was suspended a string of cartridges knotted at intervals of a few inches into a length of cord. The cord passed over the branch of a tree into which nails had been driven as guides. All these cords were gathered together in two batches of five each at a point some distance away, in such a way that one man, using both hands, could slowly lower the strings of cartridges simultaneously into all ten braziers, and so give the impression that there was firing over a front of two hundred yards. If they had had fireworks they could have saved themselves much trouble, but they had no fireworks, and Archie Sheridan was justly proud of his ingenious substitute.

Sheridan worked the "invading armies," while Kelly lay down behind a tree some distance away, sheltered from any stray bullets, and loaded his rifle. To complete the illusion it was necessary that the firing should seem to have some direction.

Sheridan, with a low whistle, signalled that he was ready, and the battle began.

The cartridges, lowered one by one into the braziers and there exploded by the heat, provided a realistic rattle up and down the line, while Kelly, firing and reloading like one possessed, sent bullets smacking into the walls of the houses and kicking up spurts of dust around the barricades. He took care not to aim anywhere where anyone might be hit.

The defence replied vigorously, though no one will ever know what they thought they were shooting at, and there were some spirited exchanges. When another whistle from Sheridan announced that the strings of cartridges were exhausted, Kelly rejoined him, and they crawled down to the road and the waiting Ford, and drove boldly towards the town, Kelly waving a nearly white flag.

The car was stopped, but Kelly was well known.

"They let me through their lines," he explained to the officer of the garrison. "That is why the firing has ceased. I was in Ondia when war was declared, and I came back at once."

He told them that he was on his way to Santa Miranda.

"Then travel quickly, and urge them not to delay sending help," said the officer, "for it is clear that we are attacked by a tremendous number, I have sent telegraphs, but you can do more by telling them what you have seen."

"I will do that," promised Kelly, and they let him drive on.

As soon as the car was clear of the town he stopped and assisted Sheridan to unearth himself from under the pile of luggage, for, being now an outlaw, Sheridan had had to hide when they passed through the towns on the journey up, and it was advisable for him to do the same for most of the return.

A little farther down the road they stopped again, and Sheridan climbed a tree and cut the telegraph wires, so that the news of the fizzling out of the attack should not reach Santa Miranda in time for the troops that had been sent out to be recalled. Instead of organizing the "invasion" they might have tapped the wire there and sent on messages from the commander of the garrison describing the progress of the battle, and so saved themselves much labour and thought, but the short road between Esperanza and Las Floras (the next town) was too well frequented for that to be practicable in broad daylight.

The Minister of the Interior was informed that it was no longer possible to communicate with Esperanza, and he could see only one explanation.

"Esperanza is surrounded," he said. "The garrison is less than a hundred. The town will fall in twenty-four hours, and the advancing armies of Maduro will meet our reinforcements at Las Floras. It will be a miracle if we can hold the invaders from Santa Miranda for five days."

"You should have kept some troops here," said Shannet. "You have sent every soldier in Santa Miranda. Once that army is defeated there will be nothing for the invaders to overcome."

"Tomorrow I will recruit the *peónes*," said Don Manuel. "There must be conscription. Pasala requires the services of every able-bodied citizen. I will draft a proclamation tonight for the President to sign."

It was then nearly five o'clock, but none of them had had a siesta that afternoon. They were holding another of many unprofitable conferences in a room in the palace, and it was significant that Shannet's right to be present was undisputed. The President himself was also there, biting his nails and stabbing the carpet nervously with the rowels of his spurs, but the other two took no notice of him. The President and de Villega were both still wearing the magnificent uniforms which they had donned for the review of the troops that morning.

Shannet paced the room, the inevitable limp unlighted cigarette drooping from his loose lower lip. His once-white ducks were as soiled and sloppy as ever. (Since they never became filthy, it is apparent that he must have treated himself to a clean suit occasionally, but nobody was ever allowed to notice this fact.) His unbrushed hair, as always, flopped over his right eye.

Since the day before, Shannet had had much to think about. Campard's amazing cable, attributing the war to a criminal gang, had arrived, and Shannet had replied with the required information. He had passed on the suggestion of his employer to the Minister for the Interior, pointing to the undoubtedly lawless behaviour of Sheridan and the unknown, but that two common outlaws could organise a war was a theory which de Villega refused to swallow.

"It is absurd," he said. "They are ordinary criminals. Two men cannot be a gang. In due time they will be caught, the man Sheridan will be imprisoned, and the man Mussolini will be hanged."

Shannet, asked for the name of the man who had assaulted him, had replied indignantly, "He told me his name was Benito Mussolini!" Since then, he had been impelled to make several protests against the conviction of the officials that this statement was to be believed, but the idea had taken too firm a root, and Shannet had to give up the attempt.

But now he had an inspiration.

"There can be no harm in finding out," he urged. "Send for the *peón* that all the trouble is about, and let us question him."

"I have a better idea than that," exclaimed de Villega, jumping up. "I will send the *peón* to the garotte tomorrow, for an encouragement to the people. They will enjoy the spectacle, and it will make them more ready to accept the proclamation of conscription. I will make a holiday . . ."

But Shannet's brain had suddenly taken to itself an amazing brilliance. In a flash it had soared above the crude and elementary idea of sending for the *peón* and forcing him to speak. He had no interest in de Villega's sadistic elaboration of the same idea. He had seen a much better solution than that.

9

Rapidly Shannet explained his inspiration to the others. It was as simple as all great inspirations. He was now firmly convinced in his mind that Sheridan and the Unknown were at the bottom of all the trouble, and this belief was strengthened by the fact that no trace of them had been found since their escape, although both police and military had searched for them. Some of the things that the Unknown had said—before and after the interlude in which words were dispensed with—came back to Shannet with a dazzling clarity. It all fitted in.

And ready to his hand lay the key to the trap in which he was in. He saw that what the Unknown had started the Unknown could stop. It was Campard's own idea, but Shannet was more conveniently placed to apply it than his master had been. Also, he had the necessary lever within a few minutes' reach.

Lilla McAndrew.

She was the master card. Sheridan, he knew, was infatuated. And Sheridan was an important accomplice of the Unknown. With Lilla McAndrew for a hostage Shannet could dictate his own terms.

"I know I have reason!" Shannet said vehemently, while he inwardly cursed the limitations of his Spanish, which prevented him driving his ideas home into the thick skulls of his audience more forcibly. "I know well the Señor Campard, for whom I have worked for years. Perhaps it sounds fantastic to you, but I know that he is not an easy man to frighten. If I had suggested this to him myself, that these two men could have plotted a war, he would have laughed me to scorn. But he has said it of his own accord, therefore I know that he must have some information."

"I think everyone has gone mad," said de Villega helplessly. "But you may proceed with your plan. At least it can do no harm. But I warn you that it is on your own responsibility. The *Señorita* McAndrew is a British subject, and questions may be asked. Then I shall say that I know nothing of it, and, if the authorities demand it, you will have to be handed over to them."

It was significant of the way in which Shannet's prestige had declined since the commencement of the war for which de Villega was inclined to blame him, but Shannet did not care. "I will take the risk," he said, and was gone.

In the Palace courtyard his horse was still being held by a patient soldier—one of the half-dozen left behind to guard the palace. Shannet clambered into the saddle and galloped out as the gates were opened for him by a sentry.

His first course took him to an unsavoury café at the end of the town, where he knew he would find the men he needed. He enrolled two. They were pleased to call themselves "guides," but actually they were half-caste cut-throats available for anything from murder upwards. Shannet knew them, for he had used their services before.

He explained what he wanted and produced money. There was no haggling. In ten minutes the three were riding out of the town.

Kelly, too late, had thought of that very possibility, as he had hinted to Sheridan in the jungle clearing that morning. But Kelly and Sheridan were still twenty miles away.

And the Saint, in the President's palatial bathroom, was leisurely completing the process of dressing himself in the clean clothes which he had found. They fitted him excellently.

Meanwhile, the men whom Shannet had left in conference were receiving an unpleasant surprise.

"God!" thundered de Villega. "How did this *peón* escape?"

"Excellency," said the abashed governor of the prison, "it was during the siesta. The man fell down moaning and writhing as if he would die. The warder went to attend him, and the man grasped him by the throat so that he could not cry out, throttled him into unconsciousness, and bound and gagged him. He also surprised the gatekeeper, and hit him in the English fashion . . ."

De Villega let out an exclamation.

"What meanest thou, pig —'in the English fashion?'"

The governor demonstrated the blow which the gatekeeper had described. It was, in fact, the simple left uppercut of the boxer, and no Latin-American who has not been infected with our methods ever hits naturally like that.

"What manner of man was this *peón*?" demanded Don Manuel, with understanding dawning sickeningly into his brain.

"Excellency, he was tall for a *peón*, and a man of the strength of a lion. If he had washed he would have been handsome, with an aristocratic nose that such a man could hardly have come by legitimately. And he had very white teeth and blue eyes . . ."

"Blue eyes!" muttered de Villega dazedly for, of course, to the Latin, all Englishmen have blue eyes.

He turned to the governor with sudden ferocity.

"*Carajo!*" he screamed. "Imbecile, dost thou not know whom thou hast let slip through thy beastly fingers? Dost thou not even know whom thou hast had in thy charge these three days?"

He thumped upon the table with his fist, and the governor trembled.

"Couldst thou not recognise him, cross-eyed carrion?" he screeched. "Couldst thou not see that he was no true *peón*? Maggot, hast thou not heard of the outlaw Benito Mussolini, for whom the *rurales* have searched in vain while he sheltered safely in the prison under thy gangrenous eyes?"

"I am a worm, and blind, Excellency," said the cringing man tactfully, for he knew that any excuse he attempted to make would only infuriate the Minister further.

De Villega strode raging up and down the room. Now he believed Shannet, wild and far-fetched as the latter's theory had seemed when he had first heard it propounded. The news of the prisoner's escape, and the—to Don Manuel—sufficient revelation of his real identity, provided incontrovertible proof that the fantastic thing was true.

"He must be recaptured at once!" snapped de Villega. "Every *guardia* in Santa Miranda must seek him without rest day or night. The *peónes* must be pressed into the hunt. The State will pay a reward of five thousand pesos to the man who brings him to me, alive or dead. As for thee, offal," he added, turning with renewed malevolence upon the prison governor, "if Sancho Quijote, or Benito Mussolini—whatever he calls himself—is not delivered to me in twelve hours I will cast thee into thine own prison to rot there until he is found."

"I will give the orders myself, Excellency," said the governor, glad of an excuse to make his escape, and bowed his way to the door.

He went out backwards, and, as he closed the door, the Saint pinioned his arms from behind, and allowed the point of his little knife to prick his throat.

"Make no sound," said the Saint, and lifted the man bodily off his feet.

He carried the governor down the passage, the knife still at his throat, and took him into a room that he had already marked down in his explorations. It was a bedroom. The Saint deposited the man on the floor, sat on his head, and tore a sheet into strips, with which he bound and gagged him securely.

"I will release you as soon as the revolution is over," the Saint promised, with a mocking bow.

Then he walked back to the other room and entered softly, closing the door behind him. De Villega was penning the announcement of the reward, and it was the President who first noticed the intruder and uttered a strangled yap of startlement.

Don Manuel looked up, and loosed an oath. He sprang to his feet, upsetting the ink-pot and his chair, as if an electric current had suddenly been applied to him.

"Who are you?" he demanded in a cracked voice, though he had guessed the answer.

"You know me best as Benito Mussolini, or Sancho Quijote," said the Saint. "My friends—and enemies—sometimes call me El Santo. And I am the father of the revolution."

He lounged lazily against the door, head back, hands rested carelessly on his hips. The Saint was himself again, clean and fresh from razor and bath, his hair combed smoothly back. The clothes he had appropriated suited him to perfection. The Saint had the priceless gift of being able to throw on any old thing and look well in it, but few things could have matched his mood and personality better than the buccaneering touch there was about the attire that had been more or less thrust upon him.

The loose, full-sleeved shirt, the flaring trousers, the scarlet sash—the Saint wore these romantic trappings with a marvellous swashbuckling air, lounging there with a reckless and piratical elegance, a smile on his lips . . .

Seconds passed before the Minister came out of his trance.

"Revolution?"

De Villega echoed the word involuntarily, and the Saint bowed.

"I am the revolution," he said, "and I have just started. For my purpose I arranged that the Army should leave Santa Miranda, so that I should have nothing to deal with but a few officials, yourselves, and a handful of *guardias*. Wonderful as I am, I could not fight an army."

"Fool!" croaked Don Manuel, in a voice that he hardly knew as his own. "The Army will return, and then you will be shot."

"Permit me to disagree," said the Saint. "The Army will return, certainly. It will be to find a new Government in power. The Army is the servant of the State, not of one man, nor even of one Government. Of course, on their return, the soldiers would be free to begin a second revolution to overthrow the new Government if they disliked it. But I do not think they will do that, particularly as the new Government is going to increase their pay. Observe the subtle difference. To have attempted to bribe the Army to support a revolution would have been treason, and rightly resented by all patriotic citizens, but to signalise the advent of the new Constitution by a bonus in cash to the Army is an act of grace and generosity, and will be rightly appreciated."

"And the people?" said Don Manuel, as in a dream.

"Will they weep to see you go? I think not. You have crushed them with taxes—we shall liberate them. They could have liberated themselves, but they had not the initiative to begin. Now I give them a lead, and they will follow."

The Saint straightened up off the door. His blue eyes, with a sparkle of mischief in them, glanced from the Minister for the Interior to the President, and back to the Minister for the Interior again. His right hand came off his hip in a commanding gesture.

"*Señores*," he said, "I come for your resignations."

The President came to his feet, bowed, and stood to attention.

"I will write mine at once, *Señor*," he said hurriedly. "It is plain that Pasala no longer needs me."

It was the speech of his life, and the Saint swept him a low bow of approval. "I thank your Excellency!" he said mockingly.

"Half-wit!" snarled de Villega over his shoulder. "Let me handle this!" He thrust the President back and came round the table.

A sword hung at his side, and on the belt of his ceremonial uniform was a revolver holster. He stood before the Saint, one hand on the pommel of his sword, the other fiddling with the little strap which secured the flap of the holster. His dark eyes met Simon Templar's bantering gaze.

"Already the revolution is accomplished?" he asked.

"I have accomplished it," said Templar.

De Villega raised his left hand to stroke his moustache.

"*Señor*," he said, "all this afternoon we have sat in this room, which overlooks the front courtyard of the palace. Beyond, as you know, is the Calle del Palacio. Yet we have heard no commotion. Is a people that has been newly liberated too full of joy to speak?"

"When the people hear of their liberation," said the Saint, "you will hear their rejoicing." De Villega's eyes glittered under his black brows.

"And your friends, *Señor*?" he pursued. "The other liberators? They have, perhaps, surrounded the palace and overcome the guards without an alarm being raised or a shot fired?"

The Saint laughed.

"Don Manuel," he said, "you do me an injustice. I said I was the father of the revolution. Can a child have two fathers? Alone, Don Manuel, I accomplished it—yet you persist in speaking of my private enterprise as if it were the work of a hundred. Will you not give me the full credit for what I have done?"

De Villega stepped back a pace.

"So," he challenged, "the people do not know. The palace guards do not know. The Army does not know. Will you tell me who does know?"

"Our three selves," said the Saint blandly. "Also two friends of mine who organised the war for me. And the governor of the prison, whom I captured on his way to mobilise the guardias against me. It is very simple. I intend this to be a bloodless revolution, for I am against unnecessary killing. You will merely resign, appointing a new Government in your places, and leave Pasala at once, never to return again on pain of death."

The holster was now undone, and de Villega's fingers were sliding under the flap. "And you—alone—demand that?"

"I do," said the Saint, and leapt at de Villega as the revolver flashed from its place.

With one arm he grasped Don Manuel around the waist, pinning his left arm to his side; with his left hand he gripped Don Manuel's right wrist, forcing it back, and twisting.

The President sprang forward, but it was all over in a couple of seconds. The revolver exploded twice, harmlessly, into the floor, and then fell with a clatter as the Saint's grip became too agonising to be borne.

The Saint hurled de Villega from him, into the President's very arms, and as de Villega staggered back his sword grated out of its sheath and remained in the Saint's right hand. The President's revolver was half-way out of its holster when the Saint let him feel the sword at his breast.

"Drop it!" ordered Simon. The President obeyed.

Templar forced the two men back to the wall at the sword's point. Then he turned quickly, using the sword to fish up the two revolvers from the floor by their trigger-guards, and turned again to halt their immediate rally with the guns impaled on his blade.

From below, through the open windows, came the shouting of the sentries, and the sound of running feet thundered in the passage outside the room.

Like lightning the Saint detached the revolvers from his sword, and held them one in each hand. They covered their owners with an equal steadiness of aim.

The two shots that de Villega had fired, though they had hit no one, had done damage enough. They hadn't entered into the Saint's plan of campaign. He had betted on being quick enough to catch de Villega before he could get his hand to his gun in its cumbersome holster—and the Saint, for once, had been a fraction of a second slow on his timing. But the error might yet be repaired.

"You, Excellency, to the windows!" rapped the Saint in a low voice. "You, de Villega, to the door! Reassure the guards. Tell them that the President was unloading his revolver when it accidentally exploded. The President will repeat the same thing from the window to the sentries below."

He dodged out of sight behind the door as it burst open, but there was no mistaking the menace of the revolvers which he still focused on the two men.

The President was already addressing the sentries below. De Villega, with one savagely impotent glance at the unfriendly muzzle that was trained upon him, followed suit, giving the Saint's suggested explanation to the guards who crowded into the doorway.

"You may go," he concluded. "No harm has been done. But remain within call—I may need you shortly."

It required some nerve to add that last remark, in the circumstances, but de Villega thought that the Saint would not betray his presence with a shot if he could possibly help it. He was right. The President came back from the window. The guards withdrew, with apologies for their excited irruption, and the door closed. The Saint slid the bolt into its socket.

"A wise precaution, Don Manuel, to warn the guards that you might need them," he said. "But I do not think it will help you."

He stuck the revolvers into his sash and picked up the sword again. It was a better weapon for controlling two men than his little knife, and much quieter than the revolvers. "Your resignations or your lives, *señores*?" said the Saint briskly. "I will take whichever you prefer to give, but I must have one or the other at once."

De Villega sat down at the table, but did not write. He unbuttoned his coat, fished out a packet of cigarettes, and lighted one, blowing out a great cloud of smoke. Through it he looked at the Saint, and his lips had twisted into a sneering grin.

"I have another thing to offer, *Señor*," he remarked viciously, "which you might prefer to either of the things you have mentioned."

"*Es decir*?" prompted Simon, with a frowning lift of his eyebrows.

De Villega inhaled again with relish, and let the smoke trickle down from his nostrils in two long feathers. There was a glow of taunting triumph in his malignant stare.

"There is the *Señorita* McAndrew," he said, and the Saint's face suddenly went very meek.

"What of her?"

"It was the *Señor* Shannet," said de Villega, enjoying his moment, "who first suggested that you were the man behind the war. We did not believe him, but now I see that he is a wise man. He left us over half an hour ago to take her as hostage. You gave me no chance to explain that when the guards entered the room just now. But I told them to remain within call for that reason—so that I could summon them as soon as you surrendered. Now it is my turn to make an offer. Stop this war, and deliver yourself and your accomplices to justice, and I will save the *Señorita* McAndrew. Otherwise . . ."

Don Manuel shrugged. "Am I answerable for the affections of the *Señor* Shannet?"

A throaty chuckle of devilish merriment shook him, and he bowed to the motionless Saint with a leering mock humility. "I, in my turn, await your decision, *Señor*," he said.

10

The Saint leaned on his sword.

He was cursing himself for the fool he was. Never before in his career had he been guilty of such an appalling lapse. Never would he have believed that he could have been capable of overlooking the probability of such an obvious counter-attack. Now his brain was whirling like the flywheel of a great dynamo, and he was considering, calculating, readjusting, summarising everything in the light of this new twist that de Villega had given to the affair. Yet his face showed nothing of the storm behind it.

"And how do I know that you will keep your bargain?" he asked.

"You do not know," replied de Villega brazenly. "You only know that, if you do not agree to my terms, the Señor Shannet will certainly take reprisals. I offer you a hope."

So that was the strength of it. And, taken by and large, it didn't strike the Saint as a proposition to jump at. It offered him exactly nothing—except the opportunity to go nap on Don Manuel's honour and Shannet's generosity, two bets which no one could have called irresistibly attractive. Also, it involved Kelly and Sheridan, who hadn't been consulted. And it meant, in the end, that all three of them would most certainly be executed, whatever de Villega decided to do about Lilla McAndrew, whom Shannet would probably claim, and be allowed, as a reward for his share in suppressing the revolution. No . . .

Where were Kelly and Sheridan? The Saint was reckoning it out rapidly, taking into consideration the age of Kelly's Ford and the reported abominable state of the roads between Esperanza and Santa Miranda. And, checking his calculation over, the Saint could only get one answer, which was that Kelly and Sheridan were due to arrive at any minute. They would learn of the abduction . . .

"The *Señora Kelly*?" asked the Saint. "What about her?"

De Villega shrugged. "She is of no importance."

Yes, Mrs. Kelly would be left behind—if she had not been shot. She was middle-aged and stout and past her attractiveness, and no one would have any interest in abducting her. So that Kelly and Sheridan, arriving at the bungalow, would hear the tale from her.

And then—there was no doubt about it—they would come storming down to the palace, *guardias* and sentries notwithstanding, with cold murder in their hearts.

The Saint came erect, and de Villega looked up expectantly. But there was no sign of surrender in the Saint's poise, and nothing relenting about the way in which he stepped up to the Minister and set the point of the sword at his breast.

"I said I came for your resignations," remarked the Saint with a deadly quietness. "That was no idle talk. Write now, de Villega, or, by the vixen that bore thee, thou diest!"

"Fool! Fool!" Don Manuel raved. "It cannot help you!"

"I take the risk," said the Saint icily. "And do not speak so loud—I might think you were trying to attract the attention of the guards. Write!"

He thrust the sword forward the half of an inch, and de Villega started back with a cry. "You would murder me?"

"With pleasure," said the Saint. "Write!"

Then there was sudden silence, and everyone was quite still, listening. For from the courtyard below the windows came the rattle of urgent hoofs.

The Saint leapt to the windows. There were three horses held by the sentries. He saw Shannet and two other men dismounting—and saw, being lifted down from Shannet's saddlebow, Lilla McAndrew with her hands tied.

He could have shouted for joy at the justification of his bold defiance. And yet, if he had thought a little longer, he might have foreseen that the girl would be brought to the palace. She was not the victim of Shannet's privateering, but an official hostage. But even if the Saint hadn't foreseen it, there it was, and he could have prayed for nothing better. He saw all the trump cards coming into his hands . . .

Then he whipped round, in time to frustrate de Villega's stealthy attack, and the Minister's raised arm dropped to his side.

The Saint speared the sword into the floor and slipped the revolvers out of his sash. For the second time he dodged behind the opening door. He saw the girl thrust roughly into the room, and Shannet followed, closing the door again behind him.

"Fancy meeting you again, honeybunch!" drawled the Saint, and Shannet spun round with an oath.

The Saint leaned against the wall, the Presidential and Ministerial revolvers in his hands. On his lips was a smile so broad as to be almost a laugh, and there was a laugh in his voice.

"Take that hand away from your hip, Shannet, my pet!" went on the Saint, in that laughing voice of sheer delight. "I've got you covered—and even if I'm not very used to these toys, I could hardly miss you at this range . . . That's better . . . Oh, Shannet, my sweet and beautiful gargoyle, you're a bad boy, frightening that child. Take the cords off her wrists, my angel . . . No, *Señor* de Villega, you needn't edge towards that sword. I may want it again myself in a minute. Gracias! . . . Is that more comfortable, Lilla, old dear?"

"Oh," cried the girl, "thank God you're here! Where's Archie?"

"On his way, old darling, on his way, as the actress said of the bishop," answered the Saint, "Are you all right?"

She shuddered a little.

"Yes, I'm all right," she said. "Except for the touch of his filthy hands. But I was very frightened . . ."

"Archie will deal with that when he arrives," said the Saint. "It's his business—he'd never forgive me if I interfered. Come here, my dear, keeping well out of the line of fire, while I deal with the specimens. I'm not the greatest revolver shot in the world, and I want to be sure that it won't matter who I hit."

He steered her to safety in a corner, and turned to Don Manuel.

"When we were interrupted," said the Saint persuasively, "you were writing. The interruption has now been disposed of. Proceed, *Señor*!"

De Villega lurched back to the table, the fight gone out of him. He could never have envisaged such an accumulation and culmination of misfortunes. It was starting to seem to him altogether like a dream, a nightmare rather—but there was nothing ethereal about the revolver that was levelled so steadily at him. The only fantastic part of the whole catastrophe was the man who had engineered it—the Saint himself, in his extraordinary borrowed clothes, and the hell-for-leather light of laughing recklessness in his blue eyes. That was the last bitter pill which De Villega had to swallow. He might perhaps have endured defeat by a man whom he could understand—a cloaked and sinister conspirator with a personality of impressive grimness. But this lunatic who laughed . . . *Que diablos*! It was impossible . . .

And then, from outside, drifted a grinding, screaming, metallic rattle that could only be made by one instrument in the world.

"Quick!" said the Saint. "Slither round behind Master Shannet, Lilla, darling, and slip the gat out of his hip pocket . . . That's right . . . Now d'you mind sticking up the gang for a sec while I bail the troops? Blaze away if anybody gets funny."

The girl handled Shannet's automatic as if she'd been born with her finger crooked round a trigger, and the Saint, with a nod of approval, crossed over to the window.

Kelly's Ford was drawn up in the courtyard, and both Kelly and Sheridan were there. Kelly was just disposing of a sentry who had ventured to question his right of way.

"Walk right in, souls!" the Saint hailed them cheerily. "You're in time to witness the abdication of the Government."

"Have you seen Lilla?" shouted a frantic Sheridan. The Saint grinned.

"She's safe here, son."

The report of an automatic brought him round with a jerk.

With the Saint's back turned, and the Saint's victory now an accomplished fact, Shannet had chanced everything on one mad gamble against the steadiness of nerve and aim of the girl who for a moment held the situation in her small hands. While Lilla McAndrew's attention was distracted by the irresistible impulse to try to hear what Archie Sheridan was saying he had sidled closer . . . made one wild leaping grab . . . missed . . .

The Saint stooped over the still figure and made a swift examination. He straightened up with a shrug, picking up his revolvers again as the first of the guards burst into the room.

"Quietly, amigos," he urged and they saw sudden death in each of his hands, and checked.

The next instant the crowd stirred again before the berserk rush of Archie Sheridan, who had heard the shot as he raced up the palace steps. A yard behind him followed Kelly, breaking through like a bull, his red head flaming above the heads of the guards.

"All clear, Archie!" called the Saint. "It was Shannet who got it." But Lilla McAndrew was already in Archie Sheridan's arms.

"Here, Kelly," rapped the Saint. "Let's get this over. Take these guns and keep the guards in order while I dispose of the Government."

Kelly took over the weapons, and the Saint stepped back and wrenched the sword out of the floor. He advanced towards the President and de Villega, who stood paralysed by the table.

"You have written?" he asked pleasantly.

De Villega passed over a piece of paper, and the Saint read it and handed it back.

"You have omitted to nominate your successors," he said. "That will be the Señor Kelly and those whom he appoints to help him. Write again."

"Half a minute," Kelly threw back over his shoulder, with his eyes on the shuffling guards. "I don't fancy being President myself—it's too risky. I'll be Minister for the Interior, and the President can stay on, if he behaves himself."

The President bowed.

"I am honoured, *Señor*," he assented with alacrity.

"Write accordingly," ordered the Saint, and it was done. The Saint took the document and addressed the guards.

"By this," he said, "you know that the President dismisses Señor Manuel Concepcion de Villega, the Minister for the Interior, and his Government, and appoints the *Señor* Kelly in his place. To celebrate his appointment, the *Señor* Kelly will in a few days announce the removal of a number of taxes which have hitherto oppressed you. Now take this paper and cause it to be embodied in a proclamation to the free people of Pasala. Let tomorrow be a public holiday and a day of rejoicing for this reason, and also because it is now proved that there is no war with Maduro. That was a rumour spread by certain malicious persons for their own ends. See that a radiogram is sent to Estados Unidos, explaining that, and saying that they may recall the warship they were sending. You may go, *amigos*."

There was a silence of a few seconds and then, as the full meaning of the Saint's speech was grasped, the room rang and echoed again to a great crash of *Vivas*!

When Kelly had driven the cheering guards out into the passage and closed the door in their faces, Simon Templar thought of something and had the door opened again to send for the governor of the prison. The man was brought quickly.

"*Señor*," said the Saint. "I apologise for the way I treated you just now. It happened to be necessary. But the revolution is now completed, and you are a free man. I bear you no malice—although I am going to insist that you disinfect your prison."

He explained the circumstances, and the prison governor bowed almost to the floor.

"It is nothing, *ilustrisimo Señor*," he said. "But if I had known I would have seen to it that your honour was given better accommodation. Another time, perhaps . . ."

"God forbid," said the Saint piously.

Then he turned and pointed to the now terrified de Villega.

"Take this man with you," he directed. "He is to leave Pasala by the next boat and meantime he is to be closely guarded. He will probably attempt either to fight or to bribe his escape. My answer to that is that if he is not delivered to me when I send for him, your life and the lives of all your warders will answer for it."

"It is understood, *señor*."

Kelly watched the departure of the governor and his prisoner open-mouthed, and when they were gone he turned to the Saint with a blank expression.

"Look here," he said, as if the thought had just struck him, "where's all this fightin' I've been told so much about?"

The Saint smiled.

"There is no fighting," he said. "This has been what I hoped it would be—a bloodless revolution. It was undertaken in the name of a justice which the law could not administer, to ruin a man more than six thousand miles away, back in London, England. He had ruined thousands, but the law could not touch him. This was my method. Your first duty as Minister for the Interior will be to revoke the original oil concession and to make out a fresh one, assigning the rights, in perpetuity, to Miss McAndrew and her heirs." He laid a hand on Kelly's shoulder. "I'm sorry to give you such a disappointment, son, and if you must have a fight, I'll have a round or two with you myself before dinner. But I had to do it this way. Any other kind of revolution would have meant the sacrifice of many lives, and I didn't really want that."

For a moment Kelly was silent and perplexed before the Saint's sudden seriousness, then he shrugged, and laughed, and took Simon Templar's hand in a huge grip.

"I don't confess to know what yez are talkin' about," he said. "And I don't care. I suppose it's been worth it—if only to see the look on de Villega's ugly face whin yez sent him to prison. And, anyway, a laughin' devil who can run a show like yez have run this one deserves to be allowed to work things his own way."

"Good scout!" smiled the Saint. "Was Mrs. Kelly all right?"

"A bit scared, but no harm done. It was Lilla she was afraid for. They just tied the missus up in a chair and left her. An' that reminds me—there was a cable waitin' for me up at the bungalow, and I can't make head or tail of it. Maybe it's something to do with you."

Kelly fumbled in his pocket and produced the form. The Saint took it over, and one glance told him that it was meant for him.

"It's from an agent of mine in London," he explained. "He wouldn't have addressed it to Archie or me in case anything had gone wrong and it was intercepted,"

He knew the code almost perfectly, and he was able to write the translation in between the lines at once.

P.O.P.s down trumped twelve thousand.—

The Saint wrote:

P.O.P.s fell heavily. Cleared twelve thousand pounds.
Campard committed suicide this morning.

It was signed with the name of Roger Conway.

"Archie!" called the Saint, thoughtfully, and again, "Archie!"

"They sneaked out minutes ago," said Kelly. "She's a sweet girl, that Lilla McAndrew . . ."

And it was so, until evening.

And at even the Saint went forth and made a tour of a number of disreputable cafés, in each of which he bought much liquor for the clientele. They did not recognise him until he started to sing—a strange and barbarous song that no one could understand. But they recognised it, having heard it sung before, with many others like it, by a certain *peón*:

The bells of Hell go ting-a-ling-a-ling.
For you but not for me;
For me the angels sing-a-ling-a-ling,
They've got the goods for me—

To this day you will hear that song sung by the peasants of Santa Miranda. And if you should ask one of them why he sings it, he will answer, with a courteous surprise at your ignorance, "That, *Señor*, is one of the songs of freedom . . ."

THE MAN WHO COULD NOT DIE

INTRODUCTION

If (as has unfortunately been observed in certain circles) I have failed to become the supreme maestro of the whodunit in my generation, I can at least truthfully plead that this is because I never seriously tried.

I have written some whodunits, but not very many, and not all of them very good. But most of the time I have tried to exploit a mutation which you might call the "whatisit."

I think it was G. K. Chesterton who first claimed in a loud voice that the short story was the only satisfactory length for a whodunit, because beyond that length it was exasperating to have to contend with an entire cast of characters with masks on, clad in deceptive raiment, speaking with disguised voices in studied ambiguities, and generally attempting to give false impressions, whatever their true characters might be, entirely for the selfish purposes of the author.

It was this cogent argument which turned my interest to the whatisit, the story in which we have no serious doubt, if any doubt at all, as to the identity of the prime villain. Our problem is to discover the facts and form of his villainy, or to find means to punish him, or to circumvent his menace to the happiness of our preferred characters.

Maxwell Smith, I believe, was one of the early proponents of this style of literary architecture in the popular detective magazines—the business of frankly presenting Desperate Desmond at the outset and centering reader interest on the task of bringing him to book through the untiring efforts of Handsome Harry. And a nice job he did of it. Of course, the classic example of this design is Hugo's *Les Misérables*, in which the indefatigable Monsieur Javert dogged the footsteps of Jean Valjean to the end of the chapter.

This yarn is one of my own first experiments with this pattern, and for that reason it may be of some interest to you tireless antiquarians.

—Leslie Charteris (1945)

1

Patricia Holm raised her fair, pretty head from *The Times*.

"What," she asked, "is an obiter dictum?"

"A form of foot-and-mouth disease," said the Saint, glibly. "Obiter—one who obits; dictum—a shirt-front. Latin. Very difficult."

"Fool," said his lady.

The Saint grinned, and pushed back his chair. Breakfast was over, a blaze of summer sunshine was pouring through the open windows into the comfortable room, the first and best cigarette of the day was canted up between the Saint's smiling lips; all was right with the world.

"What's the absorbing news, anyway?" he inquired lazily.

She passed him the paper, and, as is the way of these things, the matter which had given rise to her question was of the most ephemeral interest—and yet it interested the Saint. Simon Templar had always been the despair of all those of his friends who expected him to produce intelligent comments upon the affairs of the day. To read a newspaper not only bored him to extinction, but often gave him an actual physical pain. Therefore it followed, quite naturally, that when the mood seized him to glance at a newspaper, he usually managed to extract more meat from that one glance than the earnest, regular student of the Press extracts from years of daily labour.

It so happened that morning. Coincidence, of course, but how much adventure is free from all taint of coincidence? Coincidences are always coinciding, it is one of their peculiar attributes; but the adventure is born of what the man makes of his coincidences. Most people say, "How odd!"

Simon Templar said, "Well, well, well!"

But *The Times* really hadn't anything exciting to say that morning and certainly the column that Patricia had been reading was one of the most sober of all the columns of that very respectable newspaper, for it was one of the columns in which such hardy annuals as Paterfamilias, Lieut.-Colonel (retired), Pro Bono Publico, Mother of Ten, unto the third and fourth generation. Abraham and his seed for ever, let loose their weary bleats upon the world. The gentleman ("Diehard") who had incorporated an obiter dictum in his effort was giving tongue on the subject of motorists. It was, as has been explained, pure coincidence that he should have written with special reference to a recent prosecution for dangerous driving in which the defendant had been a man in whom the Saint had the dim beginnings of an interest.

"Aha!" said the Saint, thoughtful-like.

"Haven't you met that man—Miles Hallin?" Patricia said. "I've heard you mention his name."

"And that's all I've met up to date," answered the Saint. "But I have met a bird who talks about nothing else but Miles. Although I suppose, in the circumstances, that isn't as eccentric as it sounds."

He had, as a matter of fact, met Nigel Perry only a fortnight before, by a slightly roundabout route. Simon Templar, being in a club in Piccadilly which for some unknown reason allowed him to continue his membership, had discovered that he was without a handkerchief. His need being vital, he had strolled over to a convenient shop—without troubling to put on a hat. The rest of the story, he insisted, was Moyna Stanford's fault. Simon had bought his handkerchief, and the shop assistant had departed towards the cashier with the Saint's simoleons, when Moyna Stanford walked in, walked straight up to the Saint, and asked if he could show her some ties. Now, Moyna Stanford was very good to look upon, and there were quantities of ties prominently displayed about the shop, and the Saint could never resist anything like that. He had shown her several ties. The rightful tie-exhibitor had returned. There had been some commotion. Finally, they had lunched together. Not including the tie-exhibitor.

The rest of the story, as the Saint retailed it to Patricia Holm, was perfectly true. He had met Nigel Perry, and had liked him immediately—a tall, dark, cheery youngster, with a million-dollar smile and a two-figure bank balance. The second of those last two items Simon had not discovered until later. On the other hand, it was not very much later, for Nigel Perry had nothing approaching an inferiority complex. He talked with an engaging frankness about himself, his job, his prospects, and his idols. The idols were, at that moment, two—Moyna Stanford and Miles Hallin. It is likely that Simon Templar was shortly added to the list; perhaps in the end he headed the list—on the male side. But at the time of meeting Miles Hallin reigned supreme.

The Saint was familiar with the name of Hallin, and he was interested in the story that Nigel Perry had to tell, for all such stories were interesting to the Saint.

At that breakfast-table, under the shadow of an irrelevant obiter dictum, Simon explained.

"Hallin's a much older man, of course. Nigel had a brother who was about Hallin's age. Years ago Hallin and the elder Perry were prospecting some godless bit of desert in Australia. What's more, they found real gold. And at the same time they found that one of their water-barrels had sprung a leak, and there was only enough water to get one of them back to civilisation. They tossed for it—and for once in his life Hallin lost. They shook hands, and Perry pushed off. After Perry had been gone some time, Hallin decided that if he sat down on the gold mine waiting to die he'd go mad first. So he made up his mind to die on the move. It didn't occur to him to shoot himself—he just wouldn't go out that way. And he upped his pack and shifted along in a different direction from the one that Perry had taken. Of course he found a water-hole, and then he found another water-hole, and he got out of the desert at last. But Perry never got out. That's just a sample of Hallin's luck."

"And what happened to the gold?"

"Hallin registered the claim. When he got back to England he looked up young Nigel and insisted on giving him a half-share. But it never came to much—about a couple of thousand, I believe. The lode petered out, and the mine closed down. Still, Hallin did the white thing. Taking that along with the rest, you can't blame Nigel for worshipping him."

And yet the Saint frowned as he spoke. He had a professional vanity that was all his own, and something in that vanity reacted unfavourably towards Miles Hallin, whom a sensational journalist had once christened "The Man Who Cannot Die."

"Are you jealous?" teased Patricia, and the Saint scowled.

"I don't know," he said.

But he knew perfectly well. Miles Hallin had cropped up, and Miles Hallin had spoilt a beautiful morning.

"It annoys me," said the Saint, with what Patricia couldn't help thinking was an absurd pettishness. "No man has a right to Hallin's reputation."

"I've heard nothing against him."

"Have you heard anything against me?"

"Lots of things."

Simon grinned abstractedly.

"Yes, I know. But has anyone ever called me 'The Man Who Cannot Die?'"

"Not when I've been listening."

"It's not a matter of listening," said the Saint. "That man Hallin is a sort of public institution. Everyone knows about his luck. Now, I should think I've had as much luck as anyone, and I've always been much bigger news than Hallin will ever be, but nobody's ever made a song and dance about that side of my claim to immortality."

"They've had other things to say about you."

The Saint sighed. He was still frowning.

"I know," he said. "But I have hunches, old darling. Let me say here and now that I have absolutely nothing against Hallin. I've never heard a word against him, I haven't one reasonable suspicion about him, I haven't one single solitary fact on which I could base a suspicion. But I'll give you one very subtle joke to laugh about. Why should a man boast that he can't die?"

"He didn't make the boast."

"Well—I wonder? . . . But he certainly earned the name, and he's never given it a chance to be forgotten. He's capitalised it and played it up for all it's worth. So I can give you an even more subtle joke. It goes like this: 'For whosoever will save his life shall lose it . . . '"

Patricia looked at him curiously. If she had not known the Saint so well, she would have looked at him impatiently, but she knew him very well.

She said, "Let's hear what you mean, lad. I can't follow all your riddles."

"And I can't always give the answers," said the Saint.

His chair tilted back as he lounged in it. He inhaled intently from his cigarette, and gazed at the ceiling through a cloud of smoke.

"A hunch," said the Saint, "isn't a thing that goes easily to words. Words are so brutally logical, and a hunch is the reverse of logic. And a hunch, in a way, is a riddle, but it has no answer. When you get an answer, it isn't the answer to a riddle, or the answer to a hunch; it's the end of a story. I don't know if that's quite clear . . ."

"It isn't," said Patricia.

The Saint blew three smoke-rings as if he had a personal grudge against them.

"My great tragedy, sweetheart," he remarked modestly, "is that I'm completely and devastatingly sane. And the world we live in is not sane. All the insanities of the world used to worry me crazy, without exception—once upon a time. But now, in my old age, I'm more discriminating. Half the things in that newspaper, which I'm pleased to say I've never read from end to end, are probably offences against sanity. And if you come to a rag like the *Daily Record*, about ninety-eight per cent of its printed area is devoted to offences against sanity. And the fact has ceased to bother me. I swear to you, Pat, that I could read a *Daily Record* right through without groaning aloud more than twice. That's my discrimination. When I read that an obscure biologist in Minneapolis has said that men would easily live to be three hundred if they nourished themselves on an exclusive diet of green bananas and Vaseline, I'm merely bored. The thing is a simple offence against sanity. But when I'm always hearing about a Man Who Cannot Die, it annoys me. The thing is more than a simple offence against sanity. It sticks up and makes me stare at it. It's like finding one straight black line in a delirious patchwork of colours. It's more. It's like going to a menagerie and finding a man exhibited in one of the cages. Just because a Man Who Cannot Die isn't a simple insult to insanity. He's an insult to a much bigger thing. He's an insult to humanity."

"And where does this hunch lead to?" asked Patricia, practically.

Simon shrugged.

"I wish I were sure," he said.

Then, suddenly, he sat upright.

"Do you know," he said, in a kind of incomprehensible anger, "I've a damned good mind to see if I can't break that man's record! He infuriates me. And isn't he asking for it? Isn't he just asking someone to take up the challenge and see what can be done about it?"

The girl regarded him in bewilderment.

"Do you mean you want to try to kill him?" she asked blankly.

"I don't," said the Saint. "I mean I want to try to make him live."

For a long time Patricia gazed at him in silence. And then, with a little shake of her head, half-laughing, half-perplexed, she stood up.

"You've been reading too much G. K. Chesterton," she said. "And you can't do anything about Hallin today, anyway. We're late enough as it is."

The Saint smiled slowly, and rose to his feet.

"You're dead right, as usual, old dear," he murmured amiably. "I'll go and get out the car."

And he went, but he did not forget Miles Hallin. And he never forgot his hunch about the man who could not die. For the Saint's hunches were nearly always unintelligible to anyone but himself, and always very real and intelligible to him, and all at once he had realised that in Miles Hallin he was going to find a strange story—he did not then know how strange.

2

Miles Hallin, as the Saint had complained, really was something very like a national institution. He was never called wealthy, but he always seemed to be able to indulge his not inexpensive hobbies without stint. It was these hobbies which had confirmed him in the reputation that Simon Templar so much disliked.

Miles Hallin was so well known that the newspapers never even troubled to mention the fact. Lesser lights in the news, Simon had discovered, were invariably accounted for. They were "the famous cricketer" or "the well-known novelist" or perhaps, with a more delicate conceit, "the actor." Simon Templar always had an uneasy feeling that these explanations were put in as a kind of covering each-way bet—in case the person referred to should become well known without anyone knowing why. But Miles Hallin was just—Miles Hallin.

Simon Templar, even in his superlatively casual acquaintance with the newspapers, had had every opportunity to become familiar with the face of Miles Hallin, though he had never seen the man in the flesh. That square-jawed, pugnacious profile, with the white teeth and crinkled eyes and flashing smile, had figured in more photographs than the Saint cared to remember. Mr. Miles Hallin standing beside the wreckage of his Furillac at Le Mans—Mr. Miles Hallin being taken aboard a lug after his speedboat *Red Lady* had capsized in the Solent—Mr. Miles Hallin after his miraculous escape during the King's Cup Air Race, when his Elton "Dragon" caught fire at five thousand feet—Mr. Miles Hallin filming a charging buffalo in Tanganyika—Simon Templar knew them all. Miles Hallin did everything that a well-to-do sportsman could possibly include in the most versatile repertory, and all his efforts seemed to have the single aim of a spectacular suicide, but always he had escaped death by the essential hair's-breadth that had given him his name. No one could say that it was Miles Hallin's fault.

Miles Hallin had survived being mauled by a tiger, and had killed an infuriated gorilla with a sheath-knife. Miles Hallin had performed in bull fights before the King of Spain. Miles Hallin had gone into a tank and wrestled with a crocodile to oblige a Hollywood movie director. Miles Hallin had done everything dangerous that the most fertile imagination could conceive—and then some. So far as was known, Miles Hallin couldn't walk a tight-rope, but the general impression was that if Miles Hallin could have walked a tight-rope he would have walked a tight-rope stretched across the crater of Vesuvius as a kind of appetiser before breakfast.

Miles Hallin bothered the Saint through the whole of that weekend.

Simon Templar, as he was always explaining, and usually explaining in such a way that his audience felt very sorry for him, had a sensitivity to anything the least bit out of the ordinary that was as tender as a gouty toe. The lightest touch, a touch that no one else would have felt, made him jump a yard. And when he boasted of his subtle discriminations, though he boasted flippantly, he spoke no less than the truth. That gift and nothing else had led him to fully half his adventures—that uncanny power of drawing a faultless line between the things that were merely eccentric and the things that were definitely wrong. And Miles

Hallin struck him, in a way that he could not explain by any ordinary argument, as a thing that was definitely wrong.

Yet it so chanced, this time, that the Saint came to his story by a pure fluke—another and a wilder fluke than the one that had merely introduced him to a man whose brother had been a friend of Hallin's. But for that fluke, the Saint might to this day have been scowling at the name of Miles Hallin in the same hopeless puzzlement. And yet the Saint felt no surprise about the fluke. He had come to accept these accidents as a natural part of his life, in the same way as any other man accepts the accident of finding a newspaper on his breakfast table, with a sense (if he meditated it at all) that he was only seeing the inevitable outcome of a complicated organisation of whose workings he knew nothing, but whose naturally continued existence he had never thought to question. These things were ordained.

In fact, there was an unexpected guest at a house-party at which the Saint spent his weekend.

Simon Templar had met Teddy Everest in Kuala Lumpur, and again, years later, at Corfu. Teddy Everest was the unexpected guest at the house-party, but it must be admitted that he was unexpected only by the Saint.

"This is my lucky day," murmured Simon, as he viewed the apparition. "I've been looking for you all over the world. You owe me ten cents. If you remember, when you had to be carried home after that farewell festival in K.L., I was left to pay for your rickshaw. You hadn't a bean, I know that, because I looked in all your pockets. Ten cents plus five per cent compound interest for six years . . ."

"Comes to a lot less than you borrowed off me in Corfu," said Everest cheerfully. "How the hell are you?"

"My halo," said the Saint, "is clearly visible if you get a strong light behind me . . . Well, damn your eyes!" The Saint was smiling as he crushed the other's hand in a long grip. "This is a great event, Teddy. Let's get drunk."

The party went with a swing from that moment.

Teddy Everest was a mining engineer, and the Saint could also tell a good story; between them, they kept the ball rolling as they pleased. And on Tuesday, since Everest had to go to London on business, he naturally travelled in the Saint's car.

They lunched at Basingstoke, but it was before lunch that the incident happened which turned Teddy Everest's inexhaustible fund of reminiscence into a channel that was to make all the difference in the world to the Saint—and others.

Patricia and Simon had settled themselves in the lounge of the hotel where they pulled up, and Everest had proceeded alone into the bar to supervise the production of cocktails— Teddy Everest was something of a connoisseur in these matters. And in the bar he met a man.

"It's extraordinary how people crop up," he remarked, when he returned. "I've just seen a bloke who reminded me of a real O. Henry yarn."

And later, over the table, he told the yarn.

"I don't think I bored you with the details of my last job," he said. "As a matter of fact, this is the only interesting thing about it. There's a gold mine somewhere in South Africa that was keeping me pretty busy last year—it was going down steadily, and I was sent out to try and find a spark more life in it. Now, it happened that I'd come across that very mine the year before, and heard all about it, and I was rather bored with the job. Everyone on the spot knew that the mine was a dud, and it seemed to me that I was just going to waste my time. Still, the pay was good, and I couldn't afford to turn my nose up at it. I'd got into jolly low water over my last holiday, to tell you the truth, and I wasn't sorry to have something to do—even if it was boring. It was on the train to Marseilles, where I caught my boat, that I met this guy—he on his way to a luxurious week at Antibes, rot him! We got talking, and it turned out that he knew a bit about the game. I remember telling him about my dud mine, and asking him if he held any shares, because I said a rag-and-bone man might give him a price for them. He hadn't any shares, which rather spoils the story."

"Because the mine wasn't a dud," murmured Simon, and Everest nodded.

"It was anything but. Certainly the old borings were worked out, but I struck a new vein all on my own, and those shares are going up to the sky when my report's been passed. I gave Hallin the tip just now—I felt he deserved it."

The Saint sat still.

It was Patricia Holm who put the question.

"Did you say 'Hallin?'" she asked.

"That's right." Everest was scraping at his pipe with a penknife. "Miles Hallin—the racing chappie."

Patricia looked across at the Saint, but the overflow she was expecting did not take place.

"Dear me!" said the Saint, quite mildly.

They were sitting over coffee in the lounge when Hallin passed through. Simon recognised him at once—before he waved to Everest.

"One of the world's lucky men, I believe," Everest said, as the clamour of Hallin's car died away outside.

"So I hear," said the Saint.

And once again Patricia looked at him, remembering his discourse of a few days before. It was a characteristic of the Saint that no idea ever slipped out of his mind, once it had arrived there; any riddle that occurred to him tormented him until he had solved it. Anything that was as wrong as Miles Hallin, to his peculiar mind, was a perpetual irritation to him, much as a note out of tune on a piano would be a perpetual irritation to a musician: he had to look round it and into it and scratch it and finger it and jigger about with it until he'd got it into line with the rest of the scheme of things, and it gave him no peace until it was settled.

Yet he said nothing more about Miles Hallin that day. Still he knew nothing. Afterwards—

But those are the bare facts of the beginning of the story.

They are told as the Saint himself would tell them, simply put forward for what they are worth. Afterwards, in the light of the knowledge to which he came he could have fitted them together much more coherently, much more comprehensively, but that would not have been his way. He would have told the story as it happened.

"And the longer I live," he would have said, "the more I'm convinced that there's no end to anything in my life. Or in anyone else's, probably. If you trace the most ordinary things back to their source, you find they have the queerest beginnings. It's just one huge fantastic game of consequences. You decide to walk home instead of taking a taxi, one night, and ten years later a man commits suicide. And if you had taken the taxi, perhaps ten years later the same man might have been a millionaire. Your father stayed at one hotel instead of another, in the same town, and at the age of fifty you become Prime Minister. If he had stayed at the other hotel you would probably have ended your life in prison . . . Take this very story. If we hadn't lunched at Basingstoke that day, or if we'd never gone to that house-party, or if I hadn't once gone out without a handkerchief, or even if I'd never gone to Kuala Lumpur—leave out the same flukes in the lives of the other people involved. Well, I've given up trying to decide exactly in what year, way back in the dim and distant past, it was decided that two men would have to die to make this story."

This is exactly the point at which Simon Templar would have paused to make his philosophical reflection.

And then he would have told how, on the following Saturday evening, the posters of *The Evening Record* caught his eye, and something made him buy a copy of the paper, and he went home to tell Patricia that Miles Hallin had crashed again at Brooklands, and Miles Hallin had escaped again with hardly a scratch, but his passenger, Teddy Everest, had been burnt to death before the whole crowd.

3

"You see," Nigel Perry explained simply, "Moyna's people are frightfully poor."

"Yeah," said the Saint.

"And Miles is such a damned good chap."

"Yeah," said the Saint.

"It makes it awfully difficult."

"Yeah," said the Saint.

They lay stretched out in arm-chairs, masked by clouds of cigarette smoke, in the bed-sitting-room which was Nigel Perry's only home. And Perry, bronzed and clear-eyed from ten days' tramping in Spain, was unburdening himself of his problem.

"You haven't seen Moyna yet, have you?" said the Saint.

"Well, hang it, I've only been back a few hours! But she'll be in later—she's got to have dinner with an aunt, or something, and she'll get away as soon as she can."

"What d'you think of your chances?"

Perry ran brown fingers through his hair.

"I'm blowed if I know, Templar," he said ruefully. "I—I've tried to keep clear of the subject lately. There's such a lot to think about. If only I'd got some real money . . ."

"D'you think a girl like Moyna cares a hoot about that?"

"Oh, I know! But that's all very fine. Any sensible girl is going to care about money sooner or later. She's got every right to. And if she's nice enough to think money doesn't matter—well, a chap can't take advantage of that . . . You know, that's where Miles has been so white. That money he paid over to me as my brother's share in the mine—he's really done his best to help me to make it grow. 'If it's a matter of '£. s. d.,' he said, 'I'd like you to start all square.'"

"Did he?" said the Saint.

Perry nodded.

"I believe he worked like a Trojan. Pestered all his friends to try and find me a cast-iron investment paying about two hundred per cent. And he found one, too—at least, we thought so. Funnily enough, it was another gold mine—only this time it was in South Africa . . ."

"Hell!" said the Saint.

"What d'you mean?"

"Hell," said the Saint. "When was this—last week?"

The youngster looked at him puzzledly.

"Oh, no. That was over a year ago . . . But the shares didn't jump as they were supposed to. They've just gone slowly down. Not very much, but they've gone down. I held on, though. Miles was absolutely certain his information couldn't be wrong. And now he's just heard that it was wrong—there was a letter waiting for me . . ."

"He's offered to buy the shares off you, and make up your loss."

Perry stared.

"How did you know?"

"I know everything," said the Saint.

He sprang to his feet suddenly. There was an ecstatic expression on his face that made

Perry wonder if perhaps the beer . . .

Perry rose slowly, and the Saint's hand fell on his shoulder. "Moyna's coming tonight, isn't she?"

"I told you . . ."

"I'll tell you more. You're going to propose, my lad."

"What?"

"Propose," drawled the Saint, "If you've never done it before, I'll give you a rapid lesson now. You take her little hand in yours, and you say, huskily, you say: 'Moyna, d'you think we could do it?' 'Do what?' she says. 'Get fixed,' says you. 'Fixed?' she says. 'How?' 'Keep the party clean,' says you. 'Moyna,' you say, crrrushing her to your booosom—that's a shade north of your cummerbund—'Moyna, I laaaaaaave you!' . . . That will be two guineas. You can post me a cheque in the morning—as the actress used to say. She was a perfect lady . . . So long!"

And the Saint snatched up his hat. He was half-way to the door when Perry caught him.

"What's the idea, Templar?"

Simon turned, smiling.

"Well, you don't want me on the scene while you shoot your speech, do you?"

"You don't have to go yet."

"Oh, yes, I do."

"Where?"

"I'm going to find Miles!"

"But you've never met him."

"I haven't. But I'm going to!"

Perry blocked the doorway.

"Look here, Templar," he said, "you can't get away with this. There's a lot of things I want to know first. Hang it—if I didn't know you pretty well, I'd say you'd gone clean off your rocker."

"Would you?" said the Saint gently.

He had been looking at Perry all the time, and he had been smiling all the time, but all at once the younger man saw something leap into the Saint's gaze that had not been there before—something like a flash of naked steel.

"Then," said the Saint very gently, "what would you say if I told you I was going to kill Miles Hallin?"

Perry fell back a pace.

"You're crazy!" he whispered.

"Sure," said the Saint. "But not so crazy as Miles Hallin must have been when he killed a friend of mine the other day."

"Miles killed a friend of yours? What in God's name d'you mean?"

"Oh, for the love of Pete!"

With a shrug, the Saint turned back into the room. He sat on the edge of a table, but his poise was as restless as his perch. The last thing that anyone could have imagined was that he meant to stay sitting there.

"Listen, and I'll tell you a joke," he said. "I'm full of jokes these days . . . Once upon a time there was a man who could not die. Joke."

"I wish to Heaven you'd say what you mean!"

"If I did, you wouldn't believe me."

"Not if it was about Miles."

"Quite! And it is about Miles. So we'd have a first-class row—and what good would that do? As it is, we're getting damned near it. So why not let it go?"

"You've made suggestions—"

"Of course I have," agreed the Saint wearily. "And now I'm going to make some more. Lose your temper if you must, Nigel, old dear, but promise me two things first: promise you'll hang on to those shares, and propose to Moyna tonight. She'll accept—I guarantee it. With lots of love and kisses, yours faithfully."

The youngster's jaw tightened.

"I think you're raving," he said. "But we're going to have this out. What have you got to say about Miles?"

The Saint's sigh was as full of patience and long-suffering as the Saint could make it. He really was trying to be patient, but he knew that he hadn't a hope of convincing Nigel Perry. And to the Saint it was all so plain. He wasn't a bit surprised at the sudden blossoming of the story: it had happened in the way these things always happened, in the way he subconsciously expected them to happen. He had taken the blossoming in his stride; it was all infinitely past and over to him—so infinitely past and over that he had ceased to think about coincidences. And he sighed.

"I've got nothing to say about Miles."

"You were saying—"

"Forget it, old dear. Now, will you do what I asked you to do about Moyna?"

"That's my business. Why should you want to dictate to me about it?"

"And as for those shares," continued the Saint calmly, "will you . . ."

"For the last time," said Perry grimly, "will you explain yourself?"

Simon looked at him over a cigarette and a lighted match, and then through a trailing streamer of smoke, and Simon shrugged.

"Right!" he said. "I will. But don't forget that we agreed it was a waste of time. You won't believe me. You're the sort that wouldn't. I respect you for it, but it makes you a damned fool all the same."

"Go ahead."

"Do you remember that fellow who was killed at Brooklands yesterday, driving with Miles Hallin?"

"I've read about it."

"He was a friend of mine. Over a year ago he told Miles Hallin about some dud shares. You bought them. Under a week ago he met Hallin again and told him the shares weren't so dud. Now Hallin's going to take the shares back off you. He killed poor old Teddy because Teddy knew the story—and Teddy was great on telling his stories. If Hallin had known that the man he saw with Teddy knew you, I should probably have had my funeral first. Miles is such a damned good chap. 'If it's a matter of £s.d.,' he'd have said, 'I'd like me to start all square.'"

"By God, Templar . . ."

"Hush! . . . Deducing back from that joke to the joke about another gold mine . . ."

Perry stepped forward, with a flaming face.

"It's a lie!"

"Sure it is. We agreed about that before I started, if you recall the dialogue . . . Where was I? Oh, yes. Deducing back from that joke . . ."

"I'd like Miles to hear some of this," Perry said through his teeth.

"So would I," murmured the Saint. "I told you I wanted to find him. If you see him first, you may tell him all about it. Give him my address." The Saint yawned. "Now may I go, sweetheart?"

He stood up, his cigarette tilted up in the corner of his mouth and his hands in his pockets, and Perry stood aside.

"You're welcome to go," Perry said. "And if you ever try to come back I'll have you thrown out."

Simon nodded.

"I'll remember that when I feel in need of some exercise," he remarked. And then he smiled. For a moment he gripped the boy's arm.

"Don't forget about Moyna," he said.

Then he crossed the landing and went down the stairs, and Nigel Perry, silent in the doorway, watched him go.

The Saint went down slowly. He was really sorry about it all, though he had known it was inevitable. At least, he had made it inevitable. He was aware that he asked for most of the trouble that came to him—in many ways. But that couldn't be helped. In the end—

He was on the last flight when a man who was running up from the hall nearly cannoned into him.

"Sorry," said the man.

"Not at all," said the Saint politely.

And then he recognised the man, and stopped him with a hand on his sleeve.

"How's the trade in death?" murmured the Saint.

Miles Hallin turned, staring, and then he suddenly knew where he had seen the Saint before. For an instant the recognition flared in his eyes, then his face became a mask of indignation.

"What the devil do you mean?" he demanded.

Simon sighed. He always seemed to have something to sigh about in those days.

"I'm getting so tired of that question," he sighed. "Why don't you try it on Nigel? Perhaps he doesn't have so much of it as I do."

He turned, and continued on his way. As he opened the front door he heard Hallin resuming his ascent at a less boisterous speed, and smiled gently to himself.

It was late, and the street outside was dark and practically deserted. But in front of the house stood an immense shining two-seater that could only have belonged to Miles Hallin.

For a space of seconds the Saint regarded it, fingering his chin, at first thoughtfully, and then with a secret devil of merriment puckering the corners of his eyes.

Then he went down the steps.

He found the tool-box in a moment. And then, with loving care, he proceeded to remove the nuts that secured the offside front wheel . . .

Two minutes later, with the wheel-brace stowed away again as he had found it, and the nuts in his pocket, he was sauntering leisurely homewards, humming to the stars.

4

The Saint was in his bath when Inspector Teal arrived in Upper Berkeley Mews the next morning, but he presented himself in a few moments arrayed in a superb pair of crepe-de-Chine pyjamas and a dressing-gown that would have made the rainbow look like something left over from a sale of second-hand mourning.

Mr. Teal eyed him with awe.

"Where did you hire that outfit?" he inquired.

Simon took a cigarette.

"Have you come here to exchange genial back-chat," he murmured, "or is it business? I have an awful suspicion that it's business."

"It is business," said Mr. Teal.

"Sorry," said the Saint, "my office hours are twelve noon to midday."

Teal shifted his gum across to the east side of his mouth.

"What's your grouse against Hallin?" he asked.

"Hallin? Who's Hallin? Two aitches."

"Miles Hallin's car was wrecked last night," said Teal deliberately.

The Saint raised his eyebrows.

"Really? Was he drunk, or did he lend the divisional surgeon a fiver?"

"The offside front wheel of his car came off when he was driving down Park Lane," said Teal patiently. "He was driving pretty fast, and he swerved into a taxi. He ought to have been killed."

"Wasn't he?" said the Saint,

"He wasn't. What have you got to say about it?"

"Well, I think it's a great pity."

"A great pity he wasn't killed?"

"Yes. Probably he wanted to die. He's been trying to long enough, hasn't he? . . . And yet it mightn't have been his fault. That's the worst of these cheap cars. They fall apart if you sneeze in them. Of course, he might have had a cold. Do you think he had a cold?" asked the Saint earnestly.

The detective closed his eyes.

"When Hallin looked at the car," Teal explained, "he found that someone had removed the nuts that ought to have been keeping the wheel on."

The Saint smoothed his hair.

"Well, really, dear old broccolo," he drawled, with a pained expression, "is that all you've come to see me about? Are you going to make a habit of coming to me to air your woes about everything that happens in London? You know, I'm awfully afraid you're getting into the way of thinking I'm some sort of criminal. Teal, you must not think that of me!"

"I know all about last night," Teal replied, without altering his weary tone. "I've already seen Perry."

"And what did Perry tell you?"

"He told me you said you were going to kill Hallin."

"Beer, beer I—I mean, dear, dear!" said the Saint. "Of course he was a bit squiffy . . ." Teal's eyes opened with a suddenness that was almost startling.

"See here, Templar," he said, "it's time you and me had a straight talk."

"I beg your pardon?" said the Saint.

"You and I," said Teal testily. "I know we've had a lot of scraps in the past, and I know a lot of funny things have happened since then. I don't grudge you your success. In your way, you've helped me a lot, but at the same time you've caused disturbances. I know you've had a pardon, and we don't want to bother you if we can help it, but you've got to do your share. That show of yours down at Tenterden, for instance—that wasn't quite fair, was it?"

"It wasn't," said the Saint generously. "But I'm afraid it appealed to my perverted sense of humour."

Mr. Teal rose ponderously.

"Then do I take it you're going on as before?"

"I'm afraid you do," said the Saint. "For the present, anyway. You see, I've got rather a down on Miles Hallin. He killed a friend of mine the other day."

"He what?"

"At Brooklands. Since you're making so many inquiries about funny things that happen to cars, why don't you investigate that crash? I don't know if there was enough left of Teddy Everest to make an investigation profitable, but if it could be done, I expect you'd find that he was thoroughly doped when he got into that car. I expect you'd find, if you were a very clever investigator—or a very clever clairvoyant, like I am—that the dope took effect while they were driving. Teddy just went to sleep. Then it would be quite an easy matter for an expert driver like Hallin to crash the car without hurting himself. And, of course, it could always catch fire."

Teal looked at him curiously.

"Is that the truth?" he asked.

"No," said the Saint. "I'm just making it up to amuse you. Good morning."

He felt annoyed with Chief-Inspector Teal that day. He felt annoyed with a lot of things—the story in general, and Miles Hallin in particular. There were many things that were capable of annoying the Saint in just that way, and when Mr. Teal had departed, the Saint sat down and smoked three cigarettes with entirely unnecessary violence.

Patricia Holm, coming in just after the third of these cigarettes had been hurled through the open window, read his mood at once.

"What is it this time?" she asked.

Simon broke a match into small pieces as if it had done him a grievous injury.

"Teal, Nigel Perry, Miles Hallin," he answered, comprehensively. "Also, an old joke about Death."

It was some time before she secured a coherent explanation. The incidents of the night before she had already heard, but he had stated them without adornment, and his manner had encouraged the postponement of questions. Now he told her, in the same blunt manner, about Teal's visit, but she had to wait until after lunch, when the coffee-cups were in front of them and the Saint was gently circulating a minute quantity of Napoleon brandy around the bowl of an enormous glass, before she could get him to expound his grievance.

"When I first spoke about Miles Hallin—you remember?—you thought I was raving. I don't want to lay on any of the 'I told you so' stuff, but now you know what you do know, I want you to try and appreciate my point. I know you'll say what anyone else would say—that the whole thing simply boils down to the most unholy fluke. I'm saying it doesn't. The point is that I'm going back far beyond that share business—even beyond poor old Teddy. I'm going back to Nigel's brother, and that little story of the great open spaces that I've heard so much about. I tell you, this just confirms what I thought about that."

"You didn't say you thought anything about it," Patricia remarked.

"I wasn't asking to be called a fool," said the Saint. "I knew that as things stood I had rather less chance of convincing any sane person than I'd have of climbing the Matterhorn with my hands tied behind me and an elephant in each pocket. But you ought to see the joke now. What would you say was the most eccentric thing about a man who could not die?"

Patricia smiled at him patiently.

"I shouldn't know what to say," she answered truthfully.

"Why," said the Saint, with a kind of vast impatience, "what else should be the most eccentric thing about him but the fact that he can die, and always could? Don't you understand that whatever jokes people make about death, they never make that kind of joke? There are impossibilities that are freakish and funny, and impossibilities that are freakish and unfunny; pigs with wings belong to the first kind, but men who cannot die belong to the second kind. Now, what could induce a man to pursue that second kind of joke with such a terrible eagerness?"

The girl shrugged.

"It's beyond me, Simon."

"The answer," said the Saint, "is that he knew it wasn't true. Because he'd once looked death in the face—slow and deliberate death, not the kind that comes with a rush. And he found he was afraid of it."

"Then that story about Nigel's brother . . ."

"Perhaps we shall never know the truth of it. But I'm as certain as I've ever been about anything that the story we're told isn't the truth. I'm certain that that was the time when Miles Hallin discovered, not that he could not die, but that he couldn't bear to die. And he saved his life at the expense of his partner."

"But he's risked his life so often since . . ."

"I wonder how much of that is the unvarnished truth—how much he engineered, and how much he adorned his stories so as to give the impression he wanted to give? . . . Because I think Miles Hallin is a man in terror. Once, he yielded to his fear, and after that his fear became the keynote of his life, which a fear will become if you yield to it. And he found another fear—the fear of being found out. He was afraid of his own legend. He had to bolster it up, he had to pile miracle upon miracle—only to make one miracle seem possible. He had to risk losing his life in order to save it."

"But why should he have killed Teddy?"

The Saint took another cigarette. He gazed across the restaurant with eyes that saw other things.

"One fear breeds another," he said. "All things in a man's mind are linked up. If one cog slips, the whole machine is altered. If you will cheat at cards, you will cheat at Snakes-and-Ladders. Hallin cheated for life; it was quite natural that he should cheat for love. Because Nigel was Moyna's favourite, Hallin had to try and take away the one little thing that gave Nigel a chance. Because Teddy could have discovered the swindle, he killed Teddy. His fear drove him on, as it will keep on driving him on: it's the most ruthless master a man can have. Now, because he saw me with Teddy at Basingstoke, and then saw me last night leaving Nigel's, he will try to kill me. If he thought Nigel believed me, he would try to kill Nigel—that's why I had to tell the story in such a way that I knew Nigel wouldn't believe it. Even now, Hallin is wondering . . ."

"But if Nigel had given up the shares without suspecting anything, and then they'd soared up as Teddy said they would . . ."

"What would that have mattered?"

"Nigel would have known."

"Known what? Hallin would have said he sold the shares for the best price he could get, and Nigel would never have thought that it might be a lie . . . But now—do you remember how I said I wanted to make Hallin live?"

"Yes."

"That was the test—before I knew any of this. I wanted to see what would happen to him if he put aside his joke. I wanted to know what he would be like if he became an ordinary mortal man—a man to whom death might not be a terror, but to whom death was still no joke. And now I know."

With her chin on her hands, Patricia regarded him. Not as she had regarded him when he had spoken of Miles Hallin before, but with a seriousness that wore a smile.

"I shall never get to the end of your mind, lad," she said, and the Saint grinned.

"At the moment," he murmured, "I'm enjoying my brandy."

And he actually did forget Miles Hallin for the rest of that afternoon and evening, for Simon Templar had the gift of taking life as it came—when once he knew from what quarter it might be coming.

His impatience disappeared. It seemed as if that talk over the coffee and brandy had cleared the air for him. He knew that trouble was coming, but that was nothing unusual. He could meet all the trouble in the world with a real enjoyment, now that he had purged his mind of the kind of puzzle that for him was gloom and groping and unalloyed Gehenna. Even the reflection that Miles Hallin had still failed to die did not depress him. He had not loosened that wheel in high hopes of a swift and catastrophic denouement, for he had known how slight was the chance that the wheel would elect to part company with the car at the very moment when Hallin was treading the accelerator flat down to the flooring; the thing had been done on the spur of the moment, more in mischief than anything else, just to pep up the party's future. And it would certainly do that.

As for Teal, and Teal's horrific warnings of what would happen if the Saint should again attract the attention of the law—those were the merest details. They simply made the practical problem more amusing . . .

So the Saint, over his brandy, swung over to a contentment as genuine and as illogical as his earlier impatience had been, and was happy for the rest of that day, and nearly died that night.

He had danced with Patricia at the May Fair, and he had thought that Patricia looked particularly beautiful, and so presently they strolled home arm in arm through the cool lamplit streets, talking intently and abstractedly about certain things that are nobody's business. And the Saint was saying something or other, or it may have been Patricia who was saying something or other, as they crossed Berkeley Square, but whoever it was never finished the speech.

Some instinct made the Saint look round, and he saw the lights of a car just behind them swerve suddenly. An ordinary sight enough, perhaps, on the face of it, but he knew by the same instinct that it was not ordinary. It may have been that he had not forgotten Miles Hallin so completely, after all.

He stopped in his stride, and stooped, and Patricia felt herself swept up in his arms. There was a lamp-post close behind them, and the Saint leapt for it. He heard the screech of brakes and tyres before he dared to look round, even then he was in time to see the pillar that sheltered him bend like a reed before the impact of the car, and he moved again, this time to one side, like lightning, as the iron column snapped at the base and came crashing down to the pavement.

Then there was a shout somewhere, and a sound of running feet, and the mutter of the car stopped.

Quietly the Saint set Patricia down again.

"How very unfortunate," he remarked. "Dearie, dearie me! . . . Mr. Miles Hallin, giving evidence, stated that his nerves had been badly shaken by his smash at Brooklands. His licence was suspended for six months."

A constable and half a dozen ordinary citizens were rapidly congregating around the wreckage, and an unholy glitter came into the Saint's eyes.

"Pardon me one moment, old darling," he murmured, and Patricia found herself standing alone.

But she reached the crowd in time to hear most of his contribution to the entertainment.

"Scandalous, I call it," the Saint was saying, in a voice that trembled—possibly with righteous indignation. Or possibly not. "I shall write to *The Times.* A positive outrage . . . Yes, of course you can have my name and address. I shall be delighted to give evidence . . . The streets aren't safe . . . murderous fools who ought to be in an asylum . . . Probably only just learnt to drive . . . Disgraceful . . . disgusting . . . ought to be shot . . . mannerless hogs . . ."

It was some time before the policeman was able to soothe him, and he faded out of the picture still fuming vitriolically, to the accompaniment of a gobble of applause from the assembled populace.

And a few minutes later he was leaning helplessly against the door of his flat, his ribs aching and the tears streaming down his cheeks, while Patricia implored him wildly to open the door and take his hilarity into decent seclusion.

"Oh, but it was too beautiful, sweetheart!" he sobbed weakly, as at last he staggered into the sitting-room. "If I'd missed that chance I could never have looked myself in the face again. Did you see Miles?"

"I did."

"He couldn't say a word. He didn't dare let on that he knew me. He just had to take it all. Pat, I ask you, can life hold any more?"

Half an hour later, when he was sprawled elegantly over an armchair, with a tankard of beer in one hand and the last cigarette of the evening in the other, she ventured to ask the obvious question.

"He was waiting for us, of course," she said, and the Saint nodded.

"My prophetic report of the police-court proceedings would still have been correct," he drawled. "Miles Hallin has come to life."

He did not add that he could have prophesied with equal assurance that Chief-Inspector Teal would not again be invited to participate in the argument—not by Miles Hallin, anyway. But he knew quite well that either Miles Hallin or Simon Templar would have to die before the argument was settled, and it would have to be settled soon.

5

Nevertheless, Teal did participate again, and it may be said that his next intrusion was entirely his own idea.

He arrived in Upper Berkeley Mews the very next evening, and the Saint, who had seen him pass the window, opened the door before Teal's finger had reached the bell.

"This is an unexpected pleasure," Simon murmured cordially, as he propelled the detective into the sitting-room. "Still, you needn't bother to tell me why you've come. A tram was stolen from Tooting last night, and you want to know if I did it. Six piebald therms are missing from the Gas Light and Coke Company's stable, and you want to know if I've got them. A seventeen horse-power saveloy entered for the St. Leger has been stricken with glanders, and you want to know . . ."

"I didn't say so," observed Mr. Teal—heatedly, for him.

"Never mind," said the Saint peaceably. "We won't press the point. But you must admit that we're seeing a lot of you these days." He inspected the detective's water-line with a reflective eye. "I believe you've become a secret Glaxo drinker," he said reproachfully.

Teal gravitated towards a chair.

"I heard about your show last night," he said, Simon smiled vaguely.

"You hear of everything, old dear," he remarked, and Teal nodded seriously.

"It's my business," he said.

He put a finger in his mouth and hitched his chewing-gum into a quiet backwater, and then he leaned forward, his pudgy hands resting on his knees, and his baby blue eyes unusually wide awake.

"Will you try not to stall, Templar—just for a few minutes?"

The Saint looked at him thoughtfully. Then took a cigarette and sat down in the chair opposite.

"Sure," he said.

"I wonder if you'd even do something more than that?"

"Namely?"

"I wonder if you'd give me a straight line about Miles Hallin—and no fooling."

"I offered you one yesterday," said the Saint, "and you wouldn't listen."

Teal nodded, shifting his feet.

"I know. But the situation wasn't quite the same. Since then I've heard about that accident last night. And that mayn't mean anything to anyone but you and me—but you've got to include me."

"Have I?"

"I'm remembering things," said the detective. "You may be a respectable member of society now, but you haven't always been one. I can remember the time when I'd have given ten years' salary for the pleasure of putting you away. Sometimes I get relapses of that feeling, even now."

"So you do," murmured the Saint.

"But this isn't one of those times," said Teal. "Just now I only want to remember another part of your record. And I know as well as anyone else that you never go after a man just because he's got a wart on his nose. Usually, your reason's fairly plain. This time it isn't. And I'm curious."

"Naturally."

"Hallin's right off your usual mark. He doesn't belong to any shady bunch. If he did, I'd know it. He isn't even a borderline case, like I knew Lemuel was."

"He isn't."

"And yet he tried to bump you off last night."

The Saint inhaled deeply, and exhaled again through a Saintly smile.

"If you want to know why he did that," he said, "I'll tell you. It was because he's always been terribly afraid of death."

"Do you mean he thought you were going to kill him?"

"That's not what I said. I certainly did say I was going to kill him, but whether he believed me or not is more than I can tell you at present."

"Then what do you mean?"

Simon raised his eyebrows mournfully, but he checked the protest that was almost becoming a habit. After all, Teal was only a detective. One had to make allowances.

"Miles Hallin thought no one in the world knew the truth about him," said the Saint. "And then he found that I knew. So he wanted me to die."

Teal compressed his lips.

Then he said, "And what was this truth?"

"Simply that Miles Hallin is a coward."

"Would he try to kill you for that?"

The Saint gazed at the ceiling.

"Did you take my tip about that Brooklands affair?" he asked.

"I made some inquiries," Teal shrugged. "I'm afraid it wasn't much use. I'm told no one could prove anything."

"And yet you've come back to see me."

"After that business last night. On the level, Templar, I'd be glad of a tip. You know something that I don't know, and just this once I want you to help me. If it had looked like one of your ordinary shows, I wouldn't have done it."

"Where is the peculiar difference between this show and what you call my 'ordinary shows'?"

"You know as well as I do . . ."

"I don't!"

The Saint uncurled from his chair like a steel spring released, and his eyes were of the same steel. The detective realised that those eyes had been levelled unwinkingly at him for a long while, but he had not realised it before. Now he saw his mistake.

"I don't know anything of the kind," snapped the Saint, with those eyes of chilled steel, and the laziness had vanished altogether from his voice. "But I do know that I can't swallow the joke of your coming to see me just because you want to take one of my feathers and put it in your own cap. I've got a darned good swallowing apparatus, Teal, I promise you, but it simply won't sink that one!"

Teal blinked.

"I only wanted to ask you . . ."

"Shucks!" said the Saint tersely. "You've told me what you wanted to ask me. My yell is that you haven't told me the real reason. And that's what I'm going to know before we take the palaver any further. You asked me not to stall, now I'm telling you not to stall. Shoot!"

For a space of seconds they eyed one another in silence, and then the detective nodded fractionally, though his round, red face had not changed its expression.

"All right," he said slowly. "I'll come clean—if you'll do the same."

The Saint stood tensely. But he hesitated only for a moment. He thought, *Something's happened. Teal knows what it is. I've got to find out. It may or may not be important, but . . .*

The Saint said curtly, "That's O.K. by me."

"Then you start," answered Teal.

Simon drew breath.

"Mine's easy. I suspect that the story of Hallin's luck in Australia is a lie. I know that Hallin's crazy about the same girl that Nigel Perry's in love with. I know that Hallin tried to push Perry out of the running by persuading him to put the little money he'd got into a mine that Hallin thought was a dud. I know that Teddy Everest told Hallin the mine was a dud, and later told him it wasn't a dud after all. I know Hallin faked that crash because Teddy might be dangerous. I know Hallin had planned some story to get those shares back from Perry, and I know Hallin tried to kill me because I told Perry the truth—even if Perry didn't believe me. That's all there is to it. Your turn."

Teal's chair creaked as he moved, but his eyes were closed. He appeared to have fallen asleep. And then he spoke with a voice that was not at all sleepy.

"Moyna Stanford was kidnapped this afternoon," he said, and the Saint swore softly.

"The hell! . . ."

"That's all I know."

"Tell me about it."

"There's very little to tell. She'd been down to lunch with some friends at Windsor—she walked alone to the station—and she hasn't been seen since."

"But, burn it!—a grown girl can disappear for two or three hours without being kidnapped, can't she?"

"Ordinarily, she can," said Teal. "I'm just telling you what's happened. She was due to have tea with some friends of her mother's.

They rang up her mother to ask why she hadn't come. Her mother rang up Windsor to ask the same question. And as soon as her mother grasped the facts she went flying to the police. Of course, Mrs. Stanford didn't get much satisfaction—we haven't got time to attend to hysterical parents who get the wind up as quickly as that—but I heard about it, and it seemed to link up. Anyway . . ."

"She might have run away with Perry," said the Saint, with a kind of frantic hope that he knew instinctively to be the hope of a fool.

And the detective's reply came so pat that even Simon Templar was startled.

"She might have," said Teal grimly, "because Perry's also disappeared."

The Saint stood like a statue.

Then when he spoke again his voice was strangely quiet.

"Tell me about Perry," he said.

"Perry just went out to lunch in the ordinary way, but he never went back to the office."

The Saint removed his cigarette from his mouth. It had gone out. He gazed at it as if its extinction was the only thing in the world that mattered.

Then he said, "At the police-court this morning, Hallin was remanded for a medical examination. Was that the Beak's idea—or yours?"

"Largely mine," said Teal.

"Would Hallin know?"

"He might have guessed."

"And what happened after that?"

"Probably, he lunched with Perry. The identification isn't certain, but . . ."

"Has Hallin been seen anywhere since?"

"I've had men making inquiries. If you'll let me use your telephone . . ."

"Carry on."

The detective moved ponderously over to the instrument, and Simon, lighting another cigarette, began to stride up and down the room.

He was still pacing the carpet when Teal hung up the receiver and turned to him again.

"Hallin hasn't been seen since lunch."

The Saint nodded without speaking, and set off on a fresh route, his hands deep in his pockets. Teal watched him with exasperation.

"Haven't you got anything to say?" he demanded.

Simon raised his eyes from the floor.

"I've made a big mistake," he said, as though nothing else concerned him, and Teal seethed audibly.

"For Heaven's sake!"

"Er—not exactly."

The Saint stopped abruptly on those words, and faced about, and Teal was suddenly amazed that he could ever have associated that dark, rakish profile with trivialities.

"My mistake," said the Saint, "was in underrating Hallin's intelligence. I don't know why I did it. He'd naturally be quick on the uptake. And he'd realise that when those shares went up he'd be damned. Perry would have to believe me. And the rest follows."

"What follows?"

"He got Perry away with some yarn—probably about Moyna. Then he rushed down to Windsor, caught Moyna at the station, and offered to drive her to London. But I know where they went—Perry may be there too . . ."

"Where?"

"Wales."

"How d'you know that?"

"Hallin's got a place there. Damn it, Teal, d'you think you're the only durned General Information Bureau in this gosh-blinded burg?" Teal brushed his hat on his sleeve.

"I can get a police car round here in five minutes," he stated.

"Do it," said the Saint, and Teal went again to the telephone—very quickly.

When he had given his instructions, he put his hat down on the table, and came and stood in front of the Saint. And suddenly his hands shot out, and moved swiftly and firmly over the Saint's pockets. And the Saint smiled.

"Did you think I was carrying the missing couple around with me?" he murmured, in the mildest of expostulation, but Teal was not amused.

"I'm remembering Lemuel," he said briefly. "You may be coming with me, but you're not carrying a gun."

The Saint smiled even more gently.

"Miles Hallin is terribly afraid," he said, addressing the ceiling. "Once upon a time, he was just afraid of dying, but now he has an even bigger fear. He's afraid of dying before he's finished with life . . . I think someone had better carry a gun."

Teal understood perfectly.

6

"So there you are!" Nigel Perry flung open the door of the cottage as Hallin's car pulled up outside. "I was wondering what on earth to do. Moyna isn't here . . ."

"She isn't far away," Hallin said.

He climbed stiffly out of his seat. Perry could not see his face clearly in the gloom, but something in Hallin's tone puzzled him. And then Hallin took him by the arm with a laugh.

"Come inside," he said, "and I'll tell you all about it."

Inside, in the lighted room, Hallin's heavy features seemed drawn and strained, but of course he had just driven nearly a hundred and sixty miles at his usual breakneck pace.

"Heavens, I'm tired!"

He sat down, and passed a hand across his forehead. His eyes strayed towards the decanter on a side-table, and the younger man hurried towards it.

"Thanks," Hallin said.

"I've been bothered to death, Miles!" said Perry boyishly, splashing soda-water into the glass. "I didn't dare leave the place, in case Moyna arrived and found nobody here, and I didn't know how to get in touch with you . . ."

"And now I expect you're wondering why I'm here at all."

"I am."

Hallin took the tumbler and half-emptied it at a gulp.

"That's better! . . . Well, everything's gone wrong that could go wrong."

"Don't you know any more than you knew at lunch-time?"

"I don't know any more, but—well, I've told you it all. Moyna rang me up—she said she was in frightful trouble—your office number was engaged, and she couldn't wait. She'd got to get out of London at once. I asked her where she was going, and she didn't seem to have any idea, I said I'd leave the key of my place in Wales with my valet . . ."

"But you gave it to me!"

"I've got more than one key, you idiot! Anyway, she jumped at the chance, and I promised to send you on by the first train. It was much later when I started to think that I might be able to help you, whatever your trouble was—and I got out the car and came straight down."

"But I can't understand it!" Perry couldn't sit down; his nerves were jangled to bits with worry. "Why should Moyna have to run away out of London? She couldn't be mixed up with any crime . . ."

Hallin took another pull at his drink.

"I wish I could be as sure of that as you are."

"Miles!"

"Oh, don't be silly, Nigel. D'you think I'd believe she was in on the wrong side? There are other ways of being mixed up in crime."

"What did you mean when you said everything had gone wrong?"

Hallin lighted a cigarette.

"I discovered something else on my way here," he said.

"You said Moyna wasn't far away . . ."

"I don't think she is. I'll tell you why. As I came up the hill, I had to stop for a moment to switch over to the reserve petrol tank. While I was out of the car I heard someone speaking beside the road. He said, 'Hallin's just come by.' Then he said, 'I'll leave him to you. I'll be waiting for Templar . . .'"

"Templar?"

"That's what he said."

"But he must have known you were there."

"He must have thought I couldn't hear. It was a pure fluke that I could. I moved a couple of steps, and I couldn't hear a sound. Some trick of echoes, I expect. However, I followed the sound, keeping in the line it seemed to move in, and I almost fell over the man. He fired at me once, and missed, and then I got hold of him. He—went over the cliff. You remember . . . it's very steep there . . ."

"You killed him?"

"Of course I did," said Hallin shortly, "unless he can fall two hundred feet without hurting himself. It was him or me—and he was armed. I got back into the car and drove on. Farther up the road a man stepped out and tried to stop me, but I drove right at him. He fired after me twice, but he didn't do any damage. And that's all."

Perry's fists clenched.

"By God, if that man really was waiting for Templar . . ."

"Why shouldn't he have been? Remember all that's happened. We don't know what Templar's game is, but we know his record . . ."

"But he was pardoned a long time ago."

"That doesn't make him straight. A man like that . . ."

Perry swung round. He caught at Hallin's arm.

"For God's sake, Miles—we've got to do something . . ."

Hallin stood up.

"That's why I came to fetch you," he said.

"But what can we do?"

"Get back to that telephone—find where the line leads."

"Could you find the place again?"

"I marked it down."

"But those men who fired at you . . ."

"We can go another way. I know all the roads around here backwards. Are you game?" Perry set his teeth.

"You bet I am. But—if you'd got a gun or something . . ."

Hallin looked at him for a moment. Then he went to the desk, unlocked a drawer, and took out two automatics. One he gave to Perry, the other he slipped into his own pocket.

"That's a good idea," he said. "Now are you ready?"

"Yes—come on!"

It was Perry who led the way out of the cottage, and he had already started the car when

Hallin climbed in behind the wheel.

They moved off with a roar, and Perry leaned over and yelled in Hallin's ear.

"They'll hear us coming!"

Hallin nodded, and kicked the cut-out over. The roar was silenced.

"You're right," he said.

They tore down the hill for a quarter of a mile, and skidded deliriously round a right-angle turn; then they went bucketing down a steep and narrow lane, with the big car brushing the hedge on either side.

"This is the only way to get round them," Hallin said.

The huge headlights made the lane as light as it would have been at noon; even so, it was a nightmare path to follow at that pace. But Hallin was a perfect driver. Presently the lane seemed to come to a dead end; Hallin braked, and put the wheel over, and they broadsided into a clear road.

"It's close here," Hallin said.

The car slackened speed; after a few moments they almost crawled, while Hallin searched the side of the road. And then he jammed on the brakes, switching off the engine and the lights as he did so.

"This is the place."

He met Perry in the road, and led off at once. For a few yards they went over grass; then they threaded a way between rocks and low stunted bushes. On his right, Perry heard a distant murmur of water. Then Hallin stopped him.

"It was just here."

Perry heard the scrape of a match, and then he saw.

They stood beside a slight bump of ground, and there was a shallow cavity in the side of it, which seemed to have been worn away under a flat ledge of stone. And in the cavity was a telephone.

The light went out.

"I've got an idea," Hallin said.

"What is it?"

"Suppose you took that man's place at the telephone—spoke to the men at the other end—told them some story? I'll follow the wire. I don't think the other end is far away. Give me ten minutes, and then start. You could distract their attention—it'd give me a chance to take them by surprise."

"But I want to get near the swine myself!"

"You shall. But to start with—look here, you know you aren't used to stalking. I could get up to them twice as quietly as you could."

Perry hesitated, and then Hallin heard him groping down into the hollow.

"All right." The youngster's voice came up from the darkness. "Hurry along, Miles, and shout as soon as you can."

"I will. Just ten minutes, Nigel."

"Right-ho!"

Hallin moved away.

He did not follow any wire. He knew just where he was going.

In ten minutes he was squatting beside a heavily insulated switch. Beside him a trellised metal tower reached up towards the stars. It was one of many that had not long since sprung up all over England, carrying long electric cables across the country and bringing light and power to every corner of the land.

That Miles Hallin had left London late was only one of his inventions. He had, as a matter of fact, been in that spot for several hours. He was an expert electrician—though the job he had had to do was fairly simple. It had been the digging that had taken the time . . .

He had an ingenious mind. The Saint would have been sheerly delighted to hear the story that Nigel Perry had heard. "If you must have melodrama, lay it on with a spade," was one of the Saint's own maxims, and certainly Miles Hallin had not tyrannised his imagination.

There was also a thoroughness about Hallin which it gave the Saint great pleasure to recall in after years. Even in murder he was as thorough as he had been in fostering the legend of his charmed life. A lesser man would simply have pushed Perry over the very convenient precipice.

"But even at that time," the Saint would say, "Hallin clung to the idea that after all he might get away with something. If he'd simply shoved Nigel off the cliff he'd have had trouble with the body. So he dug a neat grave, and put Nigel in it to die, so all our sweet Miles had to do afterwards was to come back and remove the telephone and fill up the hole. You can't say that wasn't thorough."

Hallin pulled on a thick rubber glove, and then he struck a match and cupped it in his other hand. He looked once at his watch. And his face was perfectly composed as he jerked over the lever of his switch.

7

"We'd better walk from here," said the Saint.

Teal nodded.

He leaned forward and spoke a word to the driver, and the police car pulled into the side of the road, and stopped there.

The detective levered himself out with a grunt, and inspected the track in front of them with a jaundiced eye.

"We might have gone on to the top of the hill," he said, and the Saint laughed without mirth.

"We might not," said the Saint. "Hallin's place is right by the top of the hill, and we aren't here to advertise ourselves."

"I suppose not," said Teal wistfully.

The driver came round the car and joined them, bringing the electric flashlights that were part of their outfit, and Teal took one and tested it. The Saint did the same. They looked at each other in the light.

"You seem to know a lot about this place," Teal said.

The Saint smiled.

"I came down from London last week specially to have a look at it," he answered, and Teal's eyes narrowed.

"Did you bring any bombs with you?" he asked. Simon turned his flashlight up the road.

"I'm afraid I forgot to," he murmured. "And now, shall we proceed with the weight-reducing, Fatty?"

They set off in a simmering silence, Teal and the Saint walking side by side, and the chauffeur bringing up the rear. As they went, the Saint began to sing, under his breath, some ancient ballad about "Oh, How a Fat Girl Can Love," and Teal's breathing seemed to become even more laboured than was warranted by the steepness of the hill. The driver, astern, also sounded as if he was having difficulty with his respiratory effects.

They plodded upwards without speaking for some time, preoccupied with their respective interests, and at last it was Teal who stopped and broke the silence.

"Isn't that a car up there?" he said.

He pointed along the beam of his torch, and the Saint looked.

"It surely is something like a car," admitted the Saint thoughtfully. "That's queer!"

He quickened his pace and went into the lead. Then the other two caught him up again; he was standing still, a few yards from the car, with his flashlight focused on the number-plate.

"One of Hallin's cars," said the Saint.

He moved quickly round it, turning his light on the tyres; they were all perfectly sound. The petrol gauge showed plenty of fuel. He put his hand on the radiator: it was hot.

"Well, well, well!" said the Saint.

Teal, standing beside him, began to flash his torch around the side of the road.

"What's that tin doing there?" he said.

"I do not know, my chubby cherub," said the Saint.

But he reached the tin first, and lifted it up. It was an empty petrol can. He turned it upside down over his palm, and shook it.

"Did he fill up here?" said Teal, and the Saint shook his head.

"The can's as dry as a successful bootlegger's politics. It's an old one. And I should say . . . Teal, I should say it was put here to mark a place. Look at the mark in the grass!"

He left Teal to it, and moved along the road, searching the turf at the side. Then he came back on the other side. His low exclamation brought Teal trotting.

"Someone's doing a midnight cross-country," said the Saint.

He pointed.

"I can't see anything," said Teal.

"You wouldn't," said the Saint disparagingly. "Now, if they'd only thought to leave some cigarette-ash about, for you to put under a microscope, or a few exciting bloodstains . . ."

Teal choked.

"Look here, Templar . . ."

"Teal," said the Saint, elegantly, "you drip."

He sprang lightly over the ditch and headed into the darkness, ignoring the other two, and, after a moment's hesitation, they followed.

The assurance with which the Saint moved over his trail was uncanny. Neither of the others could see the signs which he was able to pick up as rapidly as he could have picked up a plain path, but they were townsmen both, trained for a different kind of tracking.

Perhaps they travelled for fifty yards. And then the Saint stopped dead, and the other two came up on either side of him. His lighted torch aimed downwards, and they followed it with their own, but again neither of them could see anything remarkable.

"What is it this time?" asked Teal.

"I saw an arm," said the Saint. "An arm and a gun. And it went into the ground. Put your lights out!"

Without understanding, they obeyed.

And, in the darkness, the Saint leapt.

His foot turned on a loose stone, throwing him to his knees, and at the same time he heard a metallic click that meant only one thing to him: an automatic had been fired—and had failed to fire.

He spun round. Holding his torch at arm's length away from him, he switched it on again. And he gasped.

"Nigel!"

The boy was wrestling with the sliding jacket of the gun. It seemed to have jammed. And he bared his teeth into the light.

"You swine!" he said.

The Saint stared.

"Nigel! It's me—Simon Templar . . ."

"I know."

The automatic reloaded with a snap, and Perry aimed it deliberately. And then Teal's hand and arm flashed down into the beam of light, caught Perry's wrist, and twisted sharply upwards. Another hand snatched the gun away.

"You devils!"

Perry got his wrist free with a savage wrench, and rolled out of the hole where he had been lying. He gathered himself, crouched, and leapt at the light. Simon put out one foot, and brought him down adroitly.

"Nigel, don't be a big boob!"

For answer the youngster squirmed to his feet again, with something like a sob, and made a second reckless rush.

The Saint began to feel bored.

He switched out his torch, and ducked. His arms fastened about Perry's waist, his shoulder nestled into Perry's chest; he tightened his grip decisively.

"If you don't stop it, Nigel," he said, "I'll break your back."

Perry went limp suddenly. Perhaps he had never dreamed of being held with such a strength. The Saint's arms locked about him like steel bands.

"What's the matter with him?" inquired Teal lethargically, and Simon grunted.

"Seems to have gone loco," he murmured.

Perry's ribs creaked as he tried to breathe.

"It's all right," he said. "I know all about you. You . . ."

"I've got him," said Teal unemotionally, and the Saint loosened his hold and straightened up.

He had dropped his torch in the scuffle. Now he stooped to grope around for it, and it was while he was stooping that another light came. It came with a sort of hissing crackle—something like blue lightning.

"What the kippered herring was that?" ejaculated Teal.

The Saint found his torch and turned its rays into the hollow where Perry had been lying. And the blue lightning came again. They all saw it.

And then the Saint laughed softly. "Good old Miles," he drawled.

"Electric," Teal said dazedly.

"Electrocution," said the Saint, mildly. There was a long silence. Then:

"Electrocution?"

Perry spoke huskily, staring at the hole in the ground, where the beams of three flashlights concentrated brilliantly.

"Good old Miles," said the Saint again.

He pointed to the blackened and twisted telephone, and a dark scar on the rock. And there was another silence.

Teal broke it, sleepily.

"Some fools are born lucky," he said. "Perry, what yarn did Hallin tell you to get you there?"

"Miles didn't do that . . ."

"I suppose I did." Teal tilted his torch over so that it illumined his own face. "You know me, Perry. You met me yesterday. I'm a police officer. Don't talk nonsense."

It was an incisive speech for Teal.

Perry said, in his throat, "Then—where's Moyna?"

"That's what I want to know," remarked the Saint. "We'll ask Miles. He'll be coming back to inspect the body. Shut your faces, and douse those glims!"

The lights went out one by one, and darkness and silence settled upon the group. Without a sound the Saint stepped to one side. He rested his torch on a high boulder, and kept his finger on the switch.

Then he heard Hallin.

At least, he heard the faint soft crunch of stones, a tiny rustle of leaves . . . He could see nothing. It was an eerie business, listening to that stealthy approach. But the Saint's nerves were like ice.

A match flared suddenly, only a few yards away. Hallin was searching the ground.

Then the Saint switched on his light. He caught Hallin in the beam, and left the light lying on the rock. The Saint himself stepped carefully away from it.

"Hullo," said the Saint unctuously.

Hallin stood rooted to the ground. The match burned down to his fingers and he dropped it.

Then his hand jerked round to his pocket . . .

"Rotten," said the Saint calmly, and his voice merged in the rattle of another shot.

From a little distance away two more lights sprang up from the darkness and centred upon Hallin. The man twisted round in the blaze, and fired again—three times. One of the lights went out. The other fell, and went out on the ground as the bulb broke. Hallin whipped round again. He sighted rapidly, and his bullet smashed the Saint's torch where it lay.

"Teal, did he get you?"

The Saint stepped swiftly across the blackness, and Teal's voice answered at his shoulder.

"No, but he got Mason."

The Saint's fingers touched Teal's coat, so lightly that the detective could have felt nothing. They crept down Teal's sleeve, jumped the hand, and closed upon the torch . . .

"Thanks," said the Saint. "See you later."

He jerked at the torch as he spoke, and got it away. The detective made a grab at him, but Simon slipped away with a laugh. He could hear Hallin blundering through the darkness, and he followed the noise as best he could. Behind him was another blundering noise, and a shout from Teal, but the Saint was not waiting.

Simon went on in the dark. He had eyes like a cat, anyway, and, in the circumstances, there might be peculiar dangers about a light . . . Then it occurred to him that there might be other live wires about, and he had no urge to die that way. He stopped abruptly.

At the same time he found that he could no longer hear Hallin. On his right he heard a muffled purling of water; behind him Teal was still stumbling sulphurously through the gloom, hopelessly lost. The detective must have been striking matches, but Simon could not see them. A rise of ground must have cut them off.

Warily the Saint felt around for another boulder, and switched on his torch as he had done before. The result startled him. Hallin's face showed up instantly in the glare, pale and twisted, scarcely a yard away; then Hallin's hand with the gun; beyond Hallin, the ground simply ceased . . .

"Precious," said the Saint, "I have been looking forward to this."

He hurled himself full length, in a magnificent standing tackle, his arms twined around Hallin's knees. Over his head, the automatic banged once, but the light did not go out. Then they crashed down together.

The Saint let go, and writhed up like an eel. He caught Hallin's right wrist, and smashed the hand against a stone. The gun dropped.

Simon snatched it up, scrambling to his feet as he did so, and one sweep of his arm sent the weapon spinning far out into the gulf.

The Saint laughed, standing up in the light.

"In the name of Teddy Everest," he said, "this is our party. Get up, Miles Hallin, you dog!"

8

Hallin got up.

He was shorter than the Saint by three or four inches, but twice as heavy in the bone, with tremendous arms and shoulders. And he came in like a charging buffalo.

Simon side-stepped the first rush with cool precision, and shot in a crisp left that caught Hallin between the eyes with a smack like a snapped stick, but Hallin simply turned, blinking, and came again.

The Saint whistled softly through his teeth.

He really wasn't used to people taking those punches quite so stoically. When he hit a man like that, it was usually the beginning of the end of the fight, but Hallin was pushing up his plate for a second helping as if he liked the diet. Well, maybe the light was bad, thought the Saint, and accurate timing made a lot of difference . . . And again he side-stepped, exactly as before, and felt the blow which he landed jolt right up his arm, but this time he collected a smashing drive to the ribs in return. It hurt him, but Hallin didn't seem to be hurt . . .

The Saint whistled even more softly.

So there was something in Hallin, after all. The man fought in a crouch that made scoring difficult. His arms covered his body, and he kept his chin well down in his chest; he wasn't easy . . .

The Saint circled round to get his back to the light, and for the third time Hallin rushed at him. Simon went in to meet him. His left swung over in a kind of vertical hook that stroked down Hallin's nose, and Hallin raised his arms involuntarily. Lashing into the opening, the Saint went for the body—right, left, right. He heard Hallin grunt to the thud of each blow, and he smiled.

They closed.

Simon knew what would come next. He was old in the game. He wrenched his body round, and took the upward kick of Hallin's knee on the muscles under his thigh. At the same moment he jerked Hallin's other leg from under him, and they went down together.

Hallin fought like a fiend. His strength was terrific. They rolled over and over, away out of the light of the torch, into the darkness, with Hallin's hands fumbling for the Saint's eyes . . . The Saint knew that one also. He grabbed one of Hallin's fingers, and twisted; it broke with a sharp crack, and Hallin screamed . . .

The Saint tore himself away. He was rising to one knee when his other foot seemed to slip into space. He clutched wildly, and found a hold on the roots of a bush, then Hallin caught him again. With a superhuman heave the Saint dragged himself another foot from the edge of the precipice, and then his handhold came clean out of the ground, bringing a lump of turf with it. He dashed it into Hallin's face.

They fought on the very brink of the precipice. Simon lost count of the number of blows he took, and the number he gave. In the darkness it was impossible to aim, and just as impossible to guard. One of them would get a hand free, and hit out savagely at the dark, then the other would do the same; sometimes they scored, sometimes they missed.

The rocks bruised them at every movement; once they crashed through a bush, and the twigs tore the Saint's face.

Then he landed again, a pile-driving half-arm jolt that went home, and Hallin lay still. Gasping, the Saint relaxed . . .

And at once Hallin heaved up titanically under him, and something more than a fist struck the side of the Saint's head.

If it had struck a direct blow Simon's skull would have been cracked like an eggshell, but Hallin had misjudged his mark by a fraction. The stone glanced from the Saint's temple; even so, it was like being kicked by a mule. It shook the Saint more than anything else in the whole of that mad struggle, and sent him toppling sideways with a welter of tangled lights zipping before his eyes. He felt Hallin slip from his grasp, and slithered desperately away to his left. Something went past his cheek, so close that he felt it pass, and hit the ground beyond him with a crunching thud . . .

He touched another bush, and crawled dizzily round it. On the other side he dragged himself up—first to his knees, then, shakily, to his feet. He could hear Hallin stumbling about in the blackness, searching for him, but he had to rest. Every muscle of his body ached; his head was playing a complete symphony . . .

Then he heard the bush rustle; and he had not moved.

He strained his eyes into the obscurity. The steady beam of the torch was a dozen yards away; suddenly he saw Hallin silhouetted against it. Hallin must have seen him at the same moment. The Saint ducked instantaneously, and the rock that Hallin hurled at him went over his head. Simon saw that rock also, for the fraction of a second, in the same silhouette: it was the size of a football.

Hallin came after it without a pause. Simon could see him clearly. With a gigantic effort the Saint gathered his strength and met the rush with a long straight left that packed every ounce of power he could muster. Hallin was coming in carelessly now: the blow took him squarely on the mouth and sent him flying.

The Saint stood still. As long as he could keep his position he had a precarious advantage. He saw Hallin's silhouette again, for a moment—but only for a moment. Then nothing. He realised that Hallin had also seen the point . . .

He began to edge away, with his ears alert for the slightest warning sound. And then he saw another light—the light of a match, moving through the darkness a few points from his torch. At the same time Teal's shout reached him faintly.

Without hesitation Simon plunged towards the electric torch.

Again he guessed exactly what Hallin would do—and he was right. The man had already crept round behind him—that gave the Saint a lead—but, as he ran, Simon heard the other coming up behind. A hand touched his arm, then Hallin cursed, and the Saint heard him fall.

Simon reached the light, switched it out, and swerved away. He heard Hallin running again, but the man went right past him and did not turn back.

"Where are you, Templar?"

He heard Teal's voice, closer at hand; as the Saint blundered after Hallin, his path took him towards the voice; presently he switched on his light again, and Teal himself showed up, red-faced and perspiring.

"Have you seen him?" rapped the Saint.

"No," said the detective shortly. "Didn't you kill him?"

Simon answered with the ghost of a laugh.

"Unfortunately I failed. But there's still time. He must have gone between us. Come on!"

He started off again, and Teal had to follow.

As they ran the Saint said, "This'll take us towards the road, anyway. He's sure to make for that. Where's Perry?"

"I sent him back to the car," said Teal short-windedly. "With Mason."

"Which car?"

"Hallin's."

"You sap! That's where Hallin'll be making for—"

"Perry's got his gun back."

"Oh! . . . How's Mason? Dead?"

"Don't know. Shot through the lungs. Perry carried him."

"Learn anything from Perry?"

"Not much. I didn't wait."

They went on quickly. Hallin could no longer be heard, but the Saint was certain about the road. And the road would take Hallin to something else . . .

They came out of the scrub on to level turf, where the going was easier. Down to his left the Saint saw a pair of headlights. He turned, hurrying on.

"Mind the ditch."

He lighted the detective over, and followed with a leap. As his feet touched the road he heard Perry's challenge.

"Stop where you are!"

"But this is us," said the Saint.

The car turned a little, and the headlights picked him up. In a moment the car itself swept up beside them.

"You haven't seen Miles?" demanded Simon, with one foot on the step.

"Not a sign."

"And you haven't heard anything?"

"Only you. I thought . . ."

"Damnation!" said the Saint, in his gentle way. He looked up and down the road, listening intently, but he could hear nothing. Then he swung on to the running board.

"He's sure to have struck the road somewhere," he said crisply. "Teal, hustle yourself round the other side . . . Can you put this thing along, Nigel?"

"I'll do my best."

"Off you go, then."

Teal climbed on to the step at the other side, and the car started again with a jerk, and gathered speed. As Perry changed up, Teal leaned over to be pessimistic.

"He'll see us coming a mile away if he is on the road," he said.

"I know," said the Saint savagely. "Perhaps you'd rather run."

He did not care to admit how pessimistic he himself felt. He was certain that Hallin must make for the road sooner or later, but he also knew that Teal's remark was perfectly justified. In fact, if it had been merely a question of capturing a fugitive, the Saint would have given it up forthwith. But there was another reason for the chase, and this very reason also gave it a faint chance of success. It was Perry who made the Saint speak of it.

"He told me Moyna wasn't far away," Perry said. "Have you any idea what he meant?"

"What he said," answered the Saint grimly. "He brought Moyna with him, but he didn't take her to the cottage. I don't know where he took her, but I'll bet he told you the truth. She won't be far away."

Perry said, in a strained voice, "Oughtn't we to be looking for her, instead of chasing him?"

"We're doing both at the same time," said the Saint quietly. "Wherever she is, that's where he's gone. Miles Hallin is going to have his life."

"I—I can hardly believe it, even now," said the youngster huskily. Simon's hand rested on his shoulder.

"I hope you won't see it proved," he said. "But I know that Hallin has gone to find Moyna."

Teal cleared his throat.

"He can't have got as far as this, anyway," he remarked.

"Right as usual, Claud Eustace." The Saint's voice was preternaturally calm. "He must have gone down the hill. Turn the car round, Nigel, and we'll try the other line."

Teal understood, and held his peace. Of course Hallin might easily have gone up the hill. He would have stepped off the road, and they might have passed him . . . But Perry could be spared the argument . . . And yet Teal did not know how sincerely the Saint was clinging to his hope. Simon himself did not know why he should have clung to the hope as he did, against all reason, but the faith that spurred him on was above reason. The Saint simply could not believe that the story would end—the way Teal thought it must end . . .

"This is where we started from." The Saint spoke to the lad at the wheel in tones of easy confidence. "We could stop the engine and coast down, couldn't we? Then we'd hardly make any noise . . ."

They went on with no sound but the soft rustle of the tyres. Simon did not have to mention the headlights. Those would give their approach away even more surely than the drone of the engine, but Simon would have invented any fatuous remark to save Perry's nerves.

They reached the bottom of the hill, and Teal was the first to see the police car standing by the road where they had left it. He pointed it out as Perry applied the brakes.

"He can't have come this way, either," Teal said. "If he had, he'd have taken that car."

"I wonder if he saw it," said the Saint.

He dropped off into the road, and his flashlight spilled a circle of luminance over the macadam. The circle moved about restlessly, and Teal stepped from the car and followed it.

"Looking for footprints?" inquired the detective sardonically, as he came up behind the

Saint, and at that moment the light in the Saint's hand went out.

"Blood," said the Saint, very quietly.

"That's a nasty word," murmured Teal.

"You everlasting mutt!" Simon gripped his arm fiercely. "I wasn't swearing. I was telling you something!" He turned. "Nigel, turn those headlights out!"

The detective was fumbling with a matchbox, but the Saint stopped him.

"It's all right, old dear," he drawled. "This gadget of yours is still working. I just thought we'd better go carefully. Hallin's been past here. He didn't take the car, so he can't have had much farther to go."

"But what's this about blood? Did you use a knife?"

"No," said the Saint, smiling in the darkness. "I hit him on the nose."

9

Moyna Stanford had been awake for a long time.

She had roused sickly from a deeper sleep than any she had ever known, and it had been more than half an hour before she could recall anything coherently, or even find the strength to move.

And when her memory returned—or, rather, when she had forced it to return—she was not much wiser. She remembered meeting Miles Hallin at Windsor station. He had insisted on driving her back to London, and she had been glad to accept the invitation. In Slough he had complained of an intolerable thirst; they had stopped at a hotel, and she had been persuaded to join him in an early cup of tea. Then they had returned to the car . . .

She did not know how long she had slept.

When she awoke, she was in darkness. She lay on something soft, and, when she could move, she gathered that it was a bed. She had already discovered that her wrists and ankles were securely bound . . .

Presently she had learned one or two other things. That it was night, for instance, she learned when she rolled over and saw a square of starlight in one wall; but her hands were tied behind her back, and she could not see her wrist-watch to find out what hour of the night it might be. Then she lay still, listening, but not the faintest sound broke the silence. The house was like a tomb.

She had no idea how long she lay there. She did not cry out—there would be no one to hear. And she could see no help in screaming. Later, the sound of a car passing close by told her that she was not far from a road—a country road, or there would have been more cars. There was never such a silence in London. Later still—it was impossible to keep track of time—she scrambled off the bed, and hobbled slowly and laboriously to the window. It was very dark outside; she could see nothing but a black expanse of country, in which no particular features were distinguishable, except that the horizon was ragged against the dimness of the sky, as if it were formed by a line of hills. She might have been anywhere in England. The window was open, and she stood beside it for a long while, wondering if another car would pass, and if the road would be near enough for anyone in the car to hear if she called, but no other car came. After a time she struggled back to the bed and lay down again; it was difficult and wearying for her to stand with her feet tightly lashed together, and her head was swimming all the while.

Then the drug she had been given must have put forth one final kick before it was finished with her, for she awoke again with a start, though she had no recollection of falling asleep. The sky through the window looked exactly the same: she was sure that she had only dozed.

She was shivering—she did not know why. Strangely enough, when she had first awoken she had been aware of no fear; that part of her brain seemed to have stayed sunken in sleep. But now she found herself trembling. There was a tightness about her chest, and she waited, tense with a nameless terror, hardly breathing, certain that some distinct sound had roused her.

Then the sound was repeated, and she would have cried out then, but her throat seemed paralysed.

Someone was coming up the stairs.

A faint light entered the room. It came from under the door, and traced a slow arc around half the floor. The creak of another board outside sent an icy qualm prickling up her spine; her mouth was dry, and her heart pounded thunderously . . . The next thing would be the opening of the door. She waited for that, too, in the same awful tenseness: it was like watching a card-castle after a sudden draught has caught it; she knew what must come, it was inevitable, but the suspense was more hideous than the active peril . . . The rattle of a key in the lock made her jump, as if she had been held motionless by a slender thread and the thread had been snapped by the sound . . .

Involuntarily she closed her eyes. When she opened them again Miles Hallin was re-locking the door on the inside, and the bare room was bright with the lamp that he carried.

Then he turned, putting the lamp down on a rough wooden chair, and she saw him properly. She was amazed and aghast at his appearance. His clothes were torn and shapeless and filthy; his collar had burst open, and his tie was half-way down his chest; his hair was dishevelled; his face was smeared and stained with blood.

"Are you awake?" he said.

She could not answer. He advanced slowly to the bed, peering at her.

"You are awake. I've come back. You ought to be glad to see me. I've nearly been killed."

He sat down, and put his head in his hands for a moment. Then he looked at her again.

"Killed!" His voice was rough and shaky. "One of your friends tried to kill me. That man Templar. I nearly killed him, though. I'd have done it if I'd been alone. We were on the precipice. There's a two hundred foot drop. Can you imagine it? You'd go down—and down—and down—down to the bottom—and break like a rotten apple—ugh!" He shuddered uncontrollably, "It was terrible. Have you ever thought about death, Moyna? I think it must be dreadful to die. I don't want to die!"

His hand plucked at her sleeve, and she stared at him, fascinated. His quivering terror was more horrible than anything she had ever imagined.

"I can't die!" he babbled. "Don't you know that? It's in all the newspapers. Miles Hallin—The Man Who Cannot Die! I'm big, strong—Templar couldn't kill me, and he's strong—I can't—go down—and lie still and—get cold—and never move any more. And you rot. All your flesh—rots . . . In the desert, I thought about it. D'you hear about Nigel's brother? We tossed for who was to die, and he won. And he didn't seem to mind dying. I pretended I didn't mind, either. And I walked with him a long way. And then—I hit him when he wasn't looking. I took the water—and left him. He—he died, Moyna. In the sun. And—shrivelled up. He's been dead—years. Sometimes I can see him . . ."

The girl moistened her lips. She could not move.

"Ever since then I've been dead, too. I've never been alive. You see, I couldn't tell anyone. Acting—all the time. So—I've always been alone. Never been able to tell anyone—never been with anyone who knew all about it—who—who was frightened, like I was. Until I met you. I knew you'd understand. You could share the secret. I was going—to tell you. And then Templar found out. I don't know how. Or he guessed. He sees everything—his eyes—I knew he'd try to take you away from me. So I brought you here. I'm going to—live. With you. He won't find us here. I bought this place for you—long ago. It's beautiful. I don't think anyone's ever died here. Moyna! Moyna! Moyna!"

"Yes?" Her voice was faint.

"I wish you'd speak. I was—afraid—you might be going to die. I had to drug you. You know I drugged you? I couldn't explain then—I had to bring you here, where we could be alone. Now I'll untie you."

His fingers tugged at the ropes he had put on her. Presently her hands were free, and he was fumbling with her feet, crooning like a child. She tried to master her trembling.

"Miles, you must let me go!"

"I'm letting you go," He held up the cords for her to see, "And now—we're all right. Just you and me. You'll be—nice to me—won't you, Moyna?"

His arms went round her, dragging her towards him.

"Miles," she strove to speak calmly, though she was weak with fear, "you must be sensible! You've got to get me back to London. Mother will be wondering what's happened to me . . ."

"London?" He seemed to grasp the word dully. "Why?"

"You know I can't stay here. But you can come and see me tomorrow morning . . ."

His blank eyes gazed at her.

"London? Tomorrow? I don't understand." Suddenly he seized her again. "Moyna, you wouldn't run away! You're not going to—to leave me. I can't go to London. You know I can't. I shall be killed. We've got to stay here . . ."

She was as helpless as a babe in his hands. He heard nothing more that she said.

"Moyna, I love you. I'm going to be good to you. I'm going to look after you . . . tell you . . . everything . . ."

"Miles," she sobbed, "oh, let me go . . ."

"Just . . . you and me. And we'll stay here. And we . . . won't die . . . ever. We won't die . . ."

"Oh, don't . . ."

"You mustn't be afraid. Not of me. We won't be afraid of anything. We're going to stay here . . . years . . . hundreds of years . . . thousands of years, Moyna, you mustn't be frightened. It'll be quite all right . . ."

"Take your hands off me . . ."

"But you do love me, don't you? And you're not going to leave me alone. I shan't be frightened of anything if you're here. In the dark, I can see Perry . . . sometimes. But I shan't mind . . ."

She fought back at him desperately, but against his tremendous strength she felt as weak as a kitten. She screamed aloud.

Somewhere a shout answered her. She heard a splintering crash, then someone leaping up the stairs. Another shout! "Moyna, where are you?"

She cried out again. Hallin let her go. She fell off the bed and flung herself at the door. He caught her again there. "They're coming," he said stupidly.

Then his eyes blazed. He dragged her away with a force that sent her flying across the room. In an instant he had reached her. She stared in horror at his face, pale and twisted under the smears of blood, only a few inches from her own.

"They're going to kill me," he gasped. "I'm going to die! Moyna, I'm going to die—die! . . . And I haven't lived yet. Loved you . . ."

She half rose, but he threw her down again. The strength that she had found went from her. She felt that she would faint at any moment. Her dress tore in his hands, but the sound seemed to come from an infinite distance. There was a mighty pounding on the door. "Open it. Hallin!" someone was shouting. "You can't get away!" Hallin's whole body was shaking.

"They can't kill me!" he croaked. "Moyna, you know that, don't you? I can't be killed. No one can ever kill me . . ."

"You fool!" came a voice outside. "You won't break the door down that way. Why don't you shoot the lock out?"

Hallin raised himself slowly from the bed. His eyes were like a babe's.

"Shoot out the lock," he said dreamily. "Yes . . . shoot out the lock . . ."

With her hand to her mouth Moyna Stanford watched him reel across the room. He spoke again.

"It's dreadful to die," he said.

On the landing outside, the Saint was focusing his flashlight on the door, and Teal's automatic was crowded against the keyhole.

The lock shattered inwards with a splintering crash, and Simon hurled himself forward. Inside the room he heard a heavy fall, and the door jammed half-open. Then Teal and Nigel Perry added their weight to the attack, and they went in.

"Nigel!"

The girl struggled up and stumbled, and Perry caught her in his arms.

But Teal and the Saint were looking at the man who lay on the floor, very still, with a strange serenity on his upturned face.

"He wasn't so lucky after all," said the detective stolidly. Simon shook his head.

"We never killed him," he said.

He fell on his knees beside the body, and when he stood up again his right hand was red and wet, and something lay in his palm. Teal blinked at it. It was a key.

"How did that get there?" he demanded.

"It was in the lock," said the Saint.

10

In the full panoply of silk hat, stock, black coat, flowered waistcoat, gold-mounted umbrella, white gloves, striped cashmere trousers with a razor-edged crease, white spats, and patent-leather shoes (reading from north to south), Simon Templar was a vision to dazzle the eyes, and Chief-Inspector Claud Eustace Teal, meeting the Saint in Piccadilly in this array, was visibly startled.

"Where are you going?" he asked.

"I have already been," said the Saint. "They do these things at the most ungodly hours. If you want to know, an infant has this day been received into the Holy Catholic Church. I personally sponsored the reception."

The detective was suitably impressed.

"Moreover," said the Saint, "it was christened Simon. Now I call that real handsome."

"What does Perry call it?" inquired Teal, and the Saint was shocked.

They walked a little way together in silence, and then Teal said, "The Commissioner's been waiting for an answer to his letter."

"I have meditated the idea," said the Saint. "As a matter of fact, I thought of heading down to see him this afternoon."

"What were you going to say?"

Simon's umbrella swung elegantly in his hand. He sighed.

"The idea is amusing," he murmured. "And yet I can't quite see myself running on the side of Law and Order. As you've so kindly pointed out on several occasions, dear old horseradish, my free-lance style is rather cramped now that you all know so much about me, but I'm afraid—oh, Teal, my bonny, I'm terribly afraid that yours is not the only way. I should become so hideously respectable before you finished with me. And there is another objection."

"What's that?"

The Saint removed his shining headpiece and dusted it lovingly with a large silk handkerchief.

"I could not wear a bowler hat," he said.

Teal stopped, and turned.

"Are you really going to refuse?" he asked, and Simon nodded.

"I am," he said sadly. "It would have been a hopeless failure. I should have been fired in a week anyway. Scotland House would become a bear-garden. The most weird and wonderful stories would be told in the Old Bailey. Gentlemen would write to *The Times*—Teal, I don't want to become a wet blanket. But I might want that arm again . . ."

"Templar," said the detective glumly, "that's the worst news I've heard for a long time."

"Is it?" drawled the Saint, appearing slightly puzzled. "I thought everyone knew. It's the hand I drink with."

"I mean, if you really are going on in the same old way . . ."

"Oh, that!"

The Saint smiled beatifically. He glanced at his watch.

"Let us go and have lunch," he said, "and weep over my wickedness. I'm such a picturesque villain, too." He sighed again. "Tell me, Teal, where can a policeman and a pirate lunch together in safety?"

"Anywhere you like," said Teal unhappily. Simon Templar gazed across Piccadilly Circus.

"I seem to remember a very good restaurant in the Law Courts themselves," he remarked. "I lunched there one day just after I'd murdered someone or other. It gave me a great sensation. And this, I think, is my cue to repeat the performance. Come, Archibald, and I will tell you the true story about the Bishop and the Actress."

PUBLICATION HISTORY

Like in the previous Saint books, the stories in *Featuring the Saint* originated in *The Thriller* magazine. "The Logical Adventure" appeared in issue 68, dated 24 May 1930 under the title of "Without Warning"; "The Wonderful War" was published in issue 17, dated 1 June 1929 as "The Judgement of the Joker"; and "The Man Who Could Not Die" appeared in issue 88, dated 11 October 1930, and was then called "Treachery."

The book was first published by Hodder & Stoughton in February 1931. An American edition, of sorts, appeared in November 1931 when Doubleday Crime Club published an edition entitled *Wanted for Murder* (later republished as *The Saint: Wanted for Murder* in March 1943). It collected the stories from *Featuring the Saint* and *Alias the Saint* in one volume.

Just to muddy the American bibliographic waters, when A. L. Burt and Co. published a hardback of *Wanted for Murder* in 1936, they added the stories from *The Saint and Mr Teal* and *The Saint in London.* Still with me? Good, because it gets worse.

In 1945, Jacobs Publishing brought out a volume called *Paging the Saint*, which comprised one story from *Featuring the Saint* ("The Man

Who Could Not Die") and one story from *Alias the Saint* ("The Story of a Dead Man," since you ask). And in 1956, when Avon published an edition of *Wanted for Murder*, they included two stories from *Alias the Saint* ("The Story of a Dead Man" and "The Impossible Crime") and none from *Featuring the Saint*!

But let's get back to the subject . . .

Two of the three stories in this book have been used elsewhere: "The Wonderful War" was adapted for the second season of the Roger Moore series of *The Saint* (and aired as episode 33 on 2 January 1964). The episode was directed by the show's producer, Robert S. Baker, and followed the original's plot fairly closely, though the setting changed to a fictional Middle Eastern country called Saveda (you'll find it just between Iraq and Kuwait). "The Man Who Could Not Die" was adapted by Terry Nation for the fourth season of the show and aired as episode 68 on 31 July 1965.

Foreign editions of *Featuring the Saint* weren't as plentiful as other Saint books; it seems to have been overlooked in favour of other more memorable adventures. A Czech edition entitled *A opět Svatý* was published by Volesky in 1937; a Spanish version, *Protagonista el Santo*, was published by Ediciones G.P. in 1961; and Garzanti brought out an Italian translation, *Protagonista il Santo*, in 1970.

French publisher Fayard also opted to pick and choose from the stories available, including "The Wonderful War" in the 1945 volume *Le Saint s'en va-t-en guerre* and "The Logical Adventure" and "The Man Who Could Not Die" in the 1947 collection *La marque du Saint*.

The most recent reprint was an April 1980 paperback edition published by Charter, which neglected to include "The Man Who Could Not Die."

ABOUT THE AUTHOR

I'm mad enough to believe in romance. And I'm sick and tired of this age—tired of the miserable little mildewed things that people racked their brains about, and wrote books about, and called life. I wanted something more elementary and honest—battle, murder, sudden death, with plenty of good beer and damsels in distress, and a complete callousness about blipping the ungodly over the beezer. It mayn't be life as we know it, but it ought to be.

—Leslie Charteris in a 1935 BBC radio interview

Leslie Charteris was born Leslie Charles Bowyer-Yin in Singapore on 12 May 1907.

He was the son of a Chinese doctor and his English wife, who'd met in London a few years earlier. Young Leslie found friends hard to come by in colonial Singapore. The English children had been told not to play with Eurasians, and the Chinese children had been told not to play with Europeans. Leslie was caught in between and took refuge in reading.

"I read a great many good books and enjoyed them because nobody had told me that they were classics. I also read a great many bad books which nobody told me not to read . . . I read a great many popular scientific articles and acquired from them an astonishing amount of general knowledge before I discovered that this acquisition was supposed to be a chore."[1]

One of his favourite things to read was a magazine called *Chums.* "The Best and Brightest Paper for Boys" (if you believe the adverts) was a monthly paper full of swashbuckling adventure stories aimed at boys, encouraging them to be honourable and moral and perhaps even "upright citizens with furled umbrellas."[2] Undoubtedly these types of stories would influence his later work.

When his parents split up shortly after the end of World War I, Charteris accompanied his mother and brother back to England, where he was sent to Rossall School in Fleetwood, Lancashire. Rossall was then a very stereotypical English public school, and it struggled to cope with this multilingual mixed-race boy just into his teens who'd already seen more of the world than many of his peers would see in their lifetimes. He was an outsider.

He left Rossall in 1924. Keen to pursue a creative career, he decided to study art in Paris—after all, that was where the great artists went—but soon found that the life of a literally starving artist didn't appeal. He continued writing, firing off speculative stories to magazines, and it was the sale of a short story to *Windsor Magazine* that saved him from penury.

He returned to London in 1925, as his parents—particularly his father—wanted him to become a lawyer, and he was sent to study law at Cambridge University. In the mid-1920s, Cambridge was full of Bright Young Things—aristocrats and bohemians somewhat typified in the Evelyn Waugh novel *Vile Bodies*—and again the mixed-race Bowyer-Yin found that he didn't fit in. He was an outsider who preferred to make his own way in the world and wasn't one of the privileged upper class. It didn't help that he found his studies boring and decided it was more fun contemplating ways to circumvent the law. This inspired him to write a novel, and when publishers Ward Lock & Co. offered him a three-book deal on the strength of it, he abandoned his studies to pursue a writing career.

When his father learnt of this, he was not impressed, as he considered writers to be "rogues and vagabonds." Charteris would later recall that "I wanted to be a writer, he wanted me to become a lawyer. I was stubborn, he said I would end up in the gutter. So I left home. Later on, when I had a little success, we were reconciled by letter, but I never saw him again."[3]

X Esquire, his first novel, appeared in April 1927. The lead character, X Esquire, is a mysterious hero, hunting down and killing the businessmen trying to wipe out Britain by distributing quantities of free poisoned cigarettes. His second novel, *The White Rider*, was published the following spring, and in one memorable scene shows the hero chasing after his damsel in distress, only for him to overtake the villains, leap into their car . . . and promptly faint.

These two plot highlights may go some way to explaining Charteris's comment on *Meet—the Tiger!*, published in September 1928, that "it was only the third book I'd written, and the best, I would say, for it was that the first two were even worse."[4]

Twenty-one-year-old authors are naturally self-critical. Despite reasonably good reviews, the Saint didn't set the world on fire, and Charteris moved on to a new hero for his next book. This was *The Bandit*, an adventure story featuring Ramon Francisco De Castilla y Espronceda Manrique, published in the summer of 1929 after its serialisation in the *Empire News*, a now long-forgotten Sunday newspaper. But sales of *The Bandit* were less than impressive, and Charteris began to question his choice of career. It was all very well writing—but if nobody wants to read what you write, what's the point?

"I had to succeed, because before me loomed the only alternative, the dreadful penalty of failure . . . the routine office hours, the five-day week . . . the lethal assimilation into the ranks of honest, hard-working, conformist, God-fearing pillars of the community."[5]

However his fortunes—and the Saint's—were about to change. In late 1928, Leslie had met Monty Haydon, a London-based editor who was looking for writers to pen stories for his new paper, *The Thriller*—"The Paper with a Thousand Thrills." Charteris later recalled that "he said he was starting a new magazine, had read one of my books and would like some stories from me. I couldn't have been more grateful, both from the point of view of vanity and finance!"[6]

The paper launched in early 1929, and Leslie's first work, "The Story of a Dead Man," featuring Jimmy Traill, appeared in issue 4 (published on 2 March 1929). That was followed just over a month later with "The Secret of Beacon Inn," starring Rameses "Pip" Smith. At the same time, Leslie finished writing another non-Saint novel, *Daredevil*, which would be published in late 1929. Storm Arden was the hero; more notably, the book saw the first introduction of a Scotland Yard inspector by the name of Claud Eustace Teal.

The Saint returned in the thirteenth issue of *The Thriller*. The byline proclaimed that the tale was "A Thrilling Complete Story of the Underworld"; the title was "The Five Kings," and it actually featured Four Kings and a Joker. Simon Templar, of course, was the Joker.

Charteris spent the rest of 1929 telling the adventures of the Five Kings in five subsequent *The Thriller* stories. "It was very hard work, for the pay was lousy, but Monty Haydon was a brilliant and stimulating editor, full of ideas. While he didn't actually help shape the Saint as a character, he did suggest story lines. He would take me out to lunch and say, 'What are you going to write about next?' I'd often say I was damned if I knew. And Monty would say, 'Well, I was reading something the other day . . .' He had a fund of ideas and we would talk them over, and then I would go away and write a story. He was a great creative editor."[7]

Charteris would have one more attempt at writing about a hero other than Simon Templar, in three novelettes published in *The Thriller* in early 1930, but he swiftly returned to the Saint. This was partly due to his self-confessed laziness—he wanted to write more stories for *The Thriller* and other magazines, and creating a new hero for every story was hard work—but mainly due to feedback from Monty Haydon. It seemed people wanted to read more adventures of the Saint . . .

Charteris would contribute over forty stories to *The Thriller* throughout the 1930s. Shortly after their debut, he persuaded publisher Hodder & Stoughton that if he collected some of these stories and rewrote them a little, they could publish them as a Saint book. *Enter the Saint* was first published in August 1930, and the reaction was good enough for the publishers to bring out another collection. And another . . .

Of the twenty Saint books published in the 1930s, almost all have their origins in those magazine stories.

Why was the Saint so popular throughout the decade? Aside from the charm and ability of Charteris's storytelling, the stories, particularly those published in the first half of the '30s, are full of energy and joie de vivre. With economic depression rampant throughout the period, the public at large seemed to want some escapism.

And Simon Templar's appeal was wide-ranging: he wasn't an upper-class hero like so many of the period. With no obvious background and no attachment to the Old School Tie, no friends in high places who could provide a get-out-of-jail-free card, the Saint was uniquely classless. Not unlike his creator.

Throughout Leslie's formative years, his heritage had been an issue. In his early days in Singapore, during his time at school, at Cambridge University or even just in everyday life, he couldn't avoid the fact that for many people his mixed parentage was a problem. He would later tell a story of how he was chased up the road by a stick-waving typical

English gent who took offence to his daughter being escorted around town by a foreigner.

Like the Saint, he was an outsider. And although he had spent a significant portion of his formative years in England, he couldn't settle.

As a young boy he had read of an America "peopled largely by Indians, and characters in fringed buckskin jackets who fought nobly against them. I spent a great deal of time day-dreaming about a visit to this prodigious and exciting country."[8]

It was time to realise this wish. Charteris and his first wife, Pauline, whom he'd met in London when they were both teenagers and married in 1931, set sail for the States in late 1932; the Saint had already made his debut in America courtesy of the publisher Doubleday. Charteris and his wife found a New York still experiencing the tail end of Prohibition, and times were tough at first. Despite sales to *The American Magazine* and others, it wasn't until a chance meeting with writer turned Hollywood executive Bartlett McCormack in their favourite speakeasy that Charteris's career stepped up a gear.

Soon Charteris was in Hollywood, working on what would become the 1933 movie *Midnight Club*. However, Hollywood's treatment of writers wasn't to Charteris's taste, and he began to yearn for home. Within a few months, he returned to the UK and began writing more Saint stories for Monty Haydon and Bill McElroy.

He also rewrote a story he'd sketched out whilst in the States, a version of which had been published in *The American Magazine* in September 1934. This new novel, *The Saint in New York*, published in 1935, was a significant advance for the Saint and Leslie Charteris. Gone were the high jinks and the badinage. The youthful exuberance evident in the Saint's early adventures had evolved into something a little darker, a little more hard-boiled. It was the next stage in development for the author and his creation, and readers loved it. It became a bestseller on both sides of the Atlantic.

Having spent his formative years in places as far apart as Singapore and England, with substantial travel in between, it should be no surprise that Leslie had a serious case of wanderlust. With a bestseller under his belt, he now had the means to see more of the world.

Nineteen thirty-six found him in Tenerife, researching another Saint adventure alongside translating the biography of Juan Belmonte, a well-known Spanish matador. Estranged for several months, Leslie and Pauline divorced in 1937. The following year, Leslie married an American, Barbara Meyer, who'd accompanied him to Tenerife. In early 1938, Charteris and his new bride set off in a trailer of his own design and spent eighteen months travelling round America and Canada.

The Saint in New York had reminded Hollywood of Charteris's talents, and film rights to the novel were sold prior to publication in 1935. Although the proposed 1935 film production was rejected by the Hays Office for its violent content, RKO's eventual 1938 production persuaded Charteris to try his luck once more in Hollywood.

New opportunities had opened up, and throughout the 1940s the Saint appeared not only in books and movies but in a newspaper strip, a comic-book series, and on radio.

Anyone wishing to adapt the character in any medium found a stern taskmaster in Charteris. He was never completely satisfied, nor was he shy of showing his displeasure. He did, however, ensure that copyright in any Saint adventure belonged to him, even if scripted by another writer—a contractual obligation that he was to insist on throughout his career.

Charteris was soon spread thin, overseeing movies, comics, newspapers, and radio versions of his creation, and this, along with his self-proclaimed laziness, meant that Saint books were becoming fewer and further between. However, he still enjoyed his creation: in 1941 he indulged himself in a spot of fun by playing the Saint—complete with monocle and moustache—in a photo story in *Life* magazine.

In July 1944, he started collaborating under a pseudonym on Sherlock Holmes radio scripts, subsequently writing more adventures for Holmes than Conan Doyle. Not all his ventures were successful—a screenplay he was hired to write for Deanna Durbin, "Lady on a Train," took him a year and ultimately bore little resemblance to the finished film. In the mid-1940s, Charteris successfully sued RKO Pictures for unfair competition after they launched a new series of films starring George Sanders as a debonair crime fighter known as the Falcon. But he kept faith with his original character, and the Saint novels continued to adapt to the times. The transatlantic Saint evolved into something of a private operator, working for the mysterious Hamilton and becoming, not unlike his creator, a world traveller, finding that adventure would seek him out.

"I have never been able to see why a fictional character should not grow up, mature, and develop, the same as anyone else. The same, if you like, as his biographer. The only adequate reason is that—so far as I know—no other fictional character in modern times has survived a sufficient number of years for these changes to be clearly observable. I must confess that a lot of my own selfish pleasure in the Saint has been in watching him grow up."[9]

Charteris maintained his love of travel and was soon to be found sailing round the West Indies with his good friend Gregory Peck. His forays abroad gave him even more material, and he began to write true-crime articles, as well as an occasional column in *Gourmet* magazine.

By the early '50s, Charteris himself was feeling strained. He'd divorced his second wife in 1943 and got together with a New York radio and nightclub singer called Betty Bryant Borst, whom he married in late 1943. That relationship had fallen apart acrimoniously towards the end of the decade, and he roamed the globe restlessly, rarely in one place for longer than a couple of months. He continued to maintain a firm grip on the exploitation of the Saint in various media but was writing little himself. The Saint had become an industry, and Charteris couldn't keep up. He began thinking seriously about an early retirement.

Then in 1951 he met a young actress called Audrey Long when they became next-door neighbours in Hollywood. Within a year they had married, a union that was to last the rest of Leslie's life.

He attacked life with a new vitality. They travelled—Nassau was a favoured escape spot—and he wrote. He struck an agreement with *The New York Herald Tribune* for a Saint comic strip, which would appear daily and be written by Charteris himself. The strip ran for thirteen years, with Charteris sending in his handwritten story lines from wherever he happened to be, relying on mail services around the world to continue the Saint's adventures. New Saint books began to appear, and Charteris reached a height of productivity not seen since his days as a struggling author trying to establish himself. As Leslie and Audrey travelled, so did the Saint, visiting locations just after his creator had been there.

By 1953 the Saint had already enjoyed twenty-five years of success, and *The Saint Detective Magazine* was launched. Charteris had become adept at exploiting his creation to the full, mixing new stories with repackaged older stories, sometimes rewritten, sometimes mixed up in "new" anthologies, sometimes adapted from radio scripts previously written by other writers.

Charteris had been approached several times over the years for television rights in the Saint and had expended much time and effort during the 1950s trying to get the Saint on TV, even going so far as to write sample scripts himself, but it wasn't to be. He finally agreed a deal in autumn 1961 with English film producers Robert S. Baker and Monty Berman. The first episode of *The Saint* television series, starring Roger Moore, went into production in June 1962. The series was an immediate success, though Charteris himself had his reservations. It reached second place in the ratings, but he commented that "in that distinction it was topped by wrestling, which only suggested to me that the competition may not have been so hot; but producers are generally cast in a less modest mould." He resented the implication that the TV series had finally made a success of the Saint after twenty-five years of literary obscurity.

As long as the series lasted, Charteris was not shy about voicing his criticisms both in public and in a constant stream of memos to the producers. "Regular followers of the Saint saga . . . must have noticed that I am almost incapable of simply writing a story and shutting up."[10] Nor was he shy about exploiting this new market by agreeing to a series of tie-in novelisations ghosted by other writers, which he would then rewrite before publication.

Charteris mellowed as the series developed and found elements to praise too. He developed a close friendship with producer Robert S. Baker, which would last until Charteris's death.

In the early '60s, on one of their frequent trips to England, Leslie and Audrey bought a house in Surrey, which became their permanent base. He explored the possibility of a Saint musical and began writing some of it himself.

Charteris no longer needed to work. Now in his sixties, he supervised the Saint from a distance whilst continuing to travel and indulge himself. He and Audrey made seasonal excursions to Ireland and the south of France, where they had residences. He began to write poetry and devised a new universal sign language, Paleneo, based on notes and symbols he used in his diaries. Once Paleneo was released, he decided enough was enough and announced, again, his retirement. This time he meant it.

The Saint continued regardless—there was a long-running Swedish comic strip, and new novels with other writers doing the bulk of the work were complemented in the 1970s with Bob Baker's revival of the TV series, *Return of the Saint*.

Ill-health began to take its toll. By the early 1980s, although he continued a healthy correspondence with the outside world, Charteris felt unable to keep up with the collaborative Saint books and pulled the plug on them.

To entertain himself, Leslie took to "trying to beat the bookies in predicting the relative speed of horses," a hobby which resulted in several of his local betting shops refusing to take "predictions" from him, as he was too successful for their liking.

He still received requests to publish his work abroad but had become completely cynical about further attempts to revive the Saint. A new Saint magazine only lasted three issues, and two TV productions—*The Saint in Manhattan*, with Tom Selleck look-alike Andrew Clarke, and *The Saint*, with Simon Dutton—left him bitterly disappointed. "I fully expect this series to lay eggs everywhere . . . the only satisfaction I have is in looking at my bank balance."[11]

In the early 1990s, Hollywood producers Robert Evans and William J. Macdonald approached him and made a deal for the Saint to return to cinema screens. Charteris still took great care of the Saint's reputation and wrote an outline entitled *The Return of the Saint* in which an older Saint would meet the son he didn't know he had.

Much of his time in his last few years was taken up with the movie. Several scripts were submitted to him—each moving further and further away from his original concept—but the screenwriter from 1940s Hollywood was thoroughly disheartened by the Hollywood of the '90s: "There is still no plot, no real story, no characterisations, no personal interaction, nothing but endless frantic violence . . ." Besides, with producer Bill Macdonald hitting the headlines for the most un-Saintly reasons, he was to add, "How can Bill Macdonald concentrate on my Saint movie when he has Sharon Stone in his bed?"

The Crime Writers' Association of Great Britain presented Leslie with a Lifetime Achievement award in 1992 in a special ceremony at the

House of Lords. Never one for associations and awards, and although visibly unwell, Leslie accepted the award with grace and humour ("I am now only waiting to be carbon-dated," he joked). He suffered a slight stroke in his final weeks, which did not prevent him from dining out locally with family and friends, before he finally passed away at the age of 85 on 15 April 1993.

His death severed one of the final links with the classic thriller genre of the 1930s and 1940s, but he left behind a legacy of nearly one hundred books, countless short stories, and TV, film, radio, and comic-strip adaptations of his work which will endure for generations to come.

> *I was always sure that there was a solid place in escape literature for a rambunctious adventurer such as I dreamed up in my youth, who really believed in the old-fashioned romantic ideals and was prepared to lay everything on the line to bring them to life. A joyous exuberance that could not find its fulfilment in pinball machines and pot. I had what may now seem a mad desire to spread the belief that there were worse, and wickeder, nut cases than Don Quixote.*
>
> *Even now, half a century later, when I should be old enough to know better, I still cling to that belief. That there will always be a public for the old-style hero, who had a clear idea of justice, and a more than technical approach to love, and the ability to have some fun with his crusades.*[12]

---

1 *A Letter from the Saint*, 30 August 1946

2 "The Last Word," *The First Saint Omnibus*, Doubleday Crime Club, 1939

3 *The Straits Times*, 29 June 1958, page 9

4 Introduction by Charteris to the September 1980 paperback reprint of *Meet—the Tiger!* (Charter), the last ever print edition.
5 *The Saint: A Complete History*, by Burl Barer (McFarland, 1993)
6 PR material from the 1970s series *Return of the Saint*
7 From "Return of the Saint: Comprehensive Information" issued to help publicise the 1970s TV show
8 *A Letter from the Saint*, 26 July 1946
9 Introduction to "The Million Pound Day," in *The First Saint Omnibus*
10 *A Letter from the Saint*, 12 April 1946
11 Letter from LC to sometime Saint collaborator Peter Bloxsom, 2 August 1989
12 Introduction by Charteris to the September 1980 paperback reprint of *Meet—the Tiger!* (Charter).

WATCH FOR THE SIGN OF THE SAINT!

THE SAINT CLUB

And so, my friends, dear bookworms, most noble fellow drinkers, frustrated burglars, affronted policemen, upright citizens with furled umbrellas and secret buccaneering dreams that seems to be very nearly all for now. It has been nice having you with us, and we hope you will come again, not once, but many times.

Only because of our great love for you, we would like to take this parting opportunity of mentioning one small matter which we have very much at heart . . .

—*Leslie Charteris,* The First Saint Omnibus *(1939)*

Leslie Charteris founded The Saint Club in 1936 with the aim of providing a constructive fanbase for Saint devotees. Before the War, it donated profits to a London hospital where, for several years, a Saint ward was maintained. With the nationalisation of hospitals, profits were, for many years, donated to the Arbour Youth Centre in Stepney, London.

In the twenty-first century, we've carried on this tradition but have also donated to the Red Cross and a number of different children's charities.

The club acts as a focal point for anyone interested in the adventures of Leslie Charteris and the work of Simon Templar, and offers merchandise that includes DVDs of the old TV series and various Saint-related publications, through to its own exclusive range of notepaper, pin badges, and polo shirts. All profits are donated to charity. The club also maintains two popular websites and supports many more Saint-related sites.

After Leslie Charteris's death, the club recruited three new vice-presidents—Roger Moore, Ian Ogilvy, and Simon Dutton have all pledged their support, whilst Audrey and Patricia Charteris have been retained as Saints-in-Chief. But some things do not change, for the back of the membership card still mischievously proclaims that . . .

> *The bearer of this card is probably a person of hideous antecedents and low moral character, and upon apprehension for any cause should be immediately released in order to save other prisoners from contamination.*

To join . . .

Membership costs £3.50 (or US$7) per year, or £30 (US$60) for life. Find us online at www.lesliecharteris.com for full details.

Made in the USA
Columbia, SC
23 November 2022

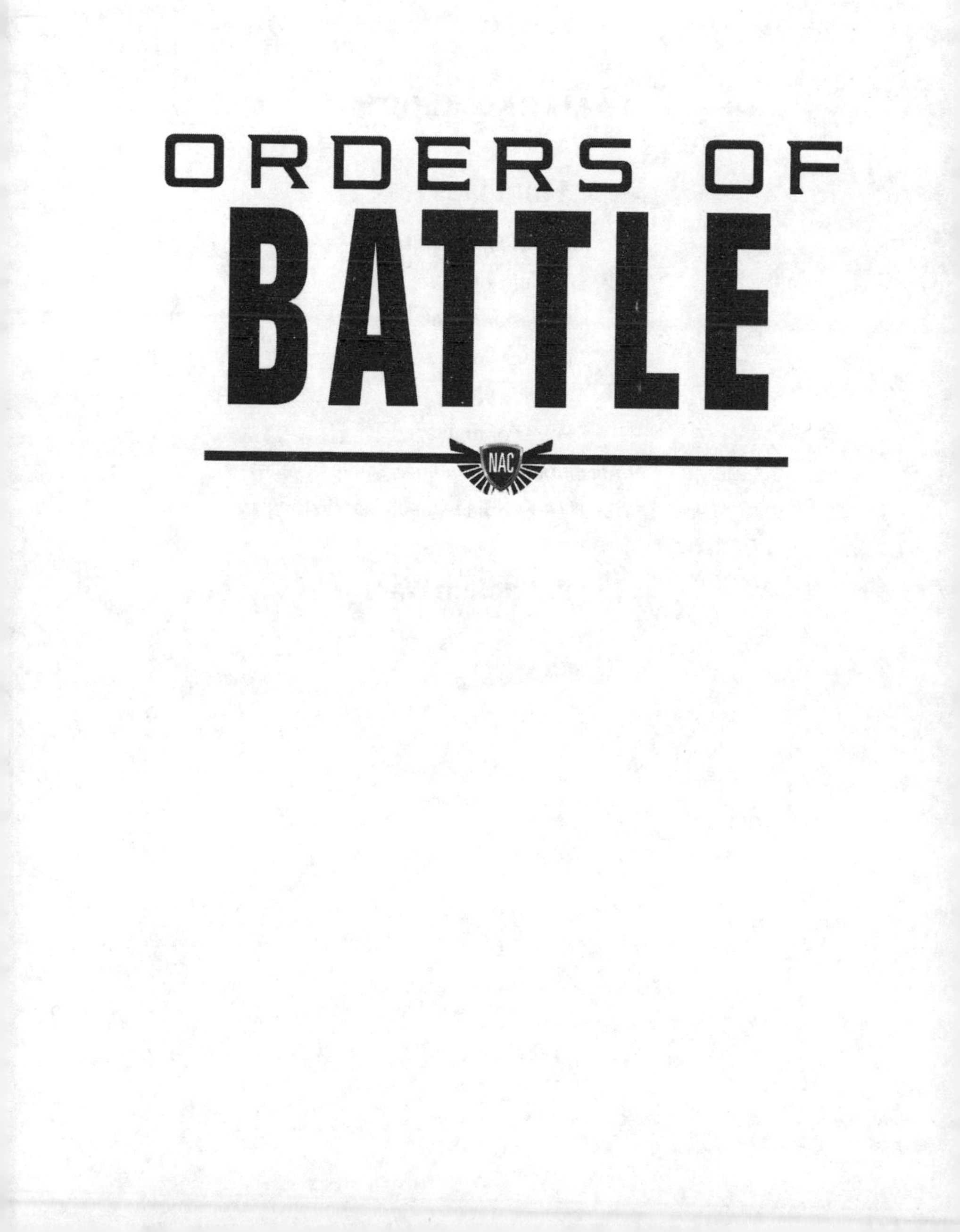
ORDERS OF
BATTLE
NAC

BY MARKO KLOOS

Frontlines

Terms of Enlistment

Lines of Departure

Angles of Attack

Chains of Command

Fields of Fire

Points of Impact

Measures of Absolution (A Frontlines Kindle novella)

"Lucky Thirteen" (A Frontlines Kindle short story)

The Palladium Wars

Aftershocks

Ballistic

ORDERS OF BATTLE

MARKO KLOOS

Published by 47North, Seattle

www.apub.com

ISBN-13: 9781542019583
ISBN-10: 1542019583

Cover design by Mike Heath | Magnus Creative

Printed in the United States of America

For Quinn, who is kind, which is the best way to be.
I love you.

CHAPTER 1

FAREWELLS

The sky above the cemetery is blue, and sunlight is streaming through the red and orange leaves on the trees. Autumn was always her favorite season, so it seems right and fitting that her funeral is today, joining her forever to the place and time she loved most. It's the middle of October, and we had our first frost a week ago. Even though the sun is out, it doesn't have the power anymore to temper the chill of the morning, and I am glad for my civilian jacket and its high-tech layers of thermal insulation. We stand by the grave and listen to the priest deliver the eulogy. When he says the words of the final prayer, I mouth them with him, even though I don't believe them anymore. But she did, and they gave her comfort when she was in bad places in her life, so I go along because this is for her and not for me.

When the priest has finished the ceremony, it's time to say good-bye for good, even though I know the woman we are laying to rest is already gone, reduced to a scoop of ashes in a little stainless steel capsule. We look on as the priest puts the capsule into the cylindrical tube where it will remain for as long as the next of kin have ledger balances to pay for the yearly maintenance fee. Even a proper grave is a 'burber luxury. In the Public Residence Clusters, you get a capsule only if there are relatives who file the request with the death certificate. Even then, the ashes are disposed of and the capsule recycled after a year to make space for someone else. Out here in Liberty Falls, remembrance has no time limit as long as someone pays the bill every year.

This is the measure of a life, I think. A tube in the ground to hold her capsule, and a little polymer plaque to mark the spot, ten centimeters high and twenty wide. It's a tiny piece of real estate, but it will be hers until I am no longer around, and I know she wouldn't care about what happens to her ashes when nobody is left to remember who she was. But for now, it's there, stark white with golden letters, and the little patch of ground it marks is more than most people with her background get to call their own, in death or before.

PHOEBE GRAYSON, it simply says. **OCTOBER 3, 2067–OCTOBER 13, 2120.**

My mother died just ten days after her fifty-third birthday. She never got to beat the average, not even the modest one for a welfare citizen. Out in the 'burbs, the average life expectancy is almost a hundred. In the PRCs, it's sixty-seven. We've managed to colonize planets a hundred light-years away, using starships that harness the energy of their own miniature suns, but we haven't managed to eradicate cancer because nobody prioritizes funding to fight a disease that mostly afflicts the population of the PRCs.

I take some comfort in knowing that Mom would have died half a decade earlier if she hadn't been out here in Liberty Falls, and that she got to spend that extra time in clean air with access to middle-class health care. She lived most of her life on someone else's terms, but the last ten years were hers alone. I'm glad she got to spend them in a place like this. Next to me, Halley leans her head against my shoulder, and I wrap an arm around her and pull her closer, drawing comfort from her presence. A dozen people have gathered this morning to say their farewells.

Chief Kopka is here, along with a handful of friends Mom made in her last decade. I accept their condolences and thank them for coming.

"You still have a place down here when you're on leave," the chief says. "Nothing changes, as far as I am concerned."

"Thank you," I say. "For everything you did for her."

"She earned her keep," the chief replies. "Several times over. Don't ever think I just took her in as a charity case. She never wanted to have anything handed to her again."

"I still owe you. For taking her on in the first place. Letting me get her out of the PRC."

"You don't owe me anything," Chief Kopka says. "Not a damn thing. None of us down here can pay back what we owe you. I know a lot of these 'burbers make the proper mouth noises when they see someone in a Commonwealth Defense Corps uniform these days. But they don't know what it's like. I damn well do. So I don't want to hear about what you think you owe. All right?"

"All right," I say. "But let me be grateful anyway. In her stead."

"How are you feeling?" Halley asks when the other funeral guests have left, and we are the only two people standing in front of the burial plot. I think about my reply for a moment.

"Diminished," I say. "I got most of the grief out the night she died. Now I just feel smaller. Like my world has shrunk down to only you and me."

Halley rests her head on my shoulder. We look at the rows and rows of nameplates on the ground, each of them marking two hundred square centimeters. Once upon a time, Earth had enough empty space for people to bury their dead as they were, whole bodies in wooden coffins. But this is the twenty-second century, the world has a hundred billion people living on it, and cremation is mandatory even in a middle-class place out in the mountains. The cemetery is divided into rows of little plots, each holding fifty burial capsules in the area where they would have buried a single person a hundred years ago.

Mom's space is almost dead center in the middle of the plot, a temporary last entry in the rows of names. Half the plot is still empty, and I know it will be a while before they fill it up—a few months, maybe a year. Out here, people live longer lives, and the town is almost insignificantly tiny compared to a PRC. In death, she will have neighbors all around her again, just like when she lived in the welfare unit. But the sky overhead will be blue more often, and there are live trees just a few dozen meters away, their leaves rustling in the cool October wind.

Halley kneels down in front of the rows of names. She runs her hand over Mom's nameplate, tracing the letters with her fingertips.

"I'll miss her," she says. "I was family to her. Sorry my parents couldn't be the same to you. I'll never forgive them for that."

"Don't worry about it. I don't."

Halley slowly shakes her head. "Your mother didn't have anything. Didn't come from anywhere special. Didn't know anyone important. She would have been a nobody to them. But she was nice to me from the moment we first met. And they have the gall to think of themselves as better."

"Don't get angry over that. Not today," I say.

Halley stands up again and sticks her hands into the side pockets of her thermal vest. "I've never stopped being angry over that, Andrew," she says. "My world shrank down to just you and me the last time we walked out of their house."

She lets out a slow breath, then kisses me on the cheek. "You're right. This isn't the time. Sorry."

I'd said my last good-bye in person, right before Mom died, when she could still see and hear me through the fog of pain meds. It seems pointless to repeat the sentiment to a grave marker and a cylinder full of ashes. Whoever she was in life is gone now, the molecules that made up her body dispersed in the atmosphere and returned to the cosmos, to be reused in the constant cycle of life. Her consciousness is gone, and there's nothing in that little stainless tube that can hear or understand me. But it would feel callous to walk away without a final gesture, so I kneel in front of the plot and duplicate what Halley did, running my hand over the nameplate, feeling the edges of the engraved letters with my thumb.

"See you among the stars," I say. "I love you."

The cemetery is on the outskirts of town, three kilometers from the chief's place. Halley and I walk back instead of summoning a ride. We've both served mostly on spaceships for the last twelve years, and we take advantage of our unlimited access to fresh air and long walks whenever we are on leave down here.

"I'm glad she got to have a few years in peace," I say when we approach the transit station on our way back into town. "Without the threat of the Lankies hanging over her head every day."

"Four years of peace," Halley says. "If you don't count the stragglers we keep killing on Mars."

"On my last rotation, I saw *three* Lankies," I say. "In six *months*. In the beginning, we saw more than that in a single patrol. Used to be we'd come back to the barn with the missile launcher empty and nothing left in the drop ship's ammo cassettes. Now we go weeks without firing a shot."

"That's good, though. Means we've wiped most of them out."

"Maybe. Or they've learned to avoid us. Those tunnels go deep."

"Not a single Lanky ship in the solar system in four years," Halley says. "I want to believe we got almost all of them. And that the few who are left are hiding in terror."

"I hope they feel fear," I reply. "But I've never seen one hesitate or run away."

We're crossing the green in front of the transit station, and the grass is covered with red and brown leaves from the surrounding trees. Unbidden, a memory bubbles up in my brain—my mother and I, walking this same path eight years ago, just a short while after I had gotten her out of the PRC with the chief's help. There had been snow on the ground back then, and she had marveled at the clean and unspoiled layer of white on the grass. I thought I had come to terms with her death by now, but the memory makes the grief surge in my chest, gripping my heart and twisting it firmly. In a few weeks, we'll have the first snowfall of the season in the mountains, and she will not be here to see it.

I walk over to one of the nearby trees and touch the trunk to feel the rough bark under my palm just like she did when she first saw this place. It's a luxury that the middle-class people out here take for granted, but the welfare rats in the PRC can live their entire lives without once being able to touch a living tree. Halley pauses a few steps behind me and watches as I run my hand over the trunk.

"The chief said that nothing changes," I say. "But I'm not sure that's true."

"You don't want to come back here anymore now that she's gone?" Halley asks.

I turn to look at her. All around us, Liberty Falls is going about its comfortable 'burber business, oblivious of the sudden rift in my personal universe.

"I don't know. I mean, I *like* it here. We've been coming down here on leave for years. But I don't know if I can keep going back to the chief's place. Everything there is going to remind me of her."

I walk toward Halley and listen to the sound of the leaves crunching under the soles of my boots, something that nobody ever hears on a starship or in the middle of a welfare city.

"And I know that the chief won't mind if we keep using his place for free. But I feel like we'd overstay our welcome if we did. He doesn't owe us shelter and food until we retire. Even if it's only a few weeks every year."

Halley blinks into the midday sun and shrugs.

"So what's next? Do we find a new place? Or do we spend every leave from now on in some shitty RecFac? Because I have no interest in going down to San Antonio and hanging out with my folks."

"I don't know," I repeat. "I just feel out of balance right now. Ask me again when our next leave comes up."

"We don't have to decide anything. Not anytime soon. Especially not today," Halley says.

We walk down Main Street and toward Chief Kopka's restaurant, where we spend our time on leave in the little upstairs guest apartment the chief keeps available for us. With our civilian clothes, we no longer stick out on the street among the 'burbers. After four years without a Lanky ship in the solar system, we no longer have to be in uniform when we're off duty, and we don't have to carry weapons and light armor with us. At first, the feeling of going unarmed was so disconcerting that I carried my contraband M17 pistol under my civilian clothes for a while, but at some point in the last year or two, I started to leave it behind in my locker. It shouldn't feel strange to be able to walk around without a weapon, but I'm still not used to it, not after so many years of constant life on the edge of annihilation.

"Four days of family leave, and two of them are eaten up by travel," Halley says. "How very generous of the Corps."

"We're just lucky we weren't on deployment," I reply. "Takes the better part of a week to get home from Mars."

"When are you going back to Podhead University?" she asks.

"Transport to Keflavík leaves at 2030 tomorrow from Falmouth. I figure I can take the train down at 1600 and be there with time to spare. What about you?"

Halley waves her hand dismissively.

"I can hop on a ride at Burlington anytime between now and tomorrow evening. The squadron isn't due for deployment for another six months. It's all just training and maintenance right now. I'm not sure I'll ever get used to having a full pilot roster and all the drop ships I need."

"I know what you mean. I request new gear, I get it right away. It's weird."

"We're turning into a peacetime military," Halley says. "Not that I'm complaining. Haven't had to write a next-of-kin letter in a good while."

I still have a hard time thinking of ourselves as senior officers, as people who have to write official condolence letters. When we joined the military, the majors and lieutenant colonels were old to our eyes. Now we both wear the oak leaves of field-grade officers. For a short while, I managed to catch up to my wife in rank when they promoted me to major last year, but then Halley made lieutenant colonel and got her own drop-ship squadron. In the old Corps, it took at least sixteen years of service to become a light colonel, but the senior officer shortage and her exceptional service record meant that she got fast-tracked into the rank after only twelve years. At her current trajectory, she'll probably be a full colonel in another five years and a general in ten. True to form, she's not excited about that prospect because it will take her out of the cockpit for good.

"That leaves us with a little more than a day," Halley says. "What do you want to do?"

I think about her question. When we are on leave, we usually eat at the chief's place and spend time in our little guest apartment, but tonight it wouldn't feel right to carry on with that routine as if nothing had changed.

"Let's go out," I tell her.

"Out where? You got a place in mind?"

"Out of town. Away from people. We can pack one of the flexible shelters and take some food along. Go out into the mountains somewhere. Maybe that trail across the river we hiked last spring. The nights aren't that cold yet."

"Just you and me and the squirrels," Halley says. "Let's do it. Let's freeze our butts off and eat cold sandwiches under the stars. We'll be cooped up in a spaceship again soon enough."

She takes my hand and gives it a firm squeeze. My grief is still raw, and I know that I will be mourning for a long time, but as we walk down the street in the autumn sunshine side by side, the world that had felt askew this morning has righted itself again just a little.

CHAPTER 2

BETWEEN WORLDS

I don't ever delude myself into thinking that Liberty Falls is the real world. Reality is what I can see out of the window of my train compartment as the maglev glides east at three hundred kilometers per hour, slicing through neighborhoods that get denser and more cluttered the closer the train gets to the Greater Boston metroplex. This is the real world, welfare clusters with residence towers that reach half a kilometer into the sky, tens of thousands of little apartment boxes stacked on top of each other to get as many people into as small a footprint as possible. This was our life before I joined the Corps and got Mom out of the PRC.

But even that world has gotten measurably better in the last few years. The improvements are small but visible. The trains are cleaner and better maintained, and the neighborhoods we pass have fewer dilapidated and burned-out blocks among them. There aren't as many security locks in the transit stations, and I don't see a quarter of the police presence that used to be out before the PRCs caught fire and the Lankies showed up in orbit one day. Whatever we were before the Lanky war started, the threat we survived has served to realign priorities in the North American Commonwealth. For the first time in my life, I'm feeling that the majority of us are pulling on the same end of the rope for a change. The cities are still no paradise, but at least they're no longer the front lobby of hell.

I'm in uniform again, as required by the regulations for travel from and to a duty station. On our stop at Boston's South Station, the compartment fills up to the last seat, and a young man takes the spot right across from me. He nods respectfully, and I return the gesture before looking out of the window again. The uniform gets more attention now than it did before, when soldiers were mere curiosities, relics of an abstract profession that did unknowable things out in the colonies between the stars. After the Lanky incursion, everyone knows what we do and why we are here.

"Are you in the Fleet, sir?" he finally asks after glancing at my uniform for a few minutes without wanting to be obvious about it.

"Yes, I am," I reply.

"Oh, I thought you were. I've just never seen anyone with a red beret like yours."

I look at the scarlet beret that's tucked underneath the epaulette on my left shoulder.

"You won't see too many of those," I say. "It's a combat controller beret. There are maybe a hundred and fifty in the whole Fleet."

"What do you do? I mean, if you don't mind my asking. Unless it's a secret."

"Combat controllers land on enemy planets with the advance force. We call down air support and mark targets for the strike fighters, that sort of thing."

"Have you been in battle?" the kid asks. I can tell he's practically humming with barely suppressed interest. I look at him and try to figure out his origin and social status. His teeth are white and straight, and he is dressed well, so he's a 'burber out on the town. He looks like he's about eighteen or nineteen, well fed and healthy.

"I have," I say. "I've been doing this for twelve years. Since the start of the Lanky war. I think I was around for all the big fights."

"Like Mars?" he asks.

"I was there. Not a fun time, though. None of them were."

"I can imagine," he says.

Like hell you can, kid, I think.

"What . . . what's it like? Out there, I mean. Fighting those things."

I look at his earnest face, and suddenly I feel very old, even though I probably only have fifteen years on this kid. Whenever I talk to well-meaning civilians about the things that go on in war, it feels like I am communicating through a translator that never quite gets the words right. How do I tell him what it feels like to stand on the surface of another planet and see a group of twenty-meter creatures approaching your firing line, and how the weapon in your hand suddenly feels pointless and feeble? How do I wrap in words what goes through your head when you have to descend into a pitch-black tunnel to flush out monsters that can crush you into bloody paste with the swing of an arm? I may only have a decade and a half on him, but the things I've seen and done in that time are so alien to his own life experience that it's almost like we are separate species at this point. He lacks a frame of reference to put the things I could tell him into a context that would make sense.

"It's scary," I tell him instead, even though the word is entirely inadequate. But it's a word that he expects, an emotion that he can parse, so he nods knowingly.

"I put in an application with the recruiting station," he says. "I want to be on a starship. Be a weapons tech or something. But my friend says they'll put you in whatever job they think you're best for. He says I'll probably end up in the infantry because they always need people there. That I should just withdraw the paperwork while I can."

"The grunt life is hard on people. Even if it's just four years."

We ride in silence for a while. My stop is the next one on the line, so when the system announces that we're approaching Falmouth station, I get up to gather my bag and head for the door at the end of the train car.

"Any words of advice?" the kid says when I open the door of our compartment. "I mean, in case they accept me."

I know that as a Commonwealth Defense Corps officer, I should be supportive of willing new recruits, encourage them to join up and fill the ranks, present a positive image of the service. I am proud of all I have done while wearing this uniform, and I am not ashamed of the Corps in the least. But I can't bring myself to serve up some rah-rah bullshit to this fresh-faced kid, who doesn't know what it's like to have to wake up with nightmares about monstrous things in deep, dark places almost every night. He doesn't know what he's volunteering to take on, the years of cumulative trauma that will fracture his body and mind, and he doesn't know that he'll never be able to put himself together quite right no matter how hard he tries.

"Listen to your friend," I say. "He sounds like a very smart guy."

My transport is a regular supply flight to Keflavík. I sit in the back in one of the sling seats along the side of the hull, sharing the cargo hold with ten other CDC troopers and several tons of supply pallets strapped to the floor. The cargo bird is cramped and noisy, but I've been a grunt for so long that I can snatch a nap anywhere and anytime, so I prop my head against the ballistic lining of the hull and drift off for most of the three-hour flight.

I wake up when we start our descent. Unlike a military spacefaring drop ship, the atmospheric craft have windows in the cargo hold, and the early-morning sun over the ocean is painting the sky outside in diffused shades of purple and orange.

Even after four months here, the view from above hasn't gotten old. It's a clear morning over Iceland, and the rocky coastline appears below us like the shore of a distant colony moon. Joint Base Keflavík has become a busy spot in the last few years. Our flight is one of several inbound craft, all lined up like pearls on a string in the airspace above the shore, position lights blinking. A few dozen kilometers to the northeast, the skyline of Reykjavík stands outlined against the mountains. At just under a million people, the city holds three-quarters of the Icelandic population, but it's still a very quaint place compared to the metroplexes of the NAC or the big continental European cities. Iceland is mostly volcanic rock and ice, which makes it the closest thing we have on Earth to the environment of the typical upstart colony out in space, and it's situated in the North Atlantic, halfway between the NAC and the Euros. All of those factors combined make it the ideal spot for the new International Special Tactics School, where I've been a part of the NAC special operations team that's teaching our allies how to fight off-world.

The school is so new that the logistics and transport chain is still a provisional patchwork. The complex is located on the other end of the island, but the drop ships can't land there directly because the base is small and has no facilities for heavy transports yet. That means I have to disembark at Keflavík base, check in with the military transfer desk, and catch one of the old tilt-rotor craft they use for ferrying people around locally. By the time the sergeant at the transfer desk has found me an outbound flight and sent me on my way to the ISTS, I've spent more time on the ground in Keflavík than I did on the flight from Falmouth. When the ancient, noisy tilt-rotor airplane finally descends onto the short gravel runway at the ISTS base, my back hurts from sitting in uncomfortable sling seats for hours, and I am glad to step out of the bone shaker and onto the Icelandic soil.

If Liberty Falls isn't the real world, Iceland isn't exactly it, either. Almost everyone here lives in Reykjavík and a handful of smaller cities by the coast, and there are some towns and villages dotting the landscape. But most of the island is gravel and glaciers, uncluttered by people or settlements. The ISTS base is a cluster of low-slung prefabricated buildings halfway down the coastline of a narrow fjord, intentionally built with modular colonial architecture and ringed by only the barest minimum of security measures. The closest town is a fishing village at the end of the fjord, ten kilometers to the west of the base, but there's nothing but gravel and puffins in between, and no reason for anyone to even venture close. The only reminder that we are still among civilians on Earth is the occasional fishing boat making its way down the fjord toward the ocean or back home to the pier. It's every bit as unnatural an environment to me as the relaxed tranquility of Liberty Falls. Most people never get to live in a place this empty and unspoiled.

I make my way from the landing strip to the main building cluster. The gravel under my feet crunches with every step, and the air is cold and clean. Soon we will see the first snow of the season, and then this place will look a lot like New Svalbard for a few months.

It's lunchtime, and as I cross the base, I have to return salutes from soldiers who are passing me on the way to the chow hall. The ISTS trains soldiers from allied nations in the ways of special space warfare, and the uniforms here are a diverse mix of various digital camouflage patterns: German, British, French, Norwegian, Dutch, Italian. Of the twenty-nine Eurocorps countries, only half a dozen have militaries big enough for Spaceborne Infantry operations. It will take another half decade until the Euros have the gear and the training to operate their own independent off-world combat units. Until then, we show them the ropes and integrate them into our joint NAC operations. But the biggest contribution the Euros are making isn't their man power, it's their money. It let us rebuild our fleet and staff our ranks after being on the ropes against the Lankies for so long. It's a good trade, and I am happy to help bring the Euros up to speed on the finer points of fighting in space in exchange for having new gear and a full personnel roster.

"Good afternoon, sir," the corporal on duty says when I walk into the company office.

"Good afternoon, Corporal Keene. Where's the company sergeant?"

"Master Sergeant Leach is out on the range with the rest of the training flight, sir."

"Range day, huh? What are they shooting?"

Corporal Keene checks the duty roster on the screen in front of him. "Uh, rifles and sidearms, sir."

"Is that the only thing on the schedule today?" I ask.

"Yes, sir. The master sergeant scheduled a ten-klick hump in armor this morning. I'm pretty sure he's planning on having everyone march back from the range when they're done. He didn't pass down a request for vehicles except for the medical mule at the range."

I nod and check my in-box for hard-copy missives. There's a small stack waiting for me, and I pull everything out and organize the stack on the countertop.

"Coffee, sir?" Corporal Keene asks as I walk off toward my office.

"Affirmative," I say. "Unless it's Fleet swill."

"No, sir. It's the Italian stuff. From real beans."

"Then most definitely affirmative," I reply. "No creamer, just black."

"Aye, sir."

I walk into my office and put the stack of hard-copy printouts down on the desk. With every promotion, my offices have grown more spacious, and the base on Iceland is more plushly appointed than any of the NAC bases on the continent. The room is almost as large as the welfare apartment I shared with my mother in the Boston PRC, and the furniture is high-quality resin laminate from Scandinavia, stark white and functional. From my window, I can see the shoreline and the fjord beyond. Overhead, the departing tilt-rotor transport disrupts the tranquil scene momentarily as it takes off from the landing strip and ascends into the cloudy sky with the sharp drone of turboprop engines at full throttle. I watch it disappear in the low cloud ceiling and listen to the sound it trails until the droning hum fades away.

Corporal Keene walks into my office and puts a coffee mug down on my desk next to the stack of papers.

"Thank you, Corporal," I say. He nods and turns to get back to the company office. His Fleet fatigues are starched and pressed, and the sleeves are rolled very precisely and without a visible crease or wrinkle. The last time I rolled sleeves to that level of precision, I was in Basic Training, and it took a good five minutes per sleeve. It's a point of pride among special operations soldiers to show off just how far above the cut they are, and the extra effort of rolling a perfectly crisp sleeve seems to have come back into fashion among the younger, untested troops. For the second time today, I feel very old.

I take a sip of my coffee. It's dark and rich, with the kind of intense flavor you can only get by roasting actual coffee beans and grinding them up into powder. Before the Euros joined their resources to ours out of necessity, the Fleet rarely had the means to spend on real coffee for the rank and file. Since then, the quality of the food has increased every year, and now the chow in the international bases and ships is even better than it was in the boot-camp mess hall when I joined up twelve years ago, back when the availability of real food was a major recruiting incentive to PRC kids brought up on soy and cheap carbohydrates.

The status screen on the wall across from my desk shows the current duty schedule and the disposition and medical status of every instructor and trainee in the company. The school has five different training companies, each specialized in a particular aspect of spaceborne special operations. My company is the combat controller and forward observer school where the Euros learn how to call down orbital strikes and close air support against Lankies. All my instructors are senior sergeants or company-grade officers with golden drop badges and combat experience. As the years since Mars have gone by, it has become more difficult to find suitable teachers. The senior NCOs have started to take retirement, and many of the officers who commanded platoons and companies in battle have been promoted into staff officer slots and pulled out of the field.

I study the board while I drink my coffee. Most of the status cells are green. Only a few red data fields indicate an unavailable instructor or sick or injured student.

This is my life now. I am a staff officer, and until I retire, I am almost certainly destined to fly a desk and look at personnel strengths and assignments. I'll be holding a cup of coffee far more often than a rifle or a pistol. This is what Halley and I pictured as our ideal permanent careers when we got through Basic Training—a few years of excitement and danger, and then an easy life in a shore-duty billet until retirement.

But when you've been in the podhead business for so many years, sometimes you just want to break a sweat and pull a trigger.

"Corporal Keene," I call through the open door into the adjoining company office.

The front desk corporal appears in the doorway a moment later. "Sir?"

"Did the armory sergeant go up to the range with the flight this morning?"

"Yes, sir. He did. But he left Corporal Lopez in charge of the armory."

I put my half-finished coffee down on the desk and get out of my chair.

"Good. Because I think I'm going to check out my rifle and join the rest of the company at the range. If anyone comes looking for me, let them know that I'll be out in the field for the day."

"Aye, sir," Corporal Keene replies. "Do you need me to have the vehicle pool send over a mule to drive you up there?"

"Negative," I say. "I've been sitting on my ass long enough these last few days. I'm going to get into my armor and run up there on foot. It's only ten klicks."

"Yes, sir," Corporal Keene says with just a hint of surprise on his face. Few troops choose to run twenty K in armor unless they are under orders or they have comrades to impress, no matter how tightly they roll the sleeves of their fatigues. But this afternoon, I want to move my legs and smell some caseless propellant, just as a reminder that I'm still a soldier and not a glorified personnel clerk. The data fields will be waiting for me when I get back from the range.

CHAPTER 3

SWEAT AND BULLETS

The path from the base to the live-fire range is a winding trail that hugs the topographic lines of the surrounding hills and mountains. The range is ten kilometers to the southwest, nestled in a valley with a steep hill as a solid backstop. We routinely use the range as a convenient halfway point for speed marches, and the trail is well defined after a year and a half of platoons and companies in battle armor treading it several times a week.

Unlike the PACS exoskeletons, regular battle armor doesn't have a performance-boosting power assist. To save battery energy, the little servos in the armor only compensate for the added weight of the gear. I still have to do all the marching and running myself, and the hillsides here on the east coast of Iceland are steeper than they look from a distance. Five kilometers into my speed march, I am aching and sweaty, but I find that I enjoy the honest exertion. I'm all by myself, working my way along the flank of a hill, the ocean a steel-gray expanse to my left, sea blending with the gray skies far in the distance. The wind is cold and clean and strong enough to buffet me on occasion, even as I am weighed down with twenty kilos of armor and a seven-kilo rifle.

It feels odd to be out here all alone. It's so quiet and empty that it seems like I have the whole planet to myself for a while. The last time I went to a church was with my mother when I was in my early teens, before she gave up on trying to drag me along. Sometimes we just briefly stopped by, outside of service hours, because Mom wanted to light a candle for someone or duck in for a quick prayer. Even to a bored kid, there was an undeniable majestic gravitas to the huge, empty cathedral and its silent stone-vaulted ceiling. This landscape feels a lot like that cathedral did, with the dome of the storm-gray sky above my head and the silence that almost seems to have a weight of its own. Seabirds are soaring in the breeze coming from the ocean, and out on the water, the wind is whipping the tops of the waves into white froth. Mom sometimes argued that everyone worships in some way. I always disputed that notion when she was alive, but as I make my way across the hills and valleys here on this unspoiled island, I realize that maybe I had missed her point all along, and it gives me a pang of regret to know that I'll never be able to tell her she was right after all. I feel a sense of restoration and inner peace when I am out here by myself or hiking in the Vermont mountains with Halley. If Mom got the same feeling in a church, then this is my own version of that, a place where I can be reflective, in awe at the knowledge that I'm in the presence of something greater than myself, something enduring and universal. Maybe we all really do attend church in our own way, whether we believe in gods or not.

I can hear the gunfire on the range long before I round the last hill. The staccato thunderclaps of supersonic muzzle reports echo back from the surrounding mountains. The propellant in the new rifles has a peculiar sound, a hoarse cough rather than a sharp boom. From what I have heard, the R&D teams calibrated the new caseless ammo to be low in flash and report, to minimize the sensor disruptions when it's fired in underground environments.

I walk down the hill and onto the range, past the flags that mark a live-fire environment. My company NCO, Master Sergeant Leach, is standing behind the firing line with his arms folded, observing the proceedings. The range has half a dozen live-fire pits. Each of them has a Eurocorps student and an NAC instructor in it, and more Eurocorps troops are lined up in the safe zone behind each pit, waiting for their turns.

I stay behind the safety line until the course of fire has ended. When the pits change students, Master Sergeant Leach turns around to shout instructions at those in line, then walks back to where I am standing.

"Good afternoon, sir," he says. "I didn't know you were going to join us."

"I didn't know either until I got in, two hours ago," I reply. "Wasn't in the mood for sitting on my ass. Not after that ride from Keflavík."

"Understood, sir. I see you brought your boomstick."

"Don't tell me you were just about to call a cold range and pack it up. I'd hate to have dragged this thing all the way out here for nothing."

"No, sir. We still have an hour left to go."

"How are they doing?" I say with a nod at the waiting lines of trainees. Master Sergeant Leach follows my gaze.

"They're quite all right. I mean, it's clear that some of the Euro countries spend more time at the range than others. But the baseline is pretty good. The Germans and the Brits especially. They'd still get their clocks cleaned by an SI line company, though. Never mind a podhead team."

We watch as the students in the pits get their weapons ready under the watchful eyes of their instructors. All the Eurocorps trainees are noncommissioned officers with lots of special operations training, and the lowest-ranking ones are still at least corporals with two years of service. But when I look down the line at the trainees who are waiting with their helmets under their arms, they all look impossibly young to me, and I voice the thought to the master sergeant.

"Tell me about it," he says. "Buncha fucking kids. They got good training, mind. But none of them have combat experience. The most senior ones? They joined the year after Mars."

"Shit," I say, and the sergeant grins without humor.

The wind coming from the sea carries the smell of the ocean water, unadulterated by the pollution of a city, a scent so clean and inoffensive that I'd have a hard time describing it to a PRC kid who has never lived in unspoiled air. Overhead, a few seabirds are circling in the breeze, seemingly unperturbed by the ruckus of the gunshots.

"How many years have you been in, Leach? Eleven?"

"Twelve," he says.

"No shit. Same as me? You went to Basic in '08?"

Leach nods. "San Diego."

"I went to Orem," I say. "January '08."

"Then you have three months on me, sir."

"I'm shocked they haven't made you an officer, too. Damn few of the pre-war crowd left."

"Oh, they tried," Master Sergeant Leach says. "Several times. But I wasn't dumb enough to let them. No offense, Major."

"None taken. And you're smarter than I was. Those stars, they come with all kinds of baggage. Plenty of days I wish I'd remained an NCO."

"Some of us have to do it," Leach says. "And I'm glad when it's someone who knows the business. But I'm still happy it's you and not me."

He nods at the rifle that's slung across my chest.

"You want me to slot you into the firing line, sir? We brought plenty of ammo along."

"Well," I say. "I didn't bring that for decoration, I guess."

I fill my magazine pouches at the ammo station and step into my assigned firing pit. The new weapon I am carrying is something I wish we had been issued just before Mars, because it's a game-changing piece of hardware. Over the years, the weapons R&D teams back home came up with the M-80, then the M-90, and finally the M-95, each with an increase in caliber to maximize the amount of explosive gas in the projectiles. Then our people and the Eurocorps weapon designers compared notes and figured out what worked, and what could be made to work even better. The result is the rifle I am now charging with its first ten-round disposable ammunition cassette. It's the JMB, the Joint Modular Battle Rifle, which spent about ten minutes in active service before it received its nickname: Jumbo. For the first time, the spacefaring services of the NAC and the Eurocorps carry the same gun and use the same kind of ammunition, greatly simplifying logistics and training.

Jumbo is a mean piece of hardware, and all the troops love it. Where the old M-95 basically fired giant hypodermic needles filled with explosive gas, the JMB shoots a very fast high-density armor-piercing projectile that has an explosive charge behind it. The new rounds are half the size of the old ones. Now we carry twice the rounds into combat we could take along for the M-95, and the new rifles can fire both single shots and automatic bursts. To keep the recoil from knocking troops on their asses, the engineers built in a dampening system that runs on hydraulic buffer tubes and—from what I can tell—a whole lot of Black Forest magic. To an infantry grunt, it feels like having a personal autocannon.

"Ready on the firing line," the range safety officer announces when I've loaded the rifle and indicated my readiness. Up ahead, the range is a thousand-meter expanse of loosely packed soil, seeded with concealed targets that will appear according to the program the RSO has loaded into the system.

The first target pops up eight hundred meters ahead and begins moving toward me at typical Lanky walking speed. With the helmet-mounted sight, it's not a big challenge to put rounds on target. It's sized to approximate a Lanky's torso, ten meters by three, but at this range even a silhouette of that size isn't very large. The rifle is paired to my armor's targeting computer, using the ballistic information from the aiming laser and combining it with the data from the environment—temperature, air pressure, windspeed. I place the aiming reticle over the middle of the target and select single-fire mode. Then I squeeze the trigger.

The rifle barks its hoarse muzzle blast and sends a ten-millimeter slug streaking downrange at twelve hundred meters per second. The shot hits the Lanky target near the middle of its mass. I quickly send two more rounds after the first. Every time a round hits, I can see the puff of the explosive charge as it turns a ten-millimeter hole into a head-sized one. The target drops from sight, the computer satisfied that the cumulative hits have done the job.

Three more targets appear halfway down the range at three hundred meters. They pop up one after the other, with a two-second delay between them, and advance toward me. I put two rounds into each, using the same sequence in which they appeared, left to right. The Jumbo chugs out the contents of its magazine, *boom-boom-boom*, and the Lanky targets drop one by one. The last one wobbles a bit, as if the final round to hit it merely glanced off the top. My ammo counter shows one round left in the weapon, and I adjust my aim and fire it right into the center of the remaining target. It drops with a satisfying *clang* that I can hear all the way back to the firing line after a second and a half. Then the three targets are all in the dirt, and I eject the empty ammo cassette and replace it with a full one from my ammo pouch.

For the next few minutes, the computer serves up a variety of targets at different distances. Some advance toward me, some move in an oblique line, others stand still or move away. With the targeting computer and the magnification of my helmet-mounted sight, I don't miss a single one. The armor doesn't have automatic aiming servos like the PACS suits do, so the weapon can't fully aim itself, but the corrective booster servos in my arm-joint links adjust my aim a little with every shot; this compensates for my small movements and those of the weapon under recoil. I use up my second magazine, then my third, putting Lanky targets into the dust one by one.

When I insert my last full cassette, my helmet display flickers and turns itself off. The reticle projection in front of my right eye winks out of existence.

"Simulated suit malfunction," the RSO says into my ear over the range safety comms channel. "Switch to iron sights and engage manually."

The Jumbo doesn't have its own sighting optics because it uses the sensors in the shooter's battle armor for targeting. If the armor fails, the only way to aim the rifle is with a set of backup sights on the top receiver. I push the lever that releases the sights, and they pop up out of their storage position with a snap. Then I bring the gun up to my shoulder to aim through the sights, like a rifleman from the pre-electronics age.

The next target appears at five hundred meters. Without the corrective aim of the optical sight projection, I have to account for the distance myself, but the caseless ten-millimeter rounds are so fast that the heavy armor-piercing explosive projectiles don't drop very much even at this range. I put the tip of the trapezoid front sight in the center of the Lanky target and squeeze the trigger twice. One hits low and barely clips the bottom of the target, but the other smacks into the top half of the polymer silhouette and sends it crashing down into the dirt. Then two more targets pop up, much closer than the last. One is a hundred meters out and rapidly advancing. The other is less than thirty meters away, and its size makes it look like it's right on top of me. I suppress a momentary surge of instinctive panic and flick the rifle's selector switch to burst-fire mode. The closer target is the bigger threat, and I hammer it with a three-round burst that tears bits and pieces off the gel-filled polymer silhouette. It seems to teeter on the edge of falling down, so I follow it up with another three-round burst, aimed high near the head to give the silhouette the added momentum it needs to fall over. When it drops, there's a cloud of dust that momentarily obscures my field of vision. I bring the rifle to the left a little, take a bead on the advancing Lanky silhouette that is now less than thirty meters away, and fire the last three rounds in one rapid burst. Even in fully automatic fire, the Jumbo barely moves. It's intoxicating to be able to dish out this much kinetic energy and explosive power without the punishment from the savage recoil the old M-series anti-Lanky rifles inflicted when fired with live ammunition. The simulator ranges with their holographic targets are useful for staying in practice in the confined space of a warship, and it's certainly safer and more economical to shoot virtual rounds at holograms. But nothing beats the sensation of sending live ammo downrange and punching big holes into actual things.

When the course of fire ends, my helmet display comes back to life and tallies up my score. With my fifty rounds, I have killed seventeen Lankies, scoring a 91 percent effective hit rate. On the battlefield, a single soldier mowing down seventeen Lankies with nothing but a rifle and a basic combat load of ammo would get so buried in medals that they'd never again be able to put on a dress-uniform blouse without the help of two strong attendants and a forklift. This isn't real life, of course, but it's still enormously confidence building to know that even our personal weapons are now powerful enough to reliably let a single trooper stop a rush from multiple Lankies.

"Not terrible," Master Sergeant Leach says when I step back behind the safety line and show the RSO the open action of my rifle to let him verify its unloaded status.

"That gun makes it easy," I say. "Where was this stuff when we were hand-cranking rounds into the chambers one by one?"

"The tech is nice. But it won't keep them from shitting their pants and fumbling their reloads the first time there's half a dozen pissed-off Lankies rushing their position."

Behind Sergeant Leach, some of the trainees have watched my performance, and I can tell by their nods and low conversations that I haven't made a total fool out of myself in the firing pit.

"If you were trying to show off, it's working," the sergeant says.

"Hardly," I say. "They're just glad the Old Man still remembers which end of the rifle the bullets come out of."

I watch the rest of the range exercise with Sergeant Leach as the afternoon wears on. One after another, the trainees collect their allotted live ammo and take their turns in the firing pits. The RSO keeps changing up courses of fire for every round. Whenever he chooses a scenario where the Lanky targets pop up almost right in front of the pits, I get a strange, uncomfortable feeling in my stomach. The targets are only rough silhouettes of Lanky torsos, but the polymer they use for the outer layer looks disturbingly like real Lanky skin, and at short range, the effect triggers some of my dormant battle stress. I've seen too many Lankies at close range, and every time I have, people died in horrific and violent ways right beside me. I read in a book once that the howling of wolves is a racial memory to us, that it used to cause fear and discomfort in ancient humans even if they had never seen a wolf before. Wolves have been all but extinct on Earth for decades, and the sound of their howling isn't disturbing to me. But I know that from now until I die, the sight of that eggshell-colored Lanky skin will be my personal specter, the memory that keeps me close to the campfire at night.

When we are done at the range, I join the company for their speed march back to the base, voluntarily tacking two hours and a lot of sweat onto my workday. We did these sorts of marches all the time back in every podhead school I've attended over the years. A march goes quicker when the reward of a hot meal and a long shower is waiting at the end of the hump, and it gives extra motivation and dopamine on the way back. We march along the path that snakes through the majestic barren landscape, and I listen as the master sergeant makes the section leaders call out cadence and sing marching songs in their respective languages. The singing and laughter echoes from the hills and down the valleys as we make our way back to base, and it's the most enjoyable thing I have done in weeks. It feels strange to admit it to myself, but despite all the bullshit that comes with life in the service, all the chunks the war has taken out of my soul over the years, I have missed this feeling of belonging and purpose. As the trainees sweat and huff and banter on the trail back down to the little cluster of ISTS buildings that's huddled on the shore of the fjord like a little island of light in the late-afternoon dusk, I realize that it may be the only reason why I am still wearing the uniform.

CHAPTER 4

A FLY-BY OFFER

Of all the duty stations I've ever had, Iceland is hands down the best, at least as far as conventional soldier metrics go. I only break a sweat when I choose to do so. The chow on the base is excellent, the landscape is breathtaking, and the MilNet connection is superfast, with enough bandwidth to do video calls with Halley anytime I want. The commanding officer of the school is a lieutenant colonel I know back from my busy podhead days in the Fleet, and he runs his shop without superfluous bullshit. We are in the middle of the North Atlantic, far removed from the rest of Special Operations Command and the rest of the Corps establishment, so we don't have to waste much time on putting on appearances for the high-level brass or the civilian oversight committees. As far as billets go, it's the cushiest one imaginable for someone of my rank and job specialty.

I know that I don't have a right to feel any discontent. There are plenty of my friends and comrades resting in the soil of far-off colonies or scattered in space who never got the chance to make it this far. And I know that I've expended enough sweat and blood over the years for this privilege. But deep down, I feel a sense of unease, as if the universe is setting me up, that it's raising my comfort level and expectations just so I can fall so much harder whenever everything gets yanked out from underneath me again. So I try to treat the billet as the temporary reprieve I suspect it to be. I run five kilometers every morning, and sometimes in the evening as well. I make it a point to join the company for as much of the hard stuff out in the field as I can get away with. And with typical grunt paranoia, I wait for the other shoe to drop, just so it can't take me by surprise.

I keep my office door open most of the time, so nobody has to knock when they want to come in. Naturally, they all do it anyway, rapping their knuckles on the doorframe instead of the door. I look up when I hear the company sergeant's typical double-tap pattern.

"Sir, we're going to get a visit from command. I just got word from Norfolk."

I look at the calendar next to the personnel roster on the wall. Four uneventful months have passed since my mother's funeral.

"What does the brass want here in the middle of freaking February? Graduation's still a month and a half off."

"That's above my pay grade, sir. I'm just conveying the happy news."

I sit back in my chair and look at the world outside. It has been snowing since midnight, and the flurries are obscuring my view of the fjord. From the patterns of the swirls that are whipping the ground, I'm guessing the winds to be at twenty knots. The outside temperature display shows three degrees below zero, cold but not unseasonable. Iceland is surprisingly temperate in the winter, sitting as it does in the middle of the Gulf Stream currents.

"Did they say who it is?"

"It's SOCOM Actual, sir," Leach replies.

"Terrific," I say. "When is he coming in?"

The master sergeant checks his watch.

"In thirty-seven minutes, sir. The bird is already on the way. They only let me know once his transfer flight from the continent was already on the ground in Keflavík."

"A surprise visit," I say. "In this sort of weather. They'll have a fun time on the final approach. I wonder what he wants out here."

Master Sergeant Leach shrugs.

"Like I said, sir. That's above my pay grade."

I check the schedule and see that the combat controller trainees are in the Dunker, an underwater vehicle-escape simulator set up in a deep indoor pool. It takes a lot of time to configure the machinery and get everyone into the safety gear that's needed for the exercise, and there are always two medics in scuba gear present in case a trainee loses their shit while hanging upside down in the fake drop-ship hull and has to be extracted to keep from drowning. Calling them all back in for a dog-and-pony presentation for the CO of the NACDC Special Operations Command would mess up the training session and throw the schedule into disarray.

"If they didn't send any instructions along, we're going to go ahead with business as usual," I say. "They want the red carpet, they'll need to give us more than thirty minutes' advance warning."

"I don't think the general is much of a red-carpet type anyway," Master Sergeant Leach says.

"You got that right," I reply, and a cloud descends on my mood when I think about the man who's about to grace us with his compact and sour-faced presence. I get out of my chair and walk over to the door, where my cold-weather coat is hanging on a hook.

"Well," I say. "Let me go and greet our special visitor. I'll wait for him out by the landing pad."

The tilt-rotor craft descends out of the swirling snow and settles onto the landing pad in a fresh gust of frigid air that stings my face with a hundred little needles. I'm out on the apron of the little airfield by myself, because I know that the man I am meeting doesn't give the slightest shit about pomp and circumstance.

Brigadier General Khaled Masoud is a stocky, muscular man with a haggard face that makes him look ten years older than I know him to be. He steps off the tail ramp of the tilt-rotor bird in just his fatigues, without a winter coat. The floppy side of his SEAL beret is drawn so low over the side of his forehead that it almost covers his right eye. He has grown a short beard since the last time I saw him, and his close-cropped stubble is streaked with gray. He walks over to me and returns my salute, then shakes my hand.

"Major Grayson," he says, his voice raised over the sound of the nearby engines. "Good to see you again."

I merely nod instead of voicing the same sentiment in return because it would be a lie. After Leonidas, where I lost a quarter of my company due to Masoud's deception of the garrison, I had vowed to frag the little bastard the first time the opportunity arose. Over time, my feelings have mellowed, but not very much. I am not willing to serve a life sentence for the satisfaction anymore, but I still avoid him whenever I can, and I won't feel any sadness at the news of his death once that day comes. To me, he is the embodiment of both the very best and worst of our profession—exceptional at his job, but willing to burn down entire planets to see it through, with ethics relegated to the notion of a luxury for gentler times.

"Let's get out of this weather," I say, unwilling to ask him why he's here and why he didn't bother to give notice. I know that he'll tell me soon enough. "My office or the mess?"

"Let's do the mess," General Masoud says, to my mild surprise. "I hear the chow here is great. I want to put it to the test."

"Aye, sir," I reply. "This way."

Whatever brought the general to this island halfway between continents, he doesn't seem to be in a hurry to share it, and I am in no hurry to find out. We get our food and claim a table in the officers' mess, a small and comfortably appointed room with floor-to-ceiling windows that would offer a great view of the fjord in the distance if we weren't in the middle of a snow squall right now.

It's three in the afternoon, and we have the whole mess to ourselves because the handful of other officers at the base are all in their offices or leading training sessions right now. The room is quiet except for the occasional clanking of dishes and silverware from the kitchen on the other side of the food counter. My own meal consists of meat loaf and mashed potatoes. The meat is vat grown, but it's real, not some flavored soy imitation. Right now, this sort of food is still reserved for the well to do and the people the government considers the most deserving. I know that we only get it as a perk, to keep morale and retention rates high. But I've stopped letting that knowledge spoil my enjoyment.

"No shark," General Masoud says as we begin our meal.

"Sir?" I ask.

"That Icelandic specialty," he replies. "Basking shark. There wasn't any at the chow buffet. I was hoping they'd have some."

"You don't want to try that for lunch," I say. "That's more of a dare. They ferment it for a few months to get rid of all the toxins. They don't serve it in the chow hall because of the smell. And nobody but the locals would eat it anyway."

"Pity," he says. "I wanted to take them up on the dare."

"If you really want some, you can get it at the civvie terminal at Keflavík. There are stores that sell it. But I have to warn you. It smells like a gym sock that's been soaked in old piss for a month. If you get any, don't open it on the transport home, or the crew chief will throw you out of the back of his ship."

General Masoud takes a bite of the food on his plate. It's a roasted potato and sausage dish, with onions and peppers and lots of real cheese.

He nods with approval and picks up another bite with his fork. "We are an amazing species, when you think about it. We're able to survive in environments that would kill off other species in a single generation. All because we're able to turn anything into food. Even poisonous shark meat. Of course, the Lankies are even better at life than we are. Amazing adaptive skills. Their home world must be a scary fucking place."

"I hope we never find out," I reply. "As much as I want to pay them a visit. With a two-hundred-megaton planet buster as a host gift."

"Sooner or later, we will have to find out, Major Grayson. We kicked them off our turf here in the solar system. But one day they'll try again. Here or in whatever colony systems we still have left. Make no mistake. This isn't over until one of us wipes out the other."

"Billions of planets in our galaxy," I say. "Infinite space in the universe. And we fight each other to the death over a fucking grain of sand on a beach."

General Masoud shrugs. "Find a way to make them see it like that, and we can all retire. Recycle those warships, dismantle the nukes. Until then, we have to be ruthless. Because they don't saddle themselves with these moral questions. Notice how they've never tried to communicate with us, either?"

"We haven't figured out a way to talk to them. But I'm pretty sure we got the message across that we don't want to be food," I say.

"Maybe it'll stick. Or maybe whatever is making them seek out our planets for themselves is bigger than their fear of our missiles. Maybe they figure the risk is worth it."

"Could be they have no choice," I say. "But to be frank with you, I don't care why they do what they do."

"If you want to really beat an enemy, you have to care. You have to know what drives them. What makes them tick. Their greatest desires, their biggest fears. So you can kick them where it hurts the most. Kick them until they are down, and then keep kicking. Until the threat is gone for good."

I take a bite of meat loaf and chew the food slowly, deliberately, a skill I had to learn once I left the PRCs. I haven't had anything made of soy in a long time, and if I can help it, I never want to eat that stuff again. To me, flavored soy will always be the taste of welfare rations and wartime deprivation.

"You've come a long way since the first time we met. You were a sergeant. Then you made lieutenant for Arcadia," Masoud says. "Then captain. And now you're a staff officer."

"You've gone up the ranks as well since then," I say.

He looks at the gold-wreathed single star on his shoulder epaulette with something like mild disdain.

"I hate seeing gold up there," he says. "That wasn't ever a goal for me. General officers don't get to do pod drops. They don't get to move the levers on the field. They just get to push icons around on a hologram. But there are more staff and general slots open than people to fill them. The officer corps took a beating in the years before Mars."

Masoud looks at the insignia on my epaulettes, the same but in silver thread, and smiles. "But I don't need to tell you that, do I?"

"I thought I was safe," I say. "Limited-duty officer. Restricted to my occupational specialty. And then they just quietly removed the limit and ordered me to staff school."

"Combat vets have the edge in the new promotion points system," Masoud replies. "And that's a good thing. Most of the junior officers in the Fleet have never seen battle. The special tactics platoons all have veterans at the helm from company level up. But the SI, that's another story. Half the line companies have fresh captains who were still in the academy during Mars. I hear the new junior officers are standing in line to volunteer for garrison duty at Outpost Campbell. Just so they can maybe take shots at a Lanky and get a combat badge."

"All the peacetime rank-jockey bullshit all over again," I say.

General Masoud shrugs once more. “It’s what it is. And we’re stuck with those wreaths on our shoulder boards, whether we want them or not.”

He shakes his head and takes another bite of his potato-and-sausage scramble. Then he looks at me appraisingly.

“Unless I have you all figured wrong. I mean, it’s an easier life now. Especially at our rank.”

He gestures with his fork to indicate the empty mess and the loaded trays at the buffet counter. “Good food. Hot water on demand. Liberty in the evenings and on the weekends. Regular leaves. Seeing sky overhead instead of deck plating. What kind of fool would rather be in armor and freezing their ass off out on a colony planet somewhere?”

“Only the rarest sort of imbecile,” I reply. “Someone who hasn’t learned his lesson yet.”

The general looks at me with a neutral expression for a few moments. Then he allows himself one of his tiny smiles.

“I’ll not fault you for being content with what you have now. God knows you’ve done a lot for the Corps. If anyone has earned the right to some easy duty, it’s the SOCOM vets who have bled for this peace. That’s why I am stopping by here with an offer, not an order.”

“An offer,” I repeat. “From you.”

“Not from me personally. From the head of SOCOM. Your branch’s commanding officer.”

I put down my fork. On the other side of the window next to us, the snow is blowing sideways across the landscape. It’s cold outside, at least by Earth’s standards. On New Svalbard, a day like this would be considered mild and almost balmy.

“I figured you didn’t come all the way out here just to sample the potato hash,” I say.

“Oh, I didn’t make this trip just to talk to you. I am on my way to some joint-service dog-and-pony show in Britain. This was just a convenient hop. A chance to check in with you. And offer you a shot at an assignment that just came open.”

My initial impulse is to tell him that I am not interested in anything he has to offer. There will be an ice-sculpture contest in hell before I ever trust this man again, not after he used my infantry company as bait to distract an entire planetary garrison. I am just about to open my mouth to tell him that. Then I take a few slow and deliberate breaths until the urge passes. I don't want to show any sort of weakness in front of General Masoud, and being unable to control anger is as much a weakness as an inability to control fear.

"A combat deployment," I guess. "And you need just the right person for it. I've heard that one before."

"It's a field deployment," Masoud says. "I don't know if there will be combat involved. I have a special tactics team about to go on deployment without a commanding officer. Their CO just got medevaced off the ship with a major health issue. He'll be out for at least a month. And I can't send out a company with a section commander in charge of the whole shop. That's too much lifting for a lieutenant."

"A regimental STT?" I ask, and Masoud nods.

"STT 500. Attached to the Fifth SI Regiment. They're on the *Washington* right now. Getting ready for a deterrence patrol. I need someone to take over for Major Mackenzie. Someone who knows their ass from a hole in the ground."

"I can't be the only qualified O-4 in the cupboard," I say.

"You're not. I have several other people I can order to take the slot. But you're more experienced than either by half. STT 500 is a varsity team. I want them to go into action with a varsity commander. Not a burned-out lifer trying to ride out the few years until retirement."

Major Masoud looks around in the mess.

"And you're the only one on my list who can hand over their shop and hit the ground running with the 500 without fucking up an ops cycle. You have what—a month left in this training flight?"

"A month and a half," I say.

"I can order one of the HQ staff officers from Norfolk or San Diego to serve out the rest of this cycle for you. Hell, I have half a dozen light-duty people in Norfolk alone that I'm tired of finding make-work assignments for. None can take command of a line company right now. But all of them can keep your seat warm here at the ISTS."

"So I'm the best for the job. And coincidentally the only one who's easily replaceable right now."

"You are the easiest to replace, that is true. But you're also the best for the job. Don't doubt that."

I want to tell the general that if he said snow is white, I'd feel the urge to go outside and check for myself. But he's still the head of the SOCOM branch, and it's entirely within his powers to make my life difficult for the rest of my service days. It's not smart to irritate someone who can make me take inventory of air filters and undershirts on Fleet Base Titan until I retire.

"But this is an offer. Not an order," I say.

"That's correct. You are the most qualified. But you also have more deployments than anyone else on my short list. That's why I am offering it to you instead of just sending movement orders through MilNet. If you would rather not stick your neck out, you have earned that right. We don't know what's going to happen in six months, or a year from now. The Lankies may show up again and spoil the peace. This may be the last quiet posting you'll get for a while."

He looks around again with a mildly disdainful expression, as if the thought of a quiet posting were offensive to him, and takes another bite of his food.

"Of course, the reverse may also be true," he continues. "With everyone fighting over combat command to pad the personnel file. Especially the captains who want to step up to major. It's a big jump from O-3 to O-4. Every ribbon counts in that competition. Could be you won't get another shot at a line company for a good while. Maybe you'll get another school assignment after this one. And anywhere else would be a downgrade from this luxury resort."

The little bastard is blackmailing me, I think.

There's no doubt in my mind that he has the last say in the staffing decisions for the STTs on deployment. The point system is good for promotions, but the command of a company-sized special tactics team is a badge that only the SOCOM leadership can award. He doesn't say it out loud, and the implication is subtle, but I refuse to believe that it's unintentional. If I turn down the job, he'll make sure I won't get another, and I'll be looking at a succession of rear-echelon and instructor assignments every twelve months until he gets bored of fucking with me.

"Let me think about it," I say. "Just for a day or two."

General Masoud puts his silverware on his plate and wipes his mouth with a napkin. Then he flashes his barely there smile again.

"I figured you would be jumping at the chance. STT 500 is probably the best team in the entire Fleet. If I made that offer to any other major in SOCOM, they'd offer to arm-wrestle a Lanky for it."

"My wife's the squadron commander of ATS-13. They're training at Goose Bay right now for their deployment in two months. I want to check with her before I commit myself to blowing off our joint leaves for the next year. I like being married. I want to remain married."

"That's perfectly understandable," Masoud says, with an expression that tells me he doesn't understand it at all.

"Are you staying on base for the night?" I ask.

He shakes his head. "I told the twirly-bird crew to refuel and keep their ship on standby for the hop back to Keflavík. I need to make Faslane by the end of the day. But I'll be busy with other stuff for the next seventy-two hours. I don't have to put a name into those movement orders until Monday morning. But I'll need your go/no-go by 1800 hours on Sunday. Understood?"

"Copy that, sir."

We finish our food and put our trays on the counter for the mess orderly to police. At the door, General Masoud puts his beret back on his head, yanks down the right side over his eye, and flattens the wool against his skull with the palm of his hand. Then he nods at the mess hall behind us.

"This is the sort of place that dulls our edge. Makes us soft. Gives us too much time to worry."

He opens the door to step outside, and the blast of cold air that blows into the entryway carries thick snowflakes that settle on our uniforms. General Masoud doesn't even flinch.

"I know you, Major Grayson. You enjoy the perks here. But you think about how it feels to be back on the sharp tip of the spear. Because deep down inside, you miss the war."

The low-grade irritation I always feel in Masoud's presence turns into anger in my chest.

"That's one hell of an assumption."

"But I know it's the truth. Because I miss it," he says. "And I know you'll deny it with your last breath, but we are very much alike, you and I."

He walks out into the driving snow before I have to stifle an insubordinate reply.

CHAPTER 5

A FISHHOOK IN THE STEAK

In the morning, the combat controller and forward observer trainees have comms gear instruction. I stop by and watch for a little while as my sergeants familiarize the Eurocorps soldiers with some more of our signals and communications equipment. Even after four years, the battlefield integration of units between the NACDC and the Eurocorps isn't seamless yet. We have spent half a century on weapons and tactics development in sharply diverging directions. The Euros have mostly been keeping the peace on their continent and safeguarding against Sino-Russian Alliance expansion, so they were geared to fight land wars on Earth. The Corps has been out on the colonies in a resource contest with the SRA among the stars for decades, so we were set up to fight small-scale colonial actions in other star systems. When the Lankies arrived, everyone had to radically change their R&D approach, but we were already proficient in space combat. The Eurocorps had to start their effort almost from scratch. But for a nation bloc that only started training space infantry less than half a decade ago, they're doing quite well already.

I don't linger in the classes to observe for long because it makes the instructors twitchy. When the boss is in the room, the teachers can't help but think that I'm there to evaluate them in some way, and I can always tell that it throws off the flow of their lecture. So I make myself scarce again, satisfied that my experienced SOCOM sergeants have things well in hand whether I am hovering over their shoulders or not. When I check my chrono after leaving the classroom building, it's only the middle of the morning. The snow squalls have lifted in the night, so with nothing better to do right now, I head back to my quarters to change into exercise clothes and go for a run.

Over the years, I have found that my brain works best when I give my body a mindless physical task that can be accomplished entirely on autopilot, in an environment where I don't have to pay much attention to my surroundings or get bombarded by external stimuli. Running out here in Iceland fits all those parameters better than anything else. As I make my way from the base up the trail that leads through the hills, I don't have to consciously think about anything, and there's nothing in my field of view but snow-frosted mountains and the vast lead-colored expanse of the North Atlantic off in the distance to my left.

I don't want to leave Iceland just yet. It's a serenely beautiful place, and I'm as far away from people as anyone can get in this hemisphere without pitching a tent on what's left of the ice shelf on Greenland. With all that good food and the light duty, it's easy to forget that there's a whole universe out there beyond the gray winter clouds. And with four years of no run-ins with the Lankies, it's easy to pretend that they're not still out there among the stars. Maybe they are scared of us now. Maybe they've learned to avoid us like a woodlands creature has incorporated the fear of fire into its instincts. It's possible that we bought the Earth some lasting peace—for a century, or a millennium, or even an eternity. Maybe they'll leave us alone for good, now that we have taught them to fear our nukes and our Orion missiles. With every month I spend here, the memory of their incursion grows a little more distant.

But as I pant and huff my way across the austere landscape of the eastern coast of Iceland, I suspect that all of those maybes are wishful thinking, not sober reflection. I've learned that as a species, we are exceptionally and universally good at rationalization, at accepting facts that support our biases, and explaining away or ignoring the ones that contradict them. And I know that much of my anger at General Masoud's unexpected visit comes from the fact that he told me things I did not want to hear in the moment.

A thousand years of peace, I think as I look at the sky. A few seabirds are hovering in the breeze above the coast, flapping their wings every few seconds to maintain station in the headwinds coming in from the ocean.

Or maybe they'll show up in the solar system again next week, with more seed ships than we have Orions to throw at them. We have regrouped and worked out new tactics. Who's to say they can't do the same?

I try to think about what would happen if we got an incursion alert right now. Our contingency plan still calls for all personnel to report to the nearest Corps facility to stand by for emergency deployment. I'd probably get moved to a podhead detachment on a Fleet unit somewhere, to get ready for surface action against the invasion spearheads, just like we have been practicing for half a decade now. But it would be a purely reactive action. I'd be suiting up in armor, yanked from a desk job into battle preparations without warning, tossed into a line unit with unfamiliar troops, people I've never trained or deployed with. And I realize that I am not prepared for war, even though I've kept my marksmanship skills honed and my body in fighting shape. I'm not prepared for war because I've let myself pretend that the fight is as good as over, that a desk job and three meals a day from a chow hall buffet are going to be my normal state for the rest of my days in uniform.

When I finish my run and trot back through the main gate of the ISTS base, I am angrier than I was when I left—not because Masoud was wrong, but because I have to concede the possibility that he wasn't.

"If he is offering it, there's a fishhook in that steak somewhere," Halley says when I have finished telling her about General Masoud's visit. We're talking on a high-bandwidth video link via MilNet. It's evening, and we're both in our respective quarters. She's in Goose Bay, the Fleet's big training base in Labrador, where drop ship and Shrike crews practice low-level flight over unpopulated areas.

"Oh, I know there's a catch somewhere," I say. "But if he knows the deployment plan, he's not sharing it."

"'Deterrence patrol' could mean anything. Could be taking up garrison orbit around Mars for three months."

"Could be going out to Arcadia with a task force. Or making the loop past Saturn's orbit. With some FleetEx at Titan thrown in halfway through."

"You don't think he has anything cooking on the side, do you? Like he did back when we went into Leonidas?" Halley asks.

I shake my head. "This isn't going to be a SOCOM mission. They wouldn't give him a whole Avenger task force. Whatever this is, it's got to be a Fleet thing. Not some off-the-books cloak-and-dagger shit."

"I would agree with you. But this is Masoud we're talking about here," Halley says. "Remember Leonidas?"

"I remember," I say, and I know that Halley won't ever need reminders, either. She almost died in the battle we fought at the end, when we had the renegade president of the NAC cornered in his underground bunker. The truth is that our entire team would have died that day if Masoud hadn't sprung his trap and strong-armed an entire planetary garrison into surrendering to an SI company and an understrength SEAL team. He was smart and ruthless, and he got the job done with a minimal amount of casualties. The assets he reclaimed from the renegades were instrumental in fighting the Lankies to a draw on Mars. Without his audacious plan, we wouldn't have been able to kick them out of the solar system. But I know without a doubt that if I had lost Halley that day, I would have killed him on the spot when he stepped off the drop ship with his SEAL team after the garrison surrendered.

"How do you feel about going on another deployment?" Halley asks.

"I'm fine with it," I say. "In all honesty? I've had three shore-duty assignments in a row. Chances are better than ever the next one would have been a combat billet anyway. And it's a deterrence patrol. We'll be dashing to some colony, or maybe one of the Jovian moons. Figure we'll do a live-fire FleetEx or two, put on a show for the colonials. It'll be good to get out into the field again."

"And if you don't take the slot, Masoud will write you off as a burnout," Halley says.

"I don't give a shit what he thinks of me. I just don't want to spend the next few years in charge of a SOCOM ammo dump somewhere in the outer system."

Halley chews on her lower lip for a moment as she considers the scenario.

"Well," she says. "I'm going on deployment in two months anyway. I can't ask you to stay home and play it safe if I'm not. And if we both do a combat tour at the same time, at least we'll be eligible for extended leave after. We can sync up our schedules."

"I'm glad you don't think I'm out of my mind for going," I say.

"That would make me such a hypocrite, Andrew. When I am just itching to get back onto a carrier deck myself."

She shakes her head with a smile. "I can't believe we are actually looking forward to this shit again. The Corps has messed with our heads more than I thought."

"If there's fighting to be done, I'd rather be up there in armor than down here holding a coffee mug. And if there's no fight, then it doesn't matter anyway. Then I'll just be doing a training cruise with live ammo."

With the thorny business of the impending deployment out of the way, I feel a sense of relief that General Masoud didn't manage to put a ding into my relationship with Halley, that there won't be seeds of discontent that will have a chance to blossom into arguments or bad feelings weeks and months down the road. Now that Mom is gone, the two most important things in my life are my marriage and the Corps, but if I had to sacrifice one to save the other, I would not hesitate for a moment to leave the military and hang up the uniform for good.

"How soon will you have to head out?" Halley asks at the conclusion of our nightly bedtime banter.

"Masoud said I have to give him word by Sunday evening," I say. "I expect I'll have movement orders by Monday morning. He doesn't wait around."

"You might as well start packing your shipboard bag, then."

"We won't have a chance to get together before I leave," I say.

"We've been there before," Halley replies. "Many times. I don't have to like it. But it's the life we chose, right?"

"I'm sure I'll be in-system for a while. Even if it's a colony run. Takes a few days just to get to the node for Arcadia. I'll check in once I get to the ship and settled in."

"Go, then. Have fun sweating with the other podheads. And make sure you get back in one piece. I'll see you in six months. And then we're taking a few weeks off."

"Count on it," I reply. "I love you. Remember to keep the number of landings equal to the number of takeoffs."

"That's the general idea," she says. "Good night. I love you, too."

The two-line message to General Masoud only takes thirty seconds to write, but my finger hovers over the "SEND" field for a good while as I pace the room. Halley is on board with the plan, and she'll be on deployment herself in eight weeks. This should be an easy call at this point, and I don't know why I am hesitating. Maybe it's the knowledge that Masoud has never sought me out with an assignment that did not have invisible strings attached to it somewhere.

Leonidas was seven years ago, I think.

We had the Lankies on our doorstep, and the renegades were on the run with our best gear. Now everyone is pulling on the same rope again, and there hasn't been a seed ship in the solar system in over half a decade. There's nobody left to deter with that patrol.

I send the message off to SOCOM command and put the personal data pad back onto the table. Then I take off my uniform and step into the shower for a quick pre-bedtime rinse.

When I am finished ten minutes later, the PDP's notification light blinks with the pulsing red of a new priority message. I pick it up and activate the screen to find that Masoud's reply consists of a standard transfer order, sent via the SOCOM administrative system. It's as clinical and impersonal as a reply can get, only a few terse entries in the relevant data fields.

ASSIGNED UNIT—SPECIAL TACTICS TEAM 500. DUTY STATION—CVB-63 NACS WASHINGTON. REPORT TO NEW PDS BY—1800H ZULU, MON 19 FEB 2120.

I click my tongue and toss the PDP back onto the table, where it lands with a dull clatter.

"You're fucking welcome," I say.

CHAPTER 6

WASHINGTON

I've seen Avenger-class ships close-up dozens of times, but somehow the sight never gets old to me. They are enormous, the better part of a kilometer in length, but they have a sleek appearance that belies their size and weight, all organic curves and flowing shapes. When the Fleet only fought other humans, warships were painted in flat black and gray, to make them less obvious against the background of interplanetary space. The Avengers are all painted in titanium white, and the hull markings are fluorescent orange, in blatant defiance of the old low-observance protocol. But these are new weapons, designed to fight new enemies, and the tactics had to change radically. Our foe is sensitive to active radiation, so the new gear is built around optical tracking and comms, which requires a high-visibility paint scheme to let the optical sensors pick up friendly ships more easily.

NACS *Washington* sits in her docking slip like an image from a defense contractor brochure, human warfighting prowess distilled into half a million tons of titanium and carbon composites. On the other side of the T-shaped docking outrigger, a space control cruiser is tied to the station with dozens of service lines and gangways, utterly dwarfed by its immense neighbor. We have three Avengers in the Fleet, and three more are under construction. The SRA has three as well, and there are six more distributed between our various Alliance nations. A dozen battlecarriers are now the thin white line between us and the Lankies, but the line is getting a little thicker every year. By the middle of the decade, there will be twice as many Avengers in service.

The shuttle makes its way to its own docking port at the inner ring of the station, and the pilot has to make a slow pass alongside *Washington*, so I get another opportunity to study the hull from stern to nose from just a few hundred meters away. The Avengers are too large to dock at Gateway or Independence stations, so the Fleet expanded the new battlecarrier base at Daedalus, on the far side of the moon. Now it's almost the size of Gateway, and the Fleet has steadily shifted its operations to the new station, leaving the old and capacity-strained Gateway to the orbital defense ships and the nascent combat fleets of the allied nations. It's a bit of a pain to get to the new base because it requires a transit from Earth to Luna and then another ride around the moon on a separate ship, but I rather enjoy the scenery every time I get to do that run. Something primal stirs in my chest whenever we come around Earth's moon and see the station and the gigantic battlecarriers rising above the lunar horizon in front of the shuttle. Fleet Base Daedalus has no civilian ships docked, and no cargo or passenger traffic to clutter up the approaches.

"Passengers, prepare for arrival and gravity ops at Daedalus," the flight deck announces as we approach our docking clamp. I double-check my harness and return my attention to the viewport next to my seat, where the angle of our approach gives me a good view at the forward ventral gun batteries on the hull of *Washington*, rows of armored turrets with triple rail-gun barrels for orbital bombardment and close-range ship-to-ship barrage fire.

I'm the ranking officer on the shuttle, so I get to leave the passenger deck first, a small but welcome privilege of my new seniority. When the green light comes on and the crew chief opens the hatch to the docking collar, I get out of my seat and gather my personal bag from the cargo bin. Then I return the crew chief's respectful nod and step through the hatch and onto Daedalus.

The new Fleet base is fully geared for military use, not an ounce of weight wasted on accommodating civilian and commercial operations. Everything is new and shiny. The deck liner under my feet is spotless, without the centerline rut that's evident on the decks of ships and stations that have seen the foot traffic of decades in active service. The corridors are well lit and wide enough for heavy equipment transfer between capital ships. There are clear direction markings on the bulkheads, and the paint isn't all faded and scuffed like on Gateway. It's been a long-running joke in the Fleet that we would come back to base one day and find that Gateway had finally de-orbited and crashed into the Pacific while we were on patrol. Now that Daedalus is a fully operational Fleet base, we may finally be able to decommission the eighty-year-old station and recycle it for scrap. But knowing the military, they'll keep using it until it falls apart completely.

I make my way to the main concourse of the station and look for the transfer desk, where a team of young corporals and sergeants are checking assignments and directing personnel.

"Good morning, sir," one of the desk sergeants says when I step up to his station. "Do you have your movement orders?"

I pull up my transfer order and let the sergeant scan it.

"*Washington*," he says. "The big dog. She's on the Alpha ring, docking gate Alpha 5. You want to follow the red marker all the way. Or you can let your PDP do a handshake with a PTU, and it'll get you there automatically."

"PTU?" I ask.

He nods at a nearby equipment corral, where at least a dozen two-wheeled gyro boards are lined up in a neat row.

"Personal transport units," he says.

"You didn't have those the last time I came through here."

"We got the PTUs last year, sir," he says.

Has it been over a year since I've been on a capital ship? I think and do the mental math. My internal calendar confirms the fact—I've been on two consecutive school assignments on Earth, so it has been fourteen months since I set foot onto a spaceship of any size. As I look at the little wheeled boards, a young enlisted Fleet member walks up to the rack, waves his PDP over the control panel of one of the units, and waits until it backs itself out of the rack and into the concourse. Then he steps onto the gyro board, and it takes off with a soft electric hum, carrying its passenger down the concourse at a brisk walking speed.

"Are we all too lazy to walk now?" I say as I watch with slight bewilderment.

"It's a big station, sir. It takes twenty or thirty minutes just to cross to the other side and into the Bravo ring from here. And the PTUs are more efficient. No traffic jams, no getting lost."

"Well, I guess that is an advantage," I say, remembering the frequent slow foot traffic on Gateway when three or four big warships were docked at the same time. It's a pleasant surprise to see that someone put thought into making the operations here more efficient and easier on the troops, but it's still a little jarring to see this nonessential technology. Five years ago, the Corps didn't have the money for convenience devices like these.

"I'll walk," I say. "Alpha is close by, right?"

"Yes, sir. Five minutes down the red line."

"Thank you, Sergeant."

He nods, and I shoulder my bag and walk off. I want to believe that he thinks I am too tough to let myself get ferried to my gate by a cute little automatic skateboard, and maybe he doesn't suspect I don't want to make an ass of myself by face-planting in the middle of the corridor in front of a bunch of junior enlisted troops.

Space is always at a premium on a warship, but the Avengers are roomier than any other ship class in the Fleet. The SOCOM detachment has its own deck section on the periphery of Grunt Country, where the ship's Spaceborne Infantry detachment is quartered. Each Avenger has an entire regiment of SI allocated to it, eight companies in total. Over nine hundred troops and thirty-two combat exoskeletons make up the surface combat power of the battlecarrier, supported by two strike-fighter and two drop-ship squadrons. Most of those troops are enlisted, who are stacked eight to a berth, and noncommissioned officers, who are paired up in theirs. But even with the stacking by squad, it takes a lot of deck space to house almost a thousand grunts and their battle gear, and Grunt Country takes up a big cluster of deck sections near the ship's hangar.

The SOCOM section is the farthest from the hangar. I make my way through the center of the ship in one of the three wide fore-and-aft passageways, which is busy with troops and Fleet personnel going about their pre-deployment business. There's no obligation to salute aboard an NACDC warship, but I get respectful nods and greetings from troops as I head to my assigned berth. The Fleet sailors I pass are all in the shipboard uniform they introduced a few years back, the one the troops nicknamed "blueberries" almost right away because of its teal-and-blue hue. I am in my Class A uniform, which is custom for reporting to a new duty station, and I can't wait to report to the CO and then change into the far more comfortable shipboard dress myself.

As a staff officer, I no longer have to rely on luck to score a private single berth. Staff officers get those as a matter of routine, and on Avengers, even the junior-grade officers have their own because the ship is optimized for crew comfort on long deployments. My berth has been coded to my DNA profile already, and I unlock it and step inside. The cabin looks and smells like it has never been occupied. I stow my gear and report in with the ship's MilNet system via the terminal on my new desk. Everything on this ship is new, including the terminal, which logs me on in the blink of an eye.

Before I leave the cabin again, I check my appearance in the stainless steel mirror next to the door. My Class A smock is in good shape, freshly cleaned and pressed. My professional résumé is pinned above the left breast pocket in the form of awards, four rows of ribbons with the shiny combat-drop badge in gold neatly centered on top. Back when I was in Basic, twelve years and what seems like a lifetime ago, only the old-timers had more than one or two rows of ribbons. As I take a closer look at my face to make sure my shave from this morning doesn't need a refresher, I notice the wrinkles in the corners of my eyes and the sporadic gray hairs that started to appear recently, and it occurs to me that if I don't have old-timer status already, I am definitely well on my way.

"Major Grayson. Do come in."

The master and commander of NACS *Washington,* Colonel Drake, acknowledges my greeting and nods toward the spot in front of his desk. I'm in the commanding officer's ready cabin, which is located right off the busy combat information center. Behind me, the door closes automatically and shuts out all the noise from the CIC.

Colonel Drake gets out of his chair and extends his hand across the desk. He is trim and fit, and taller than me by at least five centimeters. His hair is reddish blond and as unruly as the standard short Fleet haircut will allow.

"I've been told they had found someone to take over the STT from Major Mackenzie. Truth be told, I wasn't optimistic we'd have the slot staffed in time for deployment."

"I was two tours into a training billet on Iceland," I say. "Guess they figured I've sat on my ass long enough."

"But have you?" Colonel Drake says with a smile. "Iceland's a cushy posting, from what I hear."

"I came up from the enlisted ranks. When they pinned the stars on me, they lied to me and said I'd be a junior-grade officer for the rest of my days. I'm a podhead at heart. Not an administrator."

From the way the wrinkles in the corners of his pale-blue eyes deepen briefly, I can tell that I gave the right answer, or at least an acceptable one. Colonel Drake nods and sits back down in his chair. I put my hands behind my back and stand at parade rest. Some commanders run their ship without formal bullshit, some run it so tightly that the crew walks on their toes at all times. Until I have this one figured out, I figure it's best to err on the side of excessive formality. The special tactics team is integrated with the SI regiment, but it's still under Fleet command, so the colonel is not only the commander of the battlecarrier but also my direct superior.

"Well, welcome to *Washington*. You've served on an Avenger before in the same job, so I'm sure you know your way around. This one has a few improvements, but that's mostly just systems stuff. Layout's exactly the same."

The colonel has a pleasantly melodic accent I can't quite place. His diction is very precise, and he uses no filler words to interrupt the rhythm of his sentences.

"Too bad you had to change horses for the STT team right before heading out," I say. "I know it messes with team cohesion. But I'll do what I can to hit the ground running."

"I'm glad to hear it. You should have an easy job. Your predecessor cherry-picked the section leaders and most of the enlisted personnel. They've been training for this deployment for the last six months."

"Can you share where we're going yet?" I ask, and the colonel shakes his head.

"I would if I knew. Command hasn't seen fit to tell us anything other than our departure date and time. But we will know more in thirty-six hours. You have some time to get settled in."

"Yes, sir."

Colonel Drake taps a field on his comms screen.

"XO, could you come to the ready cabin, please?"

"Aye, sir," a female voice replies.

A few moments later, the door signal sounds, and I turn toward it as it opens with a faint pneumatic hiss.

The woman who walks into the ready room is tall and lean. She has dark-brown hair that's pulled back into a ponytail, and the back and sides are trimmed very short. Something about the curve of her jawline and the dark-brown color of her eyes reminds me of someone else, but I can't quite figure it out just yet. She looks at me and gives me an appraising once-over.

"Lieutenant Colonel Campbell, this is Major Grayson. He's the new STT boss. Major Grayson, this is my XO, Sophie Campbell."

Lieutenant Colonel Campbell offers her hand, and we shake. Her grip is firm and purposeful.

"Welcome to the ship, Major," she says. "Glad you could join us on short notice."

She doesn't smile when she offers her welcome, and something about the tone of her statement makes it sound just a little bit sarcastic. I choose to ignore the minor barb and smile noncommittally in return.

"XO, please log the major's arrival and show him around the CIC before he heads down to Grunt Country to meet the team," Colonel Drake says. "Good to have you aboard, Major. Carry on."

I follow the XO back out into the CIC. She leads me over to the command pit and stops in front of the holotable, which shows the space around the ship and the Fleet base. A handful of contacts are in various approach and departure patterns, diligently tracked by the ship's integrated defense system.

"The skipper says you've been on an Avenger before," she says.

"I was on *Ottawa* on her first deployment."

"The colony evacuation at New Svalbard," she says, and I nod.

"That was bad news," she says. "Ship did well, though."

"We splashed three seed ships," I say. "But they had already landed in force, so there was nothing more we could do other than to get the civvies off."

"I read the after-action reports. What a waste."

"It was either nuke the place or surrender it to them."

"I'm not saying it was the wrong decision," she says. "But it was a waste."

Now that I know her name, I have figured out why she looks vaguely familiar.

"Are you related to Colonel Campbell?" I ask. "The skipper of the *Indianapolis*?"

"He was my father," she says.

"I served with him on *Indy*," I say. "He was the best commander I've ever seen."

"So I hear," she says. "Everyone who served with him says the same thing. You're familiar with the special tactics station here in the CIC, right?"

She points to one of the stations that surround the command pit. I walk over and take a closer look. Everything is set up the way it was on *Ottawa*, when I took turns at the STT station with my senior NCO and the platoon leaders.

"Yes, I am," I say. "Haven't been in that chair in a little while. But it's all familiar ground."

"You have full access to the CIC, so do what you have to do to get yourself up to speed. Any questions or concerns?"

I didn't exactly expect a parade at my arrival, but the XO's frosty and brusque manner seems a little out of place even for an executive officer, the traditional heavy hat on a warship. I don't know what I've done to piss off the ship's second-in-command right out of the starting gate, but I don't want to show my irritation until I have figured out whether her low-level ire is justified, or whether she's just a natural asshole.

"No questions or concerns at this time, ma'am," I say.

"Then don't let me keep you, Major. I will see you at the command staff meeting at 0800 in the morning."

"Aye, ma'am."

I take the hint and turn to leave the CIC. Whatever chip is lodged on the XO's shoulder, this isn't the time or place to address it. But the whole interaction has served to make me feel a little uneasy as I head down the passageway and off toward the SOCOM berths. For the first time since I agreed to the transfer, I feel myself wishing for an undo button to put me back onto Iceland, with four days on the clock until my weekend liberty with Halley.

CHAPTER 7

SETTLING IN

On a smaller warship, the cabin of a unit's commanding officer also has to serve as their workspace. The Avengers are so large that each unit all the way down to company level gets a proper office just like they do on a shore installation.

When I walk into the office of STT 500, there's just one person behind the counter, someone with a high-and-tight military regulation haircut that is peppered with gray. He is typing on the input field of a terminal, and his back is turned toward the door. When he hears me entering, he turns, and I see first sergeant insignia on his shoulders.

"Good morning, sir," he says.

"Good morning, First Sergeant," I reply. As we size each other up, I can tell he's scanning my uniform credentials, which are more revealing than his because I am in my ribbon-adorned Class A uniform, and he is wearing Fleet fatigues. But from what I can see on that camouflage smock, it's more than enough to get the picture. He is wearing the golden trident of a SEAL, the Fleet's space-air-land commandos and the cream of the SOCOM branch, and a golden pod drop badge underneath.

"I'm the new CO," I say. "Major Grayson. Here to take over for Major Mackenzie."

"Yes, sir. First Sergeant Gallegos. I'm the company SNCO. Welcome to STT 500."

He gestures toward the door behind him.

"My office is behind the company office, and yours is behind mine, sir. Just like on a shore base. But a lot smaller."

"At least we have offices," I say. "This is a palace compared to a cruiser or an assault carrier."

"First time on an Avenger, sir?"

"Negative. I was the CO for the STT on *Ottawa*'s shakedown cruise."

"Then this will be familiar ground to you," he says. "All the Mark I Avengers have the same layout."

He looks at my combat controller badge and the coral-red beret under my left shoulder board.

"Captain Burns is your CCT section lead. He'll be glad to finally have a combat controller at the helm."

"What was Major Mackenzie's MOS?" I ask.

"Uh, he's a SEAL, sir."

The regulations specify that the commander of a special tactics team has to be a SOCOM-qualified officer from one of the three Fleet occupations that make up the SOCOM branch: combat controller, Spaceborne Rescue, or SEAL. Naturally, each occupation thinks of itself as the best of the lot, and almost everyone prefers to have a boss who comes from the same specialty. Captain Burns, the leader of the combat controller section, will undoubtedly be happy to have a fellow red hat as a superior, but I know that my company sergeant is probably less than happy to trade in his SEAL commanding officer for a combat controller. The interservice rivalries are fractal, and the lower down the organizational chain they go, the more intense they seem to get.

"I usually trust my section leaders to run their own business. I may get a little more hands-on with the CCT section because that's my trade. But I'm not a micromanager."

"Aye, sir."

"What kind of shape are we in, First Sergeant?" I ask.

"It's a solid team, sir. A lot of the junior NCOs aren't seasoned yet. Some of the squad leaders are a little green. We have a few fresh lieutenants who just got their tridents this year. But all the senior sergeants are combat vets. So are all the section leaders."

"I want to meet them. See if you can schedule a sit-down and find a room at some point today."

"You want an all-officer meeting, or just the section leaders, sir?" First Sergeant Gallegos asks.

I think about my answer briefly.

"Just the section leaders for now. I'll meet the rest in due course. No point yanking everyone away from their tasks."

"Aye, sir. I'll slot in a meeting and send you the data. When would you like to do the change of command ceremony? We'll have to do that on the flight deck because Grunt Country doesn't have a space that can hold the whole company. And I'll have to let the commander know ahead of time."

I grimace and shake my head.

"You know what, First Sergeant? I don't really care for pomp and ritual. And the troops have better things to do than stand around on the flight deck and watch me play with a flag. Make an entry in the company log that I assumed command of the CCT at"—I check my chrono—"1300 hours Zulu today. And send out a message to that effect on the all-company list. That should take care of the formalities."

"Aye, sir." First Sergeant Gallegos's little smile tells me that he approves of my abbreviated protocol.

"I'll be back in a little while to get set up in the new office. But first I want to get out of the travel uniform and into cammies."

"Copy that, sir. Place'll be here when you get back."

I nod and walk out of the office to head to my cabin. When I became an officer, it took me a long while to get used to being addressed as "sir." It still feels strange to hear that deferential term coming out of the mouth of a senior SEAL sergeant who is a good five years older than me, and who has been in the Corps for at least as long as I have. I do some math and realize that if I had stayed in the noncommissioned officer career track, I would be a master sergeant or first sergeant myself now, especially considering the accelerated promotion schedule the Corps adopted out of necessity over the last five years. It's easy enough to refill the ranks of young enlisted and junior noncoms. A newly minted corporal has at most two years of training behind him. But the senior noncoms, the ones who are the backbone of the military, take a very long time to train and develop, and they are difficult to replace. For probably the fiftieth time since I accepted Masoud's offer of an officer slot, I feel a tinge of regret over my decision to let them promote me out of the noncommissioned ranks. But I have no way of un-ringing that particular bell other than to resign my commission and leave the service altogether.

Back in my cabin, I change out of my Class A uniform and hang it up neatly. Then I choose my most comfortable and worn-in set of Fleet cammies. The regular Fleet personnel are wearing the blueberries, but SOCOM personnel are allowed their camouflage field uniforms to set them apart from the rank and file, emphasize their special operations status, and foster esprit de corps. Technically speaking, it's against regulations, but not even the most uptight and by-the-book Fleet commanders will dare to countermand the tradition. It's a small privilege, hard earned through grueling training and sky-high casualty rates in combat, but it's an important morale booster, and taking it away would provoke unreasonable levels of discontent among the podheads. Special operations soldiers are the most resilient and mentally flexible combat troops in the Fleet, but they get their cammies in a bunch about the strangest things if they feel their sense of tradition is violated. When the Corps switched to army-style ranks across the board in the course of unifying the branches ten years ago, it took the SEALS a while to stop using their navy ranks among each other in defiance of the sacrilegious new conventions. People who readily launched onto Lanky-occupied worlds in fragile bio-pods and spent weeks on hostile planets in extremely stressful conditions found it almost intolerable to be called "sergeant" instead of "petty officer."

When I am dressed, I check myself in the mirror. The cammies I am wearing are clean and without a wrinkle or loose thread. They have the perfect grade of saltiness, that hard-won quality of a set of utility cammies when they are worn and faded enough to mark a seasoned grunt, but not so much that they run afoul of regulations. But something still doesn't look right about my appearance.

I take off my camouflage blouse and spread it out on my bunk. Then I spend an extra ten minutes rolling up the sleeves into crisp and smooth bands of pale blouse liner, good enough to pass muster of the most uptight drill instructor. Whatever else my new troops will think of me, it won't be that I am too old or lazy to sport a perfect sleeve roll.

The four officers waiting for me in the briefing room get out of their chairs when I step through the door, and I immediately wave them off.

"As you were," I say.

They sink back into their seats. There are several empty chairs around the big table that takes up most of the room, and I sit down next to my new section leaders. The Force Recon captain is immediately obvious in his SI camouflage. The other three are wearing the same Fleet pattern I do, and I can only place them when they turn toward me and make the main qualification badges on their uniforms visible.

"Good afternoon, sir," the SEAL captain says. His name tape says "HARPER," and he's a squat and muscular man with a jawline that makes him look like a heavyweight prizefighter. The other officers in the room add their own version of the greeting.

"Good afternoon," I say. "If it's that late already. It'll take me a week to get used to shipboard watch cycles again, I'm afraid."

"I'm not even adjusted yet, and we've been on this boat for a week and a half," Captain Harper says.

I pull my PDP out of the leg pocket of my cammies and place it on the table in front of me.

"I won't take up much of your afternoon," I say. "I'm Major Andrew Grayson, the new CO of STT 500. General Masoud asked me to fill in for Major Mackenzie. I know it's a pain in the ass when you have to get used to a new boss in the middle of a deployment, so I'll try to grease the process as much as I can."

"We're still in pre-deployment prep," the Force Recon captain says. "It's all just stowing kit and getting used to the new digs."

"Anyone get wind of where we're going yet?"

All four captains shake their heads.

"No, sir. Command's holding their cards close to their chests on this one," Captain Harper replies. "Not so much as a whiff. If you discount the speculations they trade on the hangar deck, that is. You know how it goes."

"The Enlisted Underground," I say. "The only faster-than-light comms network in the Corps. Spreads bullshit at blinding speed."

The other officers chuckle.

"So we have no idea yet where we are going. Or what we are doing once we get there," I say.

"That's about the long and short of it, sir," the combat controller lead, Captain Burns, says with a smile. I know his face from somewhere, probably a combat deployment over Mars a few years back, but I've never had him as a teammate or subordinate, and I have no idea whether he remembers running into me. All four of these officers are a little younger than I am, and slightly less experienced. The time in service for a captain is ten years, and promotion to major is all but certain at that point for seasoned podhead officers because of the constant scarcity of highly qualified personnel. The men sitting at the table with me were young lieutenants when I was a captain, and now they command platoon-sized special operations teams, just like I did when Masoud made the Fleet pin officer stars onto my epaulettes seven years ago.

"Let's hope for a training milk run. But let's prepare for combat. Let me ask you this, gentlemen. If we had a surprise pod drop on the menu next week, how would you feel about the readiness of your sections? And no need to blow smoke up my ass. I don't care about starched uniforms or spit-shined boots. I care about skills and attitudes. We've had a long stretch of peace, if you don't count garrison duty bullshit on Mars. You know, where the company-grade officers stand in line for twelve weeks of platoon command so they can claim combat awards. No hard surfaces left for us podheads to hone our edge."

From their subtly shifting expressions, I know that I've picked the right tone and theme for my little pep talk—emphasizing our commonalities and setting us apart from the regular infantry and the support branches.

"Honest assessment," I continue. "Are we ready for battle? Let's hear it. SEAL section?"

"We're in good shape," Captain Harper says. "I have two second lieutenants that still have the sap coming out of their ears. But they're eager to get in the game. And all my squad leaders know their business. I've assigned the most experienced ones to the squads with the new officers. To keep them between the guard rails."

"Same here," Captain Taylor, the spaceborne rescue leader, adds. "We've made it common practice in the STT to assign the section SNCOs to the squads with the greenest second lieutenants."

"I heartily endorse that practice," I say. "No better backseat driver than a grizzled master sergeant. I can't count the times my SNCO saved me from myself when I had my first platoon. They should issue one to each new second lieutenant as soon as they get that star."

"Force recon is a go as well," the SI captain says. His name is Lawson, and he looks like a recruiting-poster model: handsome, whippet lean, and with hair buzzed to the minimum length the clippers will allow. "Same story. I've got a few more new corporals than I'd like, but the squad leaders and the command element are solid. We'll get it done, whatever it is."

"You've all served on Mars, right?" I ask. Every officer in the room nods.

"Who here was on the ground for Invictus?" I add. Invictus was the name of the operation that culminated in the Second Battle of Mars, when Earth's combined space-capable forces tried to retake the planet from the Lankies seven years ago. Only Captain Harper, the SEAL, and Captain Burns, the combat controller, raise their hands.

"Then you know what these things are like," I say to them. "When we don't have them bottled up underground. When we are in the minority. If we spend the next six months doing practice assaults on Titan, it won't break my heart. But don't plan for that. Plan for them to dunk us into a bucket of angry hornets. You know what the fight will be like if we drop onto a colony. One where they've had years to prepare the battlefield."

I pause for emphasis and look at their serious expressions. For the moment, my misgivings about being called "sir" by officers close to my own age are gone. Half of the captains in this room and all the junior officers in the STT either joined the service after the invasion of Mars, or they were still in officer school when it happened. Whatever experience they have with fighting Lankies, it's in the atypical environment of post-invasion Mars, where we have suppressed the remaining Lankies and cowed them into retreating deep underground.

None of them have ever had to hold the line with a squad or a platoon that had a dozen Lankies bearing down on them in the open, with no air support forthcoming and no PACS to shore up the flanks and lay down heavy fire. It's a terror nobody can really convey in a classroom, or in anecdotes told in a bar after hours. Every veteran of Mars I know doesn't like to talk about the battle with people who weren't there. The lack of a common reference point upon which to hang the emotional ballast makes it feel like trying to communicate in different languages. There's a sharp delineation among us between the Before and the After, between those who dropped into battle on Mars and whose who didn't, and I know it's not going to go away until the last of the survivors have left active duty.

We spend the next thirty minutes going through the administrative minutiae of a command team meeting—status reports on the individual sections, personnel concerns, coordination of team training, and half a dozen other bullet points. I don't know the other team leaders yet, so I am relegated to listening and observing the interactions of my section leads. But they know that this isn't about loading me up with information, that it's mostly about us getting a feel for each other.

"Thank you, gentlemen," I say when the captains have concluded their turns. "I'll drop by each section separately in the next day or two. I'll want to look at the training schedules and introduce myself to the squad leaders as well. If you have any needs or wants for your sections, bring your concerns to me. Now's the time to make sure all the gears are turning freely. Once we leave the dock, it's down to whatever we brought along. I strongly encourage you to take one last look at your section rosters. You know your people. This is your final opportunity to tweak the lineup if you have any reservations. Be sure that you're happy with what you have when we head out."

I get out of my chair, and the section leaders follow suit.

"One more thing," I say. "The STT is directly subordinate to the ship's CO. The next step up from my office is the commander's ready cabin. That's the place you need to go if you ever have any misgivings or complaints about your new company commander. But everything else ends at my desk. I want to keep our internal SOCOM business our own. Command has given the STT a long leash. Let's not give them a reason to take the slack out of it."

"Aye, sir," Captain Harper says, and Taylor and Lawson echo the statement.

"Copy that, sir," Captain Burns says.

Burns, Taylor, and Lawson file out of the room. From the way he's lagging behind, I can tell that Captain Harper wants to have a quick word in private.

"Anything else on your mind, Captain?" I ask when the other three have left.

Harper turns toward me and straightens out his camouflage tunic, then brushes some nonexistent lint from the flap of his chest pocket.

"You probably don't remember my face," he says. "But I was on the team that went to Leonidas with you. Seven years ago, when you were in charge of the infantry platoon."

I look at his face again. Something about it triggers a vague recollection in my brain, but I wouldn't have been able to pinpoint it to a specific time or place if he hadn't told me.

"You were on Masoud's team," I say.

Captain Harper nods.

"I was a young second lieutenant. Second combat deployment. We were the ones who stuck nuclear demolition charges on the terraformers. Spent a week sneaking around in the shadows while you were raising all kinds of hell on Arcadia."

"We didn't raise hell. We poked the hornet's nest with a stick. And then we spent most of the week running away. One platoon, with a whole garrison regiment on our asses."

"I read the after-action report," Harper says. "And the award citations."

"Lots of posthumous awards," I reply. "That's not really one of my favorite memories. Any particular reason why you're bringing that up?"

He shifts his stance a little.

"Look, I know there was some bad blood between you and Masoud after Arcadia."

"You could say that," I say.

"It wasn't right of him to do what he did. We all knew you grunts were coming along to keep the garrison busy. I didn't find out until later that he didn't tell you in advance. We all volunteer to stick our heads out every day. Nobody likes getting volunteered."

"I'm not sure I believe that the whole SEAL team was in the dark about that," I reply, trying to keep my rapidly increasing irritation out of my voice.

Captain Harper shrugs.

"What you believe is not up to me, sir. I can only tell you what happened."

"Again—why are you bringing it up now?"

"I wanted to put all the cards on the table before we head out," he says. "In case you want to ask for another SEAL section lead. I didn't want you to find out a few days from now when you read through the deployment history in my personnel file."

I study the captain's earnest face and try to discern his sincerity. With my own anger tingeing my judgment, I know that I can't make that call on the spot. But in the absence of other evidence, I decide to give him the benefit of the doubt for now. Arcadia was seven years ago, and he was just a young lieutenant fresh out of training. There's nothing to be gained in the moment from blaming him for Masoud's actions.

Still, it's not an easy absolution.

"There's still bad blood," I tell Harper. "But it's between me and the general. Not between me and the SEALs. Or you in particular. I appreciate your forthrightness."

"Thank you, sir. I'm glad there are no hard feelings."

"Of course not," I say.

But as the SEAL captain walks out of the room and leaves me alone with my thoughts, I find that I'm not so sure about that after all.

CHAPTER 8

KEEPING UP WITH THE KIDS

The top of the platform is two meters above my head, and the wall in front of me is too smooth to climb. I flex my legs and feel the fiber strands of my armor's power liner contract along with my muscles. A vertical jump like that would have been impossible for me to do even at the peak of my physical fitness back in Combat Controller School. But with the Mark V HEBA suit, I leap off the flight deck's rough nonslip surface and get high enough for a handhold on the first try. I hook my fingers over the edge of the platform and pull myself up. The HEBA suit weighs over thirty kilos, but the power assist from the armor liner makes the load feel inconsequential. I swing my leg over the edge and haul my bulk on top of the obstacle-course platform, where I allow myself a little pause to catch my breath and take a brief look around.

We are a week out of Daedalus, and I still don't know where we are going or what our task will be. In the absence of a concrete mission for which to prepare, we spend our days with maintenance and training. Today, we have set up an obstacle course with lightweight, collapsible modules. The course forms a loop on the deck that's a hundred meters on its long sides, but we're still only taking up a small portion of *Washington*'s cavernous flight deck. The periphery is lined with the biggest assembly of military spacecraft I have ever seen in one place. The Avenger-class battlecarriers have a full space wing allotted to them—two attack squadrons, two drop-ship squadrons, and three support squadrons. All in all, there are over a hundred attack birds and drop ships parked all around us, painted in the latest high-visibility pattern, in the bright white-and-orange color scheme of the Avengers. Exercising with all these state-of-the-art war machines beats the hell out of running on the road at a base somewhere. It makes me feel like I'm in the middle of a recruiting vid.

Two hundred years of camouflage conventions thrown out of the airlock, I think. *If we ever go up against the Sino-Russians again, we're going to be repainting a lot of gear.*

The next obstacle is a single steel bar that bridges a ten-meter gap to another platform. There are no form requirements for the course other than "finish it and don't fall on your face," and I can tackle the problem any way I choose. The power assist of the suit gives my muscles a lot of extra boost, but I don't quite trust it to give me the power for a ten-meter jump, and I don't want to bust my ass on the deck below while half the STT troops are watching. Instead, I run across the gap on top of the bar. The power assist doesn't just amplify my muscles, it also helps me keep my balance even with thirty kilos of armor wrapped around me. The fiber strands of the armor liner are made of a new flexible wire that contracts when it is electrified, and the tech wizards of the military R&D department have found a way to work it into a material that functions like an external layer of very strong muscles. Turning on the assist drains the power cell of the armor faster, but it provides a ridiculous performance boost that never fails to be intoxicating. The bug suit already gives me a near-omniscient view of my surroundings on the battlefield, and now the new power liner lets me run faster and jump higher than ever before.

The other end of the platform has another two-meter drop. I jump down and let the armor cushion the impact. The next section is a twenty-meter run of knee-high tunnel that has to be navigated while crawling. I dive to the deck and make my way through the dark tube on elbows and knees. Ever since my near-death experience in the Lanky tunnels on Greenland, I've had a phobia of dark and confined spaces, so I rush through this obstacle as quickly as I can to reach the light at the end of it.

The course is pretty grueling, even for a SOCOM troop in power-assisted battle armor. Every obstacle is designed to require the use of a different group of muscles. By the time I've reached the end, I've run, dodged, climbed, jumped, and crawled through two hundred fifty meters of increasingly demanding structures, and every part of my body aches with fatigue. But it feels good to sweat in earnest again, and the backdrop of armed spacecraft serves as a motivator, a welcome reminder that I am training for a fight again instead of a yearly physical fitness evaluation for my personnel file.

"Not bad," First Sergeant Gallegos says when I take off my helmet and walk over to the spot where he is keeping score.

"Let's see," I say, and he holds up his PDP so I can look at the screen with the results. When I see the numbers, I flinch a little. Of all the STT troops who have run the course so far, my time places me solidly toward the bottom of the middle.

"Good God. Who's Sergeant Khan? I'm a minute and a half slower."

"Khan's in the Spaceborne Rescue section. Third Squad. He's a freak of nature. I swear he could outrun a Lanky even without power assist."

"I can't keep up with these kids anymore, Gallegos. Not even with a juiced bug suit."

"Neither can I, sir," the first sergeant says. "It's a young man's game. But you're still forty-five seconds above the cutoff. I'd say you have a few years still."

"Thank you. I'm glad I know my expiration date now."

I watch as the rest of the STT troopers make their way around the obstacle course. They're all young and fit, highly trained soldiers in their physical prime. As always in joint units made up from different specialties, there's a good-natured competition going on between the sections. The ones who are finished with the course take turns motivating the others with cheers and shouted encouragements. All around the obstacle course, maintenance crew and deck hands are watching the SOCOM soldiers tearing through the exercises. These kids are the new generation of special operations troops, trained and raised to the trident or the scarlet beret after the desperate rear-guard battles we had to fight in the first five years of the war. But they're every bit as fast and strong as First Sergeant Gallegos and I ever were, and maybe more so. The food has improved greatly again, and the new tactics we bled to develop on the battlefield are now part of the classroom curriculum in Combat Controller School and SEAL training. The military is no longer underfed, stretched to the breaking point, or forced to fight unwinnable battles with unsuitable weapons. Every bit of the world's military spending and R&D in the last half decade has gone toward the effort against the Lankies, and these men and women are part of the return on that massive investment.

"That's the whole lot," Gallegos says when the last STT soldiers have made it around the concourse. "We're going to leave the obstacle course up until 1700. One of the SI companies asked to use it. They've volunteered to do the takedown and stowing for us after they're done."

"Fine with me. As long as the jarheads don't break our stuff. You know those SI grunts."

Gallegos nods with a mock expression of parental sternness.

"Lock 'em in a room with two anvils, and in ten minutes they'll have lost one and broken the other," he says.

I leave the first sergeant to his business and wander off onto the middle of the flight deck while the STT troopers gather to head back to their quarters for post-exercise showers. It's soothing to be in the center of so much new firepower, even if it's a reminder that I'm on a warship that's headed into harm's way. But it no longer feels like we are at a breaking point, and that the end of the world is just one lost battle away.

I walk along the long rows of drop ships, dozens of advanced Dragonfly-F models and a handful of Blackflies, our special operations birds. The ones we used to infiltrate the Arcadia colony were painted in a flat black that seemed to absorb the light. These new Blackflies are no longer black at all. Instead, they are wearing the same white-and-orange paint as the Dragonflies and Super Shrikes next to them. Visual stealth was good against other humans, but Lankies don't have eyes. Even the camouflage patterns on our field uniforms are pointless now, but we keep them because they make us feel more soldierly than walking around in high-visibility colors.

There's an open section on the deck between the drop-ship parking spots and the Super Shrike attack craft. It's maybe fifty meters square and marked off with a red-and-white line. Several civilian techs are busy with gear that's unfamiliar to me. One of them is standing next to a row of knee-high devices that look like enormous twenty-sided dice. A diagnostics cable is laid out on the deck, with connectors leading to each device. They make me think of mines, but I dismiss the thought immediately because there are no ordnance flags on them, and I know that neither our ammo handlers nor the civilian techs would handle live munitions or explosives without warning labels. I walk over to the tech who is holding a hand terminal that's plugged into the end of the diagnostics line.

"What on earth are those things?" I ask.

The tech turns to look at me. She wears her long brown hair tied up in a ponytail, a very uncommon sight on a warship, where almost all the female troops keep their hair short enough to fit under a helmet. The name tag on her overalls says "FISHER, C."

"They haven't really settled on an official letter salad for the designation," she says. "But they're drones. The R&D techs call them 'Wonderballs.'"

"Wonderballs," I repeat. "What's so wondrous about them? If it's not a secret, I mean."

I take a closer look at the nearest device. The surface is faceted, and every one of the facets has a variety of sensor windows set into it.

"It's basically a ball of high-powered optical sensors," she says. "Plus laser-based comms gear. All wrapped around a power cell and tied into a central processing core. It's for the new early-warning network, Arachne. But don't ask me what that stands for. We haven't come up with a cool backronym yet."

"How new is that? It's the first time I've heard about it."

"Well," Technician Fisher says. "This will be the first field deployment, actually."

She points her stylus at the row of drones.

"The ship carries a few hundred of these. They come in packs of twelve, launched with a deployment drone. We float them out a few hundred thousand kilometers, and they'll auto-deploy into formation. Extends our bubble of awareness by a factor of twenty."

"I thought seed ships were too hard to spot for mobile early-warning systems," I say.

"These don't spot Lanky seed ships. Well, not exactly."

She smiles when she sees my puzzled expression.

"We beat our heads against that wall for a while. Then we finally figured out that if we can't see what's there, we can program these to see what isn't there. Like the light from a star that blinks out when a seed ship passes in front of it. Or the light from another Wonderball."

"An optical trip wire," I say, and she nods.

"These have twenty optical lens clusters pointing in every direction. No need to turn it a certain way because all orientations are right. And the neural core does all the thinking. Every Wonderball is linked to every other one. And when one of them sees that a light is going out where it shouldn't, all the others know it, too, at the speed of light."

"Not bad," I say. "Not bad at all."

"And the best part? It's all without active radiation. There's a low-power comms laser that sends telemetry back to us, but that's it. The power cell and all the neural networking inside is EM shielded. The Lankies may notice one if they fly past and they're close enough to bump it with their hull. Other than that, it's just inert space debris."

"Clever," I say. "Let's hope they work as advertised. It would be nice if we could see a seed ship coming from a long way out."

"They'll work," Technician Fisher says with conviction. "I've been busy with the software and hardware integration for a year and a half now. You'll be able to spot seed ships for the Orions from a few hundred thousand kilometers out."

"If we deploy them along the right vector," I say, and she shrugs.

"I don't work on the tactics. Just on the nuts and bolts, and the computer code."

Something about her pleasant, earnest face and her small frame in bulky shipboard overalls triggers a vague recollection in my brain.

"Have we met?" I ask. "You look familiar. Have you been on a deployment with the Fleet before?"

She hesitates for a moment and then nods slowly.

"I was on the PACS field test team on *Ottawa*. Four years ago."

Now that she has put a missing piece into the puzzle, my brain rushes to supply the rest.

"That's right. You were one of the exo jockeys," I say with a smile. "You guys saved our asses down on New Svalbard. Without the PACS support, they would have overrun us."

"It was just supposed to be a field test," she replies. "Never thought I'd be in the back of a drop ship on the way into battle. With live ordnance on the rails. But there was nobody else around who was trained."

"Yeah, the Lankies had their own timetable. None of us thought it'd be anything more than a training cruise."

"I never want to be that close to any of those things again," she says. "I tried to tell myself it was just a day at the range. But that didn't work so well once I was on the ground."

I recognize the haunted expression that flits across her face as she recalls the memory, and I guess that her nightmares probably look a lot like mine. The civilian contractors volunteered to be dropped onto the battlefield when we were holding New Longyearbyen against what seemed like hundreds of Lankies, in the middle of a blinding snowstorm that neutralized our long-range weapons and our air support. They shored up our flanks with the PACS and stemmed the tide long enough for us to get all the colonists off the moon, but the battle was like a knife fight in a frozen meat locker. I can't imagine the terror they must have felt to be going into battle without military training or mental preparation. It was against every regulation in the book, but it let us turn a certain defeat into a draw, and the brave R&D techs saved many hundreds of lives that day.

"Andrew Grayson," I say and offer my hand. "I'm in charge of the special tactics team on this ship. I wouldn't be here if it wasn't for you and those PACS. And don't take this as a come-on, but I'd love to buy you a drink or two at the RecFac sometime."

The small and fleeting smile she gives me in reply looks like she's not quite sure whether I am serious or making fun of her. Then she accepts the handshake.

"I'm Callista Fisher. I'm the lead tech for the R&D team," she says. "I don't really drink. But I appreciate the offer. It's good to know that we made a difference."

"I felt bad that we had to leave all the exos behind. After all your efforts."

"We didn't have the time or space to load them up," she says. "I barely made the last drop ship. I think the Lankies were maybe a hundred meters behind us when we took off and left the place. But I built that machine. Drove it almost every day for over a year. It wasn't great to see it sitting there on the airfield when the tail ramp went up."

"Like an abandoned puppy," I say.

She waves her hand in a dismissive gesture. "Just a machine, right? We got to build new ones. They're just things."

"We get attached to things," I say. "Especially when they've served to save our lives. You wouldn't believe how much I love my bug suit."

Technician Fisher flashes that unsure smile again, as if she's still trying to figure out if I am genuine. Then the terminal in her hands lets out a series of low beeps, and she seems almost relieved to be able to pay attention to it.

"I don't usually drink," she says. "Only when things go really sideways. The only time I've ever really gotten drunk was when we got back in from the New Svalbard evac. The infantry guys said it would help with the shaking knees."

She taps a few things on her terminal's screen and furrows her brows.

"And right now I need to get back to figuring out why Wonderball eighty-three here is still stuck in a boot loop even after two hard resets of the processing core. But I may take you up on your offer at some point. Might be nice to try a drink for recreation instead of stress relief."

"Look me up if you do," I reply. "Those of us who were at New Svalbard made a pledge that none of the PACS drivers from that day will ever have to buy their own booze again if one of us is around."

"I will," she says. "I just hope it won't be because things have gone sideways again. I feel like I've fulfilled my lifetime quota for unexpected close combat."

Overhead, a 1MC announcement starts blaring.

"All command-level officers, report to the flag briefing room at 1730 Zulu. I repeat, all command-level officers report to the flag briefing room at 1730 Zulu."

I check my chrono. A command-level meeting can only be called by the skipper. Whatever the subject of the briefing, it's important enough to hold it on short notice. Right now it's 1633, which means I barely have time to turn in my armor and get a shower.

As I make my way to the forward bulkhead at a trot, I look back at Technician Fisher, who is focused on her hand terminal again. She's probably around my age, but somehow she looks too young in her bulky overalls among all the war material on the deck.

Let's hope it's just a bullshit briefing, I think, even though I know that no skipper with any sense calls those on short notice. I suspect that we're about to find out what task the Fleet has thought up for us, and I've been in the service for too long to hope for a milk run to a training range. Any podhead with more than six months in the Fleet who's still an optimist is either naive or a complete moron.

CHAPTER 9

MARCHING ORDERS

"Glad you could join us, Major," the XO says when I walk into the flag briefing room. All the other command officers are already assembled. I check my chrono to see that I am thirty-eight seconds late. I could point out that I am the only member of the command quintet who had to turn in a set of combat armor and shower before the short-notice briefing, but I take a seat without commenting on Lieutenant Colonel Campbell's little dig.

Everyone in the briefing room outranks me. Three of them are colonels—the ship's CO, Colonel Drake; the commander of the air and space group, Colonel Pace; and the commanding officer of the SI regiment, Colonel Rigney. The next one down the rank ladder is Lieutenant Colonel Campbell, the executive officer of the carrier. As a major, I am on the low end of the totem pole here. But as the leader of the special tactics team, I am not subordinate to either the CAG or the Spaceborne Infantry. The STT is attached to the SI regiment during combat ops, but it remains in the Fleet command structure, so my direct superior is the ship's commander. I look at Colonel Drake to see if he shares his XO's mood, but he merely nods at me and returns his attention to the PDP in his right hand. I try to divine the nature of the briefing from the expression on his face. He seems focused and somber, which is not an encouraging sign.

Here we go, I think.

"All right, listen up," Colonel Drake says. He looks around at everyone and leans forward in his chair, then folds his hands on the tabletop in front of him. "We finally have our marching orders, and they are . . . interesting."

"Uh-oh," Colonel Pace says in a wry tone. He's tall for a pilot and almost unreasonably good-looking, flashing perfect 'burber teeth in a boyish smile.

"I'm sure you're about to give us your definition of interesting," Colonel Rigney says. He's the only other person in the room wearing camouflage fatigues, a stern-faced grunt with a severe-looking gray regulation buzzcut.

"There's a lot to unpack," Colonel Drake replies. He activates the holographic projector in the middle of the briefing table and links his PDP to it. Then he brings up a star chart that depicts a slice of the inner solar system.

"All right, let's start with the setup. We are not heading for Mars, but you've all figured that out already. We are on the way to an assembly point outside of the asteroid belt. Once we get there, we will wait for the rest of our entourage for this mission. We are going to form a joint task force with ACS *Johannesburg* and her battle group. That's CVB-67, the African Commonwealth's shiny new Mark II Avenger."

Colonel Pace lets out a low whistle. "A two-Avenger task force. That's not going to be a training run, is it?"

"Only in the context of letting *Jo'burg* and her crew get some deployment experience under our experienced tutelage," Colonel Drake says. "Our combat systems will be fully integrated. This will be the first time one of the allied Avengers deploys into combat with us. They've done a turn above Mars since their commissioning, so they've fired war shots before. But this is going to be their first out-of-system deployment. So we'll be their backup, and they'll be ours."

"I'm not sure how I feel about having to teach the ropes to a green carrier crew," the XO says. "Colonial deployments could mean Lanky contact. That's a pretty unforgiving learning environment."

"They have to start pulling their weight at some point," Colonel Drake replies. "And the Fleet wants to make sure they have the most experienced Avenger crew from our side along for the ride. Truth be told, I suspect we'll be doing the heavy lifting if it comes down to that."

"So where are we going, boss?" the CAG asks.

Colonel Drake looks around the table in silence for effect. Then he brings up another hologram and shunts it next to the first one until they slowly rotate side by side for everyone to see. It's a star chart I don't recognize immediately. When I finally recall the configuration of the system, I feel a surge of anxiety welling up inside my chest.

"We're going to Capella A," Colonel Drake says. "Back to the place where it all started with the Lankies, twelve years ago."

There's some murmuring from the other officers in the room.

"We're teaming up with an inexperienced task force," I say. "To go into a hot system that the Lankies have held for over a decade."

"That's what the Fleet wants us to do," Colonel Drake says amiably. "You were there at Capella A, weren't you? Back in '08 when we made first contact?"

I nod. "I was on *Versailles*. We pulled up into Willoughby orbit and ran right into a Lanky minefield. Lost a third of the crew right there. And a bunch more on the surface. We had no idea what we were facing."

"But now we do," Colonel Drake says. "We have the experience and the gear. And we're not going to roll into Capella with a blindfold on. It's going to be a reconnaissance in force. With limited objectives in-system."

"A hit-and-run raid." Colonel Rigney leans back in his chair and folds his arms across his broad chest. "Are we going to engage in ground action?"

"That depends on what we see when we get there. But I think it's pretty safe to say that we won't be asked to reoccupy a colony the enemy has fortified for twelve years. Not even with a full regiment. If we do anything on the ground, it will be limited to targets of opportunity. We're not set up for holding territory in a hostile system. The plan is to stick our heads in, kick some asses if they present themselves for an easy kicking, then get the hell back out."

"They could have a hundred seed ships in that system by now. Could be we don't get a chance to get the hell back out once we transition in," I say.

"Like I said, we aren't going to go in with a blindfold on," Colonel Drake replies. "The Fleet has allocated a lot of recon assets to this mission. The stealth corvettes are going to precede us and map out the opposition before we commit the task force."

"Any idea why we're doing this now, sir? We haven't had a tussle with the Lankies in four years. That may change if we start going out and poking beehives," I say.

"We're still at war with those things, Major," Lieutenant Colonel Campbell says. "We can't just hole up in the systems we have left and hope they'll leave us alone. We have to press our advantage now. Before they figure out how to counter the Orions and the Avengers. Because if that happens, we won't be able to cook up something new."

"It's a risk," Colonel Drake says. "We'll be committing a sixth of Earth's operational Avenger force. If we don't make it back out, and the Lankies decide to come back for a second helping, the rest may not be enough to stem the tide. Especially since the Mark IIIs are still on their shakedown cruises and *Ottawa* is going in for her first overhaul in a few weeks."

"You podheads are usually more gung ho about locking horns with the enemy," the CAG says to me. "I'm surprised to see the SOCOM guy trying to be the voice of caution."

I look around the room to see that everyone at the table is looking at me and waiting for my reaction. A few minutes ago, the knowledge that I am the junior officer in the room might have intimidated me into acquiescence. But now that I know where we are going, I don't have any reservation about giving voice to my experience, even if it means I may be stepping on the toes of the assembled colonels.

"I know that strategic deployments aren't exactly my field of specialty," I say. "And I'm not a xenobiologist. But I've been fighting these things on the ground since the day we ran into the minefield around Willoughby. And the only thing anyone knows for sure about them is that we don't know much about them at all. Every single time we've faced them in a large-scale battle, they've managed to surprise us and blow our plans to hell."

Colonel Drake nods.

"Your concerns are justified, Major. But trust me when I tell you that I have absolutely no interest in biting off more than I can chew. We have our mission parameters. But we decide the execution every step of the way. If it looks like we're in over our heads, we are heading for the back door."

He looks at the other officers in the room.

"If any of you have misgivings at any point, I want you to bring them up to me right away. I don't intend to run this operation from the top down. You are all in charge of your own shops. Any command decision that's not an on-the-spot call, we sit down and make sure that Fleet, SI, and SOCOM are on the same page. If you see that we are about to do something stupid, don't hold back your opinion. I have specialist department leaders for a reason. The Fleet gave us the mission, but they're leaving the 'how' up to us."

The commander changes the holographic display to a side-by-side star chart of the solar system and Capella A.

"We're going in with two carriers and their combined battle groups," he says. "That's a lot of firepower. More than we've ever thrown at the Lankies. But that doesn't mean we have to use all that ordnance. We are sneaking into one of their neighborhoods, and I intend to tread as softly as I can."

"If sneaking is the objective, we can send one or two stealth corvettes and get just as much intel," Colonel Pace says. "Maybe more, because they won't see the stealth ships. We show up in their backyard with two battle groups, they may not go about their daily routines. They'll just throw everything they have at us."

"Did Fleet Command tell you what they hope to get in return for risking two Avengers?" I ask.

"We can do the recon with the stealth corvettes, that's true. But they won't be able to do anything other than sneak and peek. If they come across any targets of opportunity or immediate threats, they'll have to make the run back home and call for reinforcements," Colonel Drake says. He magnifies the chart of the Capella A system. Willoughby, officially charted as Capella Ac, is making its orbit around the parent star, but unlike the smaller map projection next to it, the Capella chart offers no up-to-date tactical information. It's as empty as an instructional hologram in astronomy class.

"Four years since our last major contact," Drake continues. "Command wants to see what they are doing out there, why they haven't made any more excursions into human-controlled space. Did they pack up and run? Are we going to walk into an empty system? Or are they biding their time and assembling a few hundred seed ships for the next invasion wave? Four years may be nothing to them. Like taking a quick breather in between rounds."

He pokes his finger at the planet we called Willoughby, once home to a settler colony of ten thousand people, and occupied Lanky territory since the year I joined the Corps.

"We need to get a feel for their posture," Colonel Drake says. "And command wants us to take their pulse right there, where it all started for us. In the place they've had under their control the longest. If their stance is defensive or avoidant, the stealth corvettes will do the job just fine. But we're taking in the two Avengers in case they're not defensive or avoidant. If we have a sudden need for big guns, we don't want to have to send for them from out-of-system and hope for a timely delivery."

He looks at me and nods.

"You are right, Major. We don't know much about these things at all. But we know they're still out there. And if we want to be prepared for the next time they come into the solar system in force, we have to find out more about them. Otherwise we'll just keep being reactive, adjust our tactics to theirs, hope we'll always come up with a last-minute fix when things get tight. It's time to turn the tables, let them react to us for a change. That's what the Fleet hopes to get in return for risking two Avengers."

"I am not disputing the logic," I say. "Or the need for the mission."

"I'm sure Fleet Command will be relieved to hear that," Lieutenant Colonel Campbell says with a smile that's dry enough for me to see dust coming off it.

"We've come a long way in twelve years," I continue. "And we know the Avengers can hold their own. I'm just saying that we need to have as many emergency exits as possible when we stick our necks out into their turf."

"You worry about the SOCOM mission," the XO says. "We will take care of the tactical aspects of the task force deployment. I know we lack your experience in direct ground combat, but we'll try not to blunder into a trap at full throttle."

"No need for turf wars," Colonel Drake admonishes. "I asked for input, after all. Let's not tear into each other over voicing reservations.

We're all pulling on the same rope. If we screw up, we'll all end up dead. Let's keep that in mind."

"Yes, sir." Lieutenant Colonel Campbell stops her staring contest and looks at the projection in the middle of the table. "What is the timeline for this little field trip?"

Colonel Drake adds the icons for the combined battle groups to the plot and moves them toward the intersection of the two sector maps.

"We will rendezvous with the *Jo'burg* battle group in thirty-three hours, then proceed to the outbound Capella A transit point and commence last-minute replenishment operations. It's a three-day ride from the rendezvous point. We'll be in Lanky space in five days. How long we stay there will depend on what we find once we transition in."

He shunts the battle group icons over into the empty sector map for Capella A.

"We'll build in plenty of emergency exits," he continues with a glance at me. "We are sending in the recon ships first. Once we get the all clear, the battle group follows. *Washington* and *Johannesburg* will stay in mutually supporting positions close to the transition point and deploy a recon network before we venture deeper into the system. If anything comes our way that we can't handle with two Avengers, we turn around and transit back out of that system as quickly as we can spool up the Alcubierre drives. No heroics, no unnecessary risks. We have nothing to gain from losing even a single ship in that place."

The colonel magnifies the projection and lets it rotate slowly between us to show the sector maps from all angles.

"Those are the parameters. Prep your departments accordingly. Give me a go/no-go by 1800 hours tomorrow. If there's anything you need, anything that concerns you, bring it to me. Oh, and the deployment destination is classified from this command level down until we come out of Alcubierre on the far side. Command wants us to keep this one quiet. Quieter than usual, I mean."

"Gosh, I wonder why," Colonel Pace says.

"To give them time to tweak the message if they end up losing two whole battle groups," Lieutenant Colonel Campbell replies.

"If we go in and kick ass, it'll be a morale booster. If they kick ours, it may cause a worldwide panic," Colonel Drake says. "But it's harder to keep a lid on this if everyone knows where we went. Keep OPSEC tight on this. We don't want a thousand people broadcasting our mission objective back home. It'll be on the Networks before we even hit the Alcubierre chute."

"A discreet mission," Colonel Campbell says, wry amusement on her face. "With a sixth of the Fleet."

"That is our script. And we will play our parts." Colonel Drake freezes the map projection and gets out of his chair.

"Readiness reports by 1800 tomorrow," he repeats. "Brief your section leaders but remember the OPSEC restrictions. I know it's a pain in the ass, but those are the orders from above."

"That's going to really put water onto the rumor mill," Colonel Rigney says. "By the time the platoon leaders brief the grunts, we'll have two dozen wild-ass theories floating around."

"Like I said, that's the script we were given. Now let's make sure we won't bomb the play. Dismissed," Colonel Drake says.

"XO, can I have a word?"

Lieutenant Colonel Campbell turns back toward me while the other officers are filing out of the briefing room after Colonel Drake.

"What's on your mind, Major?"

I wait with my reply until the room is empty except for the two of us.

"You've been snippy with me ever since I reported in. Have I done anything to offend you? Because I know we have never met before I joined this ship. And I know the XO isn't supposed to be all warm and sweet because you're the enforcer for the commander. But I'm getting a little tired of taking heat from you without knowing why."

She studies me for a moment with narrowed eyes.

"Snippy," she repeats. "You think I am snippy with you."

"I do."

Lieutenant Colonel Campbell shakes her head and smiles without the slightest trace of good humor.

"I don't think that's a discussion you want to have with me right now, Major."

"Try me. Just between the two of us. I know it has to be personal. Because I haven't been on this ship long enough for you to get an accurate assessment of my skills."

"Just between the two of us," she says. "All right. Since you insist."

She folds her arms in front of her chest.

"You annoy the shit out of me, if you must know. Just between the two of us."

"Any particular reason?" I ask.

She nods at the rank insignia on my shoulders.

"You're an upstart, Major. I looked at your file when they assigned you to this ship. I know you've done well in the field. But you act like a noncom in an officer costume. Because that's what you are."

"You're saying my rank is not legit?"

"I'm not saying it isn't legit," she says. "SOCOM pinned the stars on you. Then they saw fit to add the wreath. They can promote whomever they want. God knows they didn't have much to pick from when we were on the ropes."

She nods at her own rank insignia, the stylized geometric version they use on the teal-and-blue Fleet uniform, one horizontal bar with two round pips stacked above it.

"I only made lieutenant colonel two years ago. When you were serving with my father eight years ago, you were a staff sergeant. I was a captain. They promoted me to major a few months after he smashed his ship against that Lanky. Bumped me up in the promotion list, like they were giving me a consolation prize because of my dead father."

There's anger in her face now, but I know somehow that it doesn't really have anything to do with me, so I resist the impulse to extend my own barbs in response. Instead, I let the XO continue without comment.

"I made major after ten years," she says. "Made lieutenant colonel at the minimum time in grade, after sixteen years in the Fleet. Meanwhile, you went from staff sergeant to major in eight years."

"I had the minimum required time in grade," I say. "Even on a peacetime schedule."

"That's bullshit. On a peacetime schedule, you wouldn't even have qualified for lieutenant. And you sure as hell wouldn't be a major right now because you were just on a limited-duty officer billet to begin with."

"You're saying you doubt my qualifications?"

"Oh, I don't doubt that you're a good podhead. You've got the medals to show for it. But you aren't a field-grade officer. I don't care what the insignia on your shoulders say. You're in charge of a company. The only reason you're able to sit at the command table with us is the fact that the SOCOM company is directly subordinate to the skipper. But everyone else in the room is three command levels above you. Pace has a carrier wing under him. Seven squadrons, a hundred and twenty spacecraft. Rigney is in charge of an SI regiment. A thousand grunts. The skipper has this carrier and everything on it. Forty-eight nukes, twelve Orions. Two and a half thousand personnel. And you? You're responsible for sixty-eight people."

She nods at the table between us.

"And you sit here with the rest of us and second-guess the deployment orders from Fleet Command. Like you're qualified to judge that. You're a grunt in command of a glorified half-strength company. You have a spot at the big table as a courtesy. Don't think for a second your opinion carries the same weight as everyone else's."

I'm a little taken aback by the amount of vitriol coming from the XO, and I wrestle with my initial reflex to give in to my anger and go on the offensive in return. There's nothing good that can come from a slap fight with the ship's second-in-command. For a few moments, there's a thick silence between us as I gather my thoughts for a response to this unexpected outburst of hostility.

"Tell you what," I say. "If you can convince General Masoud to bust me back to sergeant first class, you'll have my eternal gratitude. Please ask him to have me relieved. I'll gladly go back to leading squads."

Campbell shakes her head. "It was difficult enough to get them to send a replacement for Mac on short notice. I'm afraid we're stuck with you. For better or worse."

"Then I'd ask that you save your criticism for the first time I screw up on the job," I say. "Give me the benefit of the doubt. Assume that I know my ass from a hole in the ground. You may want to consider that Masoud roped me into the officer ranks because he thought I was qualified. Or maybe because he hates me, too. Because I've done nothing but shovel shit since I got the job."

The XO smiles and shakes her head.

"I don't hate you, Major Grayson," she says. "I don't know you well enough for that yet. And I do hope you prove me wrong."

She turns around and walks toward the door. At the threshold, she pauses and turns her head toward me again.

"You may want to consider something, too. Maybe General Masoud is right, and you are more than qualified for your job. And maybe you're well outside of your lane right now. Both of those can be true at the same time, you know."

She walks out of the room, and I listen as her footsteps trail down the passageway, still rattled by her criticism.

CHAPTER 10

JUMPING OFF

"Now hear this: Replenishment personnel, stand by for transfer operations. NACS Littleton *is now coming alongside to port. I repeat, stand by for transfer operations on port stations."*

I am at the TacOps station in the CIC, which gives me a ringside seat to watch our pre-Alcubierre replenishment operation. *Littleton* is one of the Fleet's large supply ships, fifty thousand tons of mass at a standard g, but she is utterly dwarfed by the bulk of *Washington*, which is ten times as heavy and five times as long. Just a few years ago, two ships joining up in space for transfer operations had to be maneuvered into place manually, but the new integrated management systems have turned the procedure into a fully automated event. Five minutes after *Littleton* has matched speed and course with us, the projection of the docking status board hovering above the plot table shows green lights in every field.

"*Littleton*, we are green across the board for transfer ops. I show hard seals on collars one through six," the XO says into her headset.

"*Washington*, our board is green as well. Hard seal confirmed. We are commencing transfer ops."

"Affirmative, *Littleton*," Lieutenant Colonel Campbell says and taps the side of her headset to terminate her comms link.

"All right," she says. "We are topping off. Comms, hit the jukebox."

"Aye, ma'am," the lieutenant at the comms station says. A few moments later, classical music comes out of the sound projectors on every deck. It's tradition in the Fleet to play music during replenishment ops, but the choice of tunes is up to the commander, and Colonel Drake seems to be a fan of Vivaldi and Bach.

We are a few hours away from the transit point for the Alcubierre chute into the Capella A system, and I am more nervous than I can recall being since the windup to the Second Battle of Mars seven years ago. Even the stupendous amount of firepower all around us doesn't fully quell my anxiety. We are in the middle of a small fleet of warships: two battlecarriers and their respective battle groups, almost twenty ships in total. The plot is dotted with icons for friendly ships: four space control cruisers, four frigates, several scout corvettes, and two supply ships, all surrounding the two carriers at the center of the display like a cloud of satellites orbiting a binary star cluster. None of the ships in the combined task force are older than ten years. The battle group assembled in this space right now is vastly more powerful than the entire combined fleet of Earth just ten years ago, and it only represents a sixth of the new fleet. But I've been in battle against Lanky seed ships before, and I have seen just how quickly those friendly ship icons on the plot can wink out of existence one by one.

On my console screen, the external feed from the optical sensors gives me a seamless view of the space around *Washington*. Just a few kilometers away, ACS *Johannesburg* hangs seemingly motionless in the blackness of deep space, aligned in the same attitude and heading as we are so that the two carriers are in parallel formation. *Jo'burg* is a Mark II Avenger, slightly more advanced than *Washington*, but I'd be hard-pressed to tell them apart without their different paint schemes and hull markings. It's comforting to see another Avenger alongside, dozens of missile silos and a double particle-cannon mount wrapped in half a million tons of steel and titanium alloy, armor that renders her almost invulnerable to the kinetic penetrators of Lanky seed ships. Each Avenger is armed with forty-eight nuclear missiles and a dozen Orion kinetic energy missiles, and just one of these ships could bomb Earth back into the Pleistocene. The only way we could develop and field warships with that much destructive potential was to spread them around among all the contributing alliances of Earth. The NAC and the SRA have three each, and six more are crewed and financed by the smaller power blocs: the African Commonwealth, the South American Union, the Euros, the South Pacific Alliance, and Korea and Japan. It's a carefully calibrated balance of power, made necessary by the inherent tendency of our species to abuse strength. Our biggest challenge isn't going to be defeating the Lankies, but resisting the temptation to use all this new firepower against each other when the outside threat is gone.

I've checked all my systems dozens of times in the past week, but I go through the routine again as I watch the replenishment ballet. The TacOps station is tied into every tactical subsystem on the ship, and the technology infusion from the Koreans and the Euros has boosted our neural network capabilities tenfold since I last served in this chair. Every request I send is executed immediately, no matter how mundane the query, using seemingly unlimited bandwidth. My team is fully staffed with qualified people; we have all the equipment we need, and every ship in the task force has full magazines and supply racks. We're on a warship designed to hunt and kill Lankies, proven in its ability to stand toe-to-toe with them in space and on the ground. I should feel optimistic about the mission. But as I look around the CIC and watch everyone go through their own routines, I wonder if all this new technology is making us more confident than we ought to be. Maybe the half decade since the last big battle has served to blunt the memory of our fear. Or maybe it's our way of facing that fear and conquering it—to put an end to our collective nightmares. Maybe we need reassurance that the monsters in the dark aren't inevitable forces of nature, that they can be dragged into the light and killed.

As I finish my tasks and shut down my display screens, I glance over to the command pit and see that Lieutenant Colonel Campbell is watching me from across the CIC. When she realizes that I've noticed, she averts her gaze and walks over to the helm station. Now that I know who her father was, I can't fail to spot the resemblance every time I see her. She's tall and lean like he was, and she inherited some of his features, like the shape of his nose and the line of her jaw and cheekbones. Colonel Campbell died eight years ago when he sacrificed himself and NACS *Indianapolis* to stop the Lanky seed ship that had broken through Earth's last-ditch defenses, and his picture is on memorial display in a lot of Fleet facilities. Even her body language and command presence remind me of her father, and I wonder whether she adopted them consciously or naturally.

"*Cincinnati* and *Nashville* are reporting they're ready for their scouting run," the comms officer reports, and Lieutenant Colonel Campbell turns back toward the holotable.

"Very well. Give them the green light to depart the formation and wish them Godspeed," she says. "If all goes well, we'll see *Cincy* in twenty-one hours."

"Aye, ma'am," the comms officer replies.

He relays the XO's directions to the two scout ships. A few moments later, their plot icons move out of the static formation of the battle group and accelerate away toward the Alcubierre point. I request a visual from the ship's exterior sensor feed, and the neural network replies instantly, showing me high-definition imagery of both stealth corvettes as they break rank and streak off toward the transit node. While most of the Fleet's ships have switched to the new high-visibility paint scheme, the stealth ships are still coated in nonreflective flat black that seems to soak up light photons, and I am once again amazed by how difficult it is to see them against the background of space even through the high-powered optics of *Washington*'s sensor arrays.

"Scouting element is away," the XO announces. "Clock's ticking. Give me a mission timer, please."

On the forward bulkhead, a timer projection appears, then begins to count down from 21:00:00. The stealth corvettes will be at the Alcubierre point in two hours, where they will start their six-hour run into the Capella system. If all goes well, *Nashville* will remain on station right on the other side of the Alcubierre chute in Capella. *Cincinnati* will reappear in the solar system in twenty-one hours with up-to-date reconnaissance data, at which point the task force will be in position for the main advance.

"Twenty-one hours to stock up on beans and bullets," Lieutenant Colonel Campbell says. "And then the war is back on."

Some of the officers in the CIC voice their cheerful agreement. None of the ones who sound positive about the XO's proclamation look like they're old enough to have been in the service when we took on the Lankies on Mars. I know for sure that none of them were there the last time we set foot in the Capella system, because I was there, twelve years and a hundred thousand lives ago, back when we were still thinking of ourselves as the undisputed masters of the galaxy.

Be very careful what you wish for, I think. *Out there, things can go sideways in a hurry. Even in a shiny new ship.*

I know they think they're prepared, because I did back when I was in their shoes. And I know they have no idea, because I didn't, either.

After my watch, when I am back in my cabin, I check the current comms delay to Earth. We are well outside the asteroid belt, and the light-speed comms need forty-seven minutes to travel home. When Halley and I both serve on Earth or Luna, we have to contend with a delay of a second at most, which means that all our comms in the last two years have been face-to-face talks, but that's not an option when you have to wait three-quarters of an hour for a reply to your statements. On deep-space deployments, we send video messages instead, if we are allowed the bandwidth, and text missives if we aren't. *Washington* has an abundance of bandwidth, so I start up my terminal to send a video to Halley before we transition out of system. But when I see the green ready light next to the optical sensor, I don't quite know what to tell my wife in the moment, so I put the terminal on standby again to gather my thoughts.

Twelve years of good-byes. I should know all the different ways to say this by now, I think. We've done sappiness, snark, dark humor, flippancy, and a dozen other moods. But there's never an easy way to have this last talk before a combat deployment. No matter which mood we choose, or how many of them we manage to cycle through in a single conversation, it's always unnatural to have to think about the possibility that it's going to be the last time we see and talk to each other.

"Here we go," I say into the sensor when I've finally collected myself.

"We're about to jump off. The task force is under information blackout, so I can't tell you where we're headed. You know the Fleet bullshit. But it's not a training milk run.

"It's all stuff we've both done before, so don't worry too much. I'll get on comms again as soon as I can. In the meantime, I want you to know that your ass still looks good in a flight suit, and that I'll be your left-seater anytime. Even if I hate the view from up front. And if I get unlucky somehow, you know the drill. I'll see you in the hills above town at night when it's cold and the sky is clear."

Whenever we have information blackouts, I have to be careful which words I choose so the automatic censoring algorithms don't intervene and garble my message or delete it entirely. But after twelve years together, Halley and I have our own common history and vocabulary to send each other clues about what's happening without having to spell everything out. Capella A was our first deployment together, right after I managed to get myself assigned to her ship, the ill-fated *Versailles*. We both still remember vividly what happened on that mission—our close escape from the disabled frigate in the spare drop ship, with me in the cockpit next to her for the white-knuckle ride down to the surface. I've only ridden in the cockpit with her twice, and I know she'll understand the reference. If I don't return, she will at least know where I went, even if the Fleet decides to keep a top-secret lid on the mission forever.

I smile into the sensor for a moment and end the message.

We have made it a habit to only say "I love you" in person, never in a vid chat or text message. If one of us buys it while we're apart, we want our last expression of that sentiment to be a memory of a face-to-face conversation, complete with the weight of the other's presence, not a line in a text or a half second of a recording that can be replayed endlessly to refresh the grief with every passing year. And when the skies above Liberty Falls are clear, Halley has line of sight to half the galaxy at night. I know that if I die in the Capella system, it will be forty-two years before the photons from the event reach the naked eye of anyone on the northern hemisphere of Earth. But the thought is comforting to us, and we've decided that in the absence of a cemetery to visit, we'll treat the visible night sky as grave markers for each other if it comes to that.

I've been in the service for twelve years. I've done hundreds of combat missions and out-of-system deployments, and my job has me steeped in the most testosterone-soaked part of the military, where everyone is highly skilled and capable, trained to be physically tough and mentally resilient. But in all this time, I've never managed to shake the awful, unwelcome little pang of despair and loneliness I feel whenever I send off that last communication right before a combat deployment.

CHAPTER 11

BAG WORK

"New contact, bearing two by positive fourteen; distance fifty thousand," the tactical officer calls out. "Checking IFF. Contact is friendly, sir. *Cincinnati* just transitioned back out of Alcubierre."

"Very well," Colonel Drake says. "They're a little early."

On the forward bulkhead, the mission timer still has thirty-one minutes left on its countdown. The icon that just appeared on the plot hologram fifty thousand kilometers in front of the task group turns from a yellow question mark to a blue lozenge shape. After a few moments, the IFF system does its handshake with the new arrival and displays a name and hull number next to the blue icon: "OCS-2 CINCINNATI." The stealth corvette makes a ninety-degree turn, away from the Alcubierre point, and lights its engines to clear the transition spot in space in a standard traffic avoidance maneuver, just in case someone else comes through the chute unexpectedly.

"*Cincinnati*, this is *Washington*. Welcome home. Glad to see you all in one piece. When you're ready, contact *Littleton* for pattern entry instructions to commence refueling ops," the comms officer says.

"Washington, Cincinnati. *Confirm handoff to* Littleton *for refueling ops. The tactical upload is commencing. The coast is clear on the other side.*

No enemy contact, and nothing is stirring for at least five light-minutes into the system."

"Glad to hear it, *Cincinnati*," Colonel Drake replies. "Now top off your tanks and take a breather because you'll have to get ready to do it again."

"Affirmative. Cincinnati *out."*

"At least we won't be jumping into a knife fight," the skipper says. "Maybe they've packed up and left."

"Wouldn't hurt my feelings any," Lieutenant Colonel Campbell says. "Although it would be a terrible waste to bring all this firepower across forty light-years and then not use it."

"Let's go through the tactical upload from *Cincy* before we roll in like we own the neighborhood again," Drake replies. "I want to take some time to look over the recon data while we head for the node. In the meantime, let's get this procession on the way. Two-minute transition intervals, carriers first, cruisers next, then the tin cans. Let the supply ships bring up the rear. Regroup on the far end in deep-space formation, then resupply again. Whatever we find in that system, I want to have everyone topped off before we head in."

"Aye, sir," the XO replies. "Comms, give the green light to the battle group for acceleration. All ahead at one gravity, follow the carriers in two-minute intervals. Fifty-three minutes to the transition point."

"Aye, ma'am," the comms officer says and starts relaying the instructions to the rest of the combined battle group. A few moments later, the situational orb on the plot table stirs into movement as *Washington* and *Johannesburg* burn their main engines and accelerate toward the transition point at one standard Earth gravity. The artificial gravity system compensates for the acceleration so efficiently that my inner ear never even feels the movement, even though we just went from coasting in space to moving forward at almost ten meters per second squared.

One by one, the other ships of the battle group line up behind the two carriers, one taking up position in the queue every two minutes, until the fleet is strung out in space in a long line of warships that stretches thousands of kilometers. The most dangerous part of the transition will be the exit from the Alcubierre chute in the Capella system—if the Lankies manage to ambush the first ships, the rest will find themselves in the middle of a battle once they emerge because there's no way to wave them off while they're in Alcubierre. But the second most dangerous part will be the traffic caused by almost twenty warships emerging into the same spot in space in two-minute intervals. A cruiser rear-ending a carrier at hundreds of meters per second can cause every bit as much destruction as a broadside from a Lanky seed ship. We have navigation procedures just for that purpose—the ships of the battle group will take sharp turns in alternating directions once they come out on the far end—but the Fleet hasn't had a chance to execute large-scale transitions in a while, and this is the largest Alcubierre deployment I've ever seen. It would be terribly anticlimactic to die in a multi-ship pileup while exiting a transit node. But astrogation and helm are not under my control, and I wouldn't be much good at the job even if they were, so I'll have to trust in the skills and the training of the young lieutenants and NCOs who crew those stations right now.

"All departments are reporting ready for transition, sir," the XO tells Colonel Drake. He nods and drums his fingers lightly on the armrest of his command chair. If he is anxious or nervous about our impending forty-two-light-year sprint into Lanky-controlled space, it's not showing in his demeanor. Back when I joined the Fleet, the commander of a warship was the Old Man, and all of them *were* old from the perspective of a twenty-one-year-old kid from the PRCs who thought he would be young and fit forever. But now that I am in my midthirties, Colonel Drake doesn't look that much older. He has maybe fifteen years on me, and his trim frame and handsome looks make him seem younger than he is. Our generation is now in command positions, and to all the lieutenants and enlisted on the ship, *we're* the Old Guys now. It feels strange to think of myself as a leader and mentor, because part of me still feels like that young kid who stepped off the bus and onto those yellow footsteps at NACRD Orem on the first day of boot camp.

"All right," Colonel Drake says. "Put me on the 1MC, please."

"You are on the 1MC, sir," the comms officer says.

"All hands, this is the commander. We are about to make the Alcubierre hop into our target system. I can't tell you our destination until we've completed the transition. But I *can* tell you that this will not be a training mission. If you hear a Combat Stations alert from here on out, it won't be a drill. You all know your jobs. Time to put your training to the test. That is all. Commander out."

He signals to the comms officer to end the connection. Then he gets up from his chair and walks over to the holotable, where he leans in to study the procession of warships heading for the Alcubierre node.

"Well," he says. "If this one goes badly, it won't be for a lack of firepower. Warm up the Alcubierre drive. Pass the word to the battle group to transition in sequence. Let's go pick ourselves a fight."

I've been on shore and in-system duty long enough to have almost forgotten just how much I dislike Alcubierre travel, that peculiar feeling of low-level ache that seems to pull on every bone in the body at the same time like growing pains, that slightly metallic taste in the mouth, and the way everything I touch with my bare hands feels like it's charged with low levels of electricity. Over the years, I've learned that focusing on the weird sensations only makes the trip more unpleasant, and that the best way to ride it out is to find some vigorous physical activity that occupies the body and takes the mind off the odd sensory dissonance.

When we transition into Alcubierre for our six-hour dash, I leave the CIC and head down to my quarters to change into exercise gear. Then I make my way to the officer gym that's set up next to the racetrack around the nuclear missile silos.

NACS *Washington* is brand-new, and so is her workout equipment. The officer gym is well stocked with the latest in strength and cardio machinery. But I am not a fan of the weight stations or the rowing machines because I don't like repetitive workouts. Instead, I either run around the track or work on the heavy boxing bag, depending on my mood for the day.

Today, I want to punch something, but when I put on my wraps and bag gloves and walk into the gym, the heavy bag is already in use. Lieutenant Colonel Campbell has beaten me down to the facility, and she is working the bag methodically, with a quick rotation of jabs, crosses, and body punches. She has her back turned to me, and there's a dark sweat stain on her workout shirt already. We're alone for now, and there's plenty more I could be doing while she's taking up the bag, but I don't want to undo my wraps and take off the gloves again just to do a few sets of pull-ups or bench presses. Instead, I walk over to one of the wall mirrors and start shadowboxing, shuffling stances and exhaling loudly with each flurry of punches to make the XO aware that someone else may want to get some bag work in.

After a while, I work through my combinations slowly to check my form while I watch Lieutenant Colonel Campbell in the mirror to observe her skills. She is giving the heavy bag a mauling with her hard-hitting crosses and hooks, and the bag is jingling loudly with each blow as it jumps at the end of its chain attachment under the barrage. Now that she's just in her formfitting workout shirt, I can tell that the XO has quite a bit of muscle on her tall frame—not the flashy bulk from lots of lifting, but the lean and defined kind that comes from throwing lots of punches at heavy things for years. Campbell has her long hair tied back into a loose ponytail that bounces with every set of blows she lays into the bag. It's a large bag, forty or fifty kilos at least, but she hits it hard enough that she has to interrupt her combos and reposition herself every few seconds because her force is making the bag swing out of her reach.

I walk over to the bag stand and grab the bag with both arms as it swings toward me. Then I plant my feet and cup the bottom of the bag with my gloves to hold it in position for the XO, a common courtesy for another boxer wanting to do more efficient bag work without having to chase the bag around.

She pauses for a moment as I position myself, then she continues her combination of punches. Her jabs are light, but every time she hauls off with a right cross or a hook, she puts all her weight into the strike, and the force travels all the way through the bag and makes me widen my stance and lower my center of gravity to avoid getting knocked back. Lieutenant Colonel Campbell is quick, strong, and sure-footed, and she keeps up her guard perfectly even as she is getting winded. After a while of gauging her technique and taking the full force of her hits, I conclude that I only have a few centimeters of reach and maybe twenty kilos of weight on her, and if we went at it in the ring, she'd be a pretty tough opponent.

I hold the bag for her, expecting her to get tired out quickly by the relentless pace of her punches. But I keep an eye on the time readout on the bulkhead, and she keeps up her intensive tempo for five minutes, shuffling stances in between her attack flurries, breathing hard but never dropping her arms from their guard position whenever she isn't striking the bag. Finally, she steps back a little, bends over with her gloves on her knees, and lets her breath slow down for a few moments.

"Your turn," she says.

I take up the challenge and move in front of the bag while she replicates my assist position, still breathing hard, her face shiny with sweat and her workout shirt soaked.

Anything worth doing is worth overdoing, I think, and check the tightness of my gloves' wrist straps. Then I lift my hands into guard position and start my own bag workout.

It doesn't take long for me to fall into my usual rhythm of combinations. I hadn't intended to go all-out this afternoon, but the XO set the bar high with her own workout, and after my dressing-down by her after the briefing, I don't want to give her the satisfaction of knowing that she worked up more of a sweat than I did. So I do my best to return the favor and try to knock her back with the punches I am driving into the bag, probing jabs followed by hard right crosses that make the bag's attachment chain chime brightly in the otherwise silent gym. I focus on my breathing and synchronize it with my punches, exhaling to empty my lungs every time I drive home one of my strikes.

Lieutenant Colonel Campbell widens her own stance and leans into the bag, but I can tell that she's barely holding on to the weight as I drive a successively heavier series of combinations into the bag, again and again. Before she can lose her footing, I back off a little and switch to quick jabs, satisfied that I managed to move her a few centimeters. It feels good to let off a little bit of steam in a sanctioned way after getting chewed out by the XO. It's a long-standing tradition that rank doesn't count during martial arts practice, and I don't have to give deference to her insignia or her status while we are both wearing gloves and engaging in a voluntary contest out here in the gym.

My five minutes at the bag seems like two hours. I make myself stay on the offense for the same length of time as she did, but my arms feel like pudding and my lungs are burning long before my time runs out. I know that the fatigue is showing on my face and in the increasing slowness of my movements just like it did with her, but I don't want to show any weakness in front of the XO. When the counter ticks over the five-minute mark, I put in another fifteen seconds for good measure and then lower my gloves, standing hunched over to catch my breath.

"Thanks for the spotting," Campbell says. "You punch hard. But you drop your arms too much in between combinations. Especially when you get tired. Watch out if you decide to go looking for sparring partners down in Grunt Country. Lots of young and strong SI corporals who'd be happy to put a podhead officer on his ass in front of everyone."

"I know my limits," I say in between panting breaths.

She smiles curtly and undoes her bag gloves, then pulls them off her hands with her teeth. There's a towel on a workout bench nearby, and she walks over to it to pick it up and wipe her face. Then she nods at me and walks out of the gym without another word, leaving me to catch my breath and slow down my heart rate to normal again.

Now that I am alone in the gym, I have my pick of equipment without having to wait a turn or spot for someone first, but the burst of intense, violent focus has used up my stamina reserves and turned my muscles into aching jelly. The exercise has served its purpose, however—I can't feel the Alcubierre discomfort anymore underneath the fatigue, and for a little while, I wasn't thinking about the fact that we are moving a tenth of a light-year farther away from Earth and Halley with every passing minute.

CHAPTER 12

CAPELLA, REVISITED

"General quarters, general quarters. All hands, man your combat stations. Set material condition Zebra throughout the ship. This is not a drill."

I've been drawing looks from some of the new lieutenants in the CIC ever since I walked in wearing my bug suit. Now I complete the ensemble by putting on my helmet and sealing it to the collar flange. Everyone else in the CIC is wearing standard Fleet vacsuits over their regular uniforms, but SOCOM personnel and SI troops put on their battle armor for general quarters. If something goes wrong and we have to take to the pods, there will be no time to change into armor, and a grunt without battle armor is useless in space or on the ground. When I turn on my helmet and activate the heads-up display, I know that I must look alien and intimidating to the new Fleet officers. The bug suit is shiny and black like an insect carapace when the polychromatic camouflage is turned off, and the helmet has no face shield or visor because those are unnecessary weak spots, useless in the hypercapnic atmospheres of Lanky-occupied moons and planets where they would fog up almost instantly in the warm, carbon-dioxide-rich air.

Big, imperialist insect, I think as I settle back in my chair and buckle into my seat harness, and a smile crosses my face when the voice in my head has a strong Russian accent. I haven't seen my friend Dmitry since we fought together on Mars, but we've exchanged messages over the last few years, and I know that he's the SRA equivalent of a sergeant major now, the highest rung he can climb on the noncommissioned officer ladder. Like Master Sergeant Leach back at the training base in Iceland, Dmitry thinks I am a complete idiot for letting the Corps promote me into the officer ranks, and I stopped disagreeing a long time ago.

"Transitioning out of Alcubierre in T-minus five," the XO says from her seat next to the command chair, where Colonel Drake is observing the proceedings.

The situational display above the plot table is empty except for the icon for *Washington* in the center because sensors and radar don't work in the superluminal space-time bubble of an active Alcubierre drive, and the distances involved would be too vast for the ship's sensors anyway. If all the other ships of the task force followed their orders and transitioned in the right intervals, we have fifteen craft traveling in the chute behind us, one every two-tenths of a light-year, strung out in a very long line that would take years to cover at subluminal speeds outside of Alcubierre. But there's no way to verify their presence until they start to emerge from the chute after us in a few minutes. Alcubierre travel is like driving in a straight line in the middle of the night with the headlights off and the windows darkened and hitting the brakes at exactly the right fraction of a millisecond to come to a stop at the intended destination.

"All departments report ready for action, sir," Lieutenant Colonel Campbell says.

"Very well," Colonel Drake replies. "Once we are in-system, ping *Nashville* and make sure the neighborhood is still clear. Low-power tight beam. Other than that, full EMCON on the comms and main sensors. I don't want anything else broadcasting outside of the hull."

"*Cincinnati* said there's nothing stirring within five light-minutes of the node," the XO says. "I wonder why the Lankies aren't keeping an eye on the back door. They have got to know where it is by now."

"They've had the system to themselves for almost twelve years," Colonel Drake says. "Maybe they get complacent just like humans."

Lieutenant Colonel Campbell shoots me a glance as if she expects me to challenge the commander's ad hoc hypothesis. I take advantage of the opaque nature of my bug suit helmet and pretend that I am not noticing her pointed look in my direction. The chip on her shoulder is still firmly lodged there even after our training session together. I don't know why she dislikes me, but I suspect that her issues go beyond the fact that I spoke out of turn in the command staff meeting.

I watch the mission clock tick down to the transition, one second at a time, minute by long minute. Coming out of Alcubierre is always a relief because the unpleasant sensations of superluminal travel go away, and it's always a source of anxiety at the same time because of the chance for an ambush or a collision as we emerge from the far end of the transit chute. The chance of instant death is small, but it exists, and I usually close my eyes and think of Halley when we exit from Alcubierre.

"Ten seconds until transition," the lieutenant at the helm announces on the 1MC. "Seven. Six. Five . . ."

When the countdown ends and we come out of Alcubierre, it feels like the world that has been slightly out of calibration for the last six hours shifts back into its proper phase. I sit in my chair with my eyes closed, savoring the feeling of mild discomfort leaving my body.

"Alcubierre transition complete," the helmsman says. "All systems in the green. Executing exit turn to portside, ninety degrees by positive forty-five, ahead one-quarter gravity."

"Astrogation, confirm our position, please," Colonel Drake says.

"Aye, sir. Stand by for astrogation fix."

The astrogation officer brings up his console and activates data fields. A few moments later, the situational orb in the center of the command pit has a new star chart overlay, and the celestial bodies in the sector flash on one by one as the positioning system gets a fix on our surroundings.

"We are on the far end of the Alcubierre chute in the Capella A system, sir. Right where we are supposed to be."

"Signal *Nashville* and check in," Colonel Drake says. "And open the 1MC for me."

"You're on the 1MC, sir," the comms officer says. All around me, the CIC personnel resume their activities as we all let out a collective breath of relief.

"All hands, this is the commander. We have completed our transition. Welcome to the Capella system. We are the first Fleet task force to enter this sector in twelve years. As you go about your duties, never lose sight of the fact that we are now on the enemy's turf. This is hostile space. Do not get complacent. We are far from home, and if we get ourselves into a tangle, backup will be a very long way off, too far away to make a difference. Stay sharp and remain focused. And if you hear a general quarters alert, move to your combat stations like your lives depend on it, because they will. Commander out."

"Tight-beam signal from *Nashville*, sir."

"Put it on the overhead," Colonel Drake orders.

"Aye, sir."

"Washington, Nashville," the voice from the scout corvette says. *"Welcome to Capella. The neighborhood is quiet. Stand by to receive current recon data upload."*

"*Nashville, Washington* Actual," Colonel Drake replies. "We are ready for your upload."

On the plot, a blue icon appears thirty thousand kilometers in front of us. A second or two later, a label appears that marks the new contact as "OCS-9 NASHVILLE." Our stealth ship is coasting slowly through space without burning her drive. With her light-absorbing black paint and her lack of active emissions, she is silent and invisible even to the passive sensors of the carrier. Only the active data link makes *Nashville*'s position on the plot unambiguous for now, and I know that as soon as the signal ends, the stealth corvette will disappear from the plot again.

"New contact, bearing two hundred by zero. Contact is friendly. *Johannesburg* is through the chute, sir," the tactical officer says.

"Signal them to double their clearance for follow-up traffic. We have a lot more hardware coming up from behind."

"Aye, sir."

On the plot, *Johannesburg*'s icon appears behind our portside stern and immediately makes a turn to starboard, mirroring our own maneuver to the other side of the transit node until the two carriers are facing in opposite directions, opening up the space between them to make room for the armada that is about to appear in that spot one by one for the next thirty minutes.

I shift my attention back to the console screen at my station and tap into the optical feed, then I cycle through the views until I've found the system suns. Capella A is a binary system, but the two stars at its center orbit each other so closely that they look like a single star most of the time. I last saw the pale-yellow light of this binary star twelve years ago, when I was serving on NACS *Versailles* on my first spaceborne deployment, with Halley on the same ship as a junior drop-ship pilot. The thought of Halley makes me feel a pang of something like homesickness, but it's not exactly the yearning for a place. We escaped death and beat the odds together here, with almost no experience and a lot of dumb luck. It was the cornerstone of our relationship and everything that followed, though—our eventual marriage and our long campaign against the Lankies. Being here without her doesn't feel quite right. This is the place where we became an *us*. Returning here by myself feels like I am about to overwrite that memory with new ones. Masoud couldn't have known the history of our relationship before Arcadia, but I resent him for this anyway. I'm certain I would have turned down the job if I had known where it would take me, back here where my life really began. If I die here, Halley will be alone, and the last twelve years will be undone, and now that my mother is gone, my wife's memories will be the only evidence of my existence.

Always a hook in the steak, I think, remembering Halley's comment on Masoud's offer. But then I dismiss the thought of another setup on the general's part. The rational section of my brain realizes that Masoud isn't prescient, that he had no way of knowing the details of the mission or our destination ahead of time. And I took the assignment of my own free will, accepting that it would most likely lead somewhere dangerous. Whatever happens here in the Capella system, Masoud won't be around, and I resolve to banish the general from my thoughts until we get back. This time, the fate of the SOCOM team is all up to me.

An hour and a half after our transition, the battle group is back in combat formation on the Capella side of the Alcubierre chute, and we are headed away from the node at a slow and careful pace. In front of us, *Washington*'s recon drones are rushing ahead into the system, little flashlights illuminating a path for us in the vast darkness. My anxiety has lessened a little, but I still watch the plot display out of the corner of my eye as we advance, expecting to see the signal-orange icon of a confirmed Lanky contact pop up at any moment. They didn't lie in wait and ambush us at the transition point to take our fleet out one by one, so the most dangerous part of this phase is over. But I know that doesn't mean the Lankies didn't notice our ingress into their territory and send out half a dozen seed ships to intercept our battle group.

"The recon drones have covered half the distance to Willoughby," the tactical officer says from her console. "No contacts reported so far."

"We're still calling it Willoughby, are we?" The XO steps up to the plot table and leans forward to examine the deployment pattern. "I think it reverted to Capella Ac when they scraped the last of us off the rocks down there."

"It'll be Willoughby again someday," Colonel Drake says. "Just not this week. Not with what we brought. But we can knock down the odds a little for when that day comes."

When that day comes, I think. We're still prying Lankies out of the ground on Mars, seven years after beating them on the surface. When they have taken over a planet or a moon, they cling to it with a ferocity and determination that we can't match. And Willoughby—Capella Ac—was a bit of a backwater colony before the Lankies claimed it, with nothing special to distinguish it that would bump it to the top of a priority list for invasion. What we're doing now really is like poking a hornet's nest with a stick to see how many of them remain, even if it's a really big stick. That day, if it ever does come, will be too far in the future for me or Halley to see, and the certainty of that knowledge is a profound comfort. We will be the generation that stopped the tide. Pushing it back will be the task of another. There are too many of them and too few of us out among the stars for it to go any other way, no matter how many new weapons we have built in the last seven years.

In our solar system, on our own turf, the battle group seemed stupendously powerful. Sixteen state-of-the-art warships, armed with the latest weapons, more destructive power than we've ever put into space together at the same time. Kinetic energy missiles, particle cannons, nuclear warheads, automatic rail guns, enough potential energy to throw Earth itself into a long and lethal winter. But now that we're on the other side of the Alcubierre chute, with the sea of darkness cloaking the unknown all around us, our formation doesn't seem nearly as formidable as it did above Daedalus a few weeks ago. Just a few thousand humans, probing their way through the void in fragile titanium hulls, having to carry all their air and food and water along with them as they go. The situational display is zoomed out to the maximum awareness scale of the passive sensors, light-minutes of space, and the little cluster of ship icons at the center of it looks very lonely in the middle of so much unfriendly emptiness.

I hope we're enough, I think. *For whatever it is they sent us to do out here.*

CHAPTER 13

INTERCEPT

Six hours after we arrive in the Capella system, I see my first Lanky seed ship in four years.

It's almost a relief when the bright orange lozenge shape of a confirmed enemy ship appears on the plot, where it somehow becomes more significant than all the other symbols, as if the Capella system just shifted its center of gravity to it. Until this moment, the primitive part of my brain has done its best to convince me that the Lankies have found a way to avoid the passive sensors from our drones and scout ships, that we have been advancing into a cloud of seed ships without noticing them. The orange icon on the tactical display is proof to the contrary. But that same part of my brain has been primed for years to associate the signal color with mortal danger, and it reacts with the same reflexive fear that prehistoric humans would have felt at the sound of a pack of wolves howling in the darkness beyond the light of the campfire.

"Contact," the tactical officer, Captain Steadman, calls out in a voice that is unreasonably calm to my ears. "Enemy seed ship, bearing three-five-five by positive zero-one-one, range eight million, five hundred fifty thousand. *Nashville* is confirming the drone data, sir."

"Twenty-five light-seconds out," Colonel Drake says. "I was hoping for a little more range on our eyeballs. But I'll take it. Better than having one pop up inside of minimum missile range."

On the plot, the blue orb representing the former colony planet Willoughby has appeared just inside our sphere of awareness, and the orange icon is right in front of it, the bright color enhanced and emphasized by the blue background.

"Tactical, we have our first customer of the day," Colonel Drake says. He gets out of his chair and walks up to the plot table. The XO follows suit. I stay right where I am because I have no useful input on the ship's tactical disposition, and because I am quite content to remain hooked up to my chair's service umbilical. We've been at general quarters for hours, but my bug suit has kept me perfectly comfortable with its built-in cooling. The vacsuits of the rest of the CIC crew only have rudimentary comfort features, and I can tell by the sheen on the faces all around me that it's much rougher to spend six hours in a vacsuit than in HEBA armor.

"Designate target Lima-1," Captain Steadman says. "Target velocity is two hundred fifty meters per second. That's pretty much the rotational speed of Capella Ac. Looks like they're in geostationary orbit right above the planetary equator."

"One seed ship," Lieutenant Colonel Campbell says in wonder. "If that's all they have in-system, this will be a short fight."

"I'll never be one to complain about favorable odds," Colonel Drake replies. "But let's not charge in with our guns blazing just yet. Tactical, get me a firing solution on Lima-1. Comms, let *Nashville* know to sit tight and wait out the planetary rotation. I don't want us to show up in orbit and find there were six more of them hiding on the other side of that rock. Do we have enough juice left in the drones to spotlight the far side?"

"Affirmative, sir."

"Then send them around and save us some time. Send the recon data to the rest of the battle group, and inform *Johannesburg* that we intend to engage the enemy as soon as we have the full picture from the drones."

"We're not going to give them the honor of the first shot?" the XO asks. "They're probably itching to be the first allied ship with a confirmed kill."

"It's been four years since we launched a war shot at a Lanky ship. And this will be the first time we use one of the Orion Vs. I'm not too keen on putting that responsibility on a green crew. They'll get their chance soon enough, I think."

I bring up the optical feed relayed by the scout ship that is holding station five million kilometers ahead of us with its sensors trained on Capella Ac. When I was here with Halley on the frigate *Versailles* twelve years ago, I didn't have much time for sightseeing, but I remember that the planet looked different. Back then, the view was Earthlike except for the shapes of the continents. But there was lots of blue and green, patches and swirls of clouds in the atmosphere, sunlight reflecting off the surface of the oceans. Now the whole planet is shrouded in clouds, without a single gap in the cover to give me a glimpse at the surface below.

The Lankies like their worlds warm and high in carbon dioxide, and whatever they use to terraform the colony planets they steal from us can flip the atmosphere to their preference in mere months. Willoughby has been theirs for over a decade, plenty of time to turn the place into whatever they consider their ideal habitat. I remember the mortally wounded *Versailles*, shot full of holes by Lanky penetrators, already on a trajectory that would lead her down into the atmosphere and turn her into a fiery comet when Halley and I dropped out of her hangar with the spare drop ship, the last people to leave the ship before it disintegrated. I wonder if any of the major wreckage pieces made it down to the surface, and whether they sit there still, overgrown and corroded in the warm, humid air. There were scores of human dead down there as well, but I'm sure that there won't be any bodies left after all this time. We don't fully understand what the Lankies do with human remains, but we do know they collect them and carry them off. The scientific consensus seems to be that they need the proteins as building materials for the seed ships, but the most common opinion in the Fleet is that they eat the corpses, and the gruesome theory naturally has more staying power than the clinical one.

The seed ship is a streamlined black cigar shape in front of the planet's cloud cover. I feel a chill trickling down my spine when I look at the familiar outline, bumps and ridges on an irregular surface that is so black it seems to swallow the sunlight. It plods on along its orbit, seemingly motionless as it rotates in sync with the planet below, oblivious of the virtual bull's-eye our tactical officer has drawn on it already.

I wonder how many protein chains in that hull used to be my crewmates, I think with a little shudder. But I was only on *Versailles* for a few weeks, and after all this time, I find that I can't recall a single name other than that of Colonel Campbell, who was the XO of the ship and went on to command *Indianapolis*. I still remember some of the faces, however—random crew members of *Versailles*, caught by surprise by the sudden decompression of their compartments and asphyxiated, corpses with terrified expressions floating in the semidarkness of the ship's passageways. They died without seeing what had killed them, the last humans in history who would know nothing of Lankies.

"We have a firing solution on Lima-1, sir," Captain Steadman says. "Orion time on target is twenty-nine minutes, forty-two seconds."

"Keep them locked in and update the solution as we get closer. I want to be able to launch our birds at any time. Weapons, warm up Orion missiles in tubes one and two."

"Warming up Orion tubes one and two, aye," the weapons officer replies. "Launch prep initiated."

The new Orion V missiles are half the size of the old Orions we used above Mars, so each Avenger can carry twice as many. But they're still enormous ship-sized missiles that have more mass than a corvette, so even an Avenger only has eight Orions, tucked away in two rows of ventral launch silos. Between *Washington* and *Johannesburg*, the battle group can engage sixteen seed ships at long range. Not every Orion we've ever launched in anger has scored a hit, but those that did have a 100 percent kill rate. Even if a quarter of our shots miss, we can blot a dozen seed ships out of space with the rest, and we've never faced off against that many, not even when we went up against the fleet they had around Mars. With two Avengers aiming their Orions at it right now, the solitary seed ship in orbit around Capella Ac is living on borrowed time, and it will die as quickly as my shipmates did above the same planet twelve years ago when Versailles ran into a Lanky minefield. The thought of this impending karmic symmetry fills me with grim satisfaction.

For the next thirty minutes, we continue our course toward the former colony planet. The distance readout next to the seed ship's blaze-orange icon counts down with every passing second. There's no maximum range for the Orions—they will burn out their nuclear charges and then coast ballistically once they've stopped accelerating—but there's a line on the plot marking the minimum range, the point in space where a launch would be too close to the target for the kinetic warhead to build up enough energy for a certain kill. It's still a long way from reaching the orange seed ship icon, but it draws closer to it every minute. The Avengers have a very long spear and a very short sword to back it up, and nothing at all to cover the range in between.

"New contact, bearing three-five-eight by positive two," the tactical officer announces. "Distance seven million, two hundred thirty-nine thousand. Designate Lima-2. Another seed ship just popped up on the equatorial horizon. Same bearing and speed as the first one."

"Looks like *Jo'burg* will get a shot at glory after all," Colonel Drake says. "Hand off the target data to them and ask them to lock on with their Orions for a simultaneous time-on-target launch."

"Aye, sir," the tactical officer says and turns toward his console to contact his counterpart on *Johannesburg*.

The second Lanky seed ship emerges on the left side of the planet just above the horizon and makes its way around the equator line, following the course of the first seed ship. Against the vast backdrop of the world, it looks tiny and forlorn even at maximum magnification. I bring up a window with the live image from the other ship and move the outlines next to each other on my screen. The second ship is noticeably different from the first—shorter by maybe five hundred meters, with a more streamlined and even hull shape. However the Lankies manage to put these things together, standardization does not seem to be on their list of priorities.

"Give me a time to target for the Orions, please," the commander says.

"Time to target is twenty-four minutes, eleven seconds, sir. *Johannesburg* has locked on to Lima-2 and is tracking the target. They are reporting ready for launch."

Our recon drones continue their patrol arc, expanding our sphere of awareness with every passing minute. When the plot expands beyond Capella Ac and starts to show the space on the far side of the planet, I almost expect to see a cluster of two or twenty orange icons, a hidden fleet of seed ships ready to spring their trap and converge on us. But when the drones complete their sweep, the only orange markers on the plot are the two seed ships we have already spotted.

"The drones have eyeballs on the dark side," Captain Steadman says. "*Nashville* confirms that we only have two bogeys above the planet."

"Hand off terminal guidance to *Nashville* and open the launch door on tube one."

"Uplink confirmed. Opening launch door on tube one. Tube one is ready to launch, sir."

Colonel Drake looks around the CIC, where everyone seems to be holding their collective breaths.

"This is where we commit," he says. "Weapons, fire on my mark. In three. Two. One. Fire."

Lieutenant Lawrence, the weapons officer, flips the manual cover off the launch button for Orion silo number one and presses down firmly. A second later, a slight vibration goes through *Washington*'s hull as the one-thousand-ton Orion V missile leaves its launch tube, propelled by a chemical booster rocket. I watch the feed from the starboard sensors to see *Johannesburg* disgorge her own Orion from its ventral launch tube. Both missiles streak away from the formation in a wide arc. When they are a few thousand kilometers from the battle group, their guidance systems nudge them onto new courses, and I watch their trajectories on the plot curve toward the Lanky seed ships.

"Booster engines shutting off. Nuclear ignition in three . . . two . . . one," the weapons officer narrates.

On the plot, the little blue V shapes representing the Orion missiles leap ahead as if someone accelerated reality by a factor of ten. Some five thousand kilometers away from the battle group, the two missiles just started their nuclear propulsion systems, expelling atomic charges and igniting them behind the ablative pusher plates at their rears, one explosion every second. It's a crude and brutal approach to propelling a missile, but it's by far the fastest method to accelerate an object, and no other way comes even close. If we had people on the Orions, the hundreds of gravities of acceleration would overwhelm even the best artificial gravity compensators in a few milliseconds and turn the crew into a fine organic mush. But the warheads on the tips of the missiles are inert blocks of super-dense materials—depleted uranium and tungsten—crude-looking cylinders that nobody bothered to even shape into penetrating points like our rifle bullets. Whatever the Orions hit at the end of their acceleration run must absorb insane amounts of kinetic energy in a few nanoseconds, and not even seed ships are tough enough to withstand that sort of blow.

"Missiles are on the way," Captain Steadman says. "Time to target is now twenty-two minutes, thirty-one seconds."

On my screen, I still have an active overlay that shows the seed ships side by side. They're creeping along their orbital paths quietly and steadily, unaware of the warheads accelerating toward them at hundreds of gravities per second and working up apocalyptic levels of kinetic energy. If one of the missiles fails to hit its designated target, it will slice through the atmosphere of Capella Ac in mere seconds and slam into the ground with a force many times greater than all the nuclear warheads in the task force combined. We never fire Orions at seed ships when the backstop is a planet with humans on it. But Capella Ac has been Lanky soil for a long time now, and any lives we wipe out on the surface with a missed shot would only be a bonus.

Twenty-two minutes feel almost indeterminable when they are spent watching two little V-shaped icons crawling across the holographic orb of a tactical situation display. The missiles streak along at fractional light speed after using all their nuclear propellant charges, but it still takes a while to cross seven million kilometers of space, and as much as I would like, I can't will them along any faster. After clashing with the Lankies so many times, I fully expect some unforeseen twist that will put us on our heels once again. Any minute, the target ships will alter course and throw off our aim, or more seed ships will appear nearby seemingly out of nowhere and send our battle group running back to the Alcubierre node in full flight.

"Orions are tracking true," the tactical officer says when the missiles have reached the last phase of their intercept. "*Nashville* is switching the birds to autonomous terminal guidance. Velocity is one point one three percent of light speed."

"Don't nobody look out of the window over there and flinch," the XO mutters. Every set of eyeballs in the CIC is glued to the tactical display now.

"Thirty seconds to impact on Lima-1 and 2," Lieutenant Lawrence calls out.

"Put the target image on the forward bulkhead, maximum magnification," Colonel Drake says. A few moments later, the same image as on my terminal appears on the bulkhead, two long-distance visual feeds from *Nashville*'s sensors tiled next to each other. The seed ships are still making their way along their orbital track, sinister shapes contrasted against the cloud cover of the atmosphere.

The two blue icons rush toward the orange ones, increasing the gap between the missiles at the last moment to home in on their respective targets thousands of kilometers apart. The first seed ship is a few minutes away from disappearing behind the equatorial horizon. The other is a quarter of a planetary circumference behind, perfectly presented in the middle of the cloud-covered sphere like the bull's-eye in the center of a practice target.

"Ten seconds," Lieutenant Lawrence says.

On the plot, the blue Vs are close enough to the orange lozenges that I can't see any separation between them from my vantage point at the TacOps station. The time readout next to them races down toward zero. I shift my attention to the visual feeds projected onto the forward CIC bulkhead.

The Orion missiles are much too fast to show up in the image. Both seed ships disappear in brilliant flashes of light at the same instant. The fireballs are so intensely bright that they wash out the center of the sensor feed momentarily. *Nashville* zooms out a few factors of magnification until the frames show the entire planetary hemisphere. Two small suns are blooming in the spots where the Lanky seed ships were making their way around the planet just a few seconds ago.

"Kaboom," Lieutenant Colonel Campbell says softly, deep satisfaction in her voice. Her comment is drowned out by the claps and low cheers that erupt in the CIC. I stifle my own relieved cheer and pump my fist at the fireworks display on the screen instead. Whenever we engage the Lankies, I expect them to pull a new trick out of their sleeves because they have done it before more than a few times. It's a relief to see that our tactics still work even after four years, that our enemy hasn't adjusted to our new weapons yet.

"Splash two," Lieutenant Lawrence shouts into the commotion. "Intercept on Lima-1 and Lima-2."

"Good shot," Colonel Drake says. "Quiet down, everyone. Hold the parade until we have a post-strike assessment from *Nashville*."

We watch the fireworks on the visual feed for a few moments. The fireballs expand and start to dissipate, losing a little of their intense luminescence with every second. If there's anything left of the seed ships, it's too small for *Nashville*'s optics to pick up. Each seed ship just had the kinetic energy of a one-thousand-ton warhead traveling at 1 percent of light speed dumped into it, more than a gigaton released in a fraction of a second. Our species already had an amazing ability to devise ways to kill things, but the threat from the Lankies has pushed our destructive capabilities into a whole new dimension. I wish they could communicate with us, if only to make them appreciate the fact that their attempts to conquer our space has made us far more formidable foes than we were just a decade ago.

Should have finished us off when you had us on the ropes, I think. *Now this won't end until one of us wipes out the other. We're just wired that way.*

"*Nashville* confirms successful intercepts on both targets," Lieutenant Steadman reports from the tactical station. "Textbook broadside hits, no visible wreckage observed."

"Very well," Colonel Drake replies. "Send our congratulations to *Johannesburg* and inform them they can now paint a kill mark on the hull. Well done, everyone. Now let's get into orbit and see what the new management has done to the place since they kicked us out."

I'm not used to streaks of good fortune when it comes to dealing with Lankies, but it seems that the day still has some luck in store for us. When we approach Capella Ac a few hours later, the two space control cruisers take point to clear a way through the usual Lanky minefield for our initial scouting run. But when the cruisers have finished their optical survey of the space above the hemisphere, there are far fewer orange mine markers on the tactical display than I had expected. When we started our invasion of Mars, there was a cloud of Lanky proximity mines around the planet, and the Hammerhead cruisers in all the battle groups had to expend all their ammunition to blast gaps into the minefield for the drop ships. The minefield around Capella Ac is more than just patchy in comparison. After two hours of survey, the combined sensor data from both cruisers shows just a few dozen mines in the vicinity, with hundreds of kilometers of empty space between them.

"Guessing they weren't expecting visitors anymore after all these years," Lieutenant Colonel Campbell says when the cruisers have finished their data upload.

"That's fine with me. We won't have to use up half our rail-gun magazines just to get a good look at the surface."

"Something else, sir," Lieutenant Steadman says. "*Nashville* says that the mines seem to be inert. They flew one of the recon drones past a few of them, and there was no reaction."

"Really." Colonel Drake frowns at the plot, where the observed mines form a very sparse net above the hemisphere. Mapping and clearing mines is one of the main jobs of the Hammerhead cruisers. Their optical sensor suites map each mine and calculate its trajectory for the next few hours. The plot is crisscrossed with dotted orange lines.

"This is too easy," Lieutenant Colonel Campbell observes. "If they guard all their colonies like that, we can have them all back by next year."

"We haven't looked at the surface yet. Shooting seed ships out of orbit is just step one. It won't get us a square meter of ground down there," Colonel Drake says. He walks back to his chair and sits down, then takes off the helmet of his vacsuit.

"Tell the cruisers to clear whatever mines they see. I don't want those things to come close to the battle group, inert or not. Maybe they're just on standby and slow to wake up. I don't want to get too used to easy."

The colonel looks over to me and nods.

"Major Grayson, prepare to get a team assembled for a possible field trip. We're sending out recon flights as soon as the cruisers knock down those mines. Command meeting in the flag briefing room at 1400 hours."

"Aye, sir," I say and disconnect the service line that tethers me to my station. I still have a sense of unease, as if we're setting ourselves up for an elaborate trap. But right now I am glad for something else to do than look at a hologram and a set of display screens, even if it means preparing for a drop onto a planet that's most likely lousy with Lanky settlements. I never look forward to battle—no sane grunt ever does—but I had almost forgotten just how invigorating the feeling of anticipating a fight can be. The sense of tension and heightened perception that comes with an impending combat drop makes me feel more alive than anything else. It feels like my entire purpose is focused to a single razor-sharp point in place and time, with no place for uncertainty or ambiguity.

Maybe that little bastard Masoud was right, I think as I leave the CIC and head down to SOCOM Country to put the STT on alert. *Maybe I'm the fucking idiot he thinks I am, and I did miss the war after all.*

CHAPTER 14

PLANNING A FIELD TRIP

This time, I make sure to be in the flag briefing room ten minutes early just so I don't give the XO another reason to dislike me. In another life, back before I learned to put the satisfaction of my ego further down in the stack of my priorities, I would have enjoyed taking up the gauntlet. Now it's just a minor irritant, not important enough to justify the expense of energy or brain bandwidth.

"So far, so good," Colonel Drake says when we're all assembled. "We're still here, and there are two fewer seed ships in the galaxy since we arrived. If I were superstitious, I'd say it's a good omen for the remainder of the mission."

He turns on the viewscreen on the briefing room bulkhead, which changes to show a slice of the tactical plot, all sixteen ships of the task force in loose orbital formation, a fifty-kilometer chain of warships of all sizes. If we had any colonists left alive on Willoughby, they'd probably be ecstatic to see the fleet that just showed up in orbit. But we're over a decade too late for a rescue mission, so I am genuinely curious to learn why the Fleet was willing to risk two Avengers to pay the place a visit.

"Situation," Colonel Drake says. In the harsh light of the briefing room fixtures, I can see that he has faint freckles on the bridge of his nose and his cheekbones, a rarity among capital ship commanders who spend most of their time inside sealed metal hulls. His shipboard uniform is tailored to fit his frame, and it's obvious that he's very trim and slender, which is also uncommon among officers of his rank and occupation.

"The task force is in orbit around a Lanky-occupied colony, Capella Ac, formerly known as Willoughby. We neutralized the enemy orbital garrison six hours ago with Orions, and our cruiser escorts have removed all mines in the neighborhood."

"Mission," the colonel continues. "Our orders are to conduct a reconnaissance in force, and that's what we will do until we encounter unfavorable odds. Battlespace Control Squadron Fifty-Five and Strike Fighter Squadrons Fifty-One and Fifty-Two have been conducting recon flights of the surface for the last five hours."

The colonel switches the display to show a series of low-altitude shots of the surface. The Willoughby I remember was mostly barren mountains and gravel fields, as unfriendly and forbidding as most barely terraformed worlds, years away from being temperate enough to support agriculture. The imagery on the bulkhead screen shows rolling hills overgrown with green-and-blue foliage, an explosion of color that looks nothing like the memory of the place in my head.

"That's Willoughby now?" I ask.

"Affirmative," Colonel Drake says. "This was taken just three hours ago by one of the birds from BCS-55. The weather down there is a bit of a party. Ceilings at a thousand feet, with fifty-knot gusts. It'll take a while to get the full picture from that low altitude. We're going to focus around the area of the colony capital instead of trying to map out the whole planet. We're still keeping EMCON just in case there are more seed ships somewhere out there in the system. So radar mapping is out of the question for the moment. High-altitude reconnaissance will be limited to thermal imaging. We don't want to light up an electromagnetic bonfire and draw the bugs to our front porch. Even if we can zap them now."

"Any sign of our tall friends yet?" Colonel Rigney asks.

Colonel Pace, the commander of the space wing, shakes his head. "None yet. Two of the recon flights passed over what looked like Lanky settlements, but they didn't see movement on the ground."

"That doesn't mean they aren't around," I say. Even though I am not looking at the XO, I can feel her gaze trying to bore into the side of my head. "As soon as we have boots on the ground, they'll come out of their holes. Just like they did on Mars."

"On the plus side, the visibility under the cloud ceiling isn't total shit," Colonel Pace says. "The grunts will have line of sight for half a kilometer or more. And if we have eyes on the ground, we can still vector in air support. The Shrikes can drop blind from inside the soup as long as there's someone on the deck to designate targets."

"What's our objective here?" Colonel Rigney asks. "If we're putting boots down, I mean. Are we drawing them out to see how hard they will bite on the bait?"

Colonel Drake shakes his head.

"The seed ships were easy. But I don't want to lose sight of the fact that we are way out on a ledge here. I don't want to stick out more than we can pull back in a hurry. Just in case the door slams shut on us, and we need to make a fast exit. There's nothing to be gained from a few hundred dead Lankies on the ground. Not if there are still a few thousand underground. And especially not if it costs us a bunch of casualties and half our ground-attack ordnance."

"If we put the regiment on the ground, we're committed," Colonel Rigney says.

"Exactly," the commander replies. "Say we land the whole SI complement, plus the STT. All the chips on the table. We lure out the Lankies and start mowing them down with exoskeletons and close air support. And they throw everything at us. Like on Mars," he adds with a glance in my direction.

"We'd have another fighting withdrawal," Colonel Rigney says. "A tactical stalemate. And we'd pay in lives and material."

"And get nothing in return," the XO says. "Fact is, we'll have nothing to show for it even if we wipe them out on the ground. We can hold the planet with a thousand grunts. For a while, anyway. But to what end?"

"We came to do a recon run," Colonel Drake says. "Not to plant the flag again and reclaim the whole colony. Just because it was easier than expected to get into orbit doesn't mean we need to bite off more than we're ordered to chew on this one."

At least he's not a glory hound, I think with some relief. Over the years, I've known enough officers who would have seized the chance to go above and beyond, to plant the NAC flag down there and liberally invest the lives of enlisted troops in an attempt to get into the history books.

"But I'd hate to have come all this way without something for the intel division to sink their teeth into," the commander continues. "Let's make it worth their while. And ours."

He turns to the bulkhead display and moves the aerial recon images to one side, then brings up a map and enlarges it to fill most of the screen.

"This was never a bustling colony," he says. "The Lankies got here before it could really get off the ground. Not quite two thousand colonists. Just a terraforming network and one major settlement—Willoughby City. For a very flexible definition of 'city,' of course."

He makes his point by centering the map on the settlement and zooming in to magnify the view. The colony capital is smaller than some military bases I've seen. It has maybe a hundred buildings, all lined up on a neat road grid that surrounds a central administration complex. I know that the map doesn't reflect the current realities on the surface because there's a terraforming station just a kilometer away from the settlement, and I know that the Lankies destroy those first whenever they take over one of our colony planets. There's still no firm consensus whether they just hate the electromagnetic radiation the fusion plants emit, or they understand the function of the terraformers—that those large buildings make the atmosphere more suitable for us and less so for them, and that the settlements need the power from those fusion reactors to survive. Either way, I have no doubt that the terraformer on the map has been a shattered ruin for over a decade now, stomped into rubble by the Lankies shortly after they landed.

The commander brings up another aerial image and puts it next to the map. The computer rotates it and zooms in until the scale of the image matches that of the map exactly. It's recognizably the same town because the Lankies left most of the buildings alone, but even from a thousand feet up, the deterioration is obvious. I saw this place once from the same vantage point, when Halley did a slow pass over the complex after our dash from the terraforming station to see why Willoughby City wasn't responding to radio calls. Back then, the streets were strewn with dead colonists, killed by Lanky gas pods like vermin in a basement. The memory is still clear in my brain despite the time that has passed since then, and I feel a very unwelcome sense of déjà vu.

"That's a lot of green," Lieutenant Colonel Campbell says. "Should it be this overgrown already? I thought the colony wasn't yet set up for agriculture."

"When I saw it last, they barely had grass between those buildings," I say.

"No, it shouldn't be this overgrown," Colonel Drake replies. "Not from the bit of stuff the colony had growing in their greenhouses. This is whatever the Lankies bring with them when they set up shop."

The colony buildings are the standard modular concrete domes, but there's so much green on them now that they look like they've been intentionally camouflaged by a very thorough unit of combat engineers. I remember the mosslike growth I've observed on Lanky-occupied worlds, but I've never seen this much of it in one spot. It looks like a hundred years have passed since humans last walked around down there. This looks like the network shows my mother liked to watch with me when I was little, science shows about what the world would look like if humans all disappeared and let nature take over. There are no corpses on the roads and walkways between the buildings, just a carpet of green coming up through the perforated concrete slabs of the prefabricated street sections.

This is how they all ended up, I think. *Every settlement on every colony planet we've lost to these things. Like the aftermath of a natural disaster.*

"The colony administration building is still standing," Colonel Drake continues. "It's a standard Class IV hardened shelter. Reinforced concrete walls one meter thick. If they went into security lockdown, that building was sealed from the inside the moment they noticed they were under attack. As you can see, the Lankies either left it alone or they couldn't crack the place open. There's a potential treasure trove of data in the basement, and I want us to go down there and secure it for the intel division back home."

"The data storage modules for the neural network," I say.

Colonel Drake looks at me and nods with a smile.

"Very good, Major."

"I was a neural network admin before I became a podhead," I say. "And I once spent a few weeks in the ops center of a Class IV."

"Very good. Then you can take point on the retrieval mission," the commander says. "I want you to put a team together to go down there and see if the data storage facility is still intact."

"The Lankies knocked out the power to that place almost right away," Colonel Rigney says. "Is there anything on those memory modules that's worth a few hundred SI lives?"

Colonel Drake shakes his head.

"I don't want to send a few hundred SI troops down there. We've cleared the planetary orbit, but we could get jumped by more Lankies at any time. If we have to make a quick exit, it will be much easier to pick up an STT platoon than to airlift an entire infantry battalion plus heavy gear out of there."

"A platoon isn't going to be able to hold much ground if the resident Lankies start popping out of the ground in numbers," Colonel Rigney replies. "Podheads or not. I'd want at least a heavy weapons company down there with PACS."

"The skipper has a point," I say.

"I would have figured you'd rather have some heavy guns on overwatch while we're rooting around above the Lankies' heads," Colonel Rigney says.

"More guns are always better guns, Colonel. No argument there. But we had that scenario at New Svalbard, four years ago. A whole regiment on the ground, plus PACS. And when the Lankies started to roll up our line, we barely got everyone out in time. We needed the SI regiment to hold off the Lankies while we got the civvies on the drop ships. But this time we don't have to hold the line if things get tight. We can have a pair of drop ships on standby in low orbit. We take in a few STT squads, we can be out again in a few minutes," I say.

Colonel Rigney shrugs. "Don't get me wrong. It won't hurt my feelings if I don't get to send my people down there to get bloody. And I am sure you know what you are doing. But that's a long wait for backup if you find yourself needing us after all."

"Is there anything on those storage modules that's worth even setting foot in that place?" Colonel Pace asks. "Something we can't gain from just letting the recon birds map the whole place from top to bottom?"

"The neural network would have been tied into all the sensors on the planet," I say. "Every terraformer, every satellite. Every surveillance sensor. The network forensics people could dissect the entire event from start to finish. It's like the colony wrote a real-time diary of its own death."

"Well, that's a bit morbid," the XO says. "But I can see the value. I don't think we've ever had a firsthand account of a Lanky invasion."

"Even if there's no military value to that data, we lost almost two thousand colonists here," Colonel Drake says. "Four hundred eighty-nine families. I checked the files. We can't bring their bodies home. Not anymore. But we may be able to retrace their steps. Take back whatever last messages or images they left before they got wiped out without warning. If there's a chance we can recover any of that, I'd say it's worth the risk so we don't go back home and tell their relatives that we went forty-two light-years to this cemetery just to take a few pictures."

There's a moment of silence in the room.

"I'm for it," Lieutenant Colonel Campbell says. "But I'm not the one who will be sticking out my neck down there. If we go through with this, the podheads will have most of the risk."

She looks at me expectantly. "What do you say, Major? This may be a quick in and out, and everyone pats you on the shoulder. Or you have boots on the ground, and ten minutes later, you are in over your heads."

I look from her to the map imagery on the bulkhead display and shrug.

"That's pretty much our job description," I say. "But I'm not going to lie. Five hundred meters of line of sight isn't much. By the time we see them coming, they'll be almost on top of us. And then we'll be back at square one because we'll need a whole space wing's worth of close air support to extract a handful of podheads."

"We can do a little better than that," Colonel Pace says. "BCS-55 has a bunch of the new seismic mines in inventory now. With the target area being as small as it is, we won't even need to deploy a lot of them. Two dozen, maybe, and we can triangulate incoming Lankies. It's not accurate enough for close-air-support runs, but we'll know if something is headed your way. Even if it's underground."

"How much early warning are we talking about?" I ask.

"Depends on how much of a hurry they're in. But I'd say at least ten minutes. They'll be able to give you a rough vector."

"If they work as advertised," Colonel Rigney says. "Last I heard, that was still experimental gear."

"So were the PACS four years ago," I say. "Anything's better than flying blind. Ten minutes ought to be enough to call down our ride and get the hell out before the neighborhood watch shows up."

I look around at the faces of the colonels at the table. "I'm comfortable with those parameters if everyone else is fine with it. I conclude with the XO that the potential payoff is worth the risk."

"Very well," Colonel Drake says. "In that case, the mission is a go. Colonel Pace will have BCS-55 send down the recon birds to place the seismic gear. Major Grayson, assemble your team and designate a backup for the standby drop ship in case we have to come and get you. We will coordinate the mission from the CIC and give the STT team the green light for deployment as soon as we've dropped the sensors dirtside. All departments, report mission readiness by 2200."

"Aye, sir," I reply. The other officers at the table murmur their assent as well. Colonel Drake shuts off the bulkhead screen and gets out of his chair.

"I know it may be a bit of a letdown," he says. "Twelve years later, and the best we can do right now is a smash-and-grab burglary. But I don't want to commit us to a fight we can't win. We have more to lose out here than they do."

"If we get my team back up here with the data modules and no casualties, I'd file that one under 'win,'" I say.

CHAPTER 15

RIDE-ALONG

Half an hour after the briefing, I am back in my quarters and rinsing off in the shower when my comms panel trills its incoming message alert. I step out of the tiny bathroom of my cabin and walk the three steps to my desk, where the terminal base flashes a soft, pulsating red light.

"Major Grayson," I say when I accept the comm.

"Major, this is the CO," Colonel Drake's voice says. "Could you report to my ready cabin when you get a minute?"

"Of course, sir. I'll be right up."

I slip into fresh camouflage uniform trousers and spend a minute rolling the sleeves of the blouse before putting it on. When I check my appearance in the mirror, I notice that I have a few strands of gray hair now, made obvious by the harsh and unflattering light of the mirror's LED fixture.

"Fabulous," I mutter, and grab one of the little silver strands to yank it out. It comes away clean, and I look at it for a moment as it curls between my fingers.

At least I got old enough to start getting gray, I think. Then I flick the strand of hair into the garbage receptacle on the wall next to my desk and turn to walk out of my quarters.

"Major Grayson, reporting as ordered," I say when I step into the commander's ready cabin. He's standing at his desk, bent over the display screen he has tilted into an almost horizontal position, and he's typing something into a data field with both hands.

"Step up, Major," he says over his shoulder. "Have a seat. And you don't need to formally report in every time you come in here. You're part of the command staff."

"It's still your ship, sir," I say, and step closer to the table without getting too curious about the contents of the commander's screen. He finishes typing and turns off the screen with a flick of his hand.

"The XO seems to think I was an NCO for too long," I continue. "Old habits and all that."

"I've always found that the mustangs make better officers than the academy wonders," Colonel Drake says. "They know both sides of the trade. It's easy to lose the bigger picture if you're only used to looking from one angle."

"I got boosted up from limited duty, sir. I was never supposed to even make major."

"No such thing as limited duty anymore, I'm afraid."

The colonel sits down, and I follow suit only when he's settled behind his desk.

"I have a task for you that concerns the upcoming STT mission," he says. "Are you still sure you want to put boots in the dirt personally?"

"Wouldn't feel right if I didn't, sir. And as you've already pointed out, I know the layout of the place better than any of my section leads do. I won't have to spend much time getting my bearings."

"What's your team setup?"

"Like you said, sir, it's going to be a smash and grab. I'm taking the SEAL section, plus one of the Spaceborne Rescue squad leaders. If we end up needing combat control, I'll be there for that. Eighteen troopers, no heavy gear, in and out in one drop ship."

Colonel Drake nods. "That makes sense to me. But I'm a cap ship jockey, not a podhead. Whatever you need to get the job done, you know to ask for it."

"What's the task you have for me, sir?" I ask.

"You'll have to keep a seat open on the drop ship down," the CO says. "We have a science detachment from the research division along for the ride. Their xenobiologist has requested to come along for the mission. She wants to take a look around on the surface, maybe bring back samples of whatever it is that's growing all over the old colony now. This may be the only chance we get to put boots on the ground, and the science mission wants in on it."

"You want me to take a civilian along on an STT mission?" I ask.

"Technically, the research-division scientists are all officers in the Corps," Colonel Drake replies. "But they're officers in the way that Fleet dentists are officers. They do the shake-and-bake officer course you've been through for your LDO promotion. But once they're in their jobs, they don't have much to do with the regular military business."

"I don't know if that's a smart idea," I say. "If things go wrong, we may end up shooting our way out of there and back to the drop ship. If she's off picking flowers somewhere, we may not be able to wait for her. Does she know that this could end badly?"

"She does. But she wants to come anyway. She was quite adamant about it."

"You make it sound like I have an option," I say.

"The STT is your shop," Colonel Drake says. "I'm in charge of the ship and the overall mission. But I leave the department heads to their own business. Ultimately, you're the one who can make that judgment call. I can tell you that the science division would be very happy with us if we let them gather some firsthand data. But I won't order you to bring one of them along. That is your decision alone. If you think it's too risky, they'll have to get over their disappointment."

I consider the request for a few moments. Whenever I have a strong initial gut feeling to a proposal, I've learned to take a few slow breaths and refrain from a knee-jerk reaction.

"We all came a long way for this," I say. "And as you said, it may be the only chance we get to go down to the surface. I'm not wild about the idea. But I suppose she can come along. As long as she knows that she has to follow our lead and take direction. The science people saved us at New Svalbard. I figure we owe them a favor or three."

Colonel Drake nods. "I'm sure they'll be glad to hear that you see it that way, Major. I'll let the science people know that the ride-along is a go."

"Can I give her the green light in person, sir? I want to go and talk to her to make sure she understands everything she's signing up for."

"Sure," the commander says. "Like I said, it's your show. She's down in the main medlab. Ask for Dr. Vandenberg."

"Aye, sir."

I get up and almost do a formal heel turn before I remember the commander's earlier admonition about excessive formality. Colonel Drake seems to notice because there's a faint smile notched in the corners of his mouth when he nods to dismiss me.

"Oh, and Major?" he says when I am at the door.

"Yes, sir?" I turn around.

"If you do give her the green light, I would appreciate it if you would keep her very close when you get down to the surface. You know those science types. They know a lot about their field, but they don't think like soldiers. Even if they are commissioned officers."

"I'll do my best to bring her back to the ship without a dent, sir," I say.

The woman sitting in a back corner of the ship's medical lab doesn't look like the stereotypical image of a research-division scientist in my head, and she doesn't look like the typical Fleet officer, either. She's wearing overalls that are in the same color scheme as the ship we're on—white with orange trim. Her back is turned toward the aisle between the rows of work nooks, and I see that she's wearing her hair in a short blonde braid that reaches just past the collar of her overalls. She has her feet propped up on the desk of her work nook, and she's flicking through a bunch of data screens in front of her. I rap my knuckles on the partition to get her attention.

"Dr. Vandenberg?" I ask.

She takes her feet off her desk and swivels her chair around.

"I'm Major Grayson," I say. "The special tactics team lead. Your chaperone for the upcoming field trip. The skipper told me that you're asking for a ride-along."

"Hello," she says, and gets out of her chair. "Be careful with the 'doctor' around here, or people start asking me to look at their ailments."

She holds out her hand, and I shake it.

"Elin Vandenberg. Just Elin is fine. Or Captain Vandenberg, if you absolutely must," she says.

We smile and size each other up for a few heartbeats. She has the lean build of someone who does a lot of cardio exercise. There are fine wrinkles in the corners of her blue eyes, and her teeth have the slight unevenness that's the hallmark of an upbringing in the PRC, where the public dentistry focuses on basic function instead of cosmetics.

"Andrew Grayson," I say. "Just Andrew is fine. Don't call me 'major' too much, or people start looking to me for guidance."

She chuckles at the joke and tucks her hands into the back pockets of her overalls. Then she nods at the office space behind her.

"Welcome to Lanky Labs," she says. "I'd offer you a seat, but I'm not actually set up for visitors. The bio division doesn't get their own space. We have to share the medlab, so they tuck us all the way in the back."

"How many people are in the bio division?" I ask.

Elin raises her index finger and shrugs.

"It's not a permanent billing. I kind of blackmailed my boss into getting me on this ship on short notice. I figured I'd maybe get a shot at Mars. The other biologists on my team are going to lose their shit when they find out what they've missed."

"First Alcubierre trip?"

She shakes her head. "I've been to Arcadia a few times with the xenobotanists. Never been to a Lanky colony. This is like Christmas and Commonwealth Day all rolled into one."

"You may have come a long way for a short stroll. We may not be on the surface for very long. It's not a friendly neighborhood. I don't want you to be disappointed if you don't get to collect a lot of samples or set up any science gear. It may not be worth the risk."

"I'll come along even if it's just for a thirty-second stroll down there," she says. "I've been doing this for ten years, ever since I got out of college. And I've only ever had lab samples to work on. Stuff that other people brought back. These things are supposed to be my field of expertise, and I've never been in their own habitat. Feels like I ought to take the chance if it's in front of me."

"We may get a little more time than just thirty seconds," I reply. "It's a recovery mission. We'll land in Willoughby City and get the data storage units out of the basement in the admin center. It may not be the most pleasant environment. Last time I was here, I saw hundreds of dead settlers in the streets. If any of them died in the admin center, the Lankies didn't collect those bodies. It'll be like a tomb in there."

"I'm not squeamish," Elin says.

"Neither am I. But I still have bad dreams every other night."

"Emotional candor. I'm not used to that from grunts. But if you're trying to scare me off with that, it's not going to work," she says with a little smile.

I do a bit of quick math in my head and guess that she's about my age if she has a doctorate and ten years of experience in the field. But somehow, she looks like I have a decade on her, despite the little wrinkles in the corners of her eyes. Frontline grunts age faster than their peers because the job is a physical and mental grinder, and not even long stretches of shore duty are enough to halt that clock or reverse it. Dr. Vandenberg looks fit and toned, but there's a kind of softness about her that's unmistakably civilian, and the braided hair only emphasizes the effect. Few of the women who serve on a warship keep their hair long because it gets in the way of the helmets that grunts, deckhands, and pilots frequently have to wear.

"The SEALs are really good at what they do," I say. "And we will have an entire drop-ship wing in support if we need to leave in a hurry. But I won't tell you that you have no reason to be anxious. This is a Lanky planet now. It'll be the most dangerous place you'll ever set foot."

"I've been in some pretty bad neighborhoods," she says.

"A PRC has nothing on this," I reply. "Trust me. Lots of tough kids from the PRCs in the infantry. And they all shit their pants when they see their first Lanky stomping toward them on the field. It's not an experience you can get from a simulator."

"I appreciate the warnings," Elin says. "But I still want to come along. I'll have to trust you and the grunts to keep me out of trouble. I'll deal with the emotional fallout later if it comes to that. But I'd always regret it if I chickened out after coming all this way."

I try to think of another argument to put in front of her to dissuade her, but I can tell by the way her jawline has set that she has made up her mind. I shrug and shake my head.

"I gave you the fine print. And you're a grown-up professional. If I can't scare you off, you have my go-ahead to come along."

She does a little fist pump and exhales for effect.

"Thank you. I'll be a good passenger. And you may find it weird or insane, but part of me hopes that I'll get to see a live Lanky down there."

"Hope that you don't get your wish," I say. "And I want you no further than twenty meters from me at all times. And when I tell you to make a run for the drop ship, you drop everything and run."

Elin smirks.

"I run marathons," she says. "And I used to run track in college. If we have to make a dash for the drop ship, I can guarantee you that I'll be the first one up the ramp. I'm curious, Major. But I am not a moron."

CHAPTER 16

ONE HELL OF A WAY TO MAKE A LIVING

There's a ritual to combat drops, and it's always the same.

You put your armor on and call out every action as you do—"latch breastplate top left, latch breastplate bottom left, lock left pauldron rear, attach left pauldron front"—because it reduces errors when the action is brought to the conscious mind instead of letting the hands do their thing on autopilot. You button up, let someone else triple-check your seals, and triple-check theirs for them. Then you pick up your weapon and ammunition, fill your magazine pouches, and let the rifle do its calibration handshake with your armor's computer. Everything has a rhythm to it, and the never-changing routine of the act puts the mind into battle mode. But the final step of the ritual is the walk to the drop ship, and that's when my brain truly focuses itself on that single point in time and space. For me, it's the visual and aural change—walking across the cavernous, perpetually busy hangar toward the waiting tail ramp of the drop ship, and stepping into a confined space that turns almost dead quiet when the ramp goes up and seals itself against the hull.

We're in a Dragonfly today because we don't need the capabilities of the far more valuable Blackflies. The cargo deck can hold forty troopers in full kit, or sixty if they squeeze in tightly. The team going down to the surface is only eighteen people strong, and we have a lot of seats to spare on this drop. The crew chief has us close to the forward bulkhead in two rows along the sides of the hull. On the floor between our seat rows, the cargo kit attachments are flush with the floor and tucked out of the way, unnecessary because we're not taking freight or heavy gear with us. Sixteen SEALs, the Fleet's elite space-air-land commandos, sit in their jump seats, weapons in their holding brackets between the backrests, all strapped in already when I walk up the ramp with Dr. Elin Vandenberg in tow. The SEALs and I are all in bug suits, and the xenobiologist is sticking out in her hostile environment kit, a white engineering vacsuit without any armor or military hardware.

"I'll keep the passenger next to me," I tell the crew chief who comes over to help us with strapping in, and he nods. It throws off the symmetry of the seating arrangement, but Elin weighs half of what any of the SEALs do in their armor, and I want her close by in case we need to unbuckle quickly in an emergency. Combat drops in the back of a drop ship are an unnerving affair even when you've done them a thousand times. For civilians or shore-based personnel like Dr. Vandenberg, they're probably ten times as stressful. Drop ships have no windows for reference, so the passengers in the back have to do the whole flight blindly, and that circumstance combined with the knowledge that danger is waiting at the end of the ride gives the brain all kinds of opportunities to indulge in speculation. When you have no idea what is going on outside of the hull, every noise becomes a system failure, and every bump becomes an imminent crash in your mind. It's my least favorite part of any mission because I have no control over what happens until we are on the ground.

"You good?" I ask the xenobiologist over helmet-to-helmet comms when the crew chief has strapped her in and tightened her harness.

She gives me a thumbs-up and a gamely smile, but I can tell by the shade of her face behind her transparent visor that she's probably having second thoughts already about committing to this ride-along.

"Have you done a drop before?" I ask to keep her mind a little busy with something other than interpreting strange noises and sensations.

"Ferry flights," she says. "Down to Arcadia. And the atmospheric birds in training, years ago. But never a drop into a hot landing zone."

"Do four more after this one, and you qualify for combat drop wings," I say.

"How many have you done?"

"Including atmospheric patrols on Mars where I didn't leave the ship? About six hundred or so. Only counting the ones where we had skids on the ground, probably three fifty."

"Good god," Elin says. "You've done this six hundred times?"

"Give or take a few."

"That is one hell of a way to make a living."

"I can't really disagree there," I say.

A slight vibration goes through the ship, and Elin looks around to figure out the source.

"Docking clamp," I say. "Latches on to the receptacle on the top."

"Rapier Three-One is in the clamp and ready for launch. Payload team leader, give me a go/no-go for launch," the drop ship's pilot sends from the flight deck.

"Last chance to get off this elevator," I say to Dr. Vandenberg. She just shakes her head, her mouth a thin horizontal line behind the thick polyplast of her face shield.

"Three-One, payload team leader. We are go for launch back here," I send to the flight deck, and I give a thumbs-up to the crew chief sitting by the bulkhead next to the flight deck passageway. He returns the gesture and speaks into his own helmet headset. A few moments later, another rumbling vibration goes through the hull, and I feel the familiar sensation of the drop ship leaving the flight deck surface as the docking clamp hoists it up for transfer to the drop hatch.

"Dagger team, Dagger Actual. Give me a comms check, please," I send to the SEALs. "Sound off."

"Dagger One-Niner, check."

"Dagger One-One, check."

"Dagger One-Two . . ."

One by one, the SEAL team members send their acknowledgments. The radio check is a time-honored tradition from the days of flaky signals and fragile wireless equipment. I would know instantly if any of my team members dropped out of the comms link because my suit's computer would alert me right away, but the sound-off is a part of the combat drop ritual as well, so nobody ever skips it for expediency. It's a nerve balm of sorts, but by this point I suspect that it has also seeped into the realm of superstition where the troops would think it bad luck to deviate from the routine. We can travel between star systems and harness the power of the sun in our spaceships, but we're still worried about pissing off the fates if we skip the proper supplications.

The new docking arms on *Washington*'s flight deck are remarkably smooth and efficient, much easier on passengers than the abrupt and jerky ones on the old assault carriers, but I can still tell from experience when we're about to lock into the drop hatch. A few moments after the familiar sinking feeling in my stomach sets in, the drop ship stops with a little shudder of the hull, and I know that we are now down "in the pit," with nothing between us and empty space except for the armored outer hatch door.

"This is the worst part," I say to Dr. Vandenberg. "When we drop, there's a second or two of free fall until we leave the artificial gravity field. It can be a little weird if you're not used to it. But it's over before you know it."

"Thanks for the warning," Elin says. She closes her eyes and puts her head back against the headrest of her seat.

Some pilots give a courtesy warning before they hit the release button for the clamp. Others don't bother to keep the passengers in the loop about procedure, and our pilot today is one of those. Every time the clamp releases and I feel the drop, I can't help but think of an execution scaffold, the floor dropping underneath the condemned without a warning. For a second and a half, sixty tons of armored war machine are in free fall as we drop out of the belly of the carrier and into the darkness of space. Then the feeling in the pit of my stomach dissipates. The engines of the drop ship go from idle to full thrust, and we are on our way to the surface of the Lanky planet formerly known as the human colony Willoughby.

"Why don't we have armor for this sort of thing?" Elin asks against the rumbling of the hull as the drop ship slices through the atmosphere. I'm glad for her that she can't see the light show I know is taking place on the other side of the titanium skin, where the superheated plasma from the friction of our descent is making us look like a shooting star.

"We do have armor," I say and tap on the hard shell of my bug suit's breastplate. "Won't keep a Lanky from squishing me, though. There isn't anything you can wrap around a trooper to be Lanky-proof."

"I mean armored vehicles," she says. "It's weird that we'd come all this way in these sophisticated machines and then just send a bunch of people with rifles to do the work. It seems like it would be good to have wheels for driving away quickly. And a big gun on top for shooting all the stuff you can't drive away from."

"Mules," I say. "The SI has them. They weigh twenty tons, and you can fit only one into a drop ship. And the places we go, most of the time we have to disembark anyway and do the job on foot. The mules can't go into Lanky holes or up steep rocky inclines. They need lots of fuel and power cells. And you need an entire drop-ship wing to transport enough mules for a single company. You can get four times as many grunts on the ground without the armor. And if we need more mobility, we already have drop ships. Those cover way more ground anyway. The new PACS are better than anything on wheels. For what we do, anyway. But those take up space, too. Four per drop ship, versus forty troopers."

"I see," she says. "You've probably figured out by now that infantry combat is not my department."

The drop ship gets jolted roughly, and Elin grabs the side of her jump seat briefly.

"This is like the worst roller coaster ride ever," she says. "I hate roller coasters, by the way."

"Didn't they give you combat training with that commission?" I say to keep the conversation going and distract her from the bouncy ride.

"I haven't fired a rifle since Basic Training," she says. "We qualify with sidearms once a year. Fifty rounds. I don't know why they even bother. It's not like a Lanky would even feel those."

"Last-ditch defiance. It's basically a magazine full of fuck-yous," I say, and she laughs.

"Ten minutes to drop zone," the pilot sends from the flight deck. "It's going to be choppy all the way down, so don't nobody get up to go to the bathroom."

"Copy ten minutes to LZ," I send back. Then I switch to my all-platoon channel to address the SEAL team.

"Ten minutes to go-time," I say. "Final gear checks and briefing now, people."

I bring up a tactical map of the target area on my helmet's heads-up display and send it to the entire team.

"Deployment as discussed in the initial briefing," I say. "We put down on this plaza a hundred meters north of the admin center. Proceed south on the main boulevard until we reach the building. Dagger Two and Dagger Four will take up overwatch positions on the northeast and southwest corners."

I mark up the map as I go through the steps we rehearsed in the pre-mission briefing. Everyone knows their jobs and places, but this, too, is part of the ritual, and it serves to focus everyone on what's about to happen.

"Dagger One and Dagger Three will breach the admin building at the main entrance vestibules. The access panels run off solar, so they should still have juice to let us punch in the master code. If the panels are dead, we'll breach with shaped charges. We make entry, and I'll take Dagger One down to the network operations center. Secure the data modules, exfil, return to the pickup point, and call down the ship for dustoff. Any questions?"

"Rules of engagement for the overwatch squads," Lieutenant Philips says. He's the leader of Third Squad, designated Dagger Two for this mission. "If we have company showing up halfway through, how close do we let them get before we light them up?"

"We'll play it by ear," I reply. "Depends on the line of sight we have once we are on the ground. If they're headed your way and you can drop them, it's up to you. If they're too close or too many, we retreat to the admin center and let close air support take care of it."

The team members all send back their acknowledgments. I check the vitals overview on my screen for the fiftieth time on this descent. Comms green, weapons green, biometrics green. I have a team of the best special operations troops in the Corps, and they're all ready to be let off the leash for a little bit.

"Hand signals for comms whenever possible," I caution. "Keep our EM noise to the bare minimum. And no explosives if we can go in soft at all. No need to stir the neighborhood more than necessary."

Another round of acknowledgment marks shows up on my screen next to the list of team member names.

"One last word to the wise," I say. "For all those who haven't been up against these things on the ground yet. They move like they're half-asleep, but they're much faster than they look. Don't get tunnel vision, or you're in deep shit before you know it. Do not go out of your way to put rounds on target just because you have one in your sights. We get nothing out of killing a few Lankies. There will still be hundreds or thousands of them. Not even a dozen dead ones are worth trading a single one of us."

The ship gets buffeted again, hard enough to feel like we're shifting sideways in the air by a meter or two. Outside, it's noisy now because we have air on the other side of the hull, and I can hear rain lashing the titanium-alloy skin of the Dragonfly. Next to me, Elin Vandenberg looks like she is trying to disappear in the depths of her vacuum suit.

In the atmosphere nearby, a thunderclap goes off like a proximity-fused artillery shell. The ship lurches, then rights itself. On most descents, I like to tap into the eternal sensor feeds to see what's ahead of us. This time, I elect to remain blissfully unaware. Until the skids of the Dragonfly hit the dirt, our fate is entirely in the pilot's hands, and there's nothing I can do from the cargo compartment even if I see trouble coming our way.

Going out to tap-dance on a ledge in the middle of a storm again, I think. Outside, thunder rolls once more, as if to underline my thoughts.

"Thirty seconds to drop zone," the flight deck announces. "Advise against unbuckling before the green light. Lots of wind shear down here."

"Copy that," I say. "We'll stay put until the skids are down."

I look over the two rows of SEALs, all appearing identical in their bug suits except for the rank and name markers on the chest plates.

"Thirty seconds to go-time. Dagger team, lock and load."

The SEALs in the hold all take their weapons out of the transport mounts and insert magazines, then they place the rifles upright between their feet. Dr. Vandenberg watches me as I follow suit.

"We're staying strapped in until we land because of the weather," I tell her. "When the ramp goes down, I'll be the first one out. You'll be right with me. Remember what I said about staying within twenty meters. I don't want to have to look for you down there if things go to shit."

She gives me a tight-lipped nod.

A combat descent is always a wild ride, but this one is wilder than most. The ship seems to slide and pitch along every axis as we come in over the landing zone. By the time I feel the impact of the skids with the ground, I am looking forward to getting off the drop ship more than I fear whatever is on the other side of that tail ramp.

The light above the ramp switches from red to green. A second later, the ramp starts to lower itself. As soon as there's a gap in the hull, a gust of wind blows into the cargo hold, bringing droplets of rain with it. I hit the quick-release button on my harness and reach over to do the same for Elin Vandenberg.

"Dagger team, on your feet," I shout.

The ramp hits the ground, and I pick up my rifle and lead the way. Behind me, the SEALs line up in two rows as they file out. As we come down the ramp, they jump off the sides and assume their guard positions.

The weather outside is a mess. The steel-gray clouds hang low in the sky, and the rain is driving across my field of view in horizontal bands that whip against the sides of the colony buildings in sight.

"Five hundred meters' line of sight, my ass," I mutter. The ground beneath my feet is concrete, but it's slick with water and whatever plant life has attached itself to the man-made material and pushed up through the cracks and gaps over the years. My armored boots splash into ankle-deep puddles as I step off the ramp and onto the surface of Willoughby.

At my back, the last of the SEALs hop off the ramp, and they rush off to the sides to assume their overwatch guard positions, rifles at the ready. I signal the crew chief that the ramp is clear, and he slaps the switch for the ramp control. A moment later, the pitch of the drop ship's engines increases, and the Dragonfly hauls itself off the ground again. I watch as it disappears into the clouds above, which doesn't take very long. It really looks like I could stand on the roof of the admin center and jump up to reach the bottom of the cloud ceiling.

My helmet display comes alive with vision enhancements and environmental data readouts, and the image of my surroundings gets brighter and more defined. Willoughby was a cool planet when we settled humans here, with daytime temperatures no higher than ten or fifteen degrees Celsius. Right now, the air outside is thirty-two degrees, and the humidity reading from my helmet sensors is at 100 percent. In just twelve years, the Lankies have managed to turn the planet into a tropical hothouse, something that would take our terraforming units at least a century to achieve with a world of this size.

On the tactical screen overlay, I can see the drop ship overhead, clawing its way into the stormy sky to reach an altitude where it can stay reasonably close without getting pounded by the low-level winds that buffeted the hell out of us in the landing phase of our descent. One by one, the icons for the members of Dagger team pop up on my screen as their suits establish a low-power TacLink connection with mine. I signal to the section leaders, point down the road toward the admin center, and pump my fist once to signal the advance.

The colony looks like something from a post-apocalyptic drama show on the Networks. The concrete structures are so weathered that it's hard to believe we only lost this place twelve years ago. The housing domes are dark with dirt and mold, and the surfaces are pockmarked with wear as if they've suffered a hundred years of erosion. There are shaggy patches of overgrowth sticking to almost every surface in sight. I walk over to the closest building, aware of Dr. Vandenberg following on my heels. There's a large patch of the strange growth on the wall next to one of the doors. It looks like moss, but with much thicker strands and more complex patterns than the stuff on Earth. I shine my helmet light on it, and the color subtly shifts, adding a slight blue tone to the green as the cone of light passes over the patch. Elin reaches out and puts her hand on the moss, then runs her fingers through it like it's the fur of an interesting animal.

"Have you seen this before?" I ask, and she shakes her head.

"Well, sort of," she says. "From samples in the lab. Stuff they scraped off the rocks on Lanky worlds. But this is on a whole new scale. You don't need a magnifying glass to see this."

"Let's move on," I say. "You can collect samples when we're done."

She nods and pulls her hand away from the growth on the wall, then she looks at her glove as if she's checking to see whether it left any residue.

We're going to spend half the day in the decontamination chambers once we're back on the ship, I think.

The roads are standard prefabricated slabs of concrete latticework, with octagonal holes in regular intervals to reduce weight and allow for drainage. In almost every gap in the concrete, plant life has come up in strands and vines, some standing ankle high. In many spots, the plants pushing up from below have cracked the concrete strands between the holes into pieces. In another ten years, all these structures will be swallowed by whatever it is the Lankies brought with them either on purpose or by accident.

Not all the buildings in the settlement survived the Lanky invasion unscathed. As we make our way down the street toward the admin building, we see some housing units that have been reduced to rubble, with only some jagged remnants of outer wall remaining, crushed by something large with a lot of weight and force. A hundred meters down the road from the drop-off spot, some pavement slats have been crumpled and squeezed upward at a thirty-degree angle. As we get closer and start to walk around the obstacle, we can see that whatever broke the thick concrete layer of the road surface left an indentation in the soil that's half a meter deep. The hole is filled with water almost to the brim, and patches of the weird mosslike plant life are floating on the surface, swirling in the ripples whipped up by the wind. I can tell that Elin is trying to take in everything at once with her helmet's sensors. She rushes over to the water-filled crater and kneels down in front of it to get the sensors and the light of her helmet as close to the surface as she can. I tap her on the shoulder as I pass her, and she gets up with a reluctant expression on her face.

"When we're done," I remind her.

Ahead, the admin building looms out of the rain, vast and gray. The Class IV structures are three-story bunkers with thick walls, designed to serve as emergency shelter for the colony during an attack or a natural calamity. They were built before the Lankies, so the calamities they had in mind were brief colonial tussles between NAC and SRA marines or periods of exceptionally harsh weather. Even though they were not built to keep Lankies out, they do a good job of it because the walls are reinforced ferroconcrete that's over a meter thick at the weakest points. Even Lankies can't crack a Class IV, but as we get close to this particular one, we can see that it wasn't for a lack of trying. The building is shaped like a loaf of bread, sloped sides and a domed top to distribute outside loads, and the flanks of the structure are scored with dozens of long furrows that look like the world's largest cat raked its claws down the sides. Some spots have big chunks of concrete torn out of them, and the steel reinforcement bars are jutting out of the holes, twisted and rusty. But none of the dents were deep enough to make it through the outer concrete walls and breach the building, even if it didn't do the residents any good in the long run.

When we reach the end of the road that leads to the little plaza in front of the building, I signal the squad leaders. Lieutenant Philips takes Dagger Two's four troopers to the northeast corner, where they turn and assume their overwatch positions. Lieutenant Dean and his Dagger Four element dash across the plaza and disappear around the far corner to settle in out of sight at the southwest corner.

"Dagger Four in position," Lieutenant Philips reports in a few moments later.

"The clock is ticking," I say on the platoon channel. "Dagger Three, move in and check the front door. Dagger One, bring up the rear with me."

We make our way across the little plaza, jumping over half-meter cracks in the concrete that are teeming with alien plant life. The main entrance to the complex is tucked away in a concrete vestibule, and something tried to get to the door with so much vigor that the retaining walls of the vestibule are now knee-high rubble in front of the doors.

"The access panels are dead," one of the Dagger Three troopers reports. "They must have knocked out the solar panels for the backup power bank."

"Can we run a bypass with external power to juice up the system?" I ask.

"Negative, sir. No way to tap into the circuit without cracking open the walls."

"I guess we're doing it the hard way then," I say and look around. I don't really want to set off explosions in this graveyard-quiet place and make the ground shake, but if the power cells for the electronic door locks are dead, there's no way to override the mechanism with the master code.

"Master key, aye," Lieutenant Evans acknowledges. "Rees, Smith, get over here and stick some boom on the locks."

We have the schematics for the Class IV shelter doors in our data banks, so the SEALs know exactly where to place the shaped charges to defeat the locking mechanism with the fewest explosives necessary. But it's still a complex operation that requires more care than punching a numeric code into an access panel. By the time the demolition experts are done with their work, I feel like I have spent an hour on the rubble pile in front of the vestibule, even though only five minutes have passed in real time. The rain is coming in with unrelenting intensity, whipping across the plaza and seemingly changing directions every few moments as the winds shift.

"Master key is ready to go," Staff Sergeant Rees finally announces.

We move off to the side and crouch in the shadow of the building, out of the blast cone of the charges.

"Light it up, Rees," I say.

"Lighting up, aye. Fire in the hole."

The charges go off with a boom that makes the rubble in front of the vestibule bounce. They're relatively small packages of high explosive, but they still make a racket, and it's only amplified by the funnel-like nature of the concrete vestibule that directs the sound outward and to the west.

The crack from the detonation rolls across the plaza and reverberates back from the nearby buildings and alleys. We still don't know if Lankies rely at all on sound or vibration to find their way around and locate us, but the charges we just sent off generated plenty of both, and I feel a renewed sense of urgency to see the mission through as quickly as possible.

On my tactical display, Rapier Three-One, our battle taxi, is in a slow turn to port at the edge of my map scale, ten kilometers away and twenty thousand feet above the ground, a little too distant for comfort. If the Lankies rush us in the rain, the drop ship won't be down on the deck quickly enough to make a difference. The seismic mines placed by the battlespace control squadron a few hours earlier are now our only early-warning system that can see farther than our eyeballs, and I am about to wager four squads of SEALs that those mines work as advertised.

"Door's open," Lieutenant Evans says.

"Copy that. Dagger One, Dagger Three, breach formation. Let's go, let's go," I send.

I make my way to the front of the building again and climb the rubble pile by the doors. When I reach the top, I can see one-half of the double doors jammed at an angle but still mostly in place, the other blown out of the frame just enough to leave a little gap between the door halves that's wider at the bottom than at the top.

"Mind your step," I tell Dr. Vandenberg as she climbs up the rubble pile behind me, but she's unencumbered by armor or weaponry and considerably more fleet-footed than I am in my battle rattle.

The SEALs file through the gap in the door one by one in front of us. When both squads are inside, I take a look around the plaza and verify the position of the overwatch squads. Then I start the short descent into the vestibule, which looms below surface level in the semi-darkness, with its walls overgrown with moss and rubble strewn at the base. From my angle, it looks disconcertingly like a tomb.

CHAPTER 17

SQUALL LINE

As soon as I walk into the hallway beyond the entrance vestibule, the temperature seems to drop by ten degrees. Ahead of me, the light cones from the suits of the SEALs cut through the darkness and illuminate the walls and ceilings, throwing flickering shadows as they make their way down the hallway. I know that Dr. Vandenberg's suit isn't equipped with infrared or thermal imaging, so I turn on my own light, even though my bug suit provides me with augmented vision.

There's a layer of concrete dust on the floor, and debris bits of various sizes litter the hallway. We don't have to go far into the building to find our first unpleasant surprise.

"Body on the right," one of the SEALs says in a low voice and points into the open doorway of a room. As I walk up, he makes way for me to see, and I look into the room he indicated. A corpse in colonial utility overalls is splayed out on the floor next to an overturned chair. After twelve years of decomposition in this air, there isn't enough left to make out any distinguishing features or marks. I can't even tell if the corpse belongs to a man or woman because most of the colonists wear the same utility clothing on the job. There's a beverage mug on a desk next to the overturned chair, and a blank and silent data pad next to it that reflects the light from my helmet lamp. I take two steps into the room to look around. Whatever was in the mug has long since evaporated, leaving a dark crust at the bottom of the container. I know the layout of the building because the admin center in New Svalbard was a Class IV as well, but after all this time, I don't recall the use of this room at that colony.

Elin mutters a soft curse into her helmet comms as she walks in carefully behind me.

"They probably sealed the door as soon as they realized they were under attack," I say. "But the Lanky nerve agent went right through the air filters."

"That's a shitty thing to be a first for," she replies in a low murmur. Then she kneels down next to the corpse and examines the body. "Looks like it went quick at least."

"I was overhead a few days later," I say. "In a drop ship. I saw the bodies in the street. It looked like the stuff had dropped them wherever they were standing or running."

"You were here at First Contact?"

"Twelve years ago. Our ship ran into the minefield in orbit without warning. First casualties of the war," I reply.

"How are you even *alive*?"

"I've asked myself the same question more than once," I say. "Come on. Lots more rooms in this place."

We walk out of the room with the corpse and follow the SEALs, who are now twenty meters farther down the long entrance hallway and almost at the central staircase.

"Hold up at the bottom of the stairs, One-Niner," I send to Captain Harper, who is leading the Dagger One squad. "I have to check something for a second."

"Copy, hold at bottom of the stairs," Harper acknowledges and halts his squad with a hand signal.

There's an office to my left that looks immediately familiar, and I shine my light into it. It's the duty station of the colonial constable, the chief law enforcement officer on the planet. To my relief, there's no corpse in here, just an empty room with a layer of dust on every surface. On the wall to the left of the door is a weapons rack with a security lock. The power in the building has been out for a decade or more, so the batteries for the backup circuits are drained, and the only way to open the lock for the weapons rack is to use the master key that's usually on the duty constable's person. But I don't need to open the rack to get the picture. There's an M-66 carbine in every one of the six locking brackets. When the Lankies hit the city, the cops didn't even have time to get their guns out of the ready rack.

"Clock's ticking, Major," Captain Harper sends.

"Affirmative. Be there in a second," I reply.

I leave the constable's office and make my way down the hallways to join up with the SEALs, with Dr. Vandenberg two steps behind.

"Down the stairs to sublevel three, then right," I say and motion my intent to take point.

We descend into the basement levels of the admin center on light boots, as if everyone is worried about disturbing the peace of the dead. It's oppressively quiet except for the sound of our soles on the dusty concrete. Two more colonist corpses are splayed out on the bottom landing, one draped halfway on top of the other, as if they both tried to make for the safety of the basement shelter and succumbed to the nerve gas at the same moment. When I shine my helmet light down the corridor in sublevel three, thousands of dust motes drift slowly in the beam in front of me, stirred up by the movement of the air we are displacing with our bodies.

"Last door on the right," I say and indicate the spot with a hand gesture. One of the SEALs from Dagger Two walks up to the door and tries the security panel.

"Dead," he says. "But it's just a level-one setup. Tiny charge should do it. Right between the panel and the frame."

Another SEAL comes up and starts preparing a small breaching charge from a chunk of plastic explosives he pulls out of one of his armor pouches. I turn and motion for everyone to get back.

"Door demo," I say. "Turn off your helmet audio."

It only takes a few moments for the lead SEAL at the door to prep the cherry-sized charge and attach it to the right spot. He moves back for what seems like a cavalierly low number of steps, then turns away from the door.

"Fire in the hole," he says.

The breaching charge is much smaller than the shaped charges we used on the heavy entrance doors, but this is a much more confined space. When the explosive goes off, it feels like someone stepped up to me and slapped me hard on both sides of my helmet above the ears. For a few moments, the hallway is full of billowing dust.

"Open sesame," the lead SEAL says and nods at the door, which is swinging from its hinges. The part where the lock used to be now has a perfectly semicircular hole in it. The SEAL who blew open the lock steps into the room and pulls the door off the hinges completely, then leans it against the wall, with as little obvious effort as if he had moved a small stack of empty mess trays out of the way.

"Jesus, Sergeant Rees," I say as he steps aside to let me in. "Tell me you couldn't have kicked that door in just the same and saved us all the noise."

Rees just flashes a grin and shrugs.

The network center is dark and quiet as well, a wholly unnatural state for a neural network facility. These are the nerve centers of warships and shore installations, and they are always powered up in day-to-day operations, backed up by at least three redundant circuits and emergency battery banks because they control all the data traffic. Everything that runs on a circuit connects to the network center via fiber-optic links, all the way down to the air-conditioning and the water temperature in the residential building units. To see one with all its consoles dark and its status lights out is a strange experience.

I walk to the storage racks in the back of the room, where finger-thick strands of fiber bundles connect to dozens of separate control modules. My neural network administrator training is a little dusty, but the equipment in this place is the same vintage as the stuff I trained on in tech school. I follow the fiber strands down to the storage bank, where the system's memory modules are plugged into hot-swappable bays. Under normal circumstances, I'd give the system the instruction to power down the storage array before handling the modules, but this rack hasn't been energized in many years, and any potential data corruption from the final power outage has already occurred a long time ago.

I remove the latches for the access cover and expose the module bays. Then I start flipping the bay locking levers and pulling out modules one at a time. They're square little boxes the size of bricks and about as heavy, and the local storage rack has twenty of them. Every single byte of information generated by the colony's electronic devices is stored in a redundant parity system on these modules, everything from the last maintenance restart to the moment the storage bank ran out of backup battery juice. Even if the colony's neural networks administrator had just performed a wipe and a system reboot right before the Lankies landed, the backup systems would have kept recording as long as the backup circuit had power, and the batteries would have been enough to keep the system up for a few months. Halley and I got here on *Versailles* a month after the initial landings, and I realize that somewhere on these memory modules, there's probably a record of our arrival at the distant terraforming station and our subsequent battle with the Lankies. The security systems at the terraforming station would have sent their data with the nightly backups to the main hub until the station was destroyed, even though there was nobody left alive in Willoughby City to see or acknowledge the routine transmissions.

I pull out the modules one by one and stack them up next to my left boot as I go. When I am finished, I weigh the last module in the palm of my hand and look at it for a moment. Thanks to modern solid-state polymer matrix storage tech, the little square module on my palm holds the combined data of the last days of almost two thousand people—every step they took, everything they saw, and everything they managed to say to any nearby microphones, which were in every room of every building in some form. It will tell the story of how they lived their last days, and how their lives ended. I wouldn't want to go through that data for any amount of money or privileges, but I understand why the intel division would want to get their hands on these modules.

"All right," I say. "Divvy these up between Dagger One and Dagger Two. Everyone takes at least one. Tuck them into your dump pouches and treat them like they have two years' worth of your salary on them."

"Are we fucked if we lose any?" Captain Harper asks.

"Negative. The system writes across all of them at once for redundancy. We lose a few, they can reconstruct the data from the others. Just as long as at least some of us make it back."

I start handing the modules to the SEALs behind me, who pass them back down the line. Every SEAL tucks away one of the modules as instructed. Elin takes one as well, and I watch as she slips it into the leg pocket of her suit and carefully seals the cover flap. When I have passed out enough modules for everyone on the team, there are three left sitting on the ground next to my foot. I take a module off the remaining stack and hold it out to Sergeant Rees.

"You get to double up on the high-value cargo, Rees. Don't get stomped."

"Aye, sir. I'll do my best." Sergeant Rees takes the module and slips it into one of the ammo punches at the front of his armor.

I pick up the last two memory modules and stow them in my armor's dump pouch, the collapsible fabric bag we all have attached to our chest plates to hold odds and ends during missions whenever we need our hands free.

"All right. We have secured the goods. Dagger One, Dagger Three, exfil and link up with Dagger Two and Four outside. Move 'em out," I say.

We ascend the central stairwell again, a little more quickly than we came down just a few minutes ago. I'll be glad to leave this basement behind, and I know that Elin Vandenberg and the SEALs feel the same way even though nobody is voicing the sentiment out loud. The building is a crypt now, and the basement levels are the darkest and most unsettling part of it. We are the first living humans in twelve years to walk these hallways, and if we lose the Lanky war, we will also be the last.

We're on the landing of the first subfloor when there's a noise coming from the level above, quick footsteps echoing in the staircase. Then the beam of a helmet light appears above the safety rail of the ground-level landing.

"Dagger One, Dagger Three," someone calls down into the stairwell on amplified audio.

"Turn off the speakers," Captain Harper shouts back. "Use the comms. We are right below you."

"Sorry, Captain." The voice that comes over the headset of my helmet a second later is that of Sergeant Thatcher, the junior NCO of Dagger Two. "Comms don't work for shit through these walls. Lieutenant Philips says to expedite if possible. The seismic mines are pinging incoming. Looks like we're about to get some company."

Harper and I exchange a look. Then he turns toward the SEALs lined up in the staircase below us and gives the hand signal for double-time.

"Lead the way, Thatcher. We are right behind you," he says.

Outside, the rain has slacked off a little while we were below, but the visibility hasn't improved much. There's a warm, humid mist in the air that is drifting in and out of the gaps between the buildings. When I step off the rubble pile and onto the plaza, my boots splash into deep puddles. As soon as I am beyond the entrance vestibule, my TacLink screen comes to life again and populates with all the data updates I've missed while I was shielded behind the thick concrete walls of the admin building.

The recon flights placed a network of seismic mines on the ground around Willoughby City that activate whenever they detect a ground disturbance. It's such a new system that I've never seen it in action before, but as I check the readouts, I find myself disappointed at the coarseness of the information. I wasn't expecting precise locations and accurate pictographs of incoming Lankies, but I was hoping for something more concrete than the vague red-shaded sector on my map that forms a wedge extending to the west of the city. According to the map legend, the width of the wedge indicates the approximate number of incoming Lankies, and the intensity of the color indicates the rough distance. I compare the values and feel a swell of dread.

Ten-plus individuals, five kilometers or less.

"We have five minutes. Maybe ten if they're not in a big hurry," I send to the squad leaders. "Dagger team, double-time back to the pickup point. Threat vector is two seventy degrees, distance five klicks and closing fast."

"Copy that. Moving out," Captain Harper acknowledges. He signals to the assembled squads. "We are leaving, people. The neighborhood's about to get unfriendly."

Next to me, Elin looks pale and wide-eyed behind her face shield.

"Remember how you said you were hoping to see a live Lanky in the wild?" I ask. "It looks like you may be about to get your wish."

We start running after the SEALs, who are already making their way across the little plaza to head for the pickup spot. With the Lankies on the way already, I decide to throw EM emission restrictions to the wind and call down our ride. It's been a while since I've had to do battlespace coordination on the run, and I find that I haven't really missed the experience.

"Rapier Three-One, Dagger Actual," I send to the drop ship. "We need immediate evac. Dagger team is on the way to the LZ. Incoming hostiles from the west, five minutes out."

"Copy that, Dagger Actual," the response comes. *"We are on the way. ETA four minutes, twenty seconds."*

"We are on the central thoroughfare and coming into the LZ from the south. All friendlies are moving on the main drag and within a hundred and fifty meters of the pickup point. If you see any hostiles outside of those bounds when you're on final, you are cleared to engage."

"Copy cleared hot, Dagger Actual. Stand by for pickup."

I drop the channel and concentrate on running again. The torn-up roadbed and the omnipresent plant growth makes for tougher going than I would like right now as I have to hop from patch to patch to avoid getting slowed down by debris piles or overgrown patches. Next to me, Elin stumbles when she steps into a deep puddle, and I reach out to help her up again.

Guess you won't be collecting any samples today, I think. *Sorry about that.*

The LZ is an open space between the rows of housing units and a small cluster of service buildings, uncluttered by vertical obstacles that could range up a drop ship. When we landed, I didn't pay attention to the signage on the buildings, but as we reach the plaza, it jumps out at me because our helmet lights illuminate the reflective letters on the signs: **WILLOUGHBY CITY PUBLIC SCHOOL**. From the way Elin's eyes widen, I can tell that she has seen the signs as well and understands the implications.

I turn my back toward the building and make myself face west, toward the incoming threat, because I don't want my helmet light to reach through the windows or the clear polyplast view panels of the nearby doors. The scene in the admin center was dark and hopeless enough for another year or two of recurring nightmares. I don't need to see what the Lanky gas pods left behind in that school building, where the four hundred and eighty-nine families of this colony sent their children on the day of the attack. Next to me, Elin is still looking at the building as if transfixed by the message on the reflective letters. I touch her shoulder to get her attention. When she turns toward me, I shake my head slowly.

The SEALs deploy around the pickup spot in a ragged firing line, rifles pointed to the west. The sky is an angry shade of dark gray, illuminated from the inside in irregular intervals by lightning bolts. The buildings to our west are all one-level residential structures, but the visibility isn't good enough to even see where the rows of houses end and the surrounding plateau begins. Mist blooms everywhere between the buildings, drifting across our field of view and swirling in the wind like ghostly tendrils.

"ETA one minute, thirty seconds," Rapier Three-One sends.

The wedge extending to the west on my map display is now a good twenty degrees wide, and as I watch, the color changes from a coral red to a dark crimson. "DISTANCE: <1000 METERS."

A low vibration shakes the ground a little under my feet, a familiar thrumming that spikes my heart rate. Another follows, then a third, each a little stronger than the first.

"They're in the squall just beyond our line of sight," I send to the platoon. "Weapons free. Engage as soon as you get a fix. Do not wait for effect. They'll drop when you've shot them enough."

Next to me, Elin Vandenberg looks like she's starting to regret some of her recent life choices. I nudge her behind me and check the loading status of my rifle. I want to assure her that she'll be fine, that we'll stop the threat, or that there's a place she can hide if we don't. But the truth is that these things are huge and immensely strong, and that we usually draw the short end of the stick whenever we have to go toe-to-toe with groups of them at small-arms distance. If we don't hold the line, Dr. Vandenberg will die with us right here on the spot, seconds away from safety. But that was the choice she made, whether she believed the magnitude of the danger or not.

In the squall line ahead, a huge shape appears. Then the Lanky is close enough to be distinct against the backdrop of the mists and the shimmering bands of rain, twenty meters of spindly appendages and rain-slick skin the color of eggshells. For a moment, I have a strong sense of déjà vu. Twelve years ago, the first Lanky I ever saw walked out of a similar squall, only a few hundred kilometers from here, in front of the disbelieving eyes of a handful of Corps marines and stranded Fleet sailors. But back then, we were taken by surprise, defeated because we had inadequate weapons and no knowledge of our new foe. Now we know that they can be killed, and we know how to kill them.

"Light it up," I shout into the platoon comms.

The SEALs need no encouragement. The Lanky has taken two long steps out of the rainy curtain of the squall line when sixteen JMB rifles open up all at once. The bright red tracer charges of the rifle bullets look like angry, suicidal fireflies as they streak across the distance to the Lanky in the blink of an eye. Some of the tracers deflect on unfavorably angled skin and careen off into the rainy darkness, but most of them strike true.

The Lanky falters, stumbles, and lets out its earsplitting distress wail. I haven't heard that sound in years except in my dreams. It's the soundtrack of crushing fear and imminent death. Every part of my body wants to recoil from it, crawl up inside itself and refuse to share a reality with it. But instead of obeying my base instincts, I put my target marker on the Lanky's chest, and I send my own scream back at it, three-round bursts of tungsten and uranium slugs, made to punch through Lanky skin and make a path for the fifty grams of explosives that are piggybacking on each bullet.

Seventeen rounds left. Fourteen. Eleven. Eight. Five. Two.

The Lanky falls just as my magazine indicator shows empty. Struck by hundreds of armor-piercing rounds, it crashes sideways into a row of residence buildings, flattening half a dozen concrete domes as it skids along, still wailing its distress call. The new rifle rounds are not as powerful as the silver bullets we used to use, but they make up for it by being much easier to shoot and allowing for much bigger magazines.

In the squall line behind the stricken Lanky, three more of them appear, walking almost side by side in a slightly staggered line. They seem to pay no mind to their fallen mate. I eject the empty magazine block from my rifle and swap in a full one, then press the button for the automatic bolt mechanism to cycle a fresh round into the chamber. The SEALs engage the newcomers without requiring direction. A new swarm of tracers rises from our position and rushes out to meet the Lankies. I add a whole magazine on full auto to the fusillade, then reload and burn through a third. As I reload once more, I glance over at Elin Vandenberg, who is squatting on the ground with her arms over her head, as if she could plug her ears with the bulk of her suit's sleeves even through the thick laminate layer of her helmet.

"Two hundred meters," Captain Harper shouts.

As the Lankies close the distance, our rifle rounds become more effective, retaining more energy to funnel into their penetrator points. Another Lanky falls, shrieking and flailing its limbs. The one behind it stumbles over its mate and goes down with it, then starts to right itself and get back to its feet. Beyond the squall line, I see more movement, heralding new arrivals. I know that no matter how many we drop, there'll be more of them following. Whatever instincts they have, self-preservation has never been among them. Their main tactic has always been to grind us down by sheer attrition and then crush our lines with numbers, and it usually works because they have the numbers to throw away. Sooner or later we will run out of bullets, and if they still have live bodies on the field when that happens, they win by default.

"Rolling in hot," I hear over the radio. *"Dagger team, keep your heads down."*

From somewhere in the eastern sky, two insanely fast comet tails streak across the battlefield and smash into the Lanky that is still on its feet and striding toward us. The shock wave from the detonation of the missile warheads rocks the ground beneath our feet, and I lose my footing and go to one knee next to Elin. When I look up again, I see bits and pieces of the Lanky's torso flying everywhere. Part of one arm sails off into a group of housing domes and bounces off with a sickening thudding sound.

Then the drop ship is overhead.

Rapier Three-One swoops out of the low-hanging clouds like a pissed-off guardian angel. The pilot pulls out of the descent and brings his ship to a hover right above our position, fifty meters overhead. A moment later, the heavy automatic cannons mounted on the side of the fuselage open up, sending little concussive shocks from the muzzle blasts rolling across the square and making the water in the puddles jump. The pilot keeps his finger on the trigger button for what seems like half a minute, hammering a storm of tracers toward the remaining Lankies and raining empty shell casings down onto the ground all around us. When the furious thunder finally stops, the Lankies in our line of sight are all on the ground, dead or dying, finally mauled and mangled into submission.

"There are more incoming," the pilot cautions. *"Setting down for immediate dustoff. Do not dawdle."*

"Get up," I say to Elin and pull her up by the sleeve of her suit. "More Lankies in the forecast. We are getting off this rock."

She's clearly shell-shocked, but she nods to acknowledge me even as she looks around wild-eyed to take in the scene. It's hard for a civilian to fathom just how much death and destruction can be unleashed in a few minutes of combat. I've used up over half my ammunition load already, and we have only engaged four Lankies, two of which needed drop-ship assistance to be finished off. Three blocks of Willoughby City are crushed to rubble or blown to pieces in front of us. There is no training in the world that can really prepare a normal, sane human for being in the middle of this much concentrated violence.

The drop ship descends into the middle of the landing spot, its tail ramp opening even before it puts down. When the skids hit the ground, the SEALs retreat toward the ship, weapons still aimed in the direction of the threat.

"Go, go, go," the pilot shouts over the radio, as if any of us need the encouragement.

I take a knee by the side of the ramp and keep my weapon at the ready as the SEALs rush up the ramp and file into the cargo hold.

"Go now," I shout at Elin and point up into the cargo hold. She nods and follows the SEALs into the ship. When the last of the Dagger team members are inside, I get up and follow. As welcoming as the drop ship is right now, I am the ranking officer on the ground, and my pair of boots needs to be the first to step onto the planet and the last to step off.

The cargo hold is abuzz with frantic activity as the SEALs secure their weapons and hurriedly strap into their jump seats. I sit Dr. Vandenberg down in one of the empty seats and strap her in. When I finish, I give her a thumbs-up, and she nods her thanks in response.

I secure my own harness and give another thumbs-up, this one to the crew chief by the front bulkhead, who looks understandably impatient right now.

"Three-one, we're all strapped in," I say. "Tail ramp clear. *Go, go, go.*"

The pilot wastes no time hauling his bird back into the air and out of the reach of angry Lankies. The rain lashes through the open tail ramp and splashes against my helmet as we leave the ground and pick up forward speed. Underneath the ship, the housing units of

Willoughby City zoom by, still too close for comfort. Then the tail ramp blocks my view of the outside as it seals into place.

"Two hundred and climbing," the pilot sends. *"We are in the clear."*

I look around the cargo hold and take stock with my helmet display to make sure all the SEALs made the dustoff.

"Dagger team, all accounted for," I tell the pilot. "Mission accomplished."

"Glad to hear it," he responds. *"That was a bit close. Sorry for the delay, but I had to keep the ship above the weather."*

"All's well that ends well," I say. "But I am going to have a talk with the R&D people about the meaning of the term 'early warning.'"

In the seat in front of me, Elin looks like she has just run a marathon without preparation. Her face has the familiar expression I've seen on a hundred young grunts after their first brush with combat—the unfocused stare into the distance as the brain needs all available bandwidth to process what just happened, to figure out how to compartmentalize the experience and keep it well away from the sane stuff.

"You got your wish," I tell her over helmet comms. "Live Lankies, in their natural environment. What do you think?"

She looks at me for a full ten seconds before she responds.

"I *think*," she says slowly, and her voice sounds like she's speaking from the middle of a dream. "I think I am going to check and see if they have any openings in the xenobotany division."

CHAPTER 18

FLAMEOUT

The weather grew more ferocious while we were on the ground. The ascent back to the ship is much bumpier than the combat descent less than an hour ago. Even the seasoned SEALs are looking a little green after five minutes of rough flight, and I'm feeling more than a little queasy as well. But the adrenaline in my system is slow to ebb, and my anxiety just transferred from the danger of Lankies in close proximity to the danger of getting blotted out of the sky by a hardware failure. My crash on Mars a few years ago is still vivid in my memory, when material fatigue caused a wing to break off the garrison patrol ship I was flying in at the time. The ejection seat and the parachute both worked, but I've been a little more nervous on drop-ship flights ever since, especially when I am not sitting in an ejection seat.

Across the aisle from me, Elin avails herself to her suit's built-in vomit tube for the second time since we left the ground. She looks small and exhausted.

"We'll be all right," I say. "These pilots know their stuff. My wife flies one of these."

"You're married?" Elin asks, and I nod.

"How about you?"

"No time," she says. "I'm constantly on the go. Had a new duty station every year for the last six years. When you don't get out much, a year's barely enough to find out where all the good food places are."

"We have the same problem," I say. "But we've made it work for twelve years now."

"You've kept a military marriage going for twelve years? Respect."

"Married for eight. Been together for twelve. We met in boot camp, if you can believe that."

"Really." She smiles weakly and eyes the end of her puke tube again. "So how do you deal with it all? The time away from each other. The . . ." She gestures around the cargo hold vaguely. "The *this*. Going to places where things want to stomp you flat. Flying in weather that nobody should be made to fly in."

"It's always been our life, I guess. We're used to it by now. We just try to make up time whenever we are together. At least we can't ever really get sick of each other."

"That's one way to look at it, I suppose," Elin says.

"It helps to know that we could quit anytime if we wanted. Resign our commissions, leave the Corps. We wouldn't have our retirement funds. But we'd have no more *this*," I say, and make the same vague gesture to encompass the cargo hold.

She narrows her eyes and smirks as she studies me with mock intensity.

"I hate to be the bearer of bad news," she says. "But if you had the chance to walk away and didn't, you're both still in because you like it."

I give her a little shrug and a smirk of my own in reply.

"Married a drop-ship pilot—" she begins.

A mighty jolt goes through the Dragonfly, and even some of the SEALs let out shouts of anxious surprise. The lights in the cargo hold flicker and dim. A moment later, there's a muffled bang, and the engine noise on the other side of the hull changes pitch and drops by half. I can tell by the shifting feeling in my stomach that the ship is quickly leveling out from its climb. When it's clear that we are transitioning to a downward-facing attitude, my anxiety spikes again, and I taste fear at the back of my throat.

"Three-One, Dagger Actual," I send to the flight deck. "What the fuck just happened?"

It takes a few tense moments before the pilot replies. When he does, I hear the warbling of cockpit alarms in the background of the transmission.

"Sit tight," he says in a terse voice. "Lightning strike on the starboard engine. We have it under control. Stand by and keep those harnesses buckled."

"Wonderful," I reply, but the pilot has already cut the link.

A smell of ozone and burning plastic is wafting into the cargo hold. I look around for possible smoke from an onboard fire but fail to find any.

"Pilot says we lost the starboard engine," I tell the SEALs. "He says they've got it, but I am putting SAR on notice anyway."

"Fantastic idea," Captain Harper says and checks the tightness of his safety harness. "What a shitty fucking end to the day that would be."

"We have an engine out," I tell Elin. "But we're not crashing."

"Yet," she says.

I bring up my tactical screen and check the assets in the area. The close-air-support flight is still in the air a hundred klicks to our southwest, two Shrikes with twenty tons of anti-Lanky ordnance between them on their wing pylons. If we have to put this ship down, I'll be able to vector in the Shrikes to take out nearby Lankies. But a Shrike can't land on rough ground, and even if it could, the Fleet's main ground-attack craft has no space or provision for passengers. For the second time today, I decide to break EMCON.

"*Washington* TacOps, this is Dagger Actual on Rapier Three-One," I send.

"Dagger Actual, Washington *TacOps, go ahead,"* Captain Taylor's voice responds. He's the on-duty officer manning the TacOps station in the CIC, and just the man I want to talk to right now because he is the leader of the Spaceborne Rescue section.

"Rapier Three-One has an engine out," I say. "We may have to put down on the surface. Get the Ready Five search-and-rescue birds warmed up and into the pits. I'll update you as soon as I get word from the pilot."

"Copy requested launch prep for Ready Five SAR flight," Captain Taylor replies. *"Alert is out. The birds are moving into the clamps right now. Good luck."*

The sound from the remaining engine does not build confidence. It changes in pitch every few seconds as the thrust level rises and falls seemingly at random. The storm is still tossing us around, and I have the very distinct premonition that it will be a while longer before I get to take my post-mission shower today.

"Dagger Actual, Three-One," the flight deck finally sends. "Everything okay back there?"

"Three-One, we're good," I reply. "Tell me we're not about to fall out of the sky. Because that would fuck up my dinner plans."

"Starboard engine's gone. We won't be able to make orbit with the thrust from the port engine alone. I'll have to find a place to set down and call for SAR."

"I've already put them on notice. The Ready Five birds are waiting in the clamps."

"Fantastic. Stand by for updates," the pilot says.

I'm not going to die on this fucking planet, I think. *Even if it does seem to have it in for me.*

We spend the next fifteen minutes in a slow and careful descent. The usual post-mission banter among the troops has ceased entirely as everyone seems to be listening intently to the noises from the port engine and the pops and creaks coming from the hull. I follow our flight path with the tactical map to keep the strike fighters in our general vicinity. There's no telling which part of the planet has Lankies on it now, and we don't have time to get recon flights down here to scan the terrain for us ahead of our descent.

"There's a patch of decent weather fifty klicks ahead," the pilot says after a long period of radio silence from the flight deck. "I can see the surface. Means we won't have to use ground radar and alert the neighborhood."

"I'll pass the coordinates to the SAR birds," I say. "We'll be back in the air in no time."

With the search and rescue coordinated, all I can do is monitor our descent and hope that we aren't about to put down the stricken ship right on top of a subterranean Lanky hive. When I switch off the tactical screen, I see that Elin Vandenberg is looking at me, and I can tell that she's trying hard not to appear afraid.

"First time crash-landing?" I say to lift the mood a little, and she nods.

"How about you?"

"Not the first time," I say. "Let's see. Had one drop ship skewered in orbit. That was a zero-g rescue. Not nearly as much fun as you'd think it is."

She smiles weakly.

"One on Mars," I continue. "Technically not a crash landing because we had to bail. Parachute descent. *Also* not as much fun as you'd think."

"Any other close calls?"

"That's it as far as drop ships go," I say. "Not a bad accident rate, I think."

"It only ever takes one," Elin replies. "Like I said, how are you even still alive?"

"Because I'd be in deep shit with my wife if I died," I respond. This time, my answer gets a laugh out of her.

"Putting down in thirty," the pilot sends back to the cargo hold over the loudspeakers ten minutes later. *"We're down to half our usual thrust, so touchdown may be a little brisk."*

"Dagger team, check your weapons," I tell the SEALs. "Looks like our shift isn't over yet."

I inspect my own gear and see that I am down to three magazines for my rifle: two in the pouches and one in the gun. I haven't been in the field with a JMB before, and it appears that the full-auto function the troops love so much has the negative side effect of prolific ammunition use under stress. If someone had briefed me ten minutes ago and asked me to guess how many rounds I fired in the engagement at Willoughby City, I would have guessed twenty. Instead, I burned through more than twice that number.

"Squad leaders, listen up," I say. "Designate one troop per squad to hit the ship armory and grab a crate of rifle mags each before we dash off. I want us all to top off just in case," I send.

"Copy that," SEAL Captain Harper says, and the other squad leaders send their acknowledgments.

"Stand by for touchdown," the flight deck announces. We feel the ship flare for the landing, pointing up the nose and arresting its downward speed in a familiar maneuver.

What follows isn't so familiar. We hit the ground so hard that everyone takes a bounce in their seats, and something on the other side of the front bulkhead pops and squeals in structural protest. The ship clearly slides on the surface for a few meters after the skids are on the ground. Then there's another sharp crack followed by a grinding noise, and the ship dips its front by seven or eight degrees as the front skid assembly collapses.

We all release the locks of our harnesses seemingly simultaneously. When I get up to help Elin, I see that she's already unlocked her own as well, and she's shrugging the padded harness straps off her shoulders.

"Grab the ammo and let's get out of here," Captain Harper shouts. "Before something else breaks in this thing."

The surroundings outside look very different from the post-apocalyptic drab of Willoughby City. We're on a plateau somewhere, with a spectacular view of a mountain chain on the horizon, and the cloud cover here isn't nearly as heavy as over the colony city. In the distance, there are actually some breaks in the clouds, and shafts of sunlight are streaming through the cracks and painting bright patches on the landscape below.

Willoughby is much greener than I remember. Twelve years ago, it was almost entirely barren. The settlers were barely able to grow crabgrass for decoration. Now there are fields of grass and moss as far as I can see. I almost stop at the bottom of the tail ramp to look around until Sergeant Rees pushes past me with an ammo can in each hand. I clear the way for the rest of the SEALs and lead Elin away from the drop ship. We're in a ground depression that's a few hundred meters long, sandwiched between a rocky hill and a shallow ravine. At the bottom of the ravine, the fast-moving currents of a river are reflecting the sporadic sunlight. It's warm, and with the lack of rain, it feels almost pleasant.

The SEALs are setting up a perimeter guard and start refilling their magazine pouches from the drop-ship armory containers. I walk over to the nearest one and do the same, then I stick a few more magazines into my dump pouch where they join the data module from the colony. I don't expect to be here long enough to use all that ammo, but life has a weird way of confounding my expectations lately.

One of the drop-ship pilots comes jogging up to where I am standing.

"The SAR birds are on the way, sir. They've been tracking us for most of the descent. ETA seventeen minutes. They say to keep EMCON except for emergencies. We didn't see any Lanky settlements nearby, but we can't look underground."

"All right," I say. "Thanks for getting us on the ground without blowing up. Guess we'll wait for the next bus together."

Elin has walked over to a nearby rise and climbed the ten-meter slope to the top. I follow her to see what piqued her interest. A few kilometers in the distance, a squall line is moving across the plateau, the line between rain and dry air so defined that it looks like someone is dragging a transparent veil over the landscape. On the horizon, angry-looking dark clouds are swirling, slowly moving toward us in the atmospheric currents.

"It's beautiful down here," she says. "This part, anyway. I can see why people didn't mind settling in this place."

I check the map and see that we've put down over two hundred kilometers northeast of Willoughby City, right in the middle of the continent between two major mountain chains. When Halley and I landed here, we found shelter at a terraforming station three hundred klicks south of the city. It's a vast, open continent that would have held tens of millions of humans in a few decades, with clean air and plenty of space for everyone.

"It's theirs now," I say. "Even if the Lankies all went away tomorrow, it would take us fifty years to get the atmosphere back to where it was."

"Heck of a greenhouse, though," Elin says. "You have to hand it to them. Whatever they're doing with these planets they're stealing from us, it's really efficient."

"You mean you xenobiologists haven't figured out the how and why yet after all these years?"

"We know they plant terraformers of their own. We know they tip the atmosphere to ten percent carbon dioxide within a year. And we know that the plant life explodes with variety after they do. We have no idea yet why they're growing anything, or whether it's even intentional and not just a side effect of something. That's part of why I am out here. It's not exactly easy to observe all the effects on-site."

"That's the truth," I say. "The new owners are super antisocial."

Overhead, the strike fighters make their presence known. They dive out of the cloud cover and make a pass over the area, waggling their wingtips as they reach our landing spot. Then one of them splits off in a sharp left-hand turn, its wingtips carving a brilliant white condensation trail in the air. A few seconds later, the sonic boom from their flyby rolls over the hill where Elin and I are standing. Before I can wonder why they're going supersonic and alerting the entire neighborhood, the radio screen pops up on my heads-up display.

"Dagger Actual, this is Siren Six-Five. We have visual on a cluster of LHOs in your area. They're fifteen klicks to your south, ten-plus individuals on the ground and moving. Doesn't look like they're headed for you, but you may want to wait this out on higher ground anyway."

I watch as the tactical screen updates with the visual sighting from the Shrikes. A small cluster of orange icons pops into existence on the other side of the hills to our left. A Lanky can cover a kilometer in a minute, and the SAR flight is still fourteen minutes away. If they change direction and pick up the pace, those Lankies could give us the second close shave of the day.

"Siren Six-Five, Dagger Actual," I reply. "Acknowledged. We'll move away from the drop ship a little just in case they're looking for the source of the ground impact. Keep an eye on them and stand by for CAS mission if they get too close for comfort."

"Copy that. Your call down there. Steer us in if you need us."

If I had my way, I'd call down the Shrikes on the Lankies right now and let them blow everything in that map grid into microscopic scraps with their ordnance. But the ground tremors from explosions seem to clue them in almost as much as unbridled EM emissions. If I have the Shrikes start fireworks on the other side of those hills, there's no telling who will notice.

For every one of them you see on the surface, there's twenty underground, we used to tell the new guys during our long and grinding orbital garrisoning of Mars.

"Captain Harper," I shout. The SEAL captain comes trotting up the hill a moment later.

"Sir?"

"Move everyone up to that ridge and take up overwatch positions from between those rocks. We have hostiles passing through the neighborhood. If they come across that ship, we're better off covering them from an elevated position."

"Aye, sir." Harper starts signaling the SEALs.

"I'm going to go two hundred meters that way, up the hill a bit," I say. "See if I can get eyeballs on the lot."

"Is that wise, sir? It's a long run back to us if they spot you."

"If they spot me, we have two Shrikes overhead that can ruin their day comprehensively," I reply. "But I need to get line of sight if I want to designate the targets before they're just over the ridge there."

"Aye, sir. Need me to send someone with you as backup?"

"Negative. I'll be quick."

"I'll come along," Dr. Vandenberg says. "I want to get eyeballs on them, too."

"I thought you'd had your fill for the day," I say. "This might be another bad life choice."

"Track runner, remember?" she says.

"You can't outrun a Lanky at full speed. Track runner or not."

"I don't have to outrun *them*. Just you."

I laugh and shake my head.

"Bad choice, but your choice. Come on, then."

She starts to jog up the hill ahead of me, and Captain Harper raises an eyebrow. I know the kind of stuff podheads talk about over chow, and this ride-along will give grist to the rumor mill for weeks to come, in both the enlisted and officer mess halls.

"I'm starting to think that you're just a really dedicated adrenaline junkie," I call after Dr. Vandenberg, and she laughs without turning around.

"Move everyone between those rocks, Captain," I say to Harper. "And if we have to run back and she's in the lead, maybe wing her in the leg."

"In truth, I'm scared shitless," Elin says as we are walking up the hillside. "I don't think I've stopped shaking since the shooting started in the colony city."

"So why stick your neck out again?"

"Because it's better than sitting around and waiting for shit to go wrong," she replies. "And because you look like you know what you're doing."

"What gives you that impression?"

"All the shit you've survived. You're either super good at what you do, or you're very determined not to piss off your wife by dying."

"I'm okay at what I do," I say. "But I *am* very determined to not piss off my wife. The combination seems to work all right for me."

We're almost at the top of the hill, and I turn to look back at the landing site. The drop ship is standing nose-down at the end of a short furrow in the rocky ground. The ridgeline where I've ordered the SEALs to take an overwatch position is a hundred meters from the ship, and almost three hundred from where I am standing. With my bug suit's power augmentation, I could run that distance in a minute, but a Lanky could do it in twenty seconds.

On my tactical screen, the icons for the Lanky patrol have updated continuously as the Shrikes' sensors have kept eyes on them, so I know I won't see any unpleasant surprises when we crest the hill. But as we reach the top and look down into the valley below, I can't suppress a little shout.

The Lankies are a few kilometers away, but still obvious with their twenty-meter frames and their slow, ambling gait. I count eleven of them, trotting down the valley single file in a loose formation, kicking up puffs of dirt and moss with every step they take. My suit's computer analyzes the targets and feeds everything into TacNet in just a few milliseconds, calculating speed, distance, and a hundred other factors. If I give the word, the Shrikes will roll in and shoot most of those Lankies with missiles, and then cluster bomb whatever is left standing in the valley for good measure. But these Lankies aren't headed our way, so they're not a threat that justifies expending twenty tons of precious ordnance. For the first year of the war, we followed the maxim that any Lanky that can be killed should be killed, to the point where we would have used a tactical nuke on those eleven down in the valley. But as the war progressed, it became clear that there are always more Lankies than ordnance, and that using our limited resources for indiscriminate destruction just accelerated our attrition rate and made them win faster.

"Type Three cranial shields," Dr. Vandenberg says. She gets down into the prone position and peers at the group in the distance with the high-powered optics of her helmet's observation attachment. I join her on the ground. The hillside is covered in a thick layer of broad-leafed moss that feels almost comfortable enough to sleep on.

"What's that?"

"Their cranial shields," she says and points downhill into the valley. "There's five distinct types we've seen so far. These are all Type Three. All the post-invasion Lankies in one location always have the same cranial shield shape. The samples from Mars are all Type Five. We haven't been back to Willoughby, so we didn't know what type they had here. Now I get to fill in that blank."

"I never knew that," I say.

"ETA for the SAR birds is seven minutes," Captain Harper says on comms. I toggle back a wordless acknowledgment.

"It's interesting to know that there are different types of Lanky head shields," I continue. "But I'm having a hard time seeing how that helps the grunts on the ground. I mean, I already know that those shields stop autocannon rounds. But the shape of the top edge is pretty unimportant to me whenever I have one of those things in my sights."

"It may not matter in the short run," she says. "Certainly not when it comes to killing them. But think about the long term. If there's an observable pattern, it may help us to figure out how they spread out in the galaxy. And maybe even where they come from, eventually."

We watch the Lanky procession in the narrow valley below for a little while. It feels strange to have so many of them in my helmet sights without taking active measures to wipe them out. But it's undeniably interesting to see them in this context—as a sentient species of living creatures with their own needs and drives, not just as the mindless agents of death and destruction on the battlefield or the boogeymen in my nightmares.

"This is more like it," Elin says.

"What's that?" I ask.

"Decent weather. Clear line of sight. A bunch of subjects to observe in the wild. And only a medium-high risk of violent death."

"Living the dream," I say.

There's a slight vibration rippling through the ground underneath us, and we exchange looks. A few moments later, a low and ominous rumbling noise comes from the direction of the Lanky troop in the valley. I reach up to turn on my helmet's comms display and contact close air support.

"Look," Dr. Vandenberg says. "What the hell is that?"

There's more rumbling, and a Lanky wail wafts over to our position. It sounds just like their distress calls on the battlefield whenever we mortally wound one of them. A few moments ago, there were almost a dozen Lankies walking down the valley in single file. Now there are two distinct groups of three, separated by a gap of a hundred meters.

"Where'd the other ones go?" I ask.

"What the fuck," Elin says slowly.

The ground between the two groups of Lankies is in motion. We see puffs of dust as the surface of the valley floor seems to be churning somehow, as if the Lankies walked into a patch of water that just had a layer of dirt and moss on the surface. But the first group of Lankies crossed the same spot without incident, so I know that this has to be something else.

A Lanky appears from the patch of churning soil on the ground and wails another piercing distress call into the sky. It moves as if it's trying to scramble back onto solid ground. When it's almost out of the restless patch of earth, a fountain of ochre-colored earth sprays up, and something very large and very fast yanks the Lanky back into the dirt. I get a brief glimpse at something that looks like a hook or a pincer, slender and glossy black like the hull of a seed ship. Then the Lanky is gone beneath the ground again, and its wail is cut off abruptly. The soil ripples for a few more seconds after the Lanky disappears. When everything is still again, the patch that swallowed the Lanky forms a new depression in the ground, contrasting churned-up earth and rocks with the moss carpet of the surrounding valley.

"You have *got* to be shitting me," I say.

The other Lankies are not displaying any sense of concern for their lost mates. They move away from the spot at brisk speed, faster than I've ever seen one move. The group to the right of the spot is almost at the mouth of the valley, on a flatter and wider patch of ground than the others, and we watch as they drop to all fours and run away from the valley and onto the plateau in an obvious hurry. Whatever just happened has sent them into a panic, and I don't think I've ever seen a scared Lanky. The other group is walking back up the valley to the left, a little slower and on two legs instead, but with no less urgency to their movements.

Underneath, the ground rumbles again just a little.

"What the hell did we just watch?" I say into the silence that follows. In the distance, the Lanky's last distress cry is echoing back from the nearby mountain ridge, weak and insubstantial.

"I have no idea," Elin says. "I've never seen anything like it before."

"I don't think anyone has," I reply. For just a moment, I was feeling a pang of sympathy for the last Lanky that got pulled down into the ground, and that's an emotion I definitely can't integrate into my worldview right now.

The ground shakes again, stronger than before. It's not the thrumming of a nearby Lanky's footsteps. Instead, it's a short pulse of a vibration, increasing in intensity and then fading again. We wait for more tremors, but none follow. Then it's quiet again except for the sound of the wind on the plateau and the distant engines of the attack craft in the sky high above us.

"ETA two minutes," Captain Harper sends over the radio. The unexpected sound of his voice makes me jump a little.

"We need to go," I tell Elin Vandenberg. She nods and gets to her feet.

"Coming your way, Captain," I say. "You want to tell the men to stay light on their feet when you head for the pickup spot."

"Any particular reason for that?"

"I think we woke something new in the neighborhood. Something that eats Lankies whole."

The SAR drop ships arrive a few minutes later, flying a slow circle over the area before setting down next to our broken Dragonfly. The Lankies on my tactical display have moved off to the east and west in two separate groups. Considering what we just witnessed, I am certain that we won't need to worry about having to avoid them for a while. But it's not the thought of the threats on the surface that have me putting an extra spring in my step as I follow the SEALs to the cargo hold of the waiting search-and-rescue drop ship.

"Can you give me a slow pass over this area before you start your ascent?" I send to the pilot when we are seated and strapped in. I have the TacLink map on my helmet display, and I'm marking the spot where we saw the Lanky disappear.

"What's over there?" the pilot asks.

"Scientific intel," I say. "For our guest from the R&D division. We saw something that might be relevant in the future. If we ever make it back here."

"Copy that. I can give you a three-sixty before we leave."

"Good enough, Lieutenant. Thank you," I reply.

Elin Vandenberg is sitting next to me, watching the ramp as it rises with a soft hydraulic whine. I tap her on the shoulder, and she turns her head toward me.

"Your suit is not tied into TacLink," I say. "I asked the pilot for a slow pass of the valley where the Lankies went under. I'm going to make sure to pass on the footage to you when we're back on the carrier."

"I appreciate that," she says. "I have it on my own system from ground level. But that was from a few kilometers away. I have a feeling that this will make me the most popular xenobiologist in the Fleet for a while."

When we pass the valley a few moments after takeoff, the pilot does as promised and puts the ship into a slow left-hand turn to circle the area. I watch the feed from the hull cameras as the terrain pans underneath the ship. The spot where the Lankies lost half a dozen of their group is now an almost perfectly circular patch of disturbed soil and shredded vegetation. For a moment, I am worried that even five hundred feet of altitude may not be sufficient to keep us in the clear, but the pilot finishes his turn before I can voice that concern over the radio. Whatever is lurking underneath the soil down there is big and strong enough to seize a three-hundred-ton Lanky and drag it under, and it's cunning enough to lay deliberate traps for them. There's no telling if something of that size even registers humans as a potential threat or food source, but I am not curious enough to find out right now. When the pilot levels out the ship and climbs above two thousand feet, I slowly let out a breath of relief.

"What a day," Elin says. "Turns out that too much adrenaline gives you a bitch of a headache once it starts to wear off."

"And nausea," I say. "Don't forget the wonderful nausea."

CHAPTER 19

A DARK VIEW OF HUMANITY

"That colony was started fifty years ago," Colonel Drake says in wonder. "Half a century. They were blasting holes and driving anchors for terraformers on every continent down there for years. Whatever that is, nobody has encountered it before."

We're sitting around the table in the flag briefing room, watching the aerial footage from the SAR ship side by side with the helmet cam imagery we took automatically. For the last hour, I've seen the ten-second event dozens of times. Even from a few kilometers away, it's pretty clear that something ambushed the Lankies and pulled down half a dozen of them in the blink of an eye. I watch again as the straggler nearly escapes the trap, then gets pulled back in with such force and ferocity that it makes the dirt spray ten meters high.

Next to me, Dr. Vandenberg clears her throat.

"I don't really think it's indigenous," she says.

Command staff meeting are usually only for the department heads, but nobody objected to the presence of the ship's resident xenobiologist today. She looks out of place in her fresh, new pair of medical technician overalls. We've spent the last three hours on decontamination and debriefing, and from the way the day is going, we're nowhere near the finish line.

"What makes you say that?" Lieutenant Colonel Campbell says. She seems to have transferred her mild dislike of me to the outside expert I brought along to the briefing, and her verbal interactions with Elin Vandenberg are curt and matter-of-fact.

"The Lankies aren't," Elin says. "And the chances that Willoughby has an organism on it that's adapted in isolation to take them as prey is pretty much zero. Whatever this thing is, I'd bet money that it came from the same place where they evolved."

"What kind of species brings its own *predator* with it when it goes out to settle another planet?"

"It may not have been on purpose," Elin replies. "Could have been by accident. We've introduced invasive species to colonies by accident, and we have all sorts of procedures to prevent that."

I'm freshly showered and in a clean set of fatigues, but I don't feel renewed. The mandatory decontamination session after the mission was twice as long as normal, and the briefing followed right after. I'm yearning for a meal and eight uninterrupted hours of sleep because I still have the post-mission shakes, and those won't go away until I've mollified my body with some carbohydrates and reset my brain with sedative-boosted sleep. Watching the same terrifying event over and over on the briefing screens isn't helping much to soothe my frayed nerves, either.

"They accidentally introduced something that can hunt them," the XO says with a skeptical tinge in her voice.

"We've done worse shit to ourselves," I say. "As a species, I mean. By accident and on purpose."

"I like the idea of Lankies getting eaten," Colonel Rigney says. "In fact, whatever that thing is, I may make it our new regimental mascot."

"I don't have any particular problem with that, either," Colonel Drake says. "But it does take Willoughby off the list for reconquest. At least until we can figure out if that species is a danger to us."

Colonel Pace chuckles.

"Even if it's not, can you imagine the pushback? Trying to send a bunch of settlers to a planet that has subterranean monsters on it that are big enough to catch Lankies?"

"Any idea what exactly we're dealing with here?" Colonel Drake asks Elin.

She looks at the images on the screen again and makes a gesture to stop the repeating footage in a certain spot. It shows the dirt fountain erupting behind the hapless Lanky, and the pincer-like protuberance that's shooting out of the ground to snag its prey.

"Lankies are ten meters from the hip to the top of the cranial shield," she says. "On average. That grabbing appendage there is half again as long, and we don't even see what it's attached to. But with the force on display here, I'd say it's something a lot bigger and heavier. Underground ambush hunter, so it's probably what my little brother would call 'dirto-dynamic.'" She smiles an apology.

"That's a pretty vague set of parameters," the XO says.

"Like a funnel spider. Or a millipede."

"That's one hell of a millipede," Colonel Drake says. He unfreezes the footage and watches for the fiftieth time as the Lanky gets pulled back into the hole toward its unseen attacker. The thought of anything that size even remotely resembling a funnel spider makes me want to launch a twenty-megaton bunker-buster nuke at that spot.

"No shit," I say. "One moment we're looking at eleven Lankies. Next thing we know, half a dozen are gone. And it only took a few seconds."

"Your new regimental mascot came up through the ground and grabbed a combined two thousand tons of prey in a single attack," Elin says to Colonel Rigney. "I have no clue what other abilities it has, but that fact alone already makes it the strongest organism in the observed galaxy by far."

"The Lankies were freaked out," I say. "They didn't stick around to fight back or try to help their pals. They just *ran*. First time I've seen a frightened Lanky."

"If they're frightened of it, they have encountered it before," Colonel Drake says.

"We have what we came for." Colonel Pace leans back in his chair and crosses his arms. "Dagger team got the memory modules from the colony. There's nothing else of worth down there anymore. Let the Lankies keep the place and have fun with their new neighbors."

"We came for recon," Colonel Drake says. "We will keep gathering data until the Lankies run us off, or we run out of fuel and ammo."

Elin starts to raise her hand, then catches herself and lowers it again. "On that note, sir. Can I make a request on behalf of the science division?"

"You sure can, Dr. Vandenberg," the commander says. Next to him, Lieutenant Colonel Campbell's face is impassive, but I can sense the implied eye-roll.

"While we're on station, I'd like to go back to the spot on the video and drop some of the remaining seismic sensors in the area. It's not nearly as good as ground-penetrating radar. But we can get a rough idea of what's there, and how it moves around."

"We can probably do that," Colonel Drake says and looks at Colonel Pace.

"CAG, have the battlespace control squadron take stock of what's left and see how we can put it to best use."

"Will do," Colonel Pace replies. "I'll update you as soon as I have data."

"Planning on capturing one, Doc?" the XO asks.

Elin shrugs. "Maybe not the whole thing. But I wouldn't mind getting a sample."

"Just as long as you don't go down there and try to make friends with it."

"That wouldn't be such a bad thing, would it?" she replies.

Lieutenant Colonel Campbell laughs and shakes her head.

"Just think," Elin continues. "It hunts *Lankies*. It can grab six of them as fast as you can clap your hands. Imagine the amount of work we could save the military if we figured out how to set a bunch of those things loose on every Lanky-controlled world."

Colonel Pace lets out a low whistle. "I like that mental image."

"You're much more savage than you look," I say. "You just met your first one a few hours ago, and you're already thinking about how to turn it into a bioweapon."

"It's my field," she says with a shrug. "Military R&D. We're not all just flower pickers down in the biotech labs, you know."

"I don't know how long we will remain on station here," Colonel Drake says. "That depends entirely on our spindly friends in the neighborhood. We have the drone network out for early warning, and the two recon corvettes are keeping an eye on things. But we may have to leave here in a hurry. So I'd rather not commit to any extensive ground ops. Nothing that we can't pack up and haul back into orbit in thirty minutes flat. Whatever missions we execute while we're here, let's tailor them around that requirement."

"You called this mission a smash-and-grab burglary at the briefing. But this doesn't really feel like a burglary," Lieutenant Colonel Campbell says. "I feel like I snuck downstairs into the kitchen in the middle of the night to swipe some cookies. And now I'm holding my breath and waiting for my mom to turn on the light because I clonked the lid against the jar by accident."

After the briefing, I head for the main ladderwell to head down to Grunt Country and finally get a meal and some sleep. My stomach is rumbling, and I feel like I've been up for twenty-four hours even though we only left for the mission eight hours ago. Combat time passes differently from normal time, at least as far as the wear on the body is concerned.

When I reach the ladderwell, Elin is waiting for me in the passageway, hands in the pockets of her overalls.

"I was joking, you know. About turning those things into weapons."

"You were *half* joking," I say. "But it's not a bad idea. When you get bullied, go hire the biggest bully on the block to punch back."

"When I proposed the idea, you looked like I had kicked a puppy or something."

I gesture down the passageway, and she falls into step next to me.

"It's because I know what a bunch of shitheads we all are," I say. "Humans, I mean."

"In what way? Not that I don't agree with you in principle."

"Because we haven't yet designed a weapon that we didn't end up using against each other in the end," I say. "We figure out how to sic these things on the Lankies, we won't be able to resist the temptation to paint national flags on 'em once the Lankies are gone."

"That's a pretty dark view of humanity," she says.

I tap the NAC patch on my upper sleeve with my index finger.

"When I put that on for the first time, there were no Lankies to fight. I fought other people. Even our own. Hood rats, SRA, shitty little Earth militaries. And even after the Lankies arrived, it took us *years* to stop killing each other and focus on the real threat. Trust me. Ten minutes after the last Lanky dies, we'll start fucking with each other again. It's not a dark view of humanity. It's just our nature."

"Some of us are trying to be better than that," Elin says.

"I know. That's why I'm still doing this job. Just don't give the bioweapons division any terrible ideas."

She steps up to me and gives me a curt one-armed hug, then pulls back quickly as if she changed her mind in the middle of the action.

"Thanks for keeping me alive down there, Andrew. And for letting me tag along after trying to talk me out of the whole thing in the first place."

"My pleasure," I say. "Don't let it seep into your dreams."

"I hope that's not the last we'll see of each other. Come down to the medlab for a chat whenever you feel like it. We have some spectacularly shitty capsule coffee."

"Thanks. I'll keep it in mind."

She nods and turns to walk down the stairs. I watch as she disappears belowdecks, braid bouncing against the collar of her civvie tech overalls. She has some steel in her, but she's not a soldier, even if she has a commission certificate that makes her a captain in the Corps. If she's lucky, she'll never be anywhere near a battle again, and this day will be merely an anomaly, an exciting anecdote for the rest of her life. For us, it's the ordinary grind. I think about Halley, who speaks my language and understands all of this without a need for explanation, and the sudden yearning I have for her company feels like an open flame that's searing the inside of my chest cavity.

Another day closer to home, I think. Maybe the fates are kind, and this was the worst one on this deployment. I made it through a Lanky attack and a forced landing today, and that should be enough to fill my danger quota for a while.

I am halfway down the final passageway to my quarters when the lighting changes to red, and the klaxon of the ship's battle alert blares through the deck.

"General quarters, general quarters. All hands, man your combat stations. Set material condition Zebra throughout the ship. This is not a drill."

"You have *got* to be shitting me," I say into the semidarkness, after a brief look around to check if there are enlisted nearby.

CHAPTER 20

CLOSE COMBAT

When I rush into the CIC to take my spot at the TacOps station, my first glance goes to the situational orb above the holotable. There aren't too many things that can trigger General Quarters out of the blue, but until I see the color orange on the plot, there's still a sliver of hope that we're just suffering a reactor shutdown, or that some frigate in our entourage collided with the supply ship during a refueling op. But as I take my seat and strap in, I see three orange icons on the edge of the display, slowly edging in toward the cluster of friendly blue icons in the middle of the orb. I turn on my screens and secure my supply hose to the receptacle in the pedestal of my chair. This is not a drill, and it's not a refueling accident. It's death coming our way in long, black cigar-shaped form.

The CIC is controlled chaos all around me.

"Bogeys Lima-1 through 3 are now at forty-nine by positive one-ten," the tactical officer calls out. "Speed five thousand meters per second steady, distance 5,313,000, still CBDR."

"*Nashville* confirms they have visual on three seed ships, sir," the comms officer, Lieutenant March, says from his station. "They are on reciprocal heading to the bogeys and coasting ballistic."

"The quiet was fun while it lasted," Colonel Drake says. "Warm up Orion tubes two through four. Energize the particle-gun mount and shift it to standby mode. What's the story on *Jo'burg*?"

"They are coming about to intercept bearing."

"Helm, light the main drive as soon as we are clear of the formation. Tell the cruisers to shield the tin cans and form up for egress to the Alcubierre point. Bring us up and around for the intercept bearing and punch it."

The tactical display is a swirl of movement as the smaller ships maneuver out of the way to give the gigantic carriers space to turn and accelerate. Cruisers and frigates can't do anything against seed ships, so the doctrine is for the carriers to shield the fleet's retreat to the transit node and take out the approaching seed ships from long range with Orions.

"We are clear of the formation and ready to burn, sir," the helmsman reports.

"Punch it. *All ahead flank,*" Colonel Drake orders.

We accelerate toward the Lankies at twenty gravities per second. A few kilometers to our starboard, *Johannesburg* follows suit. The numbers next to the orange icons on the situational display begin to count down with worrisome speed.

"Five million is a little too close," Lieutenant Colonel Campbell says. "We should have picked them up at ten million klicks already. They came right through the drone picket."

"It's not infallible technology," the commander says. "Doesn't matter. Weapons, open outer hatches for Orion tubes two and three. Tactical, upload firing solutions for Lima-1 and Lima-2. Hand off Lima-3 to *Jo'burg*. And make sure there's absolutely no ambiguity about who shoots at what."

"Lima-1 and Lima-2 are locked in," Lieutenant Lawrence says. "Outer hatches open. Ready to fire tubes two and three."

"*Jo'burg* reports they're locked on to Lima-3 and ready to fire. Fire control is linked, sir."

Everything is happening so quickly that I haven't even had time to get properly nervous. Barely thirty seconds have passed since I rushed into the CIC, and both carriers are already on an intercept course with the enemy seed ships, with Orion missiles armed and locked on to the targets.

"All right," Colonel Drake says. "Let's take a deep breath and double-check our numbers before we launch thirty percent of our remaining long-range ordnance into space. We don't get extra points for speed right now."

"Bogeys are still CBDR," Captain Steadman says. "Distance five million, one hundred thousand. Hell of a closing rate, sir."

"You're right. No need to rush in. Cut throttle and go to ballistic, and signal *Jo'burg* to do the same. We're far enough from the rest of the task force now."

On the tactical display, the cluster of blue icons has split into two distinct groups. Both carriers are interposing themselves between the incoming seed ships and the rest of the fleet, which is making for the Alcubierre node at full acceleration. If the carriers fail to stop the seed ships, the rest of the task force will have enough of a head start to make the node.

I have no task right now, no cog I can turn in the machinery to help the ship get ready for battle. My special tactics troopers are buckled in at their action stations close to the escape pods in Grunt Country, and that's where they will remain until we are out of battle one way or the other. I have a front-row seat to the event, and I don't need to try to guess what's going on from the noises in the hull and the movements of the ship. But I haven't decided yet whether that makes sitting through a ship-to-ship combat engagement more bearable or less so. Everything happens quickly, and the life and death of the whole ship and all three thousand people on her can flip on a single number in a firing algorithm or a fraction of a second of missile flight time. And all I can do is check the tightness of my harness belts and listen to the CIC crew around me as they do their jobs. It's almost worse than getting launched through a minefield in a bio-pod. If you die in a pod, at least you have privacy.

"Particle-cannon mount is energized and on standby, sir."

"Thank you, Lieutenant Lawrence," the commander says.

"Range five million. We have a green firing solution. *Johannesburg* is still linked and ready to launch."

"Fire."

"Firing Two. Firing Three." Lieutenant Lawrence looks up from his control screen. "Sir, *Johannesburg*'s bird cleared the tube with a second-and-a-half delay."

"Fuck," Colonel Drake says in an uncharacteristic display of emotion. "Ready tube four and match firing solution for Lima-3. Open outer silo door and prepare to fire."

"Ready tube four, aye. Matching firing solution for Lima-3."

The blue missile icons on the plot rush out from the two carriers and streak toward the incoming orange icons. We watch the blue tracks extend from the center of the plot, one blip every few seconds, like the heartbeat on a medical status screen. One of the missile icons is a beat behind the other two. It doesn't seem like it should make much of a difference at these speeds, but the commander found it worrisome enough to warrant a swear, so now I am anxious about it as well.

"Bogeys are still CBDR," Captain Steadman says. "Coming in straight and dumb as usual."

"It had to be *three*," Lieutenant Colonel Campbell says. "One less, and we could have engaged them all by ourselves."

"Well, yeah, that's the way the launchers work, unfortunately," Colonel Drake says. "Two at a time. We needed that bird from *Johannesburg* in the mix."

"On the plus side, nobody's splashed three seed ships in one strike since Mars," Captain Steadman says in a tense voice. His eyes haven't left the blue missile icons on the plot since they appeared there a few minutes ago.

"The day it starts to feel like this has become easy," Colonel Drake replies, "is the day we get our asses kicked all the way up to our ears."

"*Nashville* is still tracking the bogeys. Intercept in thirty. Twenty-eight. Twenty-six."

For the second time in two days, I try to will the disembodied little icons on the screen to hurry along to their targets: *blip-blip-blip.*

"Give me the visual from *Nashville*," the commander orders. "Put it up on the bulkhead and magnify."

The screen that expands on the forward CIC bulkhead shows a vast dark square of space, and only the little red cross-shaped target markers superimposed by *Nashville*'s computer provide evidence that we're looking at something other than empty vacuum. The Indianapolis-class stealth corvettes have the most powerful surveillance optics of any ship in the Fleet, and even those high-powered lenses and their software algorithms aren't always able to pick out Lanky seed ships in deep space. But this time, we got lucky once again, and our ad hoc early-warning system gave us enough advance notice to employ our long-range firepower.

"Ten seconds to intercept." Lieutenant Lawrence counts down. "Eight. Seven . . ."

The pulses of the blue missile symbols on the tactical screen seem to be in sync with the beats of my heart now as they merge with the orange icons.

On the viewscreen, a bright flash turns the display white from edge to edge.

"Intercept," Captain Steadman calls out. "Stand by for post-strike assessment."

The flare-up on the viewscreen dims slowly to reveal an irregular cloud of glowing fragments expanding into every direction from the center. A few moments later, a small red marker appears on the right half of the image, moving in jerky little steps with every one-second update from *Nashville*'s sensors.

"Splash *two*," Captain Steadman says, with a hesitant note on the second word. "Successful intercepts on Lima-1 and Lima-2. The bird from *Johannesburg* missed Lima-3. Target is still CBDR, distance now four and a half million klicks."

"Weapons, update the Orion in tube four with the firing solution for Lima-3 and fire when ready," Colonel Drake says.

"Aye, sir." Lieutenant Lawrence moves his fingers over the data fields on his control panel so quickly that they're practically a blur. "Firing solution updated and verified. Launching tube four."

Another little blue V-shaped icon appears in the center of the tactical display and rushes outward to meet the remaining orange symbol approaching from the periphery of our awareness bubble. The other ships of the task force are halfway to the edge of our screen on the opposite side, making full speed for the safety of the Alcubierre node back to the solar system.

"Tell *Johannesburg* to ready another tube for a follow-up shot and fire on our mark." Colonel Drake has unbuckled his harness, and now he gets out of his chair and walks over to the holotable in the center of the command pit, as if he can better divine the information flow from the computer by looking at the readouts more closely.

"Aye, sir. They have a new bird ready and locked on."

"That's half our Orions gone already," the commander mutters.

The missile races for the point in space where the computer has calculated the intersection between the kinetic warhead and the Lanky seed ship, building up speed with every passing second. There's a practical minimum range for the Orion missiles where the accumulated speed isn't yet enough to create the energy for a certain kill, and we are getting closer to that line every minute.

"Ten seconds to intercept on Lima-3," Lieutenant Lawrence says.

"Sir, there's an aspect change on the bogey. Lima-3 just changed course." Captain Steadman looks up from his tactical screens.

"Lima-3 just did *what*?"

"They just made a vector change, thirty degrees to port and twenty down from their previous approach ecliptic."

"Three seconds. Two. One." There's a pause from the weapons officer, and then a sharp intake of breath. "That's a *miss*. Orion Four failed to intercept."

"The Lanky dodged at the last second," Captain Steadman says with disbelief in his voice.

"Lankies don't fucking *dodge*," the XO says. "They can't see the Orions coming. You can't dodge what you can't see."

"Another aspect change on Lima-3, sir. They turned back toward port, ten degrees offset from their original trajectory, and positive twenty on the starting ecliptic. He's definitely dodging, ma'am," Steadman replies.

"He's zigzagging," Colonel Drake says in wonder. "We gave him a warning with that missed shot, and now he knows there are sharks in the water."

"*Johannesburg* is asking if they are weapons free for a follow-up shot," the comms officer says.

"We're kissing up on minimum Orion range," Lieutenant Lawrence warns.

"God*dammit*." Colonel Drake strides back to his chair and sits down. "Tell *Jo'burg* to hold their shot. No point wasting another Orion on a dodging target."

"Aye, sir."

"Give me *Jo'burg* on comms, please," Colonel Drake says.

"Aye, sir. You are on."

"*Johannesburg*, this is *Washington* Actual. We've missed our opportunity for a clean trap. This one is tap-dancing inside our minimum intercept range now."

"Washington, Johannesburg *Actual. That's on us, unfortunately. We will be happy to take point for a close-range intercept."*

"Negative, Commander. Turn your ship around and shield the task force. We are going in for a knife fight. If they make it past us, you hold off the bogey while the battle group transitions out. And let's not argue over who gets to take it on the nose right now. We are quickly running out of elbow room here."

"Affirmative, Washington. *We will come about and take up blocking position. Good luck."*

"Same to you, Commander. *Washington* out."

Colonel Drake slips on his harness straps again and tightens them.

"Comms, lay in a direct intercept course for Lima-3," he orders.

"Intercept course for bogey Lima-3, aye."

"One gravity acceleration, nice and easy. Give us some margin on the closing rate. Light up the drive."

"One gravity acceleration ahead, aye," the helmsman acknowledges.

"Weapons, it's all on you now," Colonel Drake says to Lieutenant Lawrence. "It's a head-on engagement, so you get one shot with the particle mount before we have to take evasive action. That's a *second and a half,* Lawrence."

"It'll do, sir," Lieutenant Lawrence says.

"I hope so. Because otherwise we'll have a few million tons of seed ship coming through the forward bulkhead."

"Lima-3 changed course again, sir," Captain Steadman reports. "Now forty degrees south of the approach ecliptic, descending bearing. He's mighty nimble for his size. I'm not sure we could do the same course changes if we had to."

"Bobbing and weaving like a boxer," Colonel Drake says. "Well, let's get in there and trade blows. See who hits harder."

"Ready on the particle mount, sir," Lawrence says.

"Lock the system to auto-fire mode and hand the triggers to the fire-control computer."

"Particle-cannon mount is now armed and live, sir."

I haven't moved in five minutes, and the air-conditioning in the CIC is working just fine, but I feel sweat trickling down my back between my shoulder blades. *Washington* and the seed ship are rushing headlong toward each other like two medieval knights in a joust. We are well inside the minimum range for the Orions now, and any missiles we fire will not have enough of an impact to break the hull of the Lanky ship. That leaves the particle cannon, which is powerful but short-ranged. With the sizes and speeds of the combatants involved, ten thousand kilometers isn't a very long distance in ship-to-ship battles. Every time I've seen the footage of the two particle-mount kills we've achieved so far, it looked like the old gun-camera footage from World War II atmospheric fighters, where the firing craft is so close to its target that it takes up most of the windshield, and bits from the stricken target fly off and hit the pursuing plane.

I look over to Colonel Drake, who is checking the straps of his harness again to give his hands something to do, as if the tightness of the chair's restraints will make even the slightest bit of difference if we collide with a three-kilometer-long seed ship head-on. But I know that in the face of mortal danger, we all have our little tics and rituals, our brains' individualized ways of dealing with the stress of our possible impending death. I've run out of fasteners and latches to check, and now I'm reduced to watching the orange icon on the holographic orb.

"Lanky is changing course," Captain Steadman says. "He's turning to port again. Twenty degrees. Forty. Fifty. Seventy-five. Lima-3 is now on a perpendicular heading at twenty-five to positive twelve degrees. He's still turning, sir."

"How does he haul that much mass around this quickly?" Colonel Drake says.

On the other side of the tactical orb, *Johannesburg* has opened the gap as she's burning her drive at full throttle to catch up with the battle group, increasing the distance between us with every refresh blip of the display.

"The Lanky just started to accelerate." Captain Steadman looks from his screen to the holotable display and back. "He's on a heading back to where he came from. I . . . I think he's making a run for it, sir. We scared him off."

"Oh, *hell* no." Colonel Drake shakes his head. "That won't do. If he gets away, there's no telling what's going to come down on our heads next. Can we catch up with him at flank speed?"

Steadman checks his screen again.

"He's at two and a half g. We can catch him."

"Helm, all ahead flank. Plot an intercept course that gets us within gun range as quickly as possible. There is no way we're going to let this guy leave the neighborhood and call all his friends. Comms, inform the battle group that the remaining seed ship is trying to break contact, and that we intend to pursue and destroy."

"Pursue a Lanky ship," Lieutenant Colonel Campbell says with a dry smile. "I don't think anyone's ever put those words in that particular order."

Washington has the higher acceleration rate, but the Lanky still has a head start, and for the next hour, the distance readout above the orange icon ticks down with agonizing slowness.

"We're well past the drone picket now," Captain Steadman warns as we reach the sixty-minute mark of our stern chase. "If there's anything else out there, we may run right into it without warning."

"Then we better take care of this customer and head back to the battle group," Colonel Drake says. "But we're committed now. For better or worse."

"He'd pull away faster if he went in a straight line. But he's still zigzagging."

"I'm fine with him making our job easier. We can't use the Orions at this range anyway. And I am not about to let him open the distance and then get away when he dodges the next volley," the commander says.

"Seven minutes, thirty seconds to weapons range for the particle mount," Lieutenant Lawrence says from the weapons station.

"Tell me we still have green lights on the mount."

"That's affirmative, sir."

"Steady as she goes, then. At least the closure rate won't be a problem," Colonel Drake says.

The display is empty now except for the single orange icon that's moving closer to the center of the tactical orb with every second. Ever since we first ran into the Lankies, a solitary Fleet ship would do everything in its power to get as far away as possible from a Lanky ship. It goes against every instinct to do the opposite and try to get closer, and it's even more unnatural to see that seed ship run away from us.

We're chasing a Lanky, I think. *At some point, the universe must have flipped itself upside down somehow when I wasn't paying attention.*

As we close the distance to the Lanky, it keeps changing its course randomly, altering its heading by ten degrees or more every time it does. On the tactical screen, the weapons officer has marked the range of the particle-cannon mount with a yellow cone that stretches out toward the seed ship.

"Target Lima-3 is in weapons range in thirty seconds," Captain Steadman says. "Triggers are armed and under computer control."

"Hold still, now," the XO says to the orange icon on the display. "Just a few more moments."

"He's turning again. Forty degrees to port and negative thirty."

"Helm, match the turn. Get those guns on target again. If he keeps jinking around like that, we'll end up overshooting him before we can get the shot off," Colonel Drake says.

On the holotable, the distance between the blue and orange icons suddenly decreases rapidly. The number marker next to the Lanky starts to spool down much faster than before, the numbers blinking in an unfriendly red.

"Lanky is decelerating rapidly," Captain Steadman shouts. "He's counter-burning. *Really* counter-burning, sir. Closure rate ten kilometers per second and increasing. Eleven seconds to collision."

"Get those guns back on target, helm. Match the turn."

We've been following the seed ship at full burn for almost an hour, and our forward velocity is much higher than that of the Lanky ship, which has decelerated so quickly that it looks like they threw out an anchor and caught a comet traveling in the opposite direction. I grip the armrests of my seat so hard that the alloy creaks under my hands. It seems the Lanky has figured out that he outweighs us by a factor of ten, and that he can squash us like a pesky bug on a windshield.

"Eight seconds to collision," Steadman calls out.

"He'll kill us with his debris," the XO warns. "Helm, crash turn to port, forty-five degrees positive, emergency power. *Now.*"

The yellow cone marking the targeting envelope of the fixed particle-cannon mount swings rapidly away from the Lanky as *Washington*'s bow comes up and around in a last-second attempt to avoid the seed ship, which is still decelerating hard in what seems like a suicidal attempt to make us overshoot.

"Five seconds."

"All hands, brace for impact," Lieutenant Colonel Campbell shouts into the 1MC.

I close my eyes and breathe in slowly and deliberately, fully conscious of the fact that it may be the last thing I do in this life. I picture

Halley's face because I want her to be the last thought I have before my consciousness disappears.

"Come on, you sluggish pig," Colonel Drake mutters. "Turn *away*."

"Lima-3 passing astern in three seconds. Clearance will be less than a hundred meters."

The sounds of the frantic activity in the CIC recede into the background as I exhale slowly, focusing on the sensation of the air streaming out of my mouth and past my lips.

A vibration shakes the ship from stern to bow, a rumbling jolt that is unlike anything I've ever felt under my feet in a spaceship. A dozen alarm sounds seem to go off all at once in the CIC.

That's it, then, I think.

There's a strange sensation rushing through me, a kind of lightness that feels as if the molecules in my body have become buoyant all at once for a second and then settled back down. A sour, electric sort of taste spreads on my tongue. A high-pitched whistling drowns out all the noises in the CIC around me, and when it fades after a few moments, all the sounds return muffled and dull as if I am suddenly underwater.

For a few heartbeats, I wait for the world to come to an end.

I can feel the sweat trickling down my back. I can smell the air in the CIC, now faintly tinged with ozone. Whatever just happened, I am not dead yet. If we collided with the seed ship, it was a glancing blow, not strong enough to pulverize the ship outright. But the metallic taste in my mouth is still there, and when I move my hand along the armrest of my chair, it generates a peculiar and unpleasant tingling sensation, as if the metal is slightly electrified.

I open my eyes again. The situational orb above the holotable has disappeared. I can hear people yelling and shouting orders, but it all sounds remote and distant. My display screens have gone out as well, and the status light in the control strip is blinking, indicating a system restart. A few seconds later, the screens come back to life, and the tactical orb in the command pit at the center of the CIC expands again, showing nothing at all except the reference grid. Everyone around me seems as dazed as I feel, like I just got woken up from a deep sleep by a comms request, and my brain hasn't had time yet to adjust to conscious reality.

The sounds of my environment come rushing in again as the stuffed feeling in my ears fades away.

"What the *hell* just happened," Colonel Drake says.

"Status report on damage control," the XO orders in a breathless voice. She looks like she's shaking off a heavy blow from a sparring partner.

"Damage panel is green, ma'am," the damage control officer reports. "All compartments report integrity."

"Something just hit us," Lieutenant Colonel Campbell says. "We didn't just trade paint with a seed ship without even popping a weld somewhere. Check the system circuit for integrity."

"Get me a new target solution on the Lanky." Colonel Drake is holding on to his armrests and shaking his head slowly. "Weapons, is the particle mount still online?"

"Negative, sir. The fire-control system is restarting. All weapons are off-line."

"Same with sensors, sir," Captain Steadman says from the tactical station. "We have no eyeballs on Lima-3. Propulsion is out, too. All eight fusion reactors are restarting from emergency shutdown."

"Contact *Nashville* and tell them to give us an uplink. Restart our propulsion and bring the ship about. We just overshot that Lanky by fifty thousand klicks at least."

"Sir, I have no reference data from the navigation system," the helmsman reports. "I don't know which way to turn the ship to bring us about."

"You're saying the whole navigation system is down?"

"No, sir. It's just . . . it's just not showing anything."

"Astrogation," Colonel Drake shouts. "Do you have a fix on our position?"

The astrogation officer shakes his head.

"Nothing at all on comms," the communications officer says. "Not even static. *Nashville* is not answering."

"What the *fuck*," the XO says. She unbuckles her harness and launches herself out of her chair, then quickly steps down into the command pit. The situational orb still shows nothing at all, even though the sensor pulses are now refreshing the reference grid again once every other second.

She turns toward Colonel Drake.

"Sensors are active, but they can't detect anything outside of the hull," she says. "Comms are working but can't hear anyone. Tactical, give me a visual of the outside. Optical feed, bow sensors, on the forward bulkhead, please."

Captain Steadman complies, and a screen materializes on the forward bulkhead. Instead of the blackness of space interspersed with the pinpoint lights of distant stars, the optical sensors on the outside of the hull show a chaos of red and purple streaks, streaming past the optics like rushing rapids.

"We're in *Alcubierre*," I say. "Son of a bitch."

"Not possible," Captain Steadman says. "We never turned on our Alcubierre drive. And we're nowhere near a transit node."

The XO points at the imagery on the bulkhead screen in response.

"Major Grayson is right. Unless you're pranking me with fake sensor footage, we're inside an Alcubierre bubble. Which explains why our sensors and radios don't work."

I run my fingers along the top of my chair's armrest again. The unpleasant tingling sensation is still there whenever my skin touches the bare metal.

"She's right," I say. "Just *feel* it."

"How the *fuck* can we be in Alcubierre?" Steadman asks. "That's impossible."

"The Lanky dragged us with him," Captain Drake says. He looks from the bulkhead display to Lieutenant Colonel Campbell. "We're inside the seed ship's Alcubierre bubble. He slowed down for the transition to get away from us. That's why we almost rear-ended him."

"The Alcubierre field isn't big enough to wrap around two ships at once," Steadman insists.

"Ours isn't," the XO says. "Looks like theirs is, though. Unless you have another explanation for that." She points at the viewscreen. "Could be that we all died, and this is just the Bifrost taking us all to Valhalla, maybe."

"Reactors are back online, sir," the engineering officer says into the moment of silence that follows.

"Belay the order on propulsion," Colonel Drake says. "If we are in an Alcubierre bubble, we'll tear ourselves into pieces if we try to maneuver. Everyone, man your stations and see what your status reports say. We need data right now, not best guesses."

The CIC officers seem to be glad for something to do that falls into their area of expertise. All around me, people resume their tasks, and the stunned silence gives way to the sounds of regular operations again. I unbuckle my harness and get out of my seat for the first time in what seems like a day and a half. Lieutenant Colonel Campbell watches me as I walk up to the command pit guardrail and seize it with both hands.

"How are you doing, Major? You've had a bitch of a day so far. Looks like it's not getting any better anytime soon."

"Could have gone worse," I say. "At least I'm still around to feel tired."

"For now," she says. "Day's not over yet."

"And I think it just took a hard turn toward Shitville," I say in a low voice.

CHAPTER 21

ALONG FOR THE RIDE

"I don't see how," the astrogator, Lieutenant Cole, finally says when he reports in. "Our Alcubierre drive is cold. But I have to conclude that the XO is right. We can't get a stellar fix, not even by doing the equivalent of sticking our heads out of the window. And we are in a total comms blackout. We should be able to triangulate on something, but we can't. Everything looks like it does when we are in an Alcubierre bubble. Except for the fact that our drive isn't running."

"Occam's razor," Colonel Drake replies. "The least complex explanation is usually the correct one. Sorry about your afterlife 'mead hall' theory, XO."

"That means there's a seed ship still out there within a few kilometers of us," I say.

"Yes, there is." Lieutenant Colonel Campbell nods at the situational orb, still bereft of any information. "But we're both suspended in his Alcubierre bubble while he's dragging us along to who the fuck knows where. He can't see us; we can't see him. We can't shoot at each other."

"But once we come out on the other side, that'll change in a hurry," Colonel Drake adds.

"If we come out on the other side," Lieutenant Cole says. "No ship has ever hitched a ride in another ship's Alcubierre field before. We could slip outside of the bubble and get torn apart by the tidal forces any second."

"If that happens, we won't know it." The XO crosses her arms in front of her chest and starts pacing between the holotable and the edge of the command pit. "We'll all be dead in a millisecond. Why don't we act as though we're *not* going to die? Because when this fellow gets to where he is headed and we're still tagging along, we'll have a problem on our hands. We're going to come out of Alcubierre with a seed ship on our stern and our pants wrapped around our ankles."

Colonel Drake nods.

"Agreed," he says. "We'll come out of Alcubierre or we won't. If we do, we need to be ready to pick up the fight."

"We need a tactical analysis of the exact moment the Lanky popped us both into Alcubierre," Lieutenant Colonel Campbell says. "Bring up the last few minutes of the engagement on the table. When that bubble shuts down, those will be our starting blocks. We will have the same heading and velocity relative to each other."

Captain Steadman works his controls and starts populating the tactical display with data. The orange icon representing the Lanky ship pops back into life and starts heading outward from the center of the globe as the tactical officer is playing back the record in reverse.

"All right, hold it there," the XO says. "Skip forward fifteen seconds. Another ten. And *hold*."

The recording freezes, and Lieutenant Colonel Campbell expands the scale of the display until the orange and blue icons are taking up most of the orb.

"That was a close fucking scrape," she says. "When the Lanky jumped into Alcubierre, he was *eighty-five meters* from our starboard stern. If we had gotten out of the way two-hundredths of a second later, we'd be missing our aft half right now."

Captain Steadman adds the movement vectors and relative velocities to the screen.

"Closing rate at the time of the transition was two thousand kilometers per second," he says. Someone in the CIC lets out a low whistle.

"Assuming that the laws of Alcubierre travel are still in effect, we're both going to come out of the far end with the same momentum we had when we went in. The Lanky was putting on the brakes hard. He was at just nine hundred meters per second. We'll have an immediate velocity advantage. If we light our drive right away and go to flank speed, we can exploit it and increase the distance to give us options. We can dictate the engagement."

"We need to get him in front of the particle cannons again," Colonel Drake says. "Light the main drive, swing around, get back into firing distance before he can build up the speed to lead us on a stern chase again."

"Maybe he wasn't aiming for us after all," I say. "Could be he had to slow down to make the transition point."

Lieutenant Colonel Campbell looks at me and shrugs.

"Your guess is as good as mine, Major. Maybe he just got pissed off and wanted to show us what happens when you pull a tiger by the tail."

"It's possible that he didn't want to overshoot his node," Colonel Drake adds. "Or the Lanky way of going to Alcubierre has a speed limit. Nobody has ever seen a seed ship go into Alcubierre. Not until today."

He looks at the intersection of the ship trajectories on the display, where only the tiniest sliver of space separates the blue vector line for *Washington* and the orange one of the seed ship.

"But I'm pretty sure he didn't mean to pick up any passengers for the ride. At least I hope so. Because that would mean he'll get an unpleasant surprise when he gets to his destination."

The XO frowns at the frozen tactical display.

"That leaves one important question," she says. "What the hell *is* his destination?"

"If we are really lucky today, we will get to find out," the commander replies.

Of all the cognitive dissonance I've felt on this deployment, the strongest one by far is the experience of watching the entire CIC crew go about their business and prepare for an engagement while we are traveling in an Alcubierre bubble that is not our own, in conditions that may obliterate us any second. I don't want to leave the CIC and drop out of the command loop, so I stay in the TacOps chair and try to come to terms with the fear that is eating away at my consciousness. We are in a space-time shortcut that is not of our own making, with no control over the journey, and no idea where we will end up once the ride stops. I know that I should be doing something other than just sitting at my station and watching everyone else busy themselves. But if I die, I want to be aware of my last moment instead of just ceasing to be in the middle of some insignificant task.

"We're in good shape," the XO finally reports to Colonel Drake. "I mean, other than the fact that we're hitching an Alcubierre ride to parts unknown from a Lanky ship. Systems are green across the board. Nothing broke when we got jolted into Alcubierre."

"I guess that's something."

"Lieutenant Cole says that if the Lanky ship's Alcubierre bubble had the same relative size as the ones our drives create, his bubble would have sliced the ship in half. Part of us would have been left behind in Capella."

"There's a cheerful thought," Colonel Drake says.

I try to imagine the bisected wreckage of an Avenger-class carrier, drifting in space, cut in half by a superluminal space-time bubble so cleanly that it looks like a cross-section image from a book about warships. The people in the aft section would be able to take to the pods unless they were unlucky enough to be in one of the compartments that were sliced open and exposed to space. But the crew in the forward part would be trapped in the Alcubierre bubble, unable to launch pods, with only emergency power and limited air, destined to suffocate while riding the transit chute. I have lost count of how many times I have owed my survival to a few milliseconds or a couple of centimeters the fates nudged in my favor, and I'm sure I only know about a tenth of them at best.

"Give me a shot clock," Colonel Drake says. "Starting from the time we got pulled into Alcubierre."

On the forward bulkhead, a time readout appears, then jumps forward to show 00:31:44.

"We have no idea how long this son of a bitch intends to spend in Alcubierre," the commander says. "But we need to be ready for a fight the second we emerge on the other side."

"What's the closest networked system to Capella?" Lieutenant Colonel Campbell asks.

"Our solar system," Lieutenant Cole replies without hesitation. "Forty-two light-years. Six hours of Alcubierre."

"With our drive," Colonel Drake says. "Theirs may be a shitload more efficient. Or not efficient at all. We may be in here for six hours, or two, or twenty."

"We were nowhere near the transit node to Earth," the astrogator replies. "Whatever his jumping-off point was, it's not the one we use. This one's new. Uncharted."

After hours in the chair, my biological needs are finally pressing enough that the discomfort overrides my anxiety-fueled reluctance to leave my post. I unbuckle my harness and get out of my chair, and the ache in my joints and lower back makes me suppress a little groan.

"Hot date, Major Grayson?" the XO asks.

"Negative, ma'am" I reply. "But if we're all going to buy it, I don't want to die sitting in a puddle."

She chuckles and turns back toward the holotable. I stretch my back and walk to the CIC door on slightly unsteady legs.

There's a head adjacent to the CIC for the use of the command crew, and I relieve myself for what seems like forever. Then I step in front of the sink and wash my hands and face, savoring the feeling of the cool water on my sweaty forehead and cheeks. It's only when I dry my face and take stock of my fatigue that I realize the absence of the bone-deep discomfort that usually comes with Alcubierre travel. It still feels like any metal surfaces I touch are slightly charged with electricity, but I no longer feel like something is trying to stretch my bones.

A rumbling vibration shakes the deck under my feet and makes me lose my balance enough to cause me to grab the edge of the stainless sink. The lights in the head go out, leaving me in the dark momentarily. Then the dim emergency lighting comes on.

That'll be just my luck, to die in the fucking head after everything that's happened, I think.

I dash back to the CIC, which is bathed in the red backup lighting. All the viewscreens and consoles are dark again. As I rush over to the TacOps station and fling myself back into the chair, there's another low rumble deep inside the hull, and the consoles come back to life seemingly all at once.

"We are out of Alcubierre," Lieutenant Cole shouts.

"That means we are still alive," Colonel Drake says. "Get the sensors back up, and get that propulsion online."

"Aye, sir. Reactor restart complete in seventeen seconds. Sensor network is online."

The tactical display appears above the holotable again. It stays empty for a few moments, and then the orange icon of a seed ship appears.

"Hostile contact, bearing one-eighty-nine by negative twenty-two. Distance thirteen thousand kilometers and increasing."

"Weapons," Colonel Drake shouts. "Bring the particle mount online and set the system to live as soon as those reactors are up."

"Aye, sir. Preparing to charge coils," Lieutenant Lawrence replies.

On the plot, the distance between us and the Lanky rapidly increases. He's behind and slightly below our stern, and with every second, we gain another thousand kilometers on him.

"Reactor reboot sequence complete in *ten. Nine. Eight* . . ."

"Lay in a course that brings us around on a least-time intercept with that seed ship," the commander orders. "As soon as the drive comes back online, bring us around so we can blow that son of a bitch to hell."

"Reactors are back online. All systems green. Main propulsion is lit."

"Execute intercept maneuver. Swing us around, helm."

There's no atmospheric friction in space, no way to bank and turn a five-hundred-thousand-ton ship like a fighter from an old war documentary. Instead, we have to change direction with thrust only, a difficult act that Halley once likened to balancing a ball bearing on a dinner plate while skating across a frozen lake. The tactical display whirls around as the helmsman uses thrusters to turn the bow of the ship, then burns the main engines selectively to redirect our momentum. I've been looking at situational displays on warships for a long time, but I quickly lose track of the vector lines and projections as everything twists and swirls.

"Bogey is accelerating," Captain Steadman says. "Lima-1 is now at two thousand meters per second and climbing, two and a half g."

"Coils are charged. Particle-gun battery is ready to fire, sir."

"Lock on to the bogey and set for auto-trigger," the commander orders. "Let's finish what we started."

When the plot stabilizes, I can see that we aren't on a straight course for the Lanky. Instead, the helmsman has used our momentum and thrown the ship into a curved trajectory that looks like we are drifting around a turn in a race car. Our nose is pointing at the Lanky, though we're not close enough yet to be in our effective weapons range. But as we continue on our wide parabolic curve, I can see that each passing moment brings our arched trajectory a little closer to the Lanky's straight one. The physics involved in maneuvering in zero gravity are still a mystery to me, and I'm glad that the crew are well-trained experts, no matter how young some of them seem.

I was launching onto Lanky worlds in bio-pods when I was just twenty-three, I remind myself.

"If that's his top acceleration, there's no way he can get away before we make our pass," Lieutenant Colonel Campbell says with satisfaction.

"We almost had him in range once before. Let's not do a victory dance until that thing is an expanding cloud of superheated debris," Colonel Drake cautions. He fixes the orange icon on the holotable with a glare and drums the fingertips of his right hand on the armrest of his chair.

"The optics are having a hard time tracking him even at this short range. If we hadn't known where he started out in relation to us, we may have never gotten a lock." Captain Steadman looks concerned. "Something is off about this ship all of a sudden. It's like trying to get a visual on a black cat running across a dark cellar."

"Just don't lose track of him now, Lieutenant."

"Negative, sir. We have him."

"Firing window is five and a half seconds," Lieutenant Lawrence reports. "We're getting a nice, juicy flyby of his broadside for two seconds of that pass. And if we miss, we get another shot just past the apex."

For the next ten minutes, we watch the two icons on the tactical screen shift position ever so slightly with every refresh of the hologram. We are closing in on the Lanky with what looks like an insurmountable speed advantage. The little yellow cone that marks our particle cannon's firing arc and range creeps closer to the dotted line with agonizing slowness.

"Visual of the bogey, on-screen," Colonel Drake orders.

The image that appears on the forward bulkhead shows just the vaguest and most indistinct outline of a seed ship in the darkness, enhanced by the image intensifiers and processing algorithms of the ships' optical sensors. Where our spaceships leave the bright thermal bloom of a fusion drive in their wake, there's nothing trailing the Lanky that gives any clue about how their propulsion systems work. We have fought them for over a decade, but their technology is still almost completely unknown to us. We know what they do, but not how they do it, or how they developed the way they did. But we know that they can be killed, that their ships can be destroyed, and that's all the knowledge we need in the moment.

I wonder if you're scared, I think as I look at the shape of the seed ship on the screen. *I wonder if you've ever had to run away before. It's not a fun experience, is it? I wonder if you fear death like we do.*

"Twenty seconds to intercept," Captain Steadman says. "Coils charged, auto-trigger enabled. Reactors are at full output."

The low noise in the CIC progressively decreases in volume the closer our blue icon gets to the orange one. By the time the yellow firing cone of the particle cannon touches the dotted line where the seed ship is going to be, it's dead silent except for the static hum of the machinery and the soft whispering of the air-conditioning.

"Dodge *this*," the XO says softly.

"Five seconds. Four. Three. Two. One. *Fire.*"

The lights in the CIC dim as the twin particle-gun mounts claim almost all the available power output of the ship's bank of fusion reactors. Deep down in the hull, the cannons mounted along the centerline spew hydrogen atoms at the Lanky seed ship at just below the speed of light, carrying terajoules of kinetic energy across the intervening space.

The dark image on the screen turns into a bright white one. Ten thousand kilometers in front of *Washington*'s bow, a new sun briefly blooms in the inky black as the hull of the Lanky ship is superheated by subatomic particles that chew through the armor in a few microseconds and unleash the fury of a hundred nuclear warheads inside.

"Target," Captain Steadman shouts. "Splash one. Broadside hit. Lima-3 is history."

The CIC crew breaks out in cheers and whistles. This time, I add my own relieved shout to the chorus. Colonel Drake sinks back in his chair a little. From where I'm sitting, he looks like he has aged about ten years and shrunk ten centimeters in the last few minutes.

"Well done," he says into the din. "Cut the drive and secure weapons. Wait for the poststrike assessment before we officially break out the party hats, people. I am not taking a damn thing for granted today."

We watch the glowing debris cloud expand and dissipate slowly over the next few minutes, three kilometers of Lanky seed ship and a million tons of mass or more disassembled into its component atoms. When the glow fades, there's nothing left but the darkness of empty space.

"That's a clean kill," Captain Steadman says. "Both cannons, dead center on the hull. Scratch one seed ship."

"We came a very long way for that kill mark," Colonel Drake says. "Now let's see where the hell we are. Astrogation, give me a fix on our position, please."

"Aye, sir," Lieutenant Cole replies. "Stand by for astrogation fix."

Lieutenant Colonel Campbell looks up at the Alcubierre shot clock that is still counting on top of the CIC bulkhead.

"Stop the clock. Reset it to the moment we came back out of Alcubierre with that Lanky."

The numbers on the clock freeze, then change to 00:33.15.

"Thirty-three minutes in Alcubierre," the XO says. "Where the *fuck* did you take us in thirty-three minutes?"

Lieutenant Cole looks from his display to the XO and then back to his screen.

"I'm . . . I'm really not sure, ma'am."

"What do you mean, you're not sure, Lieutenant? Is the astrogation equipment still off-line?"

"It's working. I *think*. Everything looks the way it should. I'm getting a good signal on the positioning system fix. We're triangulating off three different pulsars. But the readout is nonsense. Maybe something got fried when the systems got bumped off-line."

"Show me that nonsense readout, please." Lieutenant Colonel Campbell strides over to the astrogation station and leans in to look at the screens.

"What the *fuck*."

"I'll run a systems check and have them recalibrate the hardware, ma'am."

The XO looks over at Colonel Drake.

"If you thought our day has been interesting so far, you're in for a laugh, Skipper."

"Don't keep me in suspense," the commander says.

Lieutenant Colonel Campbell looks around the CIC, and for the first time since I've come aboard, I can see something like worry in her face. She reaches down and punches a succession of data fields. On the holotable, the tactical display disappears, and a galactic star chart expands in its stead.

"The galactic positioning system claims we are here," the XO says. A tiny blue lozenge-shaped marker appears on the star chart and starts blinking slowly, looking forlorn in the vast sea of constellations all around it. She increases the scale of the display, and I feel a surge of despair when I see just how far the map has to zoom out before the nearest star system shows up.

"If this is right, we're in the middle of nowhere, on the ass end of the Corvus constellation. *Nine hundred* light-years from Earth."

CHAPTER 22

— A LONG WAY FROM ANYTHING —

"What's the likelihood that the system is wrong?" Colonel Drake asks. He's standing at the astrogation station with the XO, hemming in an increasingly unhappy-looking Lieutenant Cole. "Maybe the mapping data is off. Nobody has been nine hundred light-years out yet."

"We get a wrong fix sometimes, but the software always corrects it in a few seconds," Lieutenant Cole says. "This one hasn't jumped its spot since it came back on."

"What about the signal?" I ask. "Could someone be messing with it?"

Lieutenant Cole shakes his head. "It's the Galactic Positioning System, right? It triangulates off the known pulsars and their magnetic time signatures. You can't spoof it or jam it. You either get the signal or you don't."

"We can't spoof it," the XO says. "Doesn't mean the Lankies can't."

"That's a bit of a stretch. They didn't know we were going to come out of Alcubierre right here any more than we did. And there's no way our ride could have sent a message ahead from inside the bubble." Colonel Drake shakes his head.

"Occam's razor," he continues. "Assume that we are where the GPS says we are."

"Then we have a bit of a problem." Lieutenant Colonel Campbell crosses her arms in front of her chest and walks over to the holotable.

"If we're really in an empty corner of the Corvus constellation, we're a very long way from any colony system. A long way from *anything*. Nothing we can reach with a fusion drive in our lifetimes. The nearest star system is nineteen light-years away. That would take two hundred years even if we had enough fuel to get this crate up to ten percent of light speed. Not that the food and water on this ship will last us even two years."

"Let's not go down that route," the commander says in a cautioning voice. "I find it hard to believe that the Lankies put their nodes into random galactic dead ends. Whatever this one was running toward, he thought it was safety."

He looks around the CIC.

"Nobody, and I mean *nobody*, carries rumors and doomsaying out of this room. This information is restricted to CIC personnel right now. Until we have verified our situation and the enemy disposition in the neighborhood, there will be no talking about where we may be or what may have happened. This is still a fully operational NAC warship with a mission. It will cease to be that if the crew starts to panic and lose their minds."

Colonel Drake looks at the XO.

"Get on the 1MC and make an all-hands announcement that we've had a malfunction of the Alcubierre system, but that we're undamaged and back to normal. Call everyone down from combat stations and resume the watch cycle. Get me a passive sensor sweep of the area and launch the recon drones for a survey run. That Lanky didn't just run toward *nothing*. Let's find out what's out here before we start bumbling around and calling attention to ourselves with EM noise." He claps his hands sharply.

"Let's get to work, people. We ended up here *somehow*. We'll figure out how to get back *somehow*. If there's an Alcubierre entry point, there must be an outbound node somewhere as well. I have absolutely no interest in pointing this ship Earthward and going the long way."

That would be a wonderful last fuck-you from the Lanky ship, I think as I lean against the command pit railing and look at the situational display that has replaced the star chart again. *Drag us out into the middle of nowhere to a place from which we can't escape.*

I unbuckle my harness and get out of my chair again. Then I walk over to the commander, who is standing in the holotable pit with the XO. Whenever we aren't running an active STT mission, I already feel like the fifth wheel in the CIC most of the time, but now the feeling is amplified as everyone in the room except me can focus on a job.

"Something on your mind, Major?" Colonel Drake says when I step down into the pit to join them.

"There's nothing I can do from the CIC right now, sir. And quite frankly, all this sitting around is making me a bit jumpy. With your permission, I want to check on my team members and at least brief the section leaders."

Colonel Drake runs a hand through his hair and scratches the back of his head.

"I would prefer if you held off on specifics until we know exactly what our situation is out here," he says. "Check on your team but give them the same general line for now. Even your section leaders. You know how quickly the rumor mill can churn."

"I think the rumor mill is churning already anyway, sir. We won't be able to keep a lid on this for long. Not if we don't want to have to put out a hundred different bush fires. You know how grunts are."

"The recon drones are going to launch in a few minutes and do a surveillance of the neighborhood. We don't need to keep a lid on this forever. Just for a few hours. Until we have data we can act on. If you don't think you can do that, I'd prefer if you remained in the CIC, Major. But I have to tell you that you look ripe for a shower and a few hours of sleep."

"I'm not sure I could sleep if I tried, sir. Not after all of this."

"I'm ordering you to try anyway. Get some no-go pills from the druids down in medical if you must. You've been on your feet for too long. I could see you nodding off at the TacOps station while we were in Alcubierre. Go rinse off and put your head on a pillow. I don't want to see you in the CIC again for at least six hours unless there's a general quarters alarm. We won't be running any ground ops anytime soon anyway. No ground to go to right now. And make sure the SEAL team has some enforced downtime as well. Might as well let them get rest while they can."

"Aye, sir," I say with some reluctance.

When I get down to Grunt Country ten minutes later, my section leaders are already in the STT briefing room, obeying the summons I sent through my data pad before I left the CIC.

"No offense, sir, but you look like you've had a rough day," Captain Burns says.

"You could say that," I concede. "Harper, how's your section doing?"

"All is well, Major. I'm a little shocked we got out of there without any casualties. But nobody stubbed so much as a toe."

I pick one of the empty seats and drop into it with a little grunt. My body feels like someone turned up the artificial gravity since I stepped out of the CIC. I know I've done much more strenuous missions before, and I've been awake for far longer periods at a stretch, but right now I feel more tired than I've ever felt in my life.

"What's the word from upstairs, sir?"

My four section leaders look at me expectantly. They're all roughly my age or just a little younger, and once again it strikes me as strange that these men look to me for guidance and leadership, that I am someone from "upstairs" now.

"You've heard the XO," I say. "Not much to add. Our Alcubierre system had a malfunction."

"A *malfunction*," Captain Taylor repeats.

"There has to be a little bit more than that," Captain Lawson says.

I let out a slow breath while I decide how much I can tell my team without disobeying the commander's order directly.

They all have command bullshit experience, I decide. *They can read between the lines.*

"The navigation system went all wonky," I say. "We don't know where we are right now. The skipper is sending out the battlespace control squadron to get the picture. Until they get word back to us, we're kind of floating in the dark. But that info stays just on this level."

I can tell by the looks my captains are exchanging that they all know I am withholding something, but I also know that they'll pretend to accept the information at face value, at least in front of me. We're only one rank apart, but the layer between company and field-grade officer is an opaque one, and there is a mental distance between us that no amount of familiarity will be able to bridge. They are closer to their NCOs and junior officers, and I am closer to the upper command echelons, and that's the way it has always been. I am no longer a small unit leader. I am someone who takes orders from the command level and withholds information from his subordinates when it's necessary for the mission. The thought makes me feel unclean somehow.

"That's all I can tell you right now. The CO will update everyone over the 1MC once we know just what the hell is going on. Until then, that's all the info I can give you."

I get out of my chair again. It takes so much effort that I'm sorry I sat down in the first place instead of doing this short update while standing at the front of the room.

"Harper, make sure that the SEALs all get some shut-eye and a good stretch of downtime. Orders from the skipper. They probably won't need us for a little while."

"Aye, sir. I'll order them into their racks if they aren't there already. Any idea for a time frame?"

"The skipper says the recon birds will need a few hours to get the picture. I would guess we should be safe for a watch cycle or two."

"Copy that. And if you don't mind me saying—"

"I *know*," I cut him off. "I don't look too fresh, either. I am heading for my own bunk as soon as we are done here. Check on your squad leaders, everyone. Make sure they're squared away and that the troops have everything they need. And you may all want to take the opportunity to get some downtime yourselves. You know the golden rule in the field."

"Never miss an opportunity to grab chow or sleep," Captain Lawson recites dutifully. "You never know when it will come your way again."

"Damn straight. Now carry on, and I'll let you know when I have more intel to share," I say.

I watch my four captains file out of the room, and I feel a sudden pang of envy that they'll be able to take one last rest without knowing the severity of the situation, without being kept awake by the knowledge that we are nine hundred light-years from home with no obvious way to get back. And not for the first time, I find myself thinking that accepting a command rank was the worst decision of my career, and maybe my entire life.

Back in my quarters, I take a long shower, overriding the water rationer five times to keep the hot water coming even though I know that we are far away from resupply now. The water is continuously recycled anyway, and it won't be the essential thing that runs out first if we don't find a way out of this place.

When I have dried off and put on a fresh set of fatigues, I sit down at my cabin's tiny office workstation and turn on my terminal screen. I scroll through my list of messages and feel a desperate sense of longing when I see

Halley's sender ID on some of them. But they are older missives, of course, received when we were still in the solar system and in range of the MilNet relays. I've already read them several times over, but with nothing else to do and no other link to my wife at the moment, I read them again, keenly aware that they may be the last words from her I'll ever get to see. But if I was hoping for comfort, seeing our last exchanges intensifies the low-level dread I already feel, and I close the message window and return to my personal landing screen. There's an inconceivable gulf of space between us now, a distance so wide that if the ship sent an emergency signal to Earth at this moment, it would take almost a millennium to reach our home planet, fifty generations of human life spans. Even if the Earth is still around in 3020 and we have any descendants on it, they won't be able to relate to our messages any more than we could relate to handwritten notes from some of our ancestors living in 1120. We'd be no more than archaeological curiosities, historical artifacts. Halley will never know what happened to me, and any far-distant relatives down the time stream won't care.

We had our chance to quit, I think. *We should have taken it. Now we'll both get to pay the price.*

It's pointless and futile because the data banks of this ship may never synchronize with the MilNet again. But I bring up a new message window anyway and address it to Halley's node. Even if she will never see the sentiment, I don't want my last recorded message to her to be some insubstantial bantering about leave schedules, so I write a new one.

>Still kicking. Still love you. Always have. Always will.

It violates our unspoken rule that we never use those words unless we are face-to-face, but I think that she would forgive me the transgression considering the circumstances.

I send the message into the outbound queue. Then I shut down the terminal and go to my bunk, where I lie down fully clothed, expecting to drift off a little at best until the next change-of-watch alert sounds.

Instead, I fall asleep almost right away. And despite the events of the last day and a half, my sleep is deep and dreamless.

CHAPTER 23

NEEDLES AND HAYSTACKS

"Now hear this. All command-level officers, report to the flag briefing room at 0800 Zulu. I repeat, all command-level officers report to the flag briefing room at 0800 Zulu."

The 1MC announcement stirs me out of my sleep. I sit up and look around in my darkened quarters until I locate the time projection on the bulkhead. It's 0730 shipboard time, and I've slept for almost nine hours and through a change of watch. When I reach for my fatigues, I realize that I am already wearing them because I went to bed in my clothes.

I turn on the light and walk into the little wet cell. The face that looks back at me in the mirror seems too pale and tired to belong to me. I don't know if someone can run out of steam for good, if one event can sap a person of all their remaining vitality and energy, but right now it feels I am almost at that point, if it exists.

On the way to the flag briefing room, I feel my stomach growling, and I realize that I haven't had any food since before I went on the surface mission to Willoughby City. With fifteen minutes to the briefing, I don't have the time to stop by the officers' mess and have a proper meal, so I grab a leftover sandwich from last night's watch-change buffet and eat it in a hurry while I rush up the stairs to the decks above, violating officer decorum in the act.

"You're looking better, Major," Colonel Drake says when I walk into the room. "I'm glad you followed my advice."

"I didn't take it as advice, sir," I say.

"Good answer. Have a seat."

I take my place in my usual spot, next to Lieutenant Colonel Campbell and across the table from Colonels Pace and Rigney. When I am seated, Colonel Drake gets up and walks over to the door to close and seal it. Then he returns to the table and remains standing at the end of it. He punches a few data fields on the surface and activates the viewscreen at the front of the room.

"Major Grayson was present in the CIC when we came out of Alcubierre, so he already knows what I told Colonel Pace and Colonel Rigney in the ready room last night. Astrogation has verified that the GPS reading is accurate. We got dragged into a thirty-three-minute Alcubierre trip by the Lanky seed ship, and we ended up nine hundred light-years away from Earth. We are currently in deep space on the outer edge of the Corvus constellation, far away from any star systems."

The viewscreen shows a star chart of the area, encompassing the closest systems and pinpointing our relative position. When I last saw the same chart in the CIC, it was empty except for the icon representing *Washington*. Now there are several other objects nearby.

"We've deployed the recon drones for a passive sensor sweep of the neighborhood," Colonel Drake continues. "And while the nearest star system is nineteen light-years away, it seems like the Lanky ship wasn't just picking this place at random. There's a planet out there, five hundred million kilometers from our current position. The drones spotted it on infrared."

"Out here," Colonel Pace says. "A planet. Without any stars nearby."

"A rogue planet," the XO says. "It's not orbiting a star. It's orbiting the galactic center instead. From what my astronomy teacher said, the galaxy is full of 'em."

“It’s about the size of Earth, give or take ten percent,” Colonel Drake continues. “We’ve redeployed the drones to cover as much of the space between here and there as possible.”

Colonel Rigney leans back in his chair and folds his arms across his barrel chest. “I have a concern. There are a thousand troops down in Grunt Country that do nothing right now but consume calories. Three thousand per day, per head. Unless we find a moon or a planet nearby where we can farm some protein and carbohydrates, we’re going to be in deep shit once the food stocks are gone.”

“We have food reserves for six months,” the XO says. “We can probably stretch that to nine if we cut down on the daily calorie allowance, and we’re willing to deal with the hit to morale that will cause. And there are enough field and emergency rations in storage to feed the grunts and the crew for another three months at least.”

“So, twelve months.” Colonel Rigney frowns. “That’s not a rosy prospect.”

“I don’t intend to stay in this place for a year,” Colonel Drake says. “We will find a way to scout the planet because it’s the only thing within nineteen light-years, and because it looks like it may have what we need to keep ourselves alive. But our focus will be to find the exit door out of this system. And there must be one, if the Lankies travel through here with any regularity.”

“How long are we keeping the news from the crew?” I ask.

“I’ll have to make an announcement,” the commander replies. “This isn’t something we can keep under wraps for much longer. We already have sixteen drop-ship crews who are in the know. The way the deckhands and fuel jockeys can keep secrets, the whole ship will probably know by the end of the day. We’re all in it together regardless of rank. The crew have a right to know what they’re facing.”

He sits down again and glances over his shoulder at the star map.

“This is going to be a tough job even without Lankies breathing down our necks. You all know what’s at stake here. We are tasked with looking for a needle in a haystack. Only the needle is a few millimeters long, and the haystack is a trillion cubic kilometers in size. And we need to find the damn thing before we run out of food and water. With no support, no backup, and no communications with home. I'm not a betting man, but I'm pretty sure I wouldn't put too much on our odds. But the alternative is to roll over and give up."

"What about the Lankies?" I ask. "If they go in and out of this place, they must have some foothold here."

"I think we can probably rule out that planet," Lieutenant Colonel Campbell says. "These things are tough, but this is a dark system. No sun, no heat. No *light*. It's not the best place to sustain life. We know they like it warm."

"If they are here, we will deal with them as we come across them," the CO says. "We have a mission, and we have a plan. The clock is ticking, so let's get back to work. There's never been less time to waste than now."

"If I can make a suggestion, the STT has four Blackfly drop ships sitting in the hangar for covert missions," I say. "We could use them for a scouting run toward that planet. Get a better picture without putting the ship at risk."

"What can the drop ships do that the drones can't without risking a crew?" the XO asks.

"They don't need a data link back to the ship, for one. And they can carry a lot more hardware. We can put a full recon package on the pylons and see a lot more than a drone could."

"That is a very long haul for a drop ship," Colonel Drake says.

I shrug. "The Blackflies have modular cargo holds. We can set them up for a long-range mission pretty easily. Three pilots to trade off on the flight deck, three mission specialists in the back who can take turns at the recon pods. I could bring along two of my combat controller section leaders and switch off with them. They can use external tanks for extra range. And with six people on the ship, we can bring enough water and provisions for weeks."

"Are you volunteering for the job, Major?" Lieutenant Colonel Campbell says. "Because that could be a one-way ticket. If you have a critical systems failure out there, we may not be able to send a rescue ship."

"I know the recon gear on the Blackflies," I say. "Better than anyone else in the STT. I'm the least likely to have to call back to the barn for help. If we do this mission, I want to be in charge of it."

Colonel Drake scratches the back of his head. Then he looks over at Colonel Pace.

"Any objections to that plan, CAG?"

The head of the carrier's space wing shakes his head. "The major is right. A Blackfly loaded up with fuel and a rotating crew has much longer legs than a drone. And we wouldn't need to keep an uplink active. They could go out there and snoop around with passive sensors, then come back and report. Probably best to keep the EM emissions to an absolute minimum until we know what we're facing out here."

"And if they run into unfriendly neighbors?" Lieutenant Colonel Campbell asks.

"Then we'll just lose a drop ship and six people instead of the whole carrier," I say. "And you will all know which way *not* to go."

Colonel Drake ponders my reply for a few moments.

"All right," he says. "Get your team together and prep one of the Blackflies for long-range reconnaissance. I'll give you a provisional go for the mission, but you will wait until the recon drones are back in the barn. Get ready for skids-up in eighteen hours."

"Aye, sir," I reply.

"Any particular reason why you're eager to stick your head out on this one?" Lieutenant Colonel Campbell asks. "I mean, not that I don't appreciate the commitment."

"I'm not good at sitting on my hands and waiting for stuff to happen to me," I say. "I want to find a way home soon. Because my wife will be livid if I get back from this deployment a few thousand years late."

The sandwich before the briefing wasn't nearly enough to fill the hole in my stomach, so I head down to the chow hall to get a proper breakfast. The officers' mess is in the middle of its end-of-watch serving shift, so it's busy with mostly junior officers coming off their duty stations and grabbing a meal before heading for their bunks. I stand in line with the lieutenants and captains and get a plate of hash and eggs along with a mug of black Fleet coffee. It can't hold a candle to the coffee Chief Kopka serves at his restaurant, but right now it's just what I need, and the knowledge that we may soon run out of the stuff makes it taste twice as good as it usually does as I take my first sip while still at the dispenser.

When I look around for a place to sit, I spot a familiar face at one of the tables. Lieutenant Colonel Campbell is seated by herself, with a respectful buffer of several chairs between her and the closest junior officers. As the ship's XO, she's the enforcer of the commanding officer, and most younger officers would avoid her even if she wasn't naturally unapproachable already.

"Mind if I join you?" I ask.

She looks up at me and nods at the seat next to her.

"It's not my personal mess hall," she says and returns her attention to the food in front of her.

I sit down and take another sip of my coffee. Then I pick up my fork and take a stab at the hash, which is a little mushy this morning.

"When did you start boxing?" I ask.

"At the Fleet academy," she says. "I was looking for cardio that wouldn't bore the shit out of me. Some guy in my year told me I'd be good at boxing because of my reach. How about you?"

"SIMAP," I say. "Started sparring with the grunts on deployments. Ended up liking the challenge of the competition."

"Hmm," she says.

We eat in silence for a little while. Just when I've decided to finish my food without trying to engage her in more conversation, she clears her throat.

"You did all right on Willoughby," she says. "That was a hairy run. I can't believe you took a civvie along for the ride. I thought for sure she'd get herself killed."

"She did well," I reply. "And she's not a civvie."

"Yeah, yeah. They're officers, I know. But they only get their commission so they're subject to the UCMJ and all the military regs. She's a civvie. And taking her along was a bad call. Even if she did get eyes on that new Lanky-eating critter for the bio-division."

"She bought herself nightmares for a while. I tried to warn her."

"You brought them all back, so there's that," Lieutenant Colonel Campbell says. "You clearly know your business. And you weren't strutting around like a peacock after. So maybe I was unfairly harsh with you after that first command briefing. But I'm still not looking to make friends, Major."

"I thought the XO wasn't allowed friends," I say. "Read that one in the regulations."

"You got that right," she says.

"We don't have to be friends. Just don't jump my ass unless I deserve it."

She glances at me and takes another bit of her food.

"Are you still going to work out, or are you going to save the calories now that we are on borrowed time?"

"I'll still hit the bag," I say. "Gotta let off steam somehow without collecting a court-martial."

I see the faintest hint of a smile on her face.

"You should come to the gym around 1030, then. None of the oak leaves on this ship seem to know how to hold a heavy bag or a set of punching mitts. And the junior officers are too afraid they might punch the XO by accident."

She finishes her food with one last bite and washes it down with a swig of her coffee. Then she gets up and picks up her tray.

"I'll see you later, Major."

I watch with a little smile as she crosses the floor of the mess hall, ignoring the junior officers that alter their course when they spot her while trying not to be obvious about it.

We can roll over and give up, I think. *Or we can keep forging on and see what happens. And maybe it turns out that we were wrong about the odds after all.*

CHAPTER 24

CARRYING ON

The XO is already in the gym when I walk in. It's the first hour after the watch change, so there are a few more people than usual on the weight and cardio machines, but the boxing area is empty except for Lieutenant Colonel Campbell. She has her long dark hair tied back in a ponytail, and once again I am struck by how much she resembles her father.

She tosses me a set of speed pads, and I catch them as they sail toward my face.

"Your father once chewed me out because he thought I was show-boating," I say as I undo the straps and squeeze my hands into the mitts. "It appears you have that in common with him."

"Really," she says.

"I was reporting to him when I got aboard *Versailles*," I say. "He was the XO. Thought I had spruced up my smock because I was fresh out of tech school and wearing a valor award and a Purple Heart."

"I assume they were legit because you're still here," she says. "He'd have people kicked out with a dishonorable discharge for wearing unearned awards."

"They were legit," I confirm. "I was a lateral transfer from the Territorial Army. But for a second or two, I was still scared shitless."

I finish wrapping the straps around my wrists and hold up the punching surfaces for Lieutenant Colonel Campbell to try out. She's tall and strong, but now she shows that she also has the speed to go with the strength and the reach. She hits the pads with a fast combination of strikes, then another, pulling her hands back into a perfect guard position in between combos. I vary the position of the pads and the sequence of the presentation—high, low, sideways, one hand, both hands. She shifts her combinations smoothly, with good footwork and no wasted movements. For a while, we are circling each other, and the only sounds from our corner of the gym are the XO's hard breathing and the slaps of her gloves on the striking surfaces of the pads. Some of the junior officers on the machines nearby have slowed or paused their own sets to watch the ship's second-in-command lay waste to some punching pads. Finally, she wears herself out for a little while, and she gestures for me to pull off the pads and switch it up.

I peel the pads off my hands and wait while she catches her breath. Then she tosses me the light gloves and takes the speed pads in exchange.

"Don't hold back," she says when she has slipped the mitts onto her hands and secured the straps.

She presents the pads, and I launch into my own workout. I can tell that she does her best to replicate the combos I made her do—high and low, straights and uppercuts, hooks and crosses, alternating sides. To a bystander, it doesn't look as ferocious or impressive as a heavy bag workout, but it's just as tiring. Three minutes in the ring is an eternity, but three minutes of full effort on the mitts feels even longer than a proper fight. By now, we are definitely the center of attention in the gym, even if the junior officers in the room aren't staring outright.

"Good," Campbell says when I finally pull back to catch my breath. "Take a breather. Heavy bag next?"

Overhead, the 1MC signal sounds, and all movement in the gym pauses.

"All hands, this is the commander. Listen up, everyone.

"Twelve hours ago, we entered Alcubierre while engaged with a Lanky seed ship. The Alcubierre field we entered was not our own, as some of you may already suspect. I have held off on sharing the complete details with you until now to allow our recon drones to do a full survey of our surroundings.

"The hard truth is this: We are in uncharted space. The Lanky's Alcubierre bubble transported us a distance of nine hundred light-years. We are presently in the constellation of Corvus, far away from Earth or any human colony. We engaged and destroyed the seed ship that got us here, so we are no longer in immediate danger. But now we are facing the prospect of having to find a way out of this place.

"We have made this journey without the rest of the battle group, so we have no backup, no resupply, and no support. But this ship is built for long missions in unfriendly space, so we are equipped for exactly this sort of task. Furthermore, we have located a nearby planet, so there may be a watering hole around here somewhere.

"That is the situation. It is challenging, but it is not hopeless. I expect everyone to do their duty to the utmost of their abilities. We depend on each other more than ever now. Work hard and be kind to each other, and do not lose heart. We are about to do things that no ship in the Fleet has ever done before. We're going to see things no human eye has ever seen before. And then we are going to go home and tell the rest of the world about it.

"Carry on. Commander out."

The XO and I look at each other.

"Cat's out of the bag," she says. "He had something in there about us being the *high-water mark of humanity* if we don't get back home. I'm glad he took that one out in the end. It was a little too depressing."

"'High-water mark of humanity' sounds so much better than *We'll all be dead in a year if this doesn't work out.*"

"I don't know," Lieutenant Colonel Campbell says. "Personally, I find the second one a lot more motivating."

She pulls the pads off her hands and chucks them to the side.

"Well, you heard the man. Carry on. Unless you want to pack it in already."

I step behind the heavy bag and brace myself against the bottom.

"After you, Colonel," I say.

She walks over to the edge of the mat and picks up her bag gloves. Then she comes over to the heavy bag and gives me a curt smile.

"Sophie," she says. "But only in here. Remember, rank doesn't count when you have gloves on."

I return the smile, surprised at the amount of pleasure I feel at her extension of this personal courtesy.

"All right, then," I say. "After you, Sophie."

There are no day and night cycles on a spaceship, but we still think of the day in relation to the clock even in the absence of light and dark skies because we're used to it. For some reason, I always think of the flight deck as a nighttime environment even though it's the most brightly lit place in the entire ship. Maybe it's because the huge open space reminds me of the plazas between the PRC high-rises, flooded with artificial light in the evening hours when people come out for entertainment and socializing. Whenever I am on one of the nighttime watches, I like to step out on the flight deck before I go up to the CIC just to soak in the atmosphere a little and pretend I'm in a bustling city again.

Tonight, the flight deck is quieter than usual. A few ammunition handlers and refueling guys are using the vast expanse for running laps between rows of parked attack craft. There's maintenance going on as always, and on the far end of the deck, the armed Ready Five drop ships are waiting silently below their docking clamps, standing by to be called upon even in the absence of a planet within five hundred million kilometers. Rumor has it that the next generation of carriers will include some sort of atmospheric exclusion field that can let drop ships and Shrikes pass through while keeping air in, and then we'll be able to have carriers with decks that are open to space and don't need drop hatches anymore. I am looking forward to that development mainly because then every flight deck will have a perpetual view of space.

Halfway down the deck, near the area where we set up our obstacle course, I see a familiar face in the middle of a group of deckhands. It's the technician I met shortly after I got on board. The group is standing around a piece of equipment on the deck, and as I get closer, I see that it's one of the deployment drones for the new optical Arachne system sensors, the ones the tech called "Wonderballs."

"Technician Fisher," I say when I join the group. "At ease," I add as some of the deckhands start their supplication ritual when they see my rank insignia.

"Major Grayson," Callista Fisher says. "How have you been?"

"Oh, I've been okay," I say. "All things considered. How about you?"

"I'm not wild about the fact that my six-month commitment seems to have turned into a possible nine-hundred-year commitment," she says. "Other than that, things are pretty okay here, too. All things considered."

I point at the deployment drone that's sitting on a maintenance rack. The access hatch on one side is open all along the drone, exposing a payload bay that stretches for most of the length of the device. Much of the bay is empty except for two nooks that have translucent containers in them. A third container of the same kind is sitting on the floor next to the drone. Inside I can see a pile of metal tabs.

"What's going on here? Are you gambling with the crew?" I ask.

"Oh, it's nothing like that. It's a message in a bottle."

I kneel in front of the plastic container and take a closer look at the metal tabs.

"We have a surplus of these drones," Technician Fisher says. "And we had the idea to use one to launch toward Earth. You know, in case we don't find the way out of here."

"A radio signal would take nine hundred years," I say. "*This* would take several millennia. There may not be anyone around to receive it. Not that it'll do us any good."

"It'll get there after we're all gone either way," she says. "And then the scale won't matter to us, will it? It's just a morale thing. Some of the other techs thought it was weird. But I kind of like it. A piece of evidence, out there for someone else to find in the future."

"These are dog tags," I say.

"People have been stopping by all day to drop theirs off," Technician Fisher explains. "They break off the bottom half and engrave it with their name and hometown and next of kin. Do you want to add yours, too? I have an electric engraving pen sitting over there."

The deckhands look at me expectantly. Once again, I feel the burden of the command rank on my shoulders. If I spoil their fun, it'll harm shipboard morale. If I contribute to the project, I semi-officially condone the practice, and then I may get into trouble with the skipper or the XO if they oppose it later. But I can't really see the harm in the gesture, even if I suspect that the skipper won't let them use the resources to send a drone full of dog tags on a ten-thousand-year journey.

"Sure," I say and reach into my fatigues blouse to pull out my own dog tag. Some of the deckhands voice their approval.

The military tags are square stainless steel plates with rounded corners, roughly perforated in the middle so the grave detail can easily separate them if needed. I am not particularly attached to this grim piece of jewelry that will only be useful after I'm dead. They've changed the formats a few times over the years, and I've lost one or two on deployment. They're easy enough to replace, and nobody gets into trouble for having to ask for a new one. I snap mine in half and tuck the chain with the attached half back into my shirt.

There's an engraving pen sitting in a charging bracket on a low stack of crates over to the side. I pick it up and look for the activation button. Technician Fisher placed a sheet of thin steel the size of a mess tray on top of the crate next to the pen, and I can see where people have tried out the device to get used to the way it writes. I do the same, taking my cue from the other trial scribbles and writing my name in slow and deliberate letters until I have figured out the pen. Then I put my dog tag half down on the crate and turn it so the blank back faces up.

Andrew Grayson
Liberty Falls, Vermont, NAC
Husband to Halley

The space on the back of the half tag is just enough for those three lines. It seems a good distillation of my important metrics, far more so than the letters and numbers on the official side of the tag that list my service number, blood type, service branch, and religious preference.

I put the pen back into its charging bracket and claim my inscribed tag from the top of the crate. The letters I etched into the stainless steel are shaky and uneven, but indisputably made by a human hand, and I'm pleased at the thought that this record will survive in my own handwriting. Maybe some future historian will find and decipher it, but it will be out there with all the other dog tags long after we're gone, whether we make it back home or not.

I walk over to the open container and kneel in front of it again. Then I add my dog tag half to the pile that has already accumulated on the bottom, hundreds of brief hand-carved messages for the distant future. It lands with a bright little metallic chime.

"Happy trails," I say. "I really hope someone on Earth will be able to read my handwriting in ten thousand years."

I get up and step out of the way so the next person can add their tag to the growing pile.

"We'll still have to get clearance from upstairs to launch that drone," Technician Fisher says. "So those tags may never go further than this deck. But someone's bound to find them sooner or later, right? Stainless steel lasts a lot longer than data banks do. I'll vacuum seal the containers once they are full."

"Tell you what," I say. "I am heading upstairs right now. When I get an idle moment or two with the skipper, I'll tell him about your idea and put in a good word for the project."

"That would be wonderful," she replies.

"The ordnance guys used to write messages on the payloads in the old days," I say. "Maybe you can use the outside of the drone for a canvas once you've got the cargo buttoned up. I'm not sure what you can use for a medium that will be readable after a long vacuum exposure, but it's a thought."

"I'll work on that," Technician Fisher says. "Thanks for the suggestion. It may seem a little silly, but the crew really started to take to the idea."

I look at the container with the pile of dog tags inside, each a shard of evidence that a living and breathing human once existed and wanted the universe to know about it.

"It's not silly at all," I say. "Not even a little."

When I leave the flight deck to head for the CIC and my duty station to prepare for the upcoming scouting mission, I stop at the painted threshold in front of the forward bulkhead that marks the official deck line for reporting in. The ship's seal is painted on the bulkhead in a five-meter-tall mural: **NACS WASHINGTON CVB-63—PREPARED FOR WAR.**

I turn around to look at the flight deck. It stretches for hundreds of meters, the biggest open space by far in this immense warship. As quiet as it is tonight, there are still hundreds of people out there doing their jobs or utilizing the space for training or coming down from their watch. As I take in the sensations of the place one last time before I have to head up into the confines of the upper decks, I realize that the feeling of low-level dread that has been coiling in the base of my brain since we unexpectedly went into Alcubierre with the Lanky has disappeared. I don't know what has triggered the feeling of inner peace that has replaced that dread. Maybe it's the acceptance of the fact that on the cosmic timescale, our existences are a blip in the collective consciousness of the universe anyway, and that I got to live my little life span with more agency and autonomy than most. I got to have a purpose and someone to fight for, and that's more than most people get these days.

We may not make it back, I think. *But even if we don't, it will be all right in the end.*

Overhead, the bell sounds over the speakers, signaling the change of watch, eight strikes of the bell rung in pairs: *ding-ding, ding-ding.* It's a signal to everyone on board that the routines and heartbeats of this ship and her crew have not stopped, regardless of where we are in space or what the next few weeks and months may bring.

I turn and walk across the threshold, toward the passageway that will lead me back to my duty station.

CHAPTER 25

– A SLINGSHOT IN THE DARKNESS –

"It is darker than *shit* out here."

It's quiet in the Blackfly's cargo hold except for the low whispering of the environmental controls, and we aren't wearing helmets, so I can hear Master Sergeant Drentlaw's softly muttered assessment clearly as he cycles through the feeds on his screens. We're in one of the coasting stages of our dash-and-coast trajectory profile, and the engines have been silent for almost an hour. Every sixty minutes, the pilots burn the engines for five minutes to build up more velocity, and then we coast ballistically for another sixty minutes so we're a black hole in space most of the time, with no thermal bloom to give us away or interfere with the reconnaissance sensors.

"Like sneaking through a dark cellar at midnight," I say.

"It's funny," the master sergeant says. "Fifteen years in the job, and I don't think I've ever really appreciated just how fucking empty it is out here."

I check my own screens, which show the current feed from the passive sensor pods mounted on the drop ship's wing pylons. The mission clock shows that we're seventy-nine hours into the scouting run, and so far there's nothing at all on our sensors except for a hot spot on infrared, now less than fifty million kilometers ahead. The planet that is our mission objective is looming in the darkness of deep space, huge and silent.

"We're further away from Earth than anyone has ever been," I say.

"I don't think the Fleet gives out an achievement badge for that," Drentlaw replies. "But I guess there's one good thing about it. It means I am also as far away from my ex-wife as I'll ever get."

I chuckle at the joke, even though it's a reminder that I am now as far away from Halley as I've ever been. The carrier is nine hundred light-years from Earth, an almost unfathomable gulf in space and time. Our Blackfly drop ship is a hundred million kilometers farther out, coasting across the space between the carrier and the nearby rogue planet, with nothing but vacuum all around us for trillions of cubic kilometers. Right now, the six of us on this ship are the most isolated human beings in the entire universe.

I check the mission timer again, where the countdown bar for the watch cycle has almost reached the end of its run.

"Ten minutes until watch change," I say. "Do you want to rest first?"

Drentlaw considers my question and shakes his head curtly.

"I'm still riding out the last dose of go pills, sir. If it's all the same to you, I'll let you take the first rest and clock out when you're done in four hours."

"It's all the same to me," I confirm.

The cargo hold of a Blackfly is usually big enough for a whole platoon of troops: forty personnel and all their gear. The inside of this particular bird is a lot more cramped, but I don't mind the tighter quarters because it almost feels cozy now. We have mission modules that can be set up in the cargo hold for various tasks, and half the hold is taken up by additional fuel and water tanks. The other half is configured for a high-endurance recon mission, a pair of surveillance workstations on the front bulkhead flanked by a galley and a separate rest module for the off-duty team members. Master Sergeant Drentlaw and I are at the controls, and Staff Sergeant Murray and the off-duty pilot are sleeping in the rest module. Looking at screens and data readouts is tiring, so we rotate the duty stations every four hours.

Drentlaw swivels his chair and unbuckles his harness.

"I'm going to warm up chow. Do you want me to throw in some for you before you hit the rack, sir?"

"Sure," I reply.

"Any preference?" he asks.

"Just pull one at random. They all taste like crap anyway."

"Truth," Drentlaw says and gets up to make his way to the tiny galley space where we can heat food and refill our water bladders from the ship's supply.

When he comes back a minute later, he puts a little food tray on the console in front of me and sits down with his own.

"Thank you, Master Sergeant." I peel the lid off the tray and inspect the contents. "Beef lasagna," I say and pry the plastic utensil off the bottom of the lid. "I've never found any beef in there."

"You know what I hate about the mission chow the most?" Drentlaw asks. "Every time I crack one open, I get pissed off at the thought that this may be the last thing I'll eat in my life."

We may be fighting each other over the scraps from these things in a few months if we don't find a way out of this place, I think. But I keep the thought to myself because I am the officer in charge of this mission, and fatalism is terrible for troop morale.

"Next burn in five minutes," the pilot on duty sends from the flight deck.

"Copy that," I reply.

I push my meal tray out of the way and check the sensors again. In a few minutes, the pilot will light the engines for our next five-minute acceleration phase, and then the heat and electromagnetic noise from the drop ship's main thrusters will interfere with the sensors and make them less accurate. Trying to get a picture from only the passive systems is time-consuming and tedious. Using radar would let us map out this galactic neighborhood a lot more efficiently, but it would light us up with electromagnetic energy that would give our presence away because Lankies can sniff out EM emissions like sharks can smell blood in the water.

Ahead of us, the rogue planet is getting more distinct on infrared with every passing minute as we hurtle toward it. I cycle through the software filters on the sensors to verify the results with a pair of imperfect human eyes. Even the highly advanced recon pods have no software that can replicate good old-fashioned gut feeling. But on this sensor pass, it's the software that catches a change in the image, something so slight that I wouldn't have spotted it with my eyes.

"Huh," I say. "Look at this for a second, Master Sergeant."

Drentlaw drops his utensil into his meal tray and puts his food aside, then he leans over to see my console screens.

"Bring up the infrared image from the planet and check the latest refresh," I say.

"Uh-oh," Drentlaw says. He returns his attention to his own screens and cycles through the modes until he is looking at the same data.

"Sector D6 to E8," he says. "I see it. Twenty-five degrees off the equatorial horizon."

"And another one at thirty-seven degrees," I say and mark the spots on the screen with a light pen.

"Think it's our friends?"

I magnify the view on the infrared sensor as far as it will let me, but the two dark blobs that have shown up in front of the rogue planet are too indistinct to make out precise shapes.

"Maybe," I say. "Doesn't really look like a seed ship to me, though."

"Computer assessment says they're different sizes." Drentlaw flicks through a few data fields and arranges them to get a better view of the values. "Anomaly One is estimated between thirty-four hundred and forty-one hundred kilometers in size. Anomaly Two is"—he whistles softly—"between fifty-five hundred and sixty-three hundred kilometers in size."

"Probably not Lanky ships, then," I say.

"Or they're just really big ones."

"Now that's a cheerful thought." I suppress a shudder at the idea of seed ships that are a thousand times larger than the ones we have seen before.

We study the heavily pixelated images on our screens for a little while and watch as the computer tries to make sense of them. We are still too far away to make out the anomalies with any degree of detail. They're just faintly different patches of color, only visible to the sensors because they block a tiny amount of infrared radiation from the rogue planet as they pass in front of it. But the indistinct shapes and large sizes don't point to seed ships.

"Those aren't Lankies," I say. "They're moons. That thing has satellites."

Drentlaw chews on his lower lip as he ponders my assessment.

"I think you're right. Course, we won't know for sure until we get a little closer."

I toggle the button for the intercom with the flight deck.

"Flight, are we still on track for a slingshot maneuver around that planet?"

"Affirmative, sir," the pilot replies. *"We are on track for a powered flyby. Unless you spot something that suggests we shouldn't. Just remember that we'll triple our mission time and fuel expense if we have to wave off the approach and go wide."*

I look at the infrared screen, where the two slightly darker blotches in front of the planet are slowly moving across the magnified display section.

"Confirm we're staying on track for the flyby, Flight. That's why we came all the way out here after all."

Without a nearby sun to illuminate the planet ahead of us, it's just a dark spot in space to the optical lenses, only noticeable by the way it blocks out the far distant stars every time it passes in front of one. We're well inside of a million kilometers before the faint light from the stars is enough for the image intensifiers to make out any details. The rogue planet is just a little bigger than Jupiter, but the lack of light makes it sinister somehow, looming in the darkness like a specter.

"Those are moons, all right," Master Sergeant Drentlaw says. "Three of 'em now. Third one just slipped over the horizon at two-thirty-nine degrees. Diameter between twenty-five hundred and twenty-seven hundred kilometers."

"I see it," I say and adjust the field of view on my infrared filter. The moons are now distinct on the sensor, tiny against the background of the much larger planet but close enough to our sensors to make out that they're spherical satellites moving at the same orbital velocity, not the cigar shapes of Lanky seed ships.

"Gotta wonder how that thing throws off enough heat to be visible on infrared from that far out," Drentlaw says. "Without a sun nearby, I mean. Figured it would be a frozen rock."

"The universe is weird," I say. "Gotta be internal heat. Isotope decay in the core, or tidal heating. Maybe both."

"What the hell is 'tidal heating'?"

I point at the moons outlined in front of the planet's infrared image. "Gravity. Planet pulls on the moons, moons pull on the planet and each other. You get plenty of that, you stir those cores around enough to warm them up."

Drentlaw looks at me and smiles wryly. "You major in astrophysics, sir?"

"I've got two years of public college," I reply. "Astrophysics wasn't on the menu down in the PRC. But I read up on the colony projects, back when I was a kid. I was dead sure we'd win the colonial lottery."

"You and a hundred million other kids," Drentlaw says, and I grin.

"There was a book about the possibility of settling rogue planets," I say. "Or their moons. It can be done, in theory. Only nobody's ever seen one close-up until now."

Master Sergeant Drentlaw looks at the optical feed, where the planet is a faint outline that looks very alien in the green tint from the image intensifier.

"Settling on a rock with no sun," he says. "Darkness twenty-four seven. Depression rates would go through the roof."

"Mission commander, this is Flight," the pilot says over the intercom. *"We are approaching the decision point for the powered flyby. You want to wave off, you have thirty minutes. After that, we are on a committed trajectory."*

"Copy that, Flight," I reply. "Stand by."

I study the screens in front of me for some last-minute divining, some evidence that would justify ordering the pilot to change our trajectory and avoid the gravity well of the planet altogether. The mission plan calls for using the rogue planet for a gravitational assist to slingshot the ship around and back the way we came. If we don't use that method for whatever reason, we have to expend onboard fuel to change direction much slower and more laboriously, and we'll have to tack over a week onto the journey. I'm not wild about the idea of spending that much extra time in a tiny drop ship with one toilet and two bunks to share among six people.

"If there are seed ships in the neighborhood, we won't see them until we're on top of them," Drentlaw says. "They don't show on infrared. And there's fuck all for sunlight out here."

"But they won't see us either," I say. "When we made the stealth run back to Earth in an Indy-class, we dodged their blockade at the Alcubierre point. And a Blackfly is a lot smaller than an Indy."

"Let's buckle in and ride the roller coaster, then," Drentlaw replies. "I better get Staff Sergeant Murray up. This is the only excitement we'll get on this field trip."

"I sincerely hope you're right, Master Sergeant," I say.

The dark rogue planet fills most of our sensor window as we begin our slingshot maneuver. Even at this short distance, the surface looks indistinct in the blackness of interstellar space, a swirling mass that seems to twist and writhe, patterns of shadows flowing like oil on a puddle. All the pod sensors are active and recording, shoveling surveillance data into the ship's memory banks for later analysis. Passing this planet in pitch-darkness at close range triggers a sense of dread in me. It feels like I am taking a swim in the ocean on a moonless night, aware of all the things that may be lurking in the deep but powerless to see any of them coming until they're close enough to yank me down into the darkness with them and swallow me. But for better or worse, we are committed to the flyby now, and all I can do is hang on and make sure all the ship's eyes and ears are taking in whatever they can.

"Six and a half minutes to the periapsis. We are really hauling ass," Staff Sergeant Murray says to my right. He has a plot on one of the displays in front of him, and a triangle-shaped representation of our drop ship is hurtling along a course projection that curves around the planet. The Blackfly has been accelerating in bursts every hour for over three days of mission time, building up more speed with every burn. We are going hundreds of kilometers per second, and if we slice through an atmosphere at this speed, we'll end up as a beautiful shower of superheated metal and alloy bits.

"Coming around the bend," the pilot sends.

On my infrared screen, an alert chirps. I turn my head to look at the display, and for a moment, my brain refuses to compute what I am seeing.

"Contact," I call out automatically even as my blood runs cold. "Multiple contacts on IR. Flight, do you have this?"

"Affirmative," the pilot replies. *"Fifteen degrees by positive twenty-one, distance six thousand. And—shit, two more. Three."*

"Make that five," Master Sergeant Drentlaw says. His gravelly voice sounds a little hoarse. "Six. Seven."

"What in the *hell*," I say.

More contacts are popping up on infrared with every passing second of our high-speed trajectory around the planet. After a few moments, nobody bothers calling out bearings and distances anymore because the values are changing so rapidly at our speed that the callouts are instantly obsolete. But as jolted as I am to find that there's something out here, it's more surprising that we are able to spot them at all.

"Flight, is our shit busted or are you seeing the same thing on IR?"

"IR is lit up like a Christmas tree, sir," the pilot says. *"Twelve seed ships and counting. We're going to pass less than fifty klicks from the closest one. Twenty-one seconds."*

"Hold the periapsis burn," I order. "Don't light those engines. We'll take the fuel penalty."

"Oh, that's a given. I'm not touching those levers."

"How the *fuck* can we even see them?" Sergeant Murray says. "Seed ships don't show on infrared."

"These sure as hell do." I look at the scattered Lanky fleet in front of us with a sudden dryness in my mouth. Every single seed ship we have encountered so far was a black hole on infrared. These seed ships are so clearly visible on the sensor screen that it looks like someone drew them onto the display in fluorescent paint.

"That's going to be a close pass," Murray says in a tense voice. "Forty-seven klicks' separation."

I watch the nearest Lanky grow bigger on the display. Nothing I can do will make a difference to our detectability, but I feel like I should be holding my breath or turning off the lights in the hold anyway, my instincts screaming at me to run and hide from the saber-toothed tiger at the cave entrance. We are well inside the weapons range of the quill-like penetrator rods the seed ships fire in enormous volleys when they engage our warships. If this one senses us, we'll get peppered by meter-thick spikes that won't even slow down as they tear through the drop ship's armor.

The Lanky ship is moving around the rogue planet in the same direction we're hurtling, but our speed advantage is so great that we pass the closest point of approach in a blink. The distance between us and the Lanky opens up to hundreds of kilometers again, then a thousand. The other seed ships are in higher and lower orbits in relation to our path, well beyond the known range of their weapons. I throw my head back against the headrest of my chair and exhale loudly.

"I feel like a minnow dashing through a school of sharks," I say.

"If we'd plotted that slingshot fifty klicks closer to atmo, we would have had a rear-end collision and a shitty day at the office," Master Sergeant Drentlaw says.

"Day's not over yet," I caution.

"We're going around the track like a missile," Sergeant Murray says. "Even if they notice us, they won't be able to catch up."

"Yeah, but they can let their friends know we're here," I say without looking away from the infrared sensor screens. The recon pods are tracking sixteen seed ships in the space around the rogue planet. As I watch, one more shows up above the planetary horizon as we complete another degree of angle on our course, and the computer tallies and tags it with velocity and distance readouts.

"Anyone want to wager a guess why they show up on IR and thermal imaging all of a sudden?" I ask.

"Maybe it's a stealth thing they do with their hulls," Lieutenant Murray offers. "Something they can turn off when they don't need it. No human's ever been in this place until now, right?"

On the plot, the drop ship reaches the periapsis of our maneuver, the spot where our trajectory is closest to the planetary atmosphere. In uncontested space, the pilot would light the engines at full throttle right now to take advantage of the kinetic energy boost, but I know that the last thing the flight crew wants to do is fire up the propulsion system and make us glow like a signal flare in the darkness. We pass the periapsis and pick up even more speed as the laws of physics make the orbital energy of the planet give us a kick in the back. Minute by minute, we're leaving the loose conglomeration of seed ships farther behind.

"Another moon," Drentlaw says and points it out on infrared. "That's four satellites around that rock. Wish we had time to stop and look closer after coming all this way."

"The recon pods did all the looking we need," I say.

"Well, that was exciting," the pilot says over the intercom.

"That's one way to put it," I reply.

"I sure as shit won't need any stim pills for a while," Master Sergeant Drentlaw says. "Four days of boredom, ten minutes of terror. Ain't that just the grunt life in a fucking nutshell."

I turn one of the sensor pods in its mounting until the infrared detection cone points toward our stern. The planet we're leaving in our wake is still filling most of the sensor's field of view, its infrared image glowing faintly with the heat from whatever process keeps the surface and the atmosphere from freezing solid in the absence of a nearby sun. Any moment, I expect to see a cigar-shaped blotch coming over the equatorial horizon in hot pursuit of our little drop ship. But the minutes tick by, and the only movement I see is the slow and steady orbit of the three moons that are on our side of the planet.

"Flight, I suggest we keep coasting ballistic for a while," I send. "I want to keep eyeballs on our six with the IR gear."

"Copy that."

I'm familiar with the drained feeling that is settling in after our brush with the unexpected Lanky presence. It's the mental residue from a brain that was firing on all cylinders, telling the body to fight or run, the flood of stress hormones that are now slowly receding in my system. I could work them off more quickly if I had an opportunity to physically exert myself. Because I am hemmed into the tight quarters of the drop ship's cargo hold, it will take a while before I'm back to normal.

But there's a kind of pleasant rush to it as well, the elation that comes with the knowledge I've once again faced death head-on and managed to avoid it. There's no substance I've ever tried that comes even close to having the same effect. I remember what Masoud said to me on Iceland a few weeks ago, but I know he was wrong when he said I miss the war. Combat soldiers don't get hooked on war. They get hooked on the exhilaration of being alive.

Next to me, Master Sergeant Drentlaw leans back in his chair so hard that it makes the hinges of the backrest creak in protest. He runs both hands through his hair and exhales a long breath.

"Join the Fleet, see the galaxy," he says. "I need to track down my recruiter and break his jaw in three places."

I laugh, and the adrenaline still in my system gives it a slightly shaky quality.

"You've been in for fifteen years, Drentlaw," I say. "Since before the Lankies. You didn't *have* a recruiter. You applied for this. Just like I did."

Master Sergeant Drentlaw tilts his head back and frowns at the ballistic liner on the cargo hold's ceiling.

"Well, sir," he says. "Then I guess we're both colossal dipshits. No offense."

"None taken," I say. "I'll never ding someone for stating the truth."

Four days of boredom, ten minutes of terror.

Once we are reasonably sure that we don't have a seed ship on our tail, we settle in for the long ride back to the carrier. Because the pilots weren't able to boost our return trip with a periapsis burn, our inbound journey will not see any time shaved off it, and we're in for another long haul that I hope will be boring and singularly uneventful.

With nothing else to do, I poke around in the petabytes of data the recon pods recorded while we were on our white-knuckle ride around the rogue planet. I am not a scientist, and even the ninety hours back to the ship won't be enough to do more than scratch the surface of so much data, but I review the sensor readouts anyway out of burning curiosity. The fact that the seed ships near the planet are plainly visible is hugely important from a tactical perspective, and it contradicts over a decade of our accumulated knowledge and experience. But that's not even the most significant thing the sensor pods have recorded on our flyby.

"I'll be damned," I say when I look at the images of the moon we spotted almost as an afterthought on the far side of the rogue planet. "Take a look at this, Murray."

Staff Sergeant Murray leans over to see the series of images on my center screen. The moon on the far side is rendered in a variety of filters, all primed for a different sensor spectrum.

"Look at that thermal image," I say and point at one of the frames.

"Warm little rock, isn't it?" Murray says. "And look at all those hotspots."

I put the IR image right next to the thermal one and point at the overlapping regions.

"I don't know about you, but that looks like geological activity to me," I say. "And that's not even the best part."

I minimize the IR and thermal screens and bring up the spectroscopic view. It shows the moon as a black circle surrounded by a halo of various colors.

"That's an atmosphere," I say.

Murray isolates a section of the spectroscopic view and expands it. Then he punches up the menu palette that shows the corresponding values for the colors.

"Not just an atmosphere," he says and looks at me with a grin. "One with water vapor."

I examine the segment Murray isolated on my screen and compare the values again. The readings are weak because there isn't much light behind the moon's horizon, but it's enough for the computer to predict an atmosphere with water molecules suspended in it.

"Thirty-one percent likelihood of water in that atmosphere," I read. "Under normal circumstances, I wouldn't be wild about putting money on those odds."

I look at the IR image from the backward-facing recon pod, where the rogue gas giant is slowly receding into the distance. Those four moons are the only port of call for us right now, with no alternative we'd be able to reach in ten lifetimes.

"We can *make* air," I say. "We can't make more water. But if that rock has it floating around in the atmosphere, I'd bet my pension that there's water somewhere on the surface, too. And if there's water, there's probably other stuff we can use."

The excitement I feel makes me drum my fingers on the edge of the console. If we weren't operating under strict EMCON, I'd get on comms back to *Washington* right now and inform them that we have hit the jackpot, that the mission has discovered exactly what we were hoping to find. As things stand, I'll have to sit on that knowledge for a few more days. We still don't know how to find a way out of this place, but a water source on that moon will buy us a lot more time to look.

I reach for the display again and move the images of the moon's spectrograph readings aside. Then I restore the view of the Lanky seed ships scattered in various orbits around the rogue planet.

"That's going to be a problem," Murray says. "One ship versus fourteen. I don't think they'll just let us pull up and fill our tanks, sir."

I look at the IR images of the Lankies, clearly visible against the backdrop of the planet and the darkness of space like signal lamps, somehow no longer invisible to our technology.

"We either take it from them, or we die of thirst in the dark," I reply. "We have to roll those dice. Whatever the odds are, at least they're above zero now."

When we get back to the carrier over a hundred hours later, I am in the cockpit, strapped into the seats behind the pilots who are on duty for the approach. From my station in the cargo hold, I have access to all the drop-ship sensors and the recon pods, so there's nothing up here I can't see much better with the filters from the sensors and their 360-degree vision. But seeing the ship with my own eyes through the transparent cockpit canopy makes it more real somehow, without all the electronic layers between the photons and my retinas.

"Twenty kilometers, turning for final," the pilot in command says and lightly touches the thruster controls to match course with the carrier. At this distance, I can only spot NACS *Washington* thanks to her brilliant-white paint coat, which reflects the minimal starlight reaching the ship from dozens and hundreds of light-years away.

As we get inside of ten kilometers, a green light appears in the near-total darkness in front of us. It's in the shape of a horizontal bar, with a white dot in the center.

"There's our meatball," the pilot says. "On track for the docking approach."

I know the function of the meatball—the pilot nickname for the Optical Landing System—because Halley is a drop-ship jock. I've seen this sight a thousand times from the back of the ship and a few times directly from the cockpit. It's just a visual aid, a large electronic light bar mounted beside the assigned docking hatch to let the pilots know they're on course and cleared for their approach. But in the darkness out here far between the stars, it's the most welcome thing I've seen in days. It's evidence that we're not alone, that other humans are still with us in this hostile nothingness, a tiny oasis of light and warmth and life.

We catch up with *Washington* and make our way along her underside, where another set of lights starts pulsing, marking our final approach to the docking hatch. The pilot triggers the forward thrusters to slow us down and match our speed with the carrier. A set of lights flashes on the cockpit console to let the flight crew know that the automated docking system has taken over for the final step of the maneuver. A few moments later, the docking clamp descends from the hatch above us and locks onto the hardpoints on the drop ship.

"Blackfly One, this is Washington *flight ops,"* a new voice says over the hardwired intercom. *"Confirm hard lock. Welcome home."*

"Thank you, Flight Ops. It's good to be back," the pilot responds. He flicks a series of switches on one of the overhead panels, and the low-pitched sound from the engines dies down gradually.

"Well, this one's over," the copilot says.

I smile as I remember those words, spoken by a different drop-ship crew member many years ago on the deck of a different carrier, when Halley and I first said good-bye to each other after Willoughby. It feels like hearing an echo from the past, and I take it as a good omen.

This one's just begun, I think.

ACKNOWLEDGMENTS

The book you are holding right now in whatever physical or digital form is my tenth published novel since 2013. That's a lot of acknowledgments to write. But if you notice that the same names tend to pop up at the end of each book, it's because I am lucky enough to have a stable support network of family, friends, editors, and trusted colleagues.

First on the list to thank is always my wife, Robin, who runs the ship and keeps things together at the Castle so I can disappear in my office every day and talk to imaginary people in my head.

Thank you to the 47North team—my editors, Adrienne and Jason; my developmental editor, Andrea Hurst; my production editor, Laura Barrett; the marketing crew; and everyone else who has had a hand in getting this book in front of readers. Last year, I had two of my short stories adapted into episodes for an animated Netflix series, and one of the unit directors told me in an e-mail that *seventy people* worked on one thirteen-minute episode for six months. Movie and TV production are pretty flashy business, and book publishing largely isn't, but I suspect that the number of people working on a book behind the scenes is probably equal to or greater than that TV team head count. I may not ever get to meet you all to thank you in person, but know that I appreciate you and the work you do.

It's June 2020 as I write this, and the world is a weird place right now. We have a global pandemic raging, the country is politically divided and seemingly on edge, and international tourism has flatlined. I haven't been able to go to any cons or family visits this year, and that probably won't change for a good while. Writing is a solitary job, and I was already used to spending a lot of time indoors by myself, so this hasn't been a radical change for me. But in times like these, our friend networks become even more important than before, and I am lucky to have good, kind, smart friends who bring joy and humor to my day. So thank you to my Doge crew: Tracie, Paul, Tam, Stacy, and Monica; my local friends Kate and Seth, Heather, Jana, Michael and Sophia, David, Christina, Kristin and Morgan; my writer pal and con buddy Melissa Olson; and my friend and collaboration partner Kris Herndon. You're all the most wonderful people, and being friends with you keeps me grounded and happy.

Thank you to George R. R. Martin, Melinda Snodgrass, and the rest of the Wild Cards crew for letting me be part of something much bigger and better than the sum of its parts, and for your friendship, support, and advice over the years.

And as much as first thanks always go to my wife, my final thanks always go out to my readers. You make it all possible, and your continued support is the main reason why I sit down to work every day. I hope you stick around for what comes next.